EDEN

MW00937244

Book Two
SPIDER WEB POWDER

JAMES ERITH

JERICO PRESS

SPIDER WEB POWDER

(Eden Chronicles, Book 2)

Published in 2015
Jerico Press

Editor: John Hudspith
Cover: Tom Moore (tom@beatmedia.co.uk)

SPIDER WEB POWDER is written in UK English.

ISBN-13: 978-1-9101340-6-1
(Available on most digital platforms)
www.JamesErith.com

It started out as a story for my Godchildren:

Isabella, Daisy, Archie and Iso.

Thank you, Team Erith!

*Charlie, Ed, Philip, Robert, Sara
... and especially Charlotte*

*Tom Moore, Marsha Moore, Neil Forbes,
Simon East, Sam Dayeh, Christie Stewart-Smith,
Adam Howard*

For Madelaine

SPIDER WEB POWDER

Previously

The de Lowe children, Isabella 14, and twins Archie and Daisy, 12, live in Eden Cottage, a large old stone farmhouse, hidden among the hills and forests on the edge of the North Yorkshire moors.

In the frequent absence of their parents on archaeological expeditions abroad, they are in the care of the housekeeper, Mrs Pye, and their elderly guardian, known to all as Old Man Wood.

In book one, The Power and The Fury, *the children were troubled by vivid, often violent and frightening dreams, particularly of a brutal murder and a devastating storm.*

Archie woke to find a strange spider-like, almost angelic creature, hovering above his sister's head. It was filtering a special powder into Daisy's mouth as she slept, and Archie concluded, rightly, that it was giving her a dream.

This powder came from the last few grains of a once vast mountain of dream powders, and only in the Garden of Eden – closed since the time of the Bible's Book of Genesis thousands of years ago – can new dream powders be made.

Unbeknown to the de Lowe children, they are the Heirs of Eden and the only people who can unlock the complex riddles put in place to open the Garden of Eden in order for the dreamspinners to retrieve these much needed supplies.

But the recent chain of events has awakened evil beings in other worlds kept away since the Garden of Eden's closure. They now have the power to cause great harm on Earth and plan to take the Garden of Eden for themselves, should it be opened.

The children tried in vain to warn their headmaster about a terrible flood, and when the dark cloud finally broke, Isabella, Archie and Daisy escaped the extraordinary violence of the storm by the skin of their teeth.

Many of their friends were not so lucky.

The storm appeared to target them and after death-defying escapades in which they suffered terrible injuries, the children stumbled upon a cavern, which had also been found by Old Man Wood.

The shattered children were miraculously restored by bathing in a curious pool, but can they now find a way out that does not involve swimming through the foul foaming waters from which they came?

Their trials and adventures have only just begun

... now read on ...

CHAPTER ONE

After The Storm, Inside The Cave

Daisy popped her head around the entrance of the hidden doorway. 'Oh for goodness' sake,' she eventually yelled out. 'I've been up and down about a thousand stairs. It really isn't hard to find—'

'I don't have weird eyes like you, remember,' Archie shot back. 'Only stupid spiky hair.'

Daisy ignored him. 'Look, it's over here!' She beckoned them to a tiny, almost invisible gap that looked identical to the cave wall from all angles. 'Clever, isn't it?' she said. 'It's recessed so that when you squeeze through, turn sharply, like this.'

'Oh!' Archie said as his fingers found the entrance and he eased himself in. 'It's a bit tight.'

'Just mind your head,' Daisy quipped, 'or you'll damage the walls. Anyway, there's a far bigger problem at the top.'

Archie shot her a look.

'You'll have to wait and see – if you're fit enough,' she said. 'It's miles up and up and up. Prepare to be disappointed.'

*

Old Man Wood's frown grew until the furrows appeared almost black and white. 'How am I supposed to get in there?' he complained. 'And what about my things?'

The children could see his point. The opening was wide enough for them, but tight for a large man like Old Man Wood.

1

'Crawl – on your side – you should be able to make it,' Daisy said, trying to be helpful.

Old Man Wood continued to stare at the gap. He was an old man, not a bendy child.

Isabella reappeared through the small slit in the wall and held out a hand. 'Your hard hat,' she said to the old man. 'Archie, as you're the smallest, grab his rucksack. Come on, let's go, I can't wait to get out of this ridiculous place.'

*

Isabella hadn't told the whole truth. The moment she woke, an unnerving sensation, as though she were being watched, made the hairs on her neck stand erect and her brow damp with fear. She connected the sensation to her nightmares in which large green alien eyes penetrated her mind and this queer feeling grew stronger and stronger until she'd woken up terrified and shaking and soaked in sweat.

Isabella tried to calm down by taking deep breaths, but her body sagged like a sack of potatoes and her brain felt like squishy dough. Perhaps this was the aftershock of surviving the great storm. Did the others feel the same?

Her thoughts turned to the twins. They had landed on the stone ledge at death's door; unconscious, frozen and lacerated with cuts that sliced into their bodies like whiplashes. Their recovery in the pool was nothing short of miraculous and in the cool light of morning, Isabella wondered if the whole thing had been part of another nightmare. Or, could it be the downside of the powerful medicine Old Man Wood had given her? What did he call it, Resplendix Mix? A gold sparkly liquid in a curious old bottle that didn't have a lid – or a use-by date. She'd taken just two drops on her tongue. And boy did it hurt – like rolling around in stinging nettles on the outside with burning hot coals inside.

Medicines that instantly healed didn't exist in the real world – or did they? But she did know that the trade-off with a powerful medicine was often a horrible side-effect. Perhaps this was what she was experiencing.

The children wound their way up and up the dark stairs, each foot feeling for the narrow risers, their feet scuffing like sandpaper. After several minutes Isabella stopped and held her sides. 'Phew!' she said. 'This is exhausting.' –

'You're seriously unfit, Bells,' Daisy said.

'Actually, I'm seriously hungry and freaked, OK? I just want to get out of here.' Her heart thumped. 'It's like the whole of yesterday was some kind of weird, crappy dream – as if we were stuck in a game where we had to stay alive—'

'Yeah,' Daisy said. 'But at least we survived.'

Isabella rested a hand on her sister's shoulder. 'I know. That's what's so crazy. You actually sort of died, Daisy. Did you know that?'

Daisy leant her head casually on the tight riser above her. 'Can't remember much.'

'Lucky you,' Isabella said as she recalled how Daisy had lain on the rocks, her body limp, her face deathly pale, her eyes shut. When Old Man Wood couldn't feel a pulse, a kind of anger had filled her and she'd screamed at Daisy with all her might not to die. And then a strange thing had happened …

'I thought it was Old Man Wood's medicine,' Daisy said. 'You know, Repulsive Mix, or whatever—'

'He calls it Resplendix Mix,' Isabella said. 'For some reason it wouldn't work on you.' She turned to Archie. 'What about you, Arch? Do you remember anything?'

Archie thought for a minute. 'Think I got fried—'

Daisy burst out laughing, the sound bouncing off the walls of the stairwell and echoing eerily back at them. 'Yup, you sure did, bro. And landed unbelievably weird hair—'

'Archie's hair isn't remotely funny,' Isabella snapped. 'Nor your red eyes and my hands.'

Daisy scowled back. 'Who said it was funny? I just said it was odd.'

'Well yes, very odd,' Isabella agreed. 'You know, Daisy, when you told us the lightning bolts were coming, did you really hear them or were you making it up?'

'Of course I heard them,' Daisy said crossly.

Isabella twisted off a sharp edge and perched on a step. 'Well, it's illogical,' she said. 'This whole thing. Water poured from the sky at a velocity far greater than Sue and I calculated – I'm convinced of it.' Isabella sucked in a huge breath. 'And we couldn't see, or hear anything, could we?' They climbed on, their footsteps almost in time. 'I still don't know how I guided us across the playing field to the bridge?' she said. 'Just imagine the devastating scene out there.' No one answered.

'Well, let's say the river is fifteen metres above sea level,' she continued, 'and we had five hours of water at a couple of inches of rain per minute. That's nearly ten metres of water – then compound that with water pouring off the hills and the spring tide and lunar situation ...' Isabella frowned and her voice dropped. 'It'll be underwater,' she continued, 'totally submerged. Only the top of York Minister—'

'Can we please get on?' Daisy interrupted. 'I want to go home, Bells.'

The children shuffled on, picking their steps carefully as Isabella continued. 'You know, I shouldn't have been able to swim against the water that swept me off the bridge, and I escaped a mudslide,' she said.

'Something egged me on. Perhaps that's what having "spirit" means.' She looked up at the climb ahead. 'Blimey. These stairs go on forever.'

'Tell me about it,' Daisy said. 'I've already done it once.'

'But you're fit—'

'Bells, stop gabbling on with theories about our great escape, and keep climbing,' Daisy said, as she pushed her sister ahead. 'Seriously, this is just the start.'

*

At long last they emerged out of the top of the narrow stone stairwell and into a large and dimly lit cavern. Beams of light filtered through tiny holes in a large circular pattern at the far end.

As the children caught their breath their eyes searched the chamber. Beneath them lay a smooth, gently undulating rock floor that gave way every now and then to a patch of mud or a pool formed from water dripping from the ceiling, which echoed in the quiet.

From the cavern roof, which was as high as a small house, jagged rocks forced their way out of the stone like misshapen teeth. Along the sides, water had shaped the rock into small alcoves creating, Archie thought, mini sleeping areas. Perhaps early humans like Neanderthals had lived and slept here thousands of years ago.

'See the problem?' Daisy said.

Now, as their eyes had adjusted, they stared at a vast boulder whose expanse sat in the ground like a massive egg in a massive eggcup. The problem was obvious; they were stuck, with no way out.

A deep boom echoed up the stairwell.

'What on earth was that?' Isabella said.

Archie turned to his twin, Daisy and raised his brows. 'Fifty pounds he's stuck.'

'You don't even have fifty quid,' Daisy said.

They hurried back to the hole.

'Are you alright?' Archie called down.

A few moments later an echo returned, the sounds crashing into one another as it reached their ears.

'I'll have to go down,' Archie said, and after a couple of minutes, encased in the musty darkness of the stairwell, he slowed. 'Where – are – you?'

'Still – at – the – bottom,' the old man replied, taking in to account the reverberating echo. 'Jammed – in, good – and – proper.'

*

Old Man Wood lay half up the stairs and half wedged in at the foot of the stairs. Sweet apples alive, he thought as he ran his leathery hands over the walls, trying to find a nodule to grip so that he could push himself back down and out. He groaned. The problem was that the more he struggled the more stuck he became.

If he could get back down – and it was a big "if" – he had no choice but to head out into the swirling waters thick with flotsam and jetsam, and swim for his life. And Old Man Wood hated swimming.

He wriggled his torso, twisting one way then another and managed to slip down a step. His outstretched foot touched on a protruding stone knob and using it to lever himself round he pressed down hard only to feel the stone retract into the step.

Before he had time to gather himself, a clunking noise filled the stairwell followed by grinding, crunching and crushing sounds. Old Man Wood covered his head with his free arm, waiting for the inevitable rocks to come crashing down.

But none came and much to his astonishment the stairwell walls began to pull back until a deep boom sounded and the noise ceased. The stairwell was now at least a foot wider.

Well, well, well, he thought as he sat down on a step and mopped his brow. That bit of stone must have been a gear cog slipping into place. Now there's a nifty bit of engineering – and just in the nick of time. What sort of person would design something like that? And why?

Old Man Wood dusted himself down, pulled himself together and stood up.

'What's – going – on – down – there?' he heard.

'Don't – you – worry,' Old Man Wood said. 'I'm coming up, littleuns! Nothing doing!'

He trundled up the stairwell finding a rhythm, stopping on three occasions to catch his breath. At the summit he sat down taking large gulps of air as the children gathered around. 'Two hundred and twenty two steps. Phew! Apples alive! And they're high steps and all.'

'What happened?' Archie asked him. 'How did you get the stairs to widen?'

Old Man Wood wiped his brow. 'Touched a lucky stone, that's all.'

'A lucky stone?' Isabella repeated.

'Yep,' Old Man Wood replied. 'Very lucky, I reckon.'

*

Isabella leant on the boulder at the entrance of the cave and groaned. It was huge – six feet high and eight feet wide with a significant amount stuck in the ground and it stood between them and freedom.

Stains marked the boulder's surface with streaky patterns where the rainwater had leeched down – the light grey stone now lined with blue and black hues.

How on earth were they going to move it? she wondered. Maybe it was one of those things that only needed a tiny push. Isabella stepped back a couple of paces and charged.

A moment later she shrieked and rubbed her shoulder.

Daisy laughed. 'I told you—'

'Shut up, Daisy,' Isabella barked. She swivelled towards Old Man Wood. 'You're good at getting out of things, aren't you, Old Man Wood?' she said, as if he might solve the conundrum for them. And then she turned, gritted her teeth and tried to push the boulder again.

Archie could hardly believe it. 'What *are* you doing? That's up there with the stupidest thing I've ever seen. Not even Daisy would try something as moronic as that.'

Daisy nodded.

'I know,' Isabella sobbed. 'It's just that … just that I'm hungry and I want to go home and I want to know if Sue and Gus survived and … this is so ridiculous and unfair and infuriating after everything we've been through.'

'But running at it isn't going to help,' Archie said quietly. 'Think about it. That boulder must weigh more than ten tonnes. You are a fraction in comparison. You're the scientist – do the maths.'

Isabella frowned, sat down and let her straight brown hair fall over her face, hiding her tears.

Archie began pacing the floor as an idea formed in his mind. He turned to Old Man Wood. 'You said you touched a lucky stone. Was it a lever or a knob – did you push it in, pull it, or did it fall to the side?'

Old Man Wood thought for a second. 'Pushed it with my foot. A chunk of rock, like a lever, I suppose—'

'Well then, if one opened the stairs up, why not another to loosen the boulder?'

Isabella looked at him curiously. 'You really think so?'

Archie shrugged. 'We haven't got much else to work with, have we, unless you've got a better idea? Whatever this place is, it's been designed by someone pretty clever

– so chances are that he built more than one. What do you think?'

The others shrugged.

'I suggest we start hunting for odd pieces of rock that stick out—'

'Stick out?' Isabella said.

'Yeah, you know – like you see in the movies.'

'Cool,' Daisy added, as she un-twiddled a blond curl from her finger.

They selected different parts of the cave and applied weight to rocks that stuck out and pushed every little cavity. But nothing worked. Not a wobble, a flicker, or a nudge. The big boulder remained exactly where it was.

*

Daisy slumped to the floor, defeated. How long had they been searching in the gloom? An hour? Two? Her tummy rumbled. 'This is nuts,' she said. 'Whatever we're looking for isn't here, I'm sure of it.'

'Well what do you suggest?' Archie said.

'What if Isabella had a point,' she replied. 'Maybe we should *all* try and push it out of the way. Who knows it may be hinged—'

'Hinged?' Archie said. *'Hinged!* Doors are hinged Daisy, not blooming great boulders.'

Daisy shot him a piercing look. 'But we haven't tried it and anyway you pulled a tree out of the ground so who says you can't move a boulder?'

'Well I can't, and anyway that was ridiculous.'

'No it wasn't.'

'Yes it was! It's like saying that Isabella could move it with her hands.'

'Well maybe she can—'

'I didn't mean that—'

'Stop it you two,' Isabella ordered. 'We need to think, work it out logically.'

Aside from the trickle of water, silence filled the large cavern as the four of them sat down on the stone floor and racked their brains.

'OK,' Archie said eventually. 'Let's try. All four of us—'

Isabella wasn't convinced and rubbed her shoulder. 'It's huge, Archie, you said it yourself.'

Archie shrugged. 'I've got nothing better to do, don't know about you.'

Archie walked over to the mouth of the cave and stood in front of the round grey bulk. 'Well come on – or do I have to do it on my own?'

Reluctantly the others joined him.

Old Man Wood and Archie took up central positions with Isabella and Daisy on either flank.

Archie counted them in. 'On the count of three. One, two … three!'

They heaved until their faces were puce, but the boulder didn't budge.

They fell to the floor.

'Anyone want to try again?' Archie said. They shook their heads. Just as Isabella said, the attempt was hopeless.

Moments later Daisy spoke up. 'Oooh. I've got an idea,' she said, and she ran the length of the cavern. 'Back in a mo,' she yelled behind her as she disappeared down the dark stairwell, her footsteps echoing behind her.

Archie stood up as though he understood what Daisy had been thinking. 'Old Man Wood – where were you when you touched this "lucky stone" ?'

'Now then,' the old man began. 'I hadn't got very far. First steps I reckon—'

'That's it!' Archie cried. 'We're looking in the wrong place. The clue must be on the walls in the chamber, down there – not up here.'

And without hesitating he shot off down the stairwell after his twin sister.

CHAPTER TWO

The Pictures In The Cave

When Archie appeared, Daisy was studying the paintings on the walls. Her lips moved as if she could read the story like a book, her eyes fixed in concentration as she scoured the simple artwork. Occasionally, she moved in to dust off the image or icon, then she'd step back and take in the whole scene. Archie was fascinated by her concentration and followed her eyes which shone as though a bright red light had been switched on inside her head.

The first section of the mural began with a circular tree and ended with figures carrying gifts. Then, the mural divided into two and kept dividing as the story progressed around the walls.

Above, and running the length of the mural was a storm, depicted by jagged lightning bolts and strong lines for heavy rain. This concluded with mountain peaks poking through water. Archie gulped.

Below this "storm mural" stood three figures in front of a setting sun and directly above them the rain lines were less dynamic. Archie instantly recognised this, for when the sun went down the night before, or so he'd been told by Isabella, the torrential rain that had sluiced from the sky abated to no more than a drizzle.

He moved on to the next mural which showed the same three characters holding a rectangular stone tablet encrusted with ornate carvings. It was not much bigger, he guessed, than a paperback book.

Here, the mural divided, as it did with each new tablet that had to be found. Three stone tablets in all, Archie thought, one for each of the three figures. And as far as he could make out, if any one of them died and at any point, then they would go to a place of skulls and withered trees. It was death. For all three.

Now that Archie studied it, it reminded him of levels on a computer game: win a level – move up a level. The difference in this game was that if one person lost a level, everyone died.

So, if these pictures were somehow connected to them and if one of them had died in the storm, then the rains would have continued on to destroy the planet until only the mountain tops were spared. A shiver ran up his spine.

He followed the mural to its conclusion where three figures basked in glorious sunlight, as if they had succeeded. Beyond the basking figures and extending over much of the rocky vaulted ceiling in the shape of a circle was the outline of a vast tree showing both roots and branches. On its upper half, animals and birds and plants and fruit hung in and around the foliage. Below, beside the roots, swam creatures of the sea.

Archie recognised some – like the seahorse, whale, elephant and crocodile – but he had no idea who the double-headed snakes were or what the birds with forked tongues and huge sharp claws were called. In fact, most of the creatures seemed to belong to an alien or medieval make-believe fantasy world.

He turned his attention to Daisy who was captivated by this strange tree. She stared at it for some time, her mouth open, a frown creasing her forehead. Archie tried to work out what she was so struck by and looked harder until he noticed, just behind the tree, the faint outline of a cross-legged woman with a crown of leaves resting upon her head. In place of eyes were dark patches as though they had been coloured in, and a cushion sat in her lap. Resting on the surface in the shape of a heart, was a locket.

Archie's mind raced and his heartbeat quickened. Was this the Ancient Woman? Was this the haggard old woman they'd dreamt of, the same person he had repeatedly killed in his dreams? Was this the same woman he'd promised Cain he would look after??

Archie rubbed his front hair spike. He noted how his follicles had hardened together like steel. So if this was them, were these cave-images … their destiny?

Archie suddenly felt rather weak and insignificant. It made him think of Kemp. Kemp, who had lost his mother when he was so very young. He tried to remember what Cain had said to them in the alleyway but the whole thing had happened so fast. If only he could find Kemp, Kemp would remember and tell him – that's if his friend was still alive.

Archie shut his eyes. Cain told them that they were the anointed ones, the Heirs of something-or-other and that everything hung on their staying alive till sunset. Wasn't that the heart of it? So if the murals were correct, he, Archie de Lowe, a rather shambolic and disorganised nearly twelve year old and his two nutty sisters had just saved the world. Wow.

But he didn't feel like a superhero.

And then it dawned on him that perhaps the whole thing was in his head – his imagination – part of a very long, extended dream. A fantasy. Yeah, that was it. Not a bit of anything that had happened was REAL. It couldn't be. Not even the paintings in front of him truly existed …

'You done?' Daisy said, waving her hands in front of his face. 'Woo-hoo! Anyone there?'

'Sorry, miles away,' Archie replied, returning to earth.

'Have you taken all of this in, absorbed as much as you can?'

Archie was a little confused. He looked around. 'God. Er... yeah. Suppose so.'

'Good,' she said, rubbing her eyes. 'As you are fully aware, my brain is completely rubbish, so from now on, I'm relying on you.' Daisy ran her hands through her curls and noted Archie's blank expression. 'Want me to explain?'

'Explain what?' Archie looked confused.

'What's going to happen, numpty.'

Archie nodded.

'Cool. Right, you see that little picture at the base of the stairwell.' Daisy pointed at it.

'Uh, right,' Archie replied, squinting. 'Yeah, didn't see that.'

'Well that shows us how we get out of here – stroke of luck Old Man Wood pushed the other one, hey?'

Archie stared at the wall. He couldn't see anything. 'Sure,' he said dumbly.

Daisy eyed him. 'You have no idea, don't you?'

'Nah. All looks like white-wash to me.'

Daisy sighed. 'Please tell me you've noticed the cave entrance recently?'

Archie reddened. He turned and his eyes led him from the steaming, bubbling pool along the stream to the entrance.

Daisy couldn't believe Archie was being such a moron. 'Jeez, Archie. This cave – *where we are right now* – is underwater. There's some kind of plastic film or glass barrier or weirdo trick holding the water back.' She marched over to the entrance, put her hands on the strange glass film and smacked it with her fist. A hollow, thick ring like a church bell replied.

'Yup, resin or glass or something,' she said nonchalantly, as though this kind of thing happened every day.

Now that his eyes adjusted, Archie could see right through the transparent barrier to the murky swirling mass of water behind it. He felt sick. 'How did it get there?'

Daisy shot him a look. 'How the hell do I know?'

Archie's voice creaked. 'What's it doing?'

'Dur! Holding back the water! Come on, Archie! What do you think it's doing?' She hit it again, this time harder. A louder "dong", rang out.

'Blimey, Daisy. Don't do that.'

'Why not? It won't break.'

'How do you know that? It might.'

Daisy ignored him. 'Look, winkle,' she said, 'when it breaks, we're dead. Very, very, very dead.'

'Just what I was thinking,' Archie said.

'But it's not going to, quite yet.' She paced back to the wall. 'So these marks,' she continued pointing to a very faint blur on the wall, 'tell us there are two levers. One to widen the stairwell and the other to release the boulder—'

'Of course,' he said rubbing his chin, 'just as I suspected.'

She moved in closer and pointed at them. 'These marks here.'

'Yeah,' said Archie moving in too high.

'No,' she said, 'these two.'

Archie shook his head. Was she playing with him?

'Now the problem is,' Daisy said, 'there's a bit of a problem.'

Archie nodded dumbly.

16

'Well, you see these funny looking icons next to them?'

Archie bent down. 'Actually, no, not really.'

Daisy tutted. 'Well they seem to indicate that the moment the boulder lever is pushed the staircase begins to retract.'

'Wow, cool.'

'No, Archie. Not cool.'

Archie frowned. 'Why not?'

'Because when that happens, winkle, the barrier breaks and water pours in.'

Archie grimaced. 'OK. Yup, not so cool.' He turned to the entrance. 'So that glass thing—'

'Collapses. The brain is stirring,' Daisy said, rather triumphantly. 'It's all here on the walls – I can't believe you're so blind.'

Archie didn't even attempt to counter her. Silence filled the cavern as they thought through their situation.

'So, if you're right.' Archie said at length. 'We're dead, whatever we do.'

'Yeah. Probably.'

'Have you got a plan?' Archie stuttered.

'What? Other than seeing what odds Isabella would give for survival? Nope. Look, that barrier is protecting a pretty big hole and as brain box kept on telling us, there's one hell of a lot of water out there. The cave entrance is a few metres above the river and the water level is higher than the top of the cave, which means water must stretch for miles above the Vale of York. And water, as you know, always finds the easiest route—'

'Hold on a minute,' Archie said trying to catch up. 'You really think water stretches across the valley?'

Daisy shot him a look as if his brain had a leak. 'Well, yes of course it does,' she said. 'So,' and she pointed at the covered entrance, 'when it goes—'

'The pressure of water flooding in would be like firing a tsunami hosepipe up the stairs,' Archie concluded.

'Correct-a-mundo,' Daisy said punching him lightly on the shoulder. 'Now you're getting the picture.'

They stared at each other.

'And the longer we wait here,' Archie whispered, 'the higher the water rises, the greater the pressure.' The magnitude of what they'd worked out was beginning to sink in.

'Yeah, winkle. Something like that.'

'God almighty. Even deader,' Archie said. 'We need Isabella's brains on this one. And, Daisy, please stop calling me winkle.'

CHAPTER THREE

Isabella's Challenge

Daisy headed up the two hundred and twenty-two steps of the stairwell with Archie in pursuit.

Isabella and Old Man Wood stood waiting for them and the moment they heard them coming leant over the stairwell firing questions.

The twins held their sides, doubled over as they caught their breath.

'So, there's good news and bad news,' Archie gasped. 'Which do you want first?'

'The good news.'

'OK,' Daisy said. 'Give me a mo.'

Daisy flexed and stretched her legs before the twins lay down on the floor to catch their breath. 'Right, the good news is, I've found the lever to activate the boulder.'

Isabella clapped her hands. 'Brilliant. And the bad news?'

'We die if we activate it.'

'Die? Really? That's pretty drastic. Are you sure?'

Daisy raised an eyebrow.

Isabella examined her siblings. 'You're … you're kidding, aren't you? It's another of your silly little jokes?'

Their serious expressions said otherwise.

'But I never saw any of this,' Isabella countered. 'Why didn't I see it?'

'I did though, Bells,' Daisy said. 'Look, sis, I'm not really sure how these eyes work, but it's scribbled on those walls, I promise. On my life.'

Isabella looked ashen but listened as Archie and Daisy explained.

Then Isabella repeated it just to be sure. 'So what you're saying is that one of us has to press this lever and run like mad up two hundred and twenty two stairs while the whole thing starts closing in and falling apart and water starts crashing through the cave opening. And then and only then will the boulder open.'

'Yup,' Daisy said blankly. 'And if we fail, it screws the world. Apparently.'

Isabella wrinkled her nose and played with her straight brown hair and then stamped her foot hard down on the ground. 'This is ridiculous.'

'Well, yes it is,' Daisy agreed, 'but the longer we wait, the greater the water pressure, the harder it gets. Anyone going to volunteer?'

Old Man Wood put his hand up. 'I'll do it.'

Daisy smiled sweetly at the old man. 'No, you're far too old, big and much too slow. Sorry. Anyone else?' she looked at the receding faces of the others.

Isabella cut in. 'Daisy you're nimble, quick … fit. It's got to be you—'

'Why don't I do everything?' Daisy replied, crossly. 'Look, my legs are pretty stiff after yesterday's match and I've just climbed up here for the third time. That's six hundred and … er—'

'Sixty-six.'

'Yes, I knew that,' Daisy fumed. 'Why don't you do it? You're two years older for goodness' sakes and you've only done it once.'

Isabella was running out of excuses. 'Archie. Come on – this is just up your street.'

Archie shook his head. 'I'm slower than Daisy and I've done it twice.'

Isabella smiled – her lips wavering. 'Oh … oh, God! All right. As usual it's going to have to be me.' Her lips quivered and then she burst into tears. 'I hate this,' she sobbed. 'I hate this kind of stupid thing. None of this makes any sense, it's … it's—'

Old Man Wood moved in and enveloped her with a big hug like a comfort blanket. 'Now then, young Bells. I'm not sure we have a choice, do we? You've always been a strong runner so you'll be just fine. I can feel it in my bones.'

This only made Isabella cry louder.

Archie couldn't bear it. 'Look, if you're going to be such a wetty about it, I'll do it!'

Isabella wiped her eyes. 'No, I'm the eldest,' she sobbed, trying to compose herself. 'And you're right, you've done it twice. It's only proper that it's me.'

Daisy smiled. 'I don't mean to be a spoil-sport,' she said, 'but the longer we wait—'

'Yes, yes I know. You've already told me,' Isabella said. 'Oh, Daisy, you're finally finding some brains!' She gave her sister a big hug, took a deep breath and steadied herself.

'Old Man Wood – you stay here with Archie. Daisy – you'd better come with me and show me how these lever things work. When I've got it, get back up the stairs. When you're at the top yell down. Everyone got that. I'll depress the lever, yell, and run for it. OK?'

Daisy spoke gently. 'No waiting, Bells, understand? When it goes, scream a warning then go as fast as you can, sis. And good luck, I know you can do it.'

Isabella smiled and turned to Archie. 'Archie, if I don't make it, please do something with that hair.'

Archie's face was as white as snow and his hair rigid. 'You'd better make it, sis,' he said softly. 'Go like the wind.'

Old Man Wood furrowed his brow. His eyes watered. 'Good luck, young'un,' he said folding her into him again. 'Believe in yourself, little Bells, and you'll be fine.'

Quietly Isabella turned and began the long walk down the steep winding stairs with Daisy following on behind.

*

At the bottom of the stairs, Isabella and Daisy came out into the bubbling cave entrance. All they could hear was the water of the pool frothing while steam floated to the ceiling. Otherwise, a nervous quiet hung about them. Isabella's heart thumped.

She searched around and found that the twins were right, the cave mouth was being held up by a most peculiar screen and beyond it, murky water swirled about. Isabella would have loved to have studied this extraordinary material and scrape off a few cells so she could analyse how it worked, but she was interrupted by Daisy.

'Right, Bells,' Daisy said taking a deep breath. 'Here are the levers. That one,' and she pointed to the top protrusion, 'is the one Old Man Wood pressed with his foot. The bottom one – here – is the dude you need to push.'

Isabella nodded. She shook like a rattle.

Daisy noticed and reached out for her hand. 'Then run, Bells. Run like you've got a seriously massive great monster after you. Got it?' Isabella's eyes were wide with fear. 'Fast as you can,' Daisy continued, 'and don't stop. Understand?' She noted how pale her sister had turned. 'Look, are you sure you can do this? I mean, I'll do it … if you can't.'

For a brief moment Isabella very nearly gave in. 'No, no. Daisy,' she said as she pulled herself together. 'You must be shattered. Get back to the cave. Call down when you're there. It'll give me time to compose myself.'

Daisy smiled trying hard not to betray her nerves and moved in close to give her sister a hug. 'Look, you can do it. Easily,' she said, her voice croaking. 'Piece of Mrs Pye's cake, sis. Easy-peasy.'

*

Isabella smiled as Daisy's footsteps receded up the stairwell like distant whispers.

She stared at the drawings on the wall for some time, just as Archie and Daisy had, thinking hard about what they'd been through and if these cave pictures had any bearing on their current circumstances. Wasn't it a coincidence, she thought, that everything on the walls seemed to bear out what they'd been through? But why them? In particular, why her?

She wondered about her best friend, Sue. Had she sent her to her death by telling her about the old rowing boat? What had she done? Suddenly she missed Sue like mad and her tears marked the dry stone floor. She would give anything for her to be here now; they always had a way of working things out.

She returned to the bottom of the stairwell, wiped her eyes and listened. Daisy must be nearing the top by now, she thought, and almost immediately she heard a croaky, eerie voice echoing down, which sounded nothing like her sister's voice.

Time to push the stone.

She ran her fingers through her hair, conscious that she was shaking almost uncontrollably. She inhaled deeply and tried to remember her relaxation classes. Centre yourself, be calm, she thought.

Breathe.

She moved out into the cave once more for a last look at the quiet gentle pool and the curious murals and the extraordinary seal covering the entrance.

She stretched her legs and moved in front of the protruding knob of stone. A terrible nausea swept through her.

OK. Here goes, time to do it.

She put her hand on the stone and leant on it with all her weight, waiting for something to give, something to click – anything.

But however hard she pushed, nothing happened.

CHAPTER FOUR

Kemp, In Cain

Trapped inside Cain's ashen body, the boy, Kemp, twisted in pain.

Why hadn't he died? He should have run off like his friend, Archie, rather than bend to the crackpot desires and charms of a deranged ghost. He would have been better off dead – rather than endure this … this relentless torture.

Cain had wanted a body in which he might move and be free and Kemp, had willingly given his.

So, Kemp thought bitterly, why didn't Cain damn well look after him? The ghost had no understanding of rest, of the needs of human beings, and now every action forced upon him was as if rods of red hot irons had permeated every nerve, muscle and sinew in his body.

Kemp remembered the moment in the alleyway when he knew that the words spoken by the ghost were neither in jest, nor madness.

The de Lowe children, Isabella, Daisy and Archie, the ghost said, were the Heirs of Eden and had to negotiate a prophecy that originated in the mists of time. He'd laughed at first but then the storm began to crash about and bolts of lightning smashed onto the rooftops and splinters of tile and brick flew through the air like shrapnel and the deafening noise made every hair on his body stand to attention and he had never been so frightened.

Kemp felt a burst of heat on his leg. He moved and the pain faded. How could those ridiculous de Lowe siblings save the world? I mean, they were crazy, nutty kids. Super-heroes, them? Even now, the thought made him chuckle … if only he wasn't so filled with pain.

A test of Mother Nature, the ghost had said. Madness the lot of it, but here he was, trapped inside the spirit of a ghost, his body reduced to ash. He'd witnessed the storm, seen the raging fury of the lightning and rain and by all accounts the de Lowes had made it alive to sundown, but only just – at least that's what he'd thought he heard Cain say. The muffled sounds of being stuck inside another body made it so difficult to hear.

If they survived, the ghost told them, the storm would cease. And when that actually happened a flash of heat shot through him so powerfully that he swore he smelt his hair burning. They must have survived.

Kemp felt his fingers burning as though currents of molten wires extended to his fingertips. Why wouldn't the ghost leave him alone for just one minute? He tried to scream but Cain didn't hear him. He needed sleep, desperately, and food and water too. How long had it been? A day or two, three? It felt like a week – a month even. He yawned and felt his body moving off, his legs clumpy as if filled with wet sand. Every time he stopped a surge of intense heat smashed into him and he had no choice but to keep moving.

Kemp could see, though not well, and the sickly vapours of singed hair and fried flesh caught at the back of his throat. Every sound was muted, like being underwater. Soon his thoughts turned to death. If he refused to go on and died within Cain, then what? He'd be burned alive, probably. But would Cain remain trapped inside him until he rotted into dust or would Cain simply slip away like the spirit he was? Kemp groaned. Cain wouldn't die – he couldn't die – he was nothing more than a spirit who might leave him at any time.

But why had Cain tried to swap him for Archie towards the end of the storm? For a moment he'd been released – tossed out naked onto the rocks and deluged by the rain. He'd seen Archie battered and smashed, his body covered in cuts and bruises, his head bloodied from a gaping wound, his body motionless, pale, deathly.

Tears came to him then, but they would not flow.

He thought instead of Archie's strange hair. Kemp managed a wry smile. He knew then that his friend was too far gone to make a choice of joining Cain willingly.

So did Cain.

He remembered how the storm had lashed him with such violence that he knew he didn't stand a chance, certainly not while naked, burnt and hungry. He had no choice but to give himself freely back to Cain. He regretted it. He should have refused then and there, died in the storm and let Cain drift off to be a ghost again.

Now, here he was, living in the darkness of the body where burns streaked him like a spray gun of hot oil. It was like being trapped in space, he thought, with no one there to hear him scream.

*

'Look at us, boy,' Cain whispered. 'Here ... look at me. Isn't it magnificent!'

Cain studied his body in a tall mirror ringed with dull gemstones. Morning light shone through a vast window. He stood alone. 'You're here, boy,' he said, as his voice echoed off the walls. 'Right here inside me – that's right; half ash, half man ... or boy ... only a fraction ghost.'

Cain examined his reflection. His borrowed eyes weren't anything like the proper article – his vision filtered by a grainy film – but what a sensation to see anything when for thousands of years he had tuned into the vibrations and presence of things using his highly developed other sense – his sixth sense.

He studied his hands and turned them over. Then back. He clapped, the noise a muted thud. Ash puffed up and floated quietly through the air.

Oh the joys of having a body, he thought, whatever form it took.

Cain removed his overcoat, took off his hat and returned, naked, in front of the mirror. His figure was the same size of the boy and his torso was covered in layers of flaky ash in every conceivable hue of grey. How utterly remarkable, he thought, as he rotated from side to side.

His chest was a boyish replica of the one he remembered, though his pectorals and abdomen were not so hard and toned as perhaps they once were, and the sinews and muscles on his thighs, calves and buttocks were pleasingly accentuated by the light.

His feet, he noted, were unusually large. He sprang up on his toes only to find that a couple of digits simply dropped off. Cain stared, fascinated, as instantly they re-grew.

In the reflection of the mirror, Cain moved close. His face appeared sallow and partially skeletal with a flaky grey chin that jutted out more than he cared. He nudged his thick plump lips, prodded his flat nose and admired his eyebrows. He touched his hair that sat in a matted mass of ash swept back off his forehead and he admired his eyes that sparkled like polished coals.

Then he noticed a strange cluster at the top of his legs. Wasn't this awfully important? Instinctively he reached for it, but to his horror – and just as he remembered its purpose – the appendage severed, slipped through his fingers and careered to the ground. The ash dispersing over the floor. Cain squealed.

His concerns were short lived. Quickly it re-grew and he and his organ were re-acquainted. Cain's mood brightened. 'Thousands of years without one,' he roared, 'and the first one falls to pieces!'

Cain was a living body of ash – a by-product, he realised, of being burnt to death all those years ago. His eyes narrowed. How could he forget the burning, when his powers were taken away from him. The deal, he remembered. Oh yes, The Deal. Part of *his* Punishment.

Cain flexed up and down on his knees, he had movement – real gravity-based movement and physical presence. Utterly marvellous. None of this floating around nonsense any more, none of this walking through walls and doors and people – although it did, from time to time, have its advantages.

He wondered if the boy would interact with him and how their relationship would work in their combined state. Would the boy do as he commanded? Who controlled who? Who was master? Cain threw his arms up in the air and clapped his hands as a shower of ash fell over his head. So far he had been in control, no doubt about it.

All of a sudden a feeling of heaviness overcame him. Was the boy asleep again? Cain clenched his fist and found that when his concentration focused on that movement alone, the fingers pulled themselves together, like it or not.

Cain pressed one foot down followed by the other. He felt a modicum of resistance, like a badly-fitting drawer that needed forcing. He willed his leg to move. 'Come on, boy – we need to be able to use these, and to good effect.' But the movement felt sluggish, sleepy. He pulled his leg back and thrust it forward in a loose kicking motion, ash spraying. 'Good lad!' he said. Now he flailed his arms, moving them faster and faster until the boy trapped inside him did exactly as he wished.

'We've places to go, my little friend, and there's not a moment to lose.' Cain said out loud. He couldn't tell if the boy inside him could hear, but a feeling told him that the boy wasn't entirely deaf. 'Do my bidding, little friend of Archie de Lowe,' he said, 'and everything will work out fine. Just fine. You never know, we may even get to like one another.'

Hard as he pushed and cajoled, the boy inside him soon slowed to a standstill. Maybe sleep was required. A couple of hours should do the trick and then he'd be off again; Cain has returned from the ashes, the rumours said. Cain the Cruel, Master of Havilah is back, the cry went round. He could almost taste their fear, smell it. The inhabitants of Havilah were terrified of his apparent re-existence, he'd been told.

Cain knew instinctively that he needed to make the most of his presence, his new form – and fast.

*

Cain ran through the sequence of events of the past few days. Archie de Lowe, that scrawny young boy, deceiving him before the storm broke. Running off, cheating death. How, in the name of Eden, had the boy and his sisters survived? Battered and broken they made it to sundown by the very skin of their teeth and with no magic except for the special gifts they had been given by the dreamspinners. But they were children. *Children*, for goodness' sakes! How many human years? Fourteen for the eldest, twelve, perhaps, for the other two, the twins?

When men lived to be a thousand years, he thought, children of this age would be considered little more than babes. Cain smirked. Maybe these days they simply grew up faster. But even so, it was hard to fathom. The whole area ravaged; destruction and death on an horrific scale, but these de Lowe children, the pathetic Heirs of Eden, survived. Were they possessed with luck, he wondered, or had he underestimated them? Maybe they had escaped because they were too small, too weak.

Cain enjoyed the thought but his mood turned darker, a rage building in him.

The boy shifted.

And how, he wondered, had the old man arrived? What did they call him now, Old Man Wood, or something preposterous like that? That bumptious, bungling old fool had dragged them into the safety of the cave where the water would mend them; of that he was certain. Cain gritted his ashen teeth noting how they disintegrated and fell away, re-growing instantaneously. But did the children, these supposed Heirs of Eden, have the faintest idea what they were doing or what awaited them? Did they really understand?

Cain sighed. No, how could they? The riddles for the finding of Eden were designed for grown men, versed in magic, educated in battle, long in wisdom and the ways of nature.

He listened for the boy inside him and heard, faintly, snores coming from within. It had a strangely calming effect. Luck – that's what it was. Maybe they had been blessed with the vagaries of fortune. But fortune, he reminded himself, never hung around for too long.

And thinking of luck, what a huge slice that the dreamspinner, Asgard, had found him. Dreamspinners, the most ancient and mysterious of creatures who spun dreams to all living things and who were hidden from all … apart from him. Who would have thought he might travel through the blue electric middle of a dreamspinner – through its electric maghole – across the worlds?

Astonishing, really.

Cain watched as a section of his ashen finger fell and collapsed in a puff of ash on the floor. Big ugly spidery things, dreamspinners, like peculiar angels, or silky, spidery clouds with long, thin, opaque legs and cavernous, oval-shaped black eyes.

Cain allowed himself a wry smile. Asgard also knew the prophecy of Eden was not meant for children and now that the dream powders in the Garden of Eden had finished Asgard had the wisdom to understand that the only way to keep dream powders coming was to seek the help of Cain the Cruel, Master of Havilah.

Cain noticed, for the very first time, a gentle rhythmical beat within his chest cavity.

A heart.

My goodness, he had a heart. He placed an ashen hand over it and pressed gently, feeling the steady rhythm of its beat. It reminded him of his mother, the Ancient Woman, stuck forever in the Atrium of the Garden of Eden. She would need protecting, but the Heirs would fail before it got to that point. In any case, Archie had sworn to protect the Ancient Woman.

He'd hold that boy to his promise over his dead body.

So what next, Cain thought. He removed his hand from his chest, shut his eyes and took a deep breath. What followed flooding? Cain smiled. Disease. Yes, of course. Disease came next. Now the memories flowed: the Heirs of Eden had seven earth days to find three tablets and understand the riddles they posed. Seven days to save the planet and the human race as they knew it. Actually, Cain calculated, if they escaped from the cave, it would be more like five and a half. Probably less.

Cain wondered what the ridiculous Heirs of Eden were doing. Still stuck, no doubt. Ha! The clues were painted on the walls of the cave, or so he'd been told.

And it required great skills of observation, strength and speed to get out. Oh, happy, happy days, he mused. With any luck the little children would end up buried there with dear, forgetful Old Man Wood. Maybe he should pay them a visit and see how they were getting along.

Cain felt an arm stretch out wide. It was the boy in him moving his limb without him. It felt quite marvellous, thrilling. He felt a long breath of air fill his new lungs as the spark of an idea gathered in his dark mind.

If the disease starts where the storm began, he thought, then maybe he ought to make things a little more lively, speed things up, put the humans out of their misery a tad earlier.

So ... what if he were to add some of the disease particles to human dreams?

He listened to the silence of the night air, thrilled with his idea. He'd work on it. If he was right, the children would be too busy trying to figure out what was going on to be in the least bit concerned.

And besides, by the time most of the world had received dreams from his dream powders made from the spider webs of Havilah, there wouldn't be a world worth saving.

Cain opened his eyes and stared through the large window, his mind buzzing with a sense of excitement he'd long forgotten.

And then the road would finally be clear, he mused. Yes, after the longest time imaginable he would lay claim to the greatest prize of all: the Garden of Eden.

CHAPTER FIVE

The Protruding Stone

At the top, Archie and Daisy listened, their ears straining, the silence unbearable. Archie nibbled his fingernails until he'd run through both hands. Occasionally he wondered if he'd heard a sound, like a click or thud and he'd peer nervously down the stairwell.

Daisy shook her legs out, shut her eyes and imagined Isabella readying herself to push the stone lever, urging her to do it. She found that when she focused, she heard, quite clearly, Isabella's gasps and groans and mutterings, but the words bounced off the walls, reaching her ears as garbled sequences of noise.

The minutes passed. Daisy slumped down the wall. 'What if she can't do it?' she whispered.

Archie shrugged. 'What if she's not doing it right?'

'There's nothing to do wrong.'

'Maybe it's stuck – you know, jammed,' Archie said. 'It must be pretty old—'

'Nah. I reckon her brain's stopped … or she's had a breakdown …'

They leaned their heads back on the hard stone and closed their eyes.

'What do you think, Old Man Wood?' Archie asked.

The old man stared at the wall as though completely lost, miles away, and shook his head. 'Don't know, littleun,' he said, a worried look on his face. 'Think I might have to go and help her.' He picked himself up and stretched out his arms.

The twins shook their heads.

'Sorry, Old Man Wood,' Daisy said sweetly, 'but it's up to Isabella. There's no way you're going down there.'

And so they waited as a dreadful eerie stillness washed over the twins who sat, heads in hands, alert for any strange noise. But all they could hear was the quiet hush of the cave and the occasional drip-dripping where water had seeped in through the ages making small pools and streams which disappeared through cracks in the rock.

Shortly, the twins heard a strange noise, a throaty, purring rhythmic sound that reverberated around the cave.

Archie stood up smartly and swivelled his head trying to pinpoint where it was coming from, but Daisy pulled at the threads of his loose tattered shirt and pointed towards the old man who sat sleeping. The twins caught each other's eye and smiled. Snores. Great big ones like a throbbing motorbike engine.

Archie sat down and closed his eyes.

'It must be fifteen minutes,' Daisy said nudging him. 'Do you think she's alright?'

'Yeah. I'm sure she's fine,' he lied.

Daisy stood up and walked over to the stairwell. 'She's down there all right – I can hear grunts and scrapes – as if she's moving a stone or a rock, or something.'

Archie joined her. 'I can't hear anything at all,' he said. 'Are you sure?'

'Yep. Quite sure,' Daisy replied. 'It's not right, Archie. Something's terribly wrong.'

*

Isabella stepped back into the cavern, took a lungful of air and tried to compose herself.

Why wouldn't the damn lever move? Perhaps she simply wasn't strong enough.

She'd spent every last morsel of energy pushing down until her arm and leg muscles cried out, but it hadn't worked. Why not?

Now she shuffled about, head down. 'Calm down, Isabella,' she said out loud, her voice mingling with the soft bubbling tones of the chamber. Isabella's hands were shaking badly, very badly.

She stretched her arms out, took a couple of long breaths and returned through the hidden door to the step. She stared at the two protruding rocks – the *supposed* levers.

What if it was stuck? Jammed in some way? She slammed her right foot down on it for the twentieth time, gritted her teeth and pushed as hard as she could. But still it would not yield.

She sat down on the stairs, exhausted. Should she ask the others? Daisy might be able to figure it out with her silly eyes or Archie with his supposed super-strength, but it would make her look such a total failure. She groaned. And then she'd get only endless taunts from the twins about how weedy and hopeless she'd been.

There's no option, she thought. I've got to do it myself, use my brain and work it out logically. She gathered her strength and approached the protruding stone from a fresh angle, positioning herself so that her foot lay directly in line with the angle of the stairs. It didn't work. In frustration she pulled and pushed and heaved again, each time getting more and more irate until a rage bubbled up inside her.

'Right, you evil stubborn, stupid rock,' she said to the protruding knob. 'I know what you need: a bloody great whack.' She marched into the cave and looked around. On the floor lay a variety of good sized stones.

'If I use a heavy one,' she said, as she found a nearly square grey lump of rock, 'and drop it from height, the downward force will be tenfold what I can do with my body mass alone.' She smiled. Triple that, she thought, as she factored in the speed and mass.

And if that fails, then – and only then – will I let Archie or Daisy have a go.

With considerable effort she rolled the rock across the floor and squeezed it through the narrow entrance. So far so good. On her knees she manoeuvred it onto the first step, and wary that it might topple off, quickly heaved it up to the second step followed by the third. On the fourth it wobbled and she caught it, pushing it back on the ledge. She took a couple of deep breaths.

Four more steps to go and with the correct aim and allowance for the circular stairs, she'd roll it off and nail the knobby stone.

Her mood lifted.

At the sixth step, she wondered whether it would be enough. Quickly she did another mass and velocity sum in her head and tried to work out if there might be enough momentum and downward force to utterly pulverise it.

Probably not. She cursed.

Up to the seventh step. Now the eighth. She was hot and angry and so utterly fixated on completing her task that she had almost forgotten about her worries. She stretched out her back and flexed her fingers.

'Right. Here you go – you horrible little, annoying, stubborn, nasty knob of rock.' Her fingers slid underneath the overhanging stone.

'You're going to be smashed into tiny little bits!'

*

Ever since she'd returned to the top, Daisy had been nagged by the thought that she may have misinterpreted the icon – the tiny, delicate picture on the wall. Perhaps the faint round markings above the image represented a touch by something like a pebble or a stone, and now that she thought hard about it, it made complete sense.

She swayed at the top of the stairs wondering whether to run down and tell Isabella. She tapped Archie on the shoulder. 'Winkle, I think I know why Isabella's struggling.'

Archie groaned and opened his eyes.

'She needs to hit it with a pebble – a stone – something hard. I've figured it out. I've got to tell her – all it needs is a tap.'

Archie woke up. 'Woah, Daisy. Hang on! What if she sets it off while you're halfway down and the walls start folding in?'

'Well so what? She's still got to run up.'

'But you've been up and down like a yo-yo and stretching your legs and stuff – they must be like jelly,' Archie said.

Daisy ruffled her hair. 'Tough. Sorry, winkle, but she needs to know. Otherwise we're stuck.'

Archie had a bad feeling about it. 'OK, but promise you'll only go down far enough so that she can hear you. The last thing we need is for you two to get in each other's way.'

Daisy nodded, and for the fourth time headed down the two hundred and twenty two steps, the noise of her feet scuffing the stones as she descended.

*

Isabella started to lift the mini boulder, her back straining, her fingers raw when a voice echoed off the walls.

Daisy. It had to be. Isabella stopped as she tried to comprehend the message. 'I'm – doing – it,' she yelled back.

Isabella suddenly found the rock unbelievably heavy and much to her horror the square lump slipped through her fingers and crashed first onto the step below and then the next, gaining momentum.

Isabella stared in disbelief, helpless to do anything. The stone spun, touched the corner of the next step and launched into the air. Isabella gasped. She hadn't figured that it would bounce! What if it missed?

It clipped the one below and as it passed by the protruding knob, a tiny stone fragment sliced off it as it flew by before smacking into the wall and shattering over the floor.

Isabella groaned and put her head in her hands. After all that, she cried, the rock missed. *It had missed!*

She sank to the floor, defeated.

Idiot – what a fool. What would the others say …

And then it happened.

Suddenly, everything shook.

Chunks of stone sprayed from the ceiling. Isabella wrapped her arms above her head, protecting herself, the shaking throwing her into the wall where she struggled to keep her footing.

Then a grinding noise; the gear mechanisms whirling, groaning and crunching all around her.

For a moment Isabella didn't understand. The next rumble threw her off her stair and she crashed down to the foot of the stairwell. Had she engaged the lever or was it an earthquake? She poked her head into the chamber and gasped.

Water seeped through cracks in the film protecting the cave entrance. Her heart thumped wildly.

My God, she'd done it.

She needed to move. But another rumble sent her sprawling against the wall. More debris flew. She felt a crack on her head. Dazed she stood up, disorientated, giddy. Isabella closed her eyes. Her head swum. She leant into the wall.

The water touching her ankle snapped her round. She opened her eyes and retched. It made her feel better instantly.

'RUN, RUN!' WHAT'S WRONG WITH YOU?' she heard.

The water was up to her knees. Isabella swore and started up the stairs, one at a time, then two – onward, upwards.

Then a boom, like a giant wave crashing into the chamber, filled her with a dread she had never believed possible.

The panel.

Isabella ran, faster and faster.

The water gaining. The passage narrowing.

She focused hard and before she knew it her hands and feet sprang off each step like a great cat until she was bounding, round and round the stairwell, faster and faster, up and up, like a blur.

Nearly there, but now the walls on either side were so tight her sides were being scraped like cheese in a grater. A blast of wind caught her now, water rushing beside, overtaking her, carrying her to the peak.

She took a last gasp of air, stretched her arms in front of her and pointed her toes like a ballerina.

When she smashed into the ceiling, her hands padded her impact but she felt herself crumple in a heap.

Her arms ached. Water sprayed everywhere.

She landed on something soft.

Then a big black veil swept over her and she felt no more.

*

Daisy was halfway down when she heard the gears shift. Isabella had done it! But instead of rushing off she waited until she heard her sister's scream, for while the passageway was rumbling and shaking it was otherwise silent.

And it remained silent.

Something must have happened. She ran down as far as she dared and screamed.

Daisy knew what was coming, she could hear it.

She waited as long as possible then fled up the stairs taking them two or three at a time urging her exhausted body on, praying that Isabella was not far behind. She feared the worst.

Near the top she could hear a noise like a dam bursting, water flashing out, gaining, chasing her. She missed a narrowing step and fell, the hard stair-lip cracking her shin. She howled but limped upwards, the rock ripping, tearing her sides.

Isabella had no chance.

A massive gust of air blasted up through the stairwell blowing her on. She knew it heralded the arrival of the water. When the water hit her she had only a few steps to go and using its momentum she flung her body out of its path and into the cave.

She stood up and gasped. Water poured from the ceiling, spraying the cavern like a fire-fighter's hose. Seconds later, she was flattened by an object that rebounded off the ceiling like a rubber ball.

Isabella's blood soaked body.

CHAPTER SIX

Sue And Gus At Sea

Sue scanned the endless horizon and whistled. 'Sublime and ridiculous.'

'What do you mean?' Gus said as he wrestled with a penknife and the lid of a can of tuna.

'We survive a monsoon in a geriatric rowing boat – with a ridiculous name—'

'There's nothing wrong with calling a boat *The Joan Of*,' Gus said, smiling.

Sue raised her eyebrows. 'Anyway, thanks to your sublime woodworking skills we're still alive, but like fools we wake up in an ocean possibly miles from anywhere in another perilous situation. Therefore, ridiculous.'

Gus flashed a toothy smile and poured the brine off the tuna and into a cup. 'Well, if you hadn't fallen asleep at your post, none of this would have happened.'

'Gus, are you blaming me?'

'Of course,' he mocked. 'I entirely blame you. You should have woken me up rather than snuggle up.'

'But you looked so sweet.' Sue couldn't believe she'd said that and instantly her face turned bright red.

Gus didn't know if he should read anything into her comment. He'd never had a girlfriend – he'd never given girls any serious thought before, but here he was, twelve and mature for his age, and most of his friends had dallied in some form of relationship. He thought about his interaction with girls and found that although he was friendly with many, like Daisy de Lowe and Poppy in his class, Sue was the first girl he'd ever really properly talked to about stuff. Stuff like life and parents and feelings. Up till now, girls could have been aliens; they did different things – odd things – and even talked in a strange way.

Gus offered Sue first go at the brine liquid that lay on top of the chopped fish.

'Oh really, do we have to?'

'Yes. Everything that can be eaten, must be eaten and that's an order. No wastage allowed.'

Although she was starving the idea of drinking raw brine didn't fill her with a great deal of joy. She rolled her eyes and pinched her nose, sipping the tangy bitter juice. It stuck to her gums.

She handed the rest over to Gus.

'You know I've never had a proper boyfriend,' she said moving next to him and leaning on his shoulder.

'And I've never had a girlfriend,' Gus said, cringing. He felt himself tense. God she smelt wonderful, like fresh fruit. And seated so close to one another there was no way of denying it; she was fabulous, even if her breath smelled a bit … fishy.

He sipped on the brine and spluttered.

She stared into his eyes. Gus was the most amazing person she'd ever come across. He'd saved her life. Not only that but he'd kept her smiling and it had given her a whole new perspective on life. If they didn't make it, he'd smile right to the bitter end, she thought. Wasn't that amazing? For some reason, she'd felt safer just being with him than anyone she could think of.

*

Gus stared back into her eyes which shone like jewels. He took a sharp intake of breath. Oh my goodness. His heart raced, blood pumping fiercely through his veins. A strange kind of electrical current passed through him. What was going on?

She leaned in and kissed him – just a peck, on his cheek and she held her mouth close. He felt her breath on his cheek. It felt so perfect, so timely. Gus felt his head swim, stood up and cracked his head on the wooden frame of the canopy above them.

'Blimey,' Sue said, chuckling. 'You've never kissed anyone before, have you?'

Gus rubbed his head. Now it was his turn to turn beetroot. 'Yeah, of course I have,' he lied, badly.

The corners of Sue's mouth turned up mischievously. 'Who?'

Gus couldn't think fast enough. His head was in a muddle. 'Oh God. Do you really have to know?'

'Yeah! Absolutely! Come on!'

Gus played for time and rubbed his head. 'Er, no … I can't—'

'Go on!' Sue demanded. 'I insist!'

'OK. It was, er, Daisy,' he said, not knowing why he'd said it.

Sue reeled. 'Daisy de Lowe, Daisy Dupree or Daisy Martin,' she fired back.

'Oh, ah, um, the first one,' he mumbled.

'Well now, you're a sneaky devil, aren't you,' she said. He was lying through his teeth like most boys his age. 'Daisy de Lowe, huh?'

Gus reddened. 'Er, yeah. Didn't last for long,' Gus said trying to sound casual and busying himself in the food box.

Sue frowned. Boys loved Daisy because she was beautiful and cool and sensational at football. But she was aloof, off in her own little world half the time. And anyway, she knew Isabella and the de Lowes better than she knew her own family and the whole thing seemed … unlikely. She reckoned Gus might have had a crush on her.

'Now, Gus,' she said. 'Let's be honest, that wasn't a great start. We could give it another go if you'd like?'

Gus drooled. His speech deserted him. He nodded like a puppy dog.

Very gently they leaned in.

The moment their lips came together, Gus smiled and tried very hard not to snicker. He lurched forward and bashed his teeth on hers. There was a clank which sounded a great deal louder to both of them than it really was.

He pulled away. 'God, sorry. That was rubbish, wasn't it?'

Sue smiled. Before he could move again, she looked deeply into his eyes, put a finger over his lips and slowly replaced her fingers with her lips.

*

Gus was so shocked that it took him a while before he joined in. Was it revolting or nice? It was most definitely slippery, he thought, and a bit fishy. His tongue appeared to be battling a mini eel.

Either way, he couldn't decide, but all of a sudden a strange shot of energy passed straight through him, like a stab of electricity. An *electric eel*, he thought.

He broke it off – a smile on his face. 'Tuna?'

Sue looked confused. 'Tuna?'

'Er. Yup.' Gus couldn't think why he'd suddenly blurted it out. Maybe it was because he felt a bit out of control, getting aroused on a boat – or more likely because he'd just opened a tin of their prized food and he was famished. Kissing could wait.

He noted her disappointed face. 'Oh no. I ruined it, didn't I?'

'No,' she said, looking a little embarrassed. 'Well, yes, you did a bit.'

'Sorry. It's just … you, er, surprised me and … I'd just opened—'

'Don't say a word,' she said. 'I'm utterly starving. Let's eat.' She prodded him gently on the arm. 'Plenty of time for practice!'

Gus divided the tuna onto the two paint pot lids they used for plates and handed out two biscuits and half an apple. It wasn't really enough, but it was better than nothing. Gus realised that running out of food was a real possibility so he divided their foodstuff into meals that might stretch to two weeks. Realistically he doubted they could hold out that long. If he could work out how to catch fish, it would, as their sports coach said, be a "game changer".

And so long as it continued raining and the three big water containers were topped up using his upside down umbrella water-catching device, they would survive. If it stopped raining for more than three days, then they were in trouble.

After chewing the food as best they could and swilling it down with a cup of water, Gus tried to not think about kissing and the quite extraordinary buzz that tingled all the way through him and set about thinking about how they could get *The Joan Of*, back to land.

They talked as he went about his tasks, the first of which was trying to make a sail. Occasionally he would ask Sue to hold things or to pass him a nail or a piece of wood. Then he gave her a length of string and Sue threaded it down a section of the tarpaulin which he'd cut with his penknife and as she did this he wrapped it around a long length of wood which was to be the mast. When this was done he wedged the upright tight between the seat and the prow of the rowing boat so that it stuck up in front of *The Joan Of.* For good measure, he nailed the timber into the prow and bound it with rope.

The course they sailed would be the direction the wind blew and he hoped like crazy they'd catch an easterly wind which would blow them back to the English coast.

Wherever they were going, perhaps now they would get there faster.

*

While Gus moved up and down the tiny boat, making adjustments and checking his ropes and trying to get wind in his sail, Sue reached into the wooden box stowed under the main seat and fetched out a fishing line. She remembered a conversation between Archie and Kemp when they'd been discussing their fishing tackle. Something to do with sweet corn as bait and shiny objects that she thought looked like large earrings. Lures. She looked in their supplies. Three tins.

She checked the nylon line. It seemed fine, as far as she could tell. She found a rounded double hook that looked like a tiny anchor which curved back on itself. Surrounding it were some faded feathers with a hint of sparkle. She opened the tin and popped two corns onto the spikes and a couple in her mouth with her fingers and savoured the sweet juice.

Carefully she removed one of her own earrings and using the fishing line, tied it close to the hook below the feathers. Very slowly she let the line out, further and further until the lure disappeared behind a gentle roll of water.

Gus popped his head down. 'Everything OK? Mind if I squeeze past. I've just got to tension the mast and then we're done.'

Sue shuffled along as Gus stood up, threw the rope above the canopy to the other end and scuttled after it.

The moment he pulled the rope, the wind caught in the tarpaulin and the boat lurched forward.

'Wa-hey! It works,' he exclaimed. He reached down and squeezed her shoulder. 'We'll get somewhere in no time,' he joked.

'Or is that nowhere in some time?' she threw back at him.

Gus beamed. The sea was calm and the lapping of water as the waves bent around the bow of the boat was a truly positive sound.

He sat down next to her. 'Now, would it be alright if we go back to just before "tuna"?'

She giggled, turned to him and they kissed, briefly.

But now Sue broke away. A look of panic filled her face.

'What is it now?' Gus said.

'Fish!'

'What?' This time it was Gus' turn to be confused. 'Hell. Where?'

'FISH!' She pushed him away. Her arm was outstretched at a ninety degree angle.

Gus stared at her with a puzzled look on his face.

She stared back. 'Help me!'

'Uh?'

'Look.' She pointed to where her other arm pointed out to sea. 'I think I've got a fish!'

Gus suddenly understood. Gently he helped her wind in the nylon line around the plastic unit. His hands on hers, keeping a steady rhythm.

'Not too fast, but you've got to keep it moving.'

'I think it's a big one,' she said, before turning pink.

Gus didn't notice. 'Let the line slack a bit and then pull it in again. Don't lose the tension!'

She did as he said and slowly started to bring it home.

'You can do it!' he said. 'Go on, land it yourself!'

Sue's arm was about to fall off and she shot him a look of panic. 'It's too heavy!'

Gus hand came back on hers. 'OK. When you think you can, we'll pull it firmly in one fluid movement into the boat.'

The fish was close and angry. Sue could see it thrashing in the water. She wound the line twice round the plastic coil, stopped and turned to Gus.

His face was beaming. 'Keep going, it won't bite!'

Sue could see its dark silvery coils, its black eyes staring back at her. Two more twists. Her fingers hurt. She pulled gently, wondering if her muscles could take it. Gus, with his big hands on top of hers steadied himself.

'One more and then up and into the boat,' he said. 'Ready?'

Together they heaved and the fish slipped out of the water and thudded into the boat.

The fish thrashed, it's tail flapping and sliding and thudding against the wooden planks, until Gus grabbed a hammer and bashed it on the head. The fish stopped, it's battle lost.

He beamed at Sue his eyes sparkling. 'You did it, Sue!' he cried. 'First go.'

He had no idea what kind of fish it was but it meant that if they drifted out to sea, at least it would give them more time. They wouldn't starve. Brilliant, brilliant Sue.

'Sushi for tea?' he said.

'Yeah! I love sushi,' Sue replied, her face radiant and her eyes sparkling.

CHAPTER SEVEN

The Boulder

Archie fell to the ground. Rock and stone dislodged from the ceiling and thudded down over the cavern floor. He rolled under an overhanging lip as the tremors shook. His heart pounded.

'Old Man Wood!' he screamed. The old man stood in the middle covering his head. 'Move! Here!'

When the tremor ceased and the noise of the gears kicked in, he wondered what sort of hell the girls must be going through deep down in the depths of the cliff.

Another tremendous rumble forced his hands over his ears. The boulder in the front of the cave began to move. Slowly, incredibly, it rose up from out of the ground. Archie jumped out from under the ledge and thumped the air.

'Come on! Keep going, keep going!' he yelled.

But as quickly as his euphoria started it ceased for the boulder simply stopped. And there it sat, the same size, the same width but with no part nestled under the ground. It was perched in the entrance.

Why didn't it roll away?

His attention was grabbed by a ghostly noise whistling up the stairs.

Hell, the girls.

He ran over. He could feel the wind, stronger now, as an awful, swirling noise grew louder and louder. Without warning and just as Daisy threw herself out of the small hole a huge jet of water smashed into the ceiling. Archie ducked as spray douched the cave.

In the following moments all hell broke loose. Going at the speed of a cannonball Isabella smashed into the ceiling, and crash-landed directly on top of Daisy.

Both lay on the ground. Motionless.

Archie's heart nearly stopped. He ran to Isabella and found her smothered in gashes – some deep dark red, others pink where skin had been peeled away by the rock. Blood ran through her hair and streamed across her face, her arms and her legs. Her body was limp, her arms shattered and bent over like towels over a washing line.

'QUICK!' he screamed at Old Man Wood. 'Quick! The girls – your potion.'

Together they carried the girls to the far end of the cave, away from the spray, and laid them down on a stone slab.

Archie turned and swore. The cavern floor was already filling with water, the boulder acting like a seal, holding the water in.

*

Old Man Wood's face was as pale as milk as he nursed Isabella. Her clothes were shredded to bits, her arms dangling.

He moved both girls as high as he could and pulled out his little bottle full of healing liquid which he placed to their lips. The Resplendix Mix would mend and make them stable. He didn't know how – but it would – so long as the bottle opened.

Almost immediately Daisy opened her eyes.

Now Isabella's turn. He pushed the bottle to her lips and she gasped as the first drop hit her tongue, coughed on the second and screamed as the third drop set to work.

Old Man Wood kissed her forehead. 'Be brave, young Bells,' he said soothingly. 'Healing, littleun, is a painful business.'

And this, he thought, as he studied her torso, was really going to hurt.

*

Archie waded through the water.

He had to move the boulder and fast. But how? He weighed it up and heard Isabella moan then scream in agony. She was alive. It spurred him on. He had to try – even if it was impossibly large. There was no other alternative.

If he could turn it a fraction, jog it a couple of millimetres, then at least some water would rush out.

He waded around to the side of the huge boulder, put his hands and chest in the water and tried to find a hand-hold. Too smooth. By the time he'd worked his way round to the other side, water lapped at his chest. He dived down and this time his fingers touched on a little ridge. Perfect. He stood up and took as big a breath as he could, sank down under the surface, bent his knees and with every ounce of strength he heaved. And he didn't stop lifting until every particle of oxygen in his frame departed.

Archie resurfaced, with only his head and shoulders above water. He gasped, drew in a huge lungful and went again. He found his hold and heaved once more.

He felt something shift. It definitely moved.

He kept it up until once again he had to surface for air. Archie stood on his tiptoes gulping. One more go. He looked over towards Old Man Wood who held the girls over his shoulder his eyes shut tight.

Archie's eyes were bulging. It had to be this time.

He ducked under. His fingers grasped the stone hold and he crouched low bending right back on his haunches. Then gritting his teeth and using every muscle in his body – he heaved. It moved again, surely, but not enough.

52

Archie resurfaced, treading water. So, so close. Maybe one more try.

He wondered whether he had enough strength left in his body. Treading water wasn't helping. Could he do one more? He swam up to the boulder and as he looked up at the sphere, an idea struck him.

Why not shove it from the top? He'd have more of a hold. Perhaps he could rock it – create a gap for the water to wash out and away.

He swam to the side and climbed on top of the stone, so that while he pawed the ceiling with his hands, his feet gripped the crown of the boulder.

Archie sucked in a couple of huge mouthful of air, bent his knees and pressed.

Nothing. He felt hopeless.

At least Old Man Wood had clambered up onto the stone ledge with the girls. He had a couple more minutes.

Archie shut his eyes as an image of him trying to push a boulder came into his head. How could he possibly be expected to move a boulder?

He grinned and then chuckled as again he saw himself, in his mind's eye, doing something so dumb, so stupid, so ridiculously impossible that it was hard to believe.

He chuckled louder, seeing himself – a boy on a boulder, trying to move it. Then he started roaring with laughter. He smacked and kicked the boulder in total hysterics.

'What a stupid, stupid fool you are, Archie de Lowe,' he sang, between howls of laughter.

As he did this he reached the top of the boulder and using the ceiling as a prop he pushed and pulled in a rocking motion singing and laughing like a maniac.

He was still laughing when he felt the extraordinary sensation of movement. Then a wobble, then a feeling of water flashing by.

Archie held on to the top of the cave like mad and only when he realised what was happening did he allow his grip to lessen.

'OH MY GOD! It's moving!' he screamed. 'HEEELP—!'

And in the nick of time, as the boulder started to rotate he threw himself off and landed in a pool of muddy water.

As he lay in a heap, he heard only the roar of water rushing by and the crash of the huge boulder smashing everything in its path as it thundered down the hillside.

CHAPTER EIGHT

Mrs Pye's Storm

A heavy drizzle from low grey clouds in the failing light matched the de Lowe's sombre mood. Looking around it was hard to imagine the place they knew so well could look so smashed, pulped to bits, beaten up. And it had all happened in a few wretched, brutal hours, almost exactly one day ago.

Boulders, rocks, sand, mud, trees, bushes and branches, lay scattered and splintered randomly with no care or enterprise. When they stumbled on a few paces and rounded a large protruding section of rock the valley opened up beneath them and even in the dank gloom they gasped. From their vantage point on top of the hill the surroundings were significantly less mangled than in the valley where the water had obliterated everything in its path. Beneath them a moving body of water stretched as far as the eye could see like a big, flat, silvery-grey monster. In the distance where the tops of the gentle valleys of the Vale of York rolled, small hillocks had emerged like little islands, stretching out like the backs of crocodiles lying in a river.

When they turned towards the school only the reflective grey of the water and the distinctive school tower and chapel roof reached up into the sky.

For several minutes the four of them stared agog at the extraordinary sight. This was destruction on a terrifying scale and from where they stood, it seemed quite possible that only they had survived.

Archie looked on while holding Daisy's hand, who in turn held Old Man Wood's hand who carried Isabella over his shoulder.

A sudden emptiness and helplessness threatened to overcome them.

'It's so quiet,' Daisy whispered, 'so, sort of … dead.' Her strange red eyes bulged, full of tears. 'Like we've discovered a different planet.'

'No birds, not a twitter,' Archie said. 'Everything churned up as though it's been in a gigantic mixer.' He felt sick.

Isabella woke, and moaned. The accelerated healing effect of the Resplendix Mix potion had knocked her out, and the pain had dropped off to mildly less excruciating. Already, astonishingly, the multiple scuffs and lacerations over her body were beginning to close. She too wanted a look.

Old Man Wood set her down, and for a while the four of them, sat quietly on the fallen bough of an old oak and viewed the landscape, a gentle wind marking their faces.

'I hope the house is still in one piece,' Daisy said at length. 'And Mrs Pye's not been flushed out.'

Old Man Wood groaned. 'Only one way to find out. Ready to go?'

Collectively they turned away and limped slowly on, their feet squelching in the mud. Old Man Wood hoisted Isabella back over his shoulder and picked out a path, mindful of larger puddles and steep banks of slippery mud.

Before long they came over the brow of the hill and looked out over where the cottage should have been.

'It's gone,' Old Man Wood said, wiping away a tear.

'No it hasn't,' Daisy said. 'Don't be daft.'

'Daisy, it isn't there anymore,' Archie said.

'Trust me, please,' Daisy said. 'It is. You're all being very dramatic.'

And as they approached, perfectly camouflaged amongst the debris at the top of the hillside, sat their stone cottage, its roof covered by moss and lichen blending in seamlessly with the greens and browns of the forest. An impressive oak tree now leaned into the courtyard in such a way that the crown of the tree enveloped the house, making the buildings all but indistinguishable from the carnage around.

Only Daisy with her extraordinary eyesight could see it.

For a while their thoughts were of the worst but when Daisy spotted a thin plume of smoke curling out of the chimney they exchanged glances and smiles, their eyes sparking into life. They knew that Mrs Pye was safe and that comfort and food and warmth and sleep were not far away.

Never had the rough misshapen stone house in the middle of the forest on the edge of the Yorkshire moors been a more welcome sight.

*

Mrs Pye sat in the kitchen fretting when she heard scuffling noises in the courtyard. Must be her imagination playing tricks again, she thought. The sound of a soccer ball being kicked over the paving slabs, a sound like sandpaper on wood, was a noise she associated with Daisy and Archie. That and shouts and laughter: happy sounds of the children.

She tried to put it out of her mind and concentrated on lighting the fire again.

Then her ears instinctively pricked up again, just as they had at every sound since she'd caught a glimpse of the old man leaving the house the day before wearing a builder's hard hat. What an astonishing rainstorm –

blasting out of the sky hour after hour. She'd never seen or heard anything like it. And as the hours slipped by she didn't dare go to bed, just in case they returned. In any case the lightning was simply terrifying. So she went round the house cleaning and mopping up water and singing loudly. For in her heart she knew something terrible was happening.

An ache, like a stubborn splinter, pierced her and for the first time in years the long scar beneath the mop of bright orange hair on her forehead throbbed, giving her a pressing headache. She pined for the children. It was as though a cord had been severed between them, as though part of her soul had become detached. She tried to put these feelings behind her and soldier on. She had to. They would return, she was sure of it. What would she do if they didn't?

A staggering amount of water had poured down the various chimneys dotted around the house. Mrs Pye had waddled round as fast as her legs would carry her placing buckets in every grate and under every chimney flue. She'd been entirely preoccupied with mopping water out of each fireplace, rolling up the hearth rugs and adjacent carpets and then emptying the buckets outside or down the sink. Round and round the house she went, from the children's bedroom in the attic to Old Man Wood's room to the parents' room, then downstairs to the kitchen and sitting room and the study, across the courtyard through sheets of rain to her apartment and then back again, and again. Each time drenched to the bone. She was thankful that the house sat at the top of a hill and had a big, oversized roof which made the water run away. Or else, she thought … or else.

In Old Man Wood's room near to where water had spilled over from the fireplace, she noticed five rectangular rugs that sat on his floor, each the size of a hearth rug. She folded them up and took them to the back door to give them a bit of shake under the wide roof trusses. As she did plumes of dust flew in every direction.

How revolting, she thought. How vile. She'd give the old man a good talking to when he returned – if he returned. They were caked, like knotted dreadlocks, their colour a blend of silvery brown and dark green and the patterns submerged beneath years of dirt. As the rain belted down upon them, a black sludge dribbled out, like slurry. Mrs Pye left the rugs in the deluge for a few moments and then decided to bring them in, draping them over a wooden clothes horse under the rickety old porch. If she left them outside, she thought, Lord only knew where they might end up.

Night fell, and to her great relief the deluge subsided. She mopped the remaining water from the fireplaces and laid a fire in both the kitchen and the sitting room, which she lit. Covering herself in a blanket, and quite overwhelmed with tiredness and worry, she nodded off in the rocking chair in the kitchen next to the warm metal range beneath the thick oak beams.

Hours later she woke suddenly and for a moment wondered where she was. She yawned and for a second thought she could hear tiny, shrill voices. She looked around. No, there was nothing there. Just imaginary things, like the noise of a football being kicked in the courtyard.

The house was as black as night so she opened a box of matches and struck one. The flame briefly shone, the bright light extending its reach into the large room before dying back. Mrs Pye felt a chill. The fire was on its last embers. She added a handful of kindling and placed two dry logs on top, stood up and stretched out, feeling the stabbing pain in her shoulder that had been with her all her life.

She took the candle and trundled to the door, made her way to the sitting room, added several logs into the large ashen grate and sank down into the sofa. She sighed. Where were they? What had become of them? She played with various scenarios. Maybe they were at school and playing with their friends, Archie with his black hair and cheeky look, the freckles around his nose that made him look naughtier than he really was and his dark lively eyes. She'd get him a whole new uniform when their parents returned. She'd insist on it. No more patched-up clothes – he was too old for that.

Then she thought of Isabella. Isabella so upright and straightforward, so bright and busy. Her straight brown hair that fell over her face when she was embarrassed, just like her mother. Her straight pointy nose and thin lips. Her alertness and confidence. Oh, and her temper!

And then there was Daisy. Funny, pretty Daisy with her blond wavy hair and red cheeks, her keen eyes and her warm smile. Why, they all had warm smiles, she thought. Nice teeth and warm smiles. Decent, well mannered kids, too. She let a tear roll down her cheeks.

Where were they?

Had they been caught in the storm trying to head home? She shivered and pulled her woollen blanket tight. Wasn't there anything she could do?

Mrs Pye had no idea how long she'd been asleep, but she woke suddenly to find a dim light filtering in through the windows and the fire smouldering in front of her. She checked her watch and with a groan, pulled herself up. The house was as quiet as she could remember and she wore her sense of loss like a ball and chain.

In the kitchen she put the kettle on the stove and stared out of the windows as morning light rose over the Vale below her. She gasped. My goodness me, she thought. A lake – or was it sea that filled the valley below?

Nearer, trees lay prostrate in a wretched jumble. Her heart sank.

She hobbled about, wondering if she should go outside and call out for them. But what if they returned only to find an empty home? That wouldn't be right, and in any case, the old man would bring them back, wouldn't he? He had a knack of doing that. After all, he'd found her all those years ago, barely alive, so they said, deep in the forest at the bottom of a gorge. He'd carried her home, apparently – for many miles. He'd do the same with the children. She felt it in the marrow of her bones. There was something right about this feeling, something special about the old man that she couldn't quite lay a finger on.

If he couldn't do it, who else could?

She continued with her chores; she made bread and finished off the washing. She added more logs to the old iron stove to bring it up to heat, and then shuffled out of the back door where she moved the wooden clothes horse and gathered up the five rugs which to her great surprise were mildly damp and not at all saturated with water.

Strange little things, she thought. Like hearth rugs but lighter and, as she realised when she gripped the fabric, far stronger. She knew Old Man Wood didn't like her in his room, and duly stayed away, but why hadn't these been washed before? She had a good mind to either throw them in the rubbish bin or pop them in the washing machine. She tutted. Without any power they would have to wait. No, she'd let them finish drying and pop them back in Old Man Wood's room, dirty though they were, and give them a proper clean when the power came back on.

*

With her jobs done and the house as spic and span as she could remember, the sweet aroma of fresh bread filling the kitchen and the dry, though filthy rugs replaced on the floor of Old Man Wood's room, Mrs Pye sat down in her rocking chair with a hot mug filled with sprigs of mint. She swayed, backwards and forwards for a minute or two, lost in her own world as she hummed Old Man Wood's peculiar song. Then her eyes began to close and she slept.

For some strange reason she thought she heard Old Man Wood's deep tone.

Her eyes opened. She'd imagined it – must have – or she'd been dreaming. She closed her eyes and as she did, she heard it again. But this time there was another voice, higher in pitch. She stood up straight away, conscious of the blood rushing into her heart. Could it be possible? Had he returned, with the children?

By the time she reached the huge studded door her pulse was racing. She withdrew the large black iron bolt and yanked on the brass knob. The door yawned open. There, in front of her, stood the old man with the three children. One was draped over his shoulder covered in blood and littered with an assortment of cuts and bruises. The others were hanging on to his coat, shivering, almost naked, their remaining clothes hanging off them, torn to shreds. One had strange spikes on his head and the other had hair matted to her face.

'It's a miracle, it's a damned ruddy miracle,' she cried as she opened her arms, her voice cracking with emotion. Daisy and Archie folded into her large midriff, tears falling freely down their cheeks. 'Oh my poor, dear children,' she cried. 'You're safe. Safe now.'

Mrs Pye ushered them in and while making a terrible fuss sat them down in front of the fire and produced a basket crammed with soft downy blankets and pillows, and shortly after that a saucepan full of thick milky chocolate appeared. She returned with homemade flapjacks and sandwiches bulging with butter and raspberry jam. Archie and Daisy tucked in, but Isabella was too sick, too broken by the looks of things, to eat. Old Man Wood was seeing to her next door.

Mrs Pye talked and cried in equal measure as she went. 'Do you have any ideas what a terrible, terrible time I've had?' she said repeatedly. 'Do you have any ideas how it's been for me, huh? Watching the storm out there and worrying meself sick,' she complained. 'And do you have any ideas how difficult it is being alone in the house with no one here?' At this point, she turned on Old Man Wood. 'What were you playing at – leaving without telling!' she shouted through to the next room. 'Left me on my own to worry – and worry I did, every minute of every night and every second of the day.'

And then she exploded into tears and told them all how much she loved them and how she would never let it happen again – over her dead body – and that she knew they'd be alright and she knew they'd come back.

Mrs Pye was normally a woman of few words so this tirade was borne out of complete and utter love and the children knew it.

Archie and Daisy exchanged smiles as if to say, "if she really knew what had happened … what then?"

CHAPTER NINE

Sue Remembers Her Phone

It was all very well catching the fish, but another matter altogether gutting it and cutting it up.

The meat came away from the bones with a lot of fiddling and a great deal of mess. Sue thought it might be a sea bass whereas Gus was convinced it was cod. It wasn't that delicious – too salty and slimy – and they joked that it would have been miles better deep fried in batter with chips, but it filled the cavernous hole in their hungry tummies. They washed it down with an additional ration of water using one of the empty baked bean tins as a cup.

As night began to fall, the rain beat a little heavier and it reminded Gus to set up his upside down umbrella rain catcher. He'd discovered Sue's umbrella on the bottom of the boat, opened it out and punctured two holes right in the centre where it met the stick. Then, he'd twisted the lid off the water container and aimed the upside-down umbrella's spike at it which he pushed fully inside. Then he tied the handle to each side support. When this was secure, he lay the wooden planks down the middle of the boat and they clambered on top, the rain tapping gently on the canopy above.

Doing nothing on the boat was exhausting.

'Pity we haven't got a camera,' Sue said. 'This should be recorded for historical purposes.'

'The intrepid adventures of Gus and Sue,' he replied. 'Survivors of the Great Yorkshire Storm.'

Sue laughed, before sitting bolt upright, her head missing the crossbeam by millimetres. Then she slapped her hands together. 'Of course! I've been incredibly dumb – I do have a camera. On my phone.'

'You forgot you had a phone,' Gus said. 'How?'

'Well, I only use it in emergencies.' She shrugged and began rummaging in her coat pockets. She pulled it out, kissed it and held it in the air as if she'd won the World Cup.

'I'll call someone – let them know we're here, wherever here is,' she said.

She pressed the power button. The lights flashed and the start up mechanism buzzed into action. They stared at it for a while. 'Oh. No reception,' she said quietly, her mood deflating.

She groaned and lay back, the presence of the phone giving her a reality check. 'I wonder if Isabella made it back – they were still playing the football match when we went past with the shopping. They had a fight on the pitch, Archie slugging away – can you believe it?'

'Archie?'

'Yeah. And Isabella doing her mad referee-bashing thing.'

Gus laughed.

'Do you think they had time to get over the bridge and up the lane to their cottage?' For the first time Sue's heart filled with a sense of loss. Before she knew it, tears were rolling down her cheeks. 'I'm sorry,' she cried, wiping them away. 'It's just bloody awful, isn't it?'

Gus put a reassuring arm around her. 'I don't know.' From the extraordinary volume of water he knew it would have been a tall order to survive. 'I'm sure loads of people are perfectly fine,' he lied. 'And more than likely Isabella's tucked up in bed with a hot chocolate having stories told to her by that very old man who lives with them.'

Sue smiled. She knew he was being nice. As she searched the depths of her soul, it didn't feel as if she had lost her friend. 'Do you think anyone survived?'

'We'll only know if we get home, I suppose.' Then he had an idea. 'Sue can I have a look at your phone.' She handed it to him. He stared at the screen for a while. 'Actually,' he said, 'better if you do it.'

'Do what?'

'Find an app with a compass. So we can start figuring out which way we're going.'

Sue started going through the various menus. 'Here, is *this* what you're after.' She handed it back to him.

Gus stared at it as if it were gold. 'Mega-tastic.' His big smile radiated back at her. He twisted the phone in his hands and the compass point moved.

'What does it say?'

Gus beamed back. 'We're heading south.'

'Is that good or bad?'

He shrugged. 'I don't know. Good, I suppose – better than heading north. Ideally, we want to head west.'

'How do we do that?' Sue said.

Gus grinned. 'A rudder for steering would help and we need to change the position of the sail.' He shifted his position and untied the sail rope before moving it into a new position on the other side of the boat. *The Joan Of* altered course slightly.

'Turn your phone off for now. We may need it later.' He clapped his hands together. 'I'm going to make a rudder with one of the planks. Can you dig out the tools?'

While Sue rummaged around at the bottom of the boat placing the tools on the seat Gus began mapping it out. 'I'll attach a small section of plank to a longer section of 2x4. Then at the bow I need to hook it over the end so it stays in place and then lever this side so that moves it one way or the other.'

Sue looked confused.

Gus smiled back. 'Just pass me things and tell me about that dream you had while I figure this out.'

As Gus set to work, Sue told him about her premonition. How she'd woken up and written down as much of her dream as possible and then studied it, altering it where she might have got it wrong. And although it made little sense, the nightmare scared her so much that she confided to Isabella. And then Isabella went berserk trying to prove it was actually going to happen. Which it did.

'And the thing is,' she said, 'Isabella had a dream about it too.' She strummed her fingers on the seat. 'Isn't that freaky?'

She paused as Gus bashed in a couple of nails and then continued. 'Most of this nightmare centred on the de Lowes and what really got me most was just how incredibly real the images appeared. It was like being on TV.'

'Give me an example,' Gus said.

'Where do I begin?' she said. 'OK, the coming of the storm, the lightning, oh, and here's one which I didn't think much of, but it felt important at the time, that they had to stay alive till sunset.'

Gus looked up. 'Well, the storm certainly happened,' he said. 'Did you tell them about the other bit?'

'About the sunset?'

'Yes. Pass me the saw.'

Sue reached into the box and handed it over. 'Yeah, but only right at the end before I ran off the pitch. I don't know why I put it off for so long. I wasn't sure I believed the nightmare would come true. It seemed too mad. And there was also another part …'

'Go on,' Gus encouraged. 'I'm all ears.'

'They had to find some clues to find three tablets or something in that old house of theirs. It was about as much as I could remember at the time.'

Gus began sawing the plank, the noise drowning out the conversation. It gave Sue time to think. 'Thing is, by the time I told them, the de Lowes were either fighting, being kicked or being hauled off the pitch.'

She ducked as Gus turned the rudder around. 'What do you make of it – do you think I'm crazy?'

Gus picked up the rudder and studied his handiwork. 'Who knows, there might be something in it. I mean you were spectacularly right about the storm, and if you remember, when nightfall came, the deluge gave way to spitting. So if they did survive, then maybe what you saw really was a premonition of some kind. Spooky, huh?'

Sue looked at Gus quizzically. For a boy he was an amazingly good listener. But she needed to get one more thing off her chest. 'Thing is, Gus, why did I have a dream about another family? And why did it feel so heart wrenchingly real?'

Gus relaxed put his tools down and faced her. 'Maybe you're related to them,' he said.

Sue guffawed.

'No, listen,' Gus continued. 'Don't get me wrong but you're incredibly similar to Isabella. You're the same height, you have the same hair. You both like the same stuff. You're as clever as each other and both of you are terrible at sport. You're just prettier.' The moment he said it, he blushed.

'Oh, that's so sweet, but I don't know about that,' she said noting Gus' discomfort. 'She's way smarter than me with a vicious temper.'

Gus smiled broadly. Isabella's sharp tongue was legendary at Upsall school and he'd been on the receiving end a couple of times. 'So what?' he said. 'Twins aren't always exactly the same—'

'Twins?'

'Yes. Maybe you're Isabella's twin. You know, separated at birth. Stranger things have happened.'

Sue had heard this theory before. 'No, I don't believe that. Loads of people look the same and act the same.'

'No one looks like me,' Gus said.

'Well you're one of a kind,' she said punching him playfully.

He raised his bushy eyebrows. 'Why don't you text Bells and remind her of all those things you said. If we get in range and they're alive you never know, it might help. There's nothing to lose apart from a bit of battery power. More than anything she'll be overjoyed to hear from you.'

'For a boy,' Sue began. 'You're quite clever.' Sue ran her fingers over the keypad while she punched in the texts. 'Tell you what, I'll send three. The first to say that we're OK, the second with all the things I've told you, and a third to my dear old mum

CHAPTER TEN

Isabella Hides Away

Where the previous day had stretched their bravery, strength and courage to the absolute limit, the following day, mental torture grabbed at each of them like a bloodsucking leech.

The world as they knew it had caved in. It was now a world where nothing made sense. The magnitude of their survival felt like a punch that simultaneously winded and broke their nose.

More so for Archie and Isabella.

Archie couldn't stop thinking of his visit from the ghost called Cain.

Every time he thought of the ghost his heart raced because everything Cain had said had come true: the fact they were the "anointed ones" with special powers – as he'd seen in the cave paintings – the fact that the storm would break and target them – as it did – and the fact that he'd seen a picture on the cave wall of a woman. Was this woman Cain's mother who he'd asked him to protect at all costs, or the hag from his dreams?

Anyway, who was Cain and how did he fit in? Archie couldn't figure if the ghost meant well or if his words fitted another agenda. He sensed that several parts of the puzzle were missing. Why did Cain really need him to protect the old woman? And how? I mean, she was a product of his imagination – his dreams, wasn't she?

And when he thought of the ghost, he worried about what had happened to his friend Kemp in the alleyway. Had Kemp joined with Cain and merged with him as

Cain had demanded? Or, had Kemp been dazzled by Cain's promise of power and strength? That was the problem with Kemp, he thought, he simply couldn't be trusted.

Archie's hair was as tight as steel and he stroked his foremost spike, odd memories returning. What about the creature that hovered over Daisy? It had to be connected to her yelling, her crazed sleep-talking. He replayed the images of the white spidery creature with the blue electric middle again and again until he felt a headache coming on. It must have been giving her a dream – or a nightmare.

He shut his eyes tight trying to erase the memory, but it persisted like a stubborn head cold. Were dreams given? Was that possible?

Archie was so confused and exhausted that for a day he simply shut down and slept and mooched about the house avoiding everyone. Although he was dying to tell Daisy about Cain, ever-present in the back of his mind was his promise to Cain that he wouldn't tell a soul.

Deep down a persistent nag told him that Cain might resurface at any time and the idea of Cain visiting him made his stomach churn. And if he did say anything, Daisy would only tease him for 'being silly' and Isabella would think he'd gone mad. So for the time being, at least, it wasn't worth mentioning.

Archie ran a hand over his head and shuddered. He didn't like his ridiculous new mace-like hairstyle – or wire-style – but it filled him with curiosity. When he relaxed the fibres softened, but when threatened or angry, the follicles tightened hard like steel. They seemed to act like antennae for his mood, for his defence.

When this happened he noted how a curious physical strength built up in him combined with an awesome sense of power, of being indestructible.

And though he dared not admit it, this strange new feeling felt wonderfully good.

*

Isabella's hands touched on the soft cotton bed sheet and she allowed herself a smile.

She couldn't remember much, just the terrible panic in the stairwell and then a pain in her arms. She clenched her fist, amazed to find there was feeling in her fingers although a strange painful electrical current tingled through the palms of each hand and through each digit. Hadn't she smashed her wrists? Then it started coming back to her: the storm, the ordeal in the cave, waking up and looking over the broken Vale of York. The excruciating pain.

It made little sense.

Her mind clouded and a frown built on her forehead like ripples of sand. Hadn't they been stuck in the water? She opened her eyes and saw the familiar sight of her section of the attic room. Home! And what of their friends, what of Sue? With a cry she sat up. Her body ached like mad and she examined her hands. A chill ran through her. *The holes.* The holes where the lightning bolt had smashed into her. She sank back into the soft pillows. She needed to sleep and think it through, work it out logically. Work it out like a scientist.

Perhaps then, it would go away.

She made her way over to the desk, and wrote in big, bold letters on a piece of A4 paper,

'DO NOT DISTURB.
DO NOT TALK TO ME
DO NOT FEED ME.'

She pinned the note to the outside of the closed thick velvet curtain that set her area apart from the rest of the attic room and shuffled back into bed where she slept, sometimes deeply, mostly fitfully, until midday.

*

'Come on, Bells,' Daisy said from the other side of the curtain as she read Isabella's notice. 'You need food. Lunch is on the table.'

Isabella groaned. She didn't want to see anyone, and she certainly didn't want to talk to anyone. Couldn't Daisy read?

'You missed breakfast and you didn't eat anything last night. You've got to eat.'

Still no response.

Daisy persevered. 'You can't hide away in your bed all day.'

I can, Isabella thought. And I will.

Daisy opened the curtain and strode in.

'GO AWAY! Can't you read?'

Daisy ignored her and sat down on the side of her bed. 'How are your arms?'

Isabella rolled over so she faced away.

Daisy sighed. 'Look, Einstein, you can't stay here all day – you'll get bed bugs and—'

'Please, Daisy. Go away, just leave me, please.'

But Daisy was in a stubborn mood, and she was bored. 'Make me.'

Isabella pulled the duvet over her head.

Daisy smiled, stood up, fluffed up her blond hair, puckered her lips and made her way to the mirror. She stared at her red eyes. 'Freaky, but kind of cool, huh? What do you think?'

Isabella groaned.

Daisy turned her attention to Isabella's neat bookshelves. 'Where's your Bible?'

'Please, Daisy—'

'Think I might do that homework – you know, the Creation story, the bit Solomon's been going on about.' Still no response. 'God, you and Archie are so boring, feeling all sorry for yourselves.' She flicked through a copy of Shakespeare's plays, read aloud two passages, folded it and tucked it under her jumper. 'Old Man Wood's disappeared again. Gone to check on his cattle – how about a game of something?' She sat down heavily on the bed and traced a finger up Isabella's body.

Isabella popped her head out. 'If I give you the Bible will you GO AWAY?'

Daisy cocked her head to one side. 'Might,' she said pouting her lips. 'On one condition – that you come down later for tea. Mrs P's knocking up a stonking curry. Helped her put the ingredients in – eleven in all – and I slipped in an extra chilli. Gonna be a corker. *And*, Banofee pie for pudding, which is your favourite.'

Isabella stirred.

'Anyway, Mrs P's been droning on and on about my eyes, it's sending me nuts. She's talked more in the last few hours than the last year put together. Hey, look at these.' Daisy popped on a pair of thin metal-rimmed pink-tinted glasses. 'Lush, eh? Found them in Mum's drawer.'

Isabella's head popped out. She pointed at the bookcase. 'Second row. Says *Bible* on it,' she said, as her head flew back under the duvet.

Daisy stood up and traced her fingers along the spines of the books. She pulled one out and sat down on the bed. 'So which bit is it? Genesis, creation or something—'

'For goodness' sakes,' Isabella cried. 'It's at the beginning of the whole thing,' she said. Did her sister have no concept of how insane the last forty-eight hours had been? Was she unaware of the scale of the disaster? 'GO AWAY!' she hissed.

Daisy stood up. 'Sure, you boring boffin. If you want to talk, chat about anything – I'm, you know, around. Not too busy today. Diary pretty much empty.'

Isabella cringed and realised Daisy was only trying to help. She popped her head out again. 'Look, I'm sorry, Daisy. I know you're trying to help … it's just that I'm not ready.'

Daisy smiled. 'Yeah, cool,' she said as she turned to leave. 'You know, Bells, whatever happened, happened. We can't change it and we don't know what's coming. That's it really. Sometimes you just have to go with the flow.' Daisy opened the curtain. 'Laters, right?' she said as she drew it behind her.

Isabella gripped her duvet in her fist. Why couldn't she go with the flow like Daisy rather than be tormented by questions and riddles and trying to make sense of things that didn't make any sense? Go with the flow – if only it was that simple.

Isabella closed her eyes and thought of Sue, her best friend in the whole world.

Tears streamed down her cheeks. She had sent Sue to her death by slipping her a bit of paper with details of a rickety old boat in a rundown boathouse. A stupid little old boat no one had even looked at for years – what was she thinking? She pictured it in her mind. Sue alone, cold, wet, begging for help, drowning. She wouldn't have stood a chance, not three minutes against that storm – not a chance in hell.

Oh Lord, she'd only tried to help – if only she'd known, if only she could have done something else.

Isabella cried until her tears ran dry as she mourned for her friend.

*

Thanks to the strange sparkly potion called Resplendix Mix, which Old Man Wood had found in the cellars beneath Eden Cottage, Isabella's injuries had very nearly healed up. She hadn't known it but when she exploded out of the stairwell and smashed into the ceiling of the cave both her arms fractured under the pressure, though incredibly, her hands had perfectly cushioned her head and didn't bear a single scrape or a blemish aside from the existing holes in her palms. Her skull, shoulders, hips and arms bore scuffs and lacerations and a patch of hair had been removed by the rocks and her face looked as if someone had taken a cheese grater to it. But overnight her bones were as good as new and her scabs had all but disappeared.

Isabella, though thrilled to have mended in astonishingly quick time, was a little confused and concerned as to how Resplendix Mix worked, and what the likely long-term side-effects might be. In all the science and medical journals she'd ever read she had never heard of anything like it. Had the potion manipulated the cells in her body to recreate the bones and tissues? Was it a form of genetic science working at a hitherto unknown level or was this a reversing potion of sorts?

But more importantly, what was Old Man Wood doing with it in the first place? Was Old Man Wood a scientist like her, or some sort of amazing chemist?

When they quizzed Old Man Wood about how it worked or what its properties were, he replied that he had no idea whatsoever, and this was the truth. And when asked where he had got it from, he took a deep breath and told them that it had been given to him a long, long time ago, most probably by an apothecary. And this was also true. But although Daisy accepted this as perfectly normal, Isabella's suspicions grew, namely because apothecaries didn't exist anymore. They were now called pharmacists or chemists.

Whatever their suspicions, the potion was like magic and, Old Man Wood told them, the faster an injury was acted upon, the quicker it healed. Hence, Isabella's arms had healed almost instantly in contrast to Archie's cuts on his legs when he crawled up the lane during the storm. The one negative effect was that as it mended the pain was excruciatingly hot.

Archie thought it was like pouring antiseptic on an open flesh wound, and eating a hot chilli at the same time, multiplied by at least ten. So when Old Man Wood had held the bottle to Isabella's lips in the cave, she had blacked out as the Resplendix Mix went to work.

As they sat down for Mrs Pye's curry at the kitchen table, Isabella moved her arm back and forth testing her limbs and said, 'I have a question for you, Old Man Wood. Why isn't Resplendix Mix prescribed in hospitals or doctors' surgeries?'

Old Man Wood raised his head for a minute, shook it before gathering a forkful of curry and cramming it in his mouth.

'I mean, look at me,' she continued, 'almost fully healed apart from these stupid holes. If it was readily available to everyone, what a huge burden it would take off the National Health Service. Think of the enormous benefits – benefits that could be used right now – out there,' she said waving towards the window, 'and its properties could probably be transferred to other schools of medicine—'

Daisy groaned. 'I preferred you when you were asleep.'

Isabella shot her a look. 'No, seriously. No hospital waiting lists, no injuries that couldn't be dealt with. No nasty scars.' She nudged Old Man Wood. 'Do you know what's in it?'

Old Man Wood shook his head.

'I'll analyse it,' Isabella said. 'Then we can manufacture it here and sell it worldwide. We'll make a fortune.'

'I don't think Mum and Dad would be too happy with that,' Daisy said.

'But they're never around, so they wouldn't know.'

'They'll be back,' Mrs Pye said. 'And at least we know they must be safe and sound.'

'Yeah, but they don't know *we're* safe, do they?' Archie added.

Isabella ignored them. 'Well, I'll do it when I'm a little older, in America or somewhere like that,' she scoffed. 'There are tons of excellent commercial scientists over there who would bend over backwards for this kind of thing.'

'Bells, I'm not sure you've thought this through,' Archie said. 'If you did make this stuff, then in one go you're wiping out all the hospitals and doctors and nurses and physios and first aiders. I mean what would all those people do?'

'And they'd brand you as a witch,' Daisy said, mischievously. 'They'd burn you alive.'

Old Man Wood hummed. 'Thing is,' he said, 'I'm not sure it works with everyone. And I've a feeling that in the wrong hands it's downright lethal.'

'Ha! So you do know what it is,' Isabella said.

Old Man Wood furrowed his brow. 'Nope. Not really littleun. It's just a feeling.'

Mrs Pye beamed at him. 'Your Old Man Wood has a ton of remarkable strings to his arrows.'

Daisy coughed. 'Isn't it, strings to his bows?'

'Or arrows to a quiver?' Archie added.

Mrs Pye shot the twins a beady look. 'Bloomers. You two getting all clever on me? You know what I means. Now eat up.'

The children didn't know what to say to this, but the medicine was part of a broader subject that needed examining and it was proving extremely difficult to expand Old Man Wood's general lack of knowledge on these things.

CHAPTER ELEVEN

Isabella Does Not Believe

The children's sense of confusion centred around the dreams they'd been given, and now that silence filled the kitchen aside from the clanging of cutlery and the odd loud slurp, Archie thought it might be a good time to revisit the topic.

'You know when we talked before about our dreams,' he began, 'when we figured out they'd been the same?' he searched around the table to see if anyone was listening. 'Well, do you think they might be coming true?' he paused. 'I mean, the flooding happened, and we all saw it coming, especially you, Bells, and don't get me wrong but there's no way we should have survived. It was only through our, you know, efforts and the other strange stuff that—'

Mrs Pye broke in. 'Well now that you're on talking about dreams, that means bed, and I is pooped. So I leaves you and loves you to get some dreams in meself.'

Old Man Wood stretched his arms wide. 'And I'm going to sit next door, softer, there.'

The children thanked Mrs Pye for the delicious curry, hugged her goodnight and shut the door.

They sat down again.

'Good point, Arch,' Daisy said leaning across the table. 'But I don't get what the old woman we dreamt about – the one you killed in my dream, Archie – has got to do with it. Maybe we've got to protect her or something so that she won't be killed.' She flashed Archie a look. 'What do you think?'

He shrugged. 'Maybe you're right,' he said as his thoughts turned to his conversation with the ghost, Cain. Archie rubbed a hard spike on his head. He didn't know what to make of the woman either but Cain wanted him to protect the Ancient Woman so perhaps that was what they had to do. The last thing he wanted was her death on his hands. 'What if there's a deeper meaning?' he added. 'Something else.'

'Cool, have you thought of anything?' Daisy said, wiping the side of her mouth.

Archie shook his head. 'Not really, Daise,' he said. 'But I was hoping we could talk about it—'

Isabella leaned back in her chair and flexed her hands. 'Come on, kids, this is ridiculous—'

Daisy put her hands up. 'Only thoughts, your brainy-ness—'

'I'm sorry, you guys,' Isabella sighed. 'Frankly it's too much for me to get to grips with right now, so I'd rather we didn't talk about the old woman.'

Daisy shot her sister a look. 'Well actually, boffin-brains, I think we should. We're in this together and dreaming of the Ancient Woman is our only common denominator.'

'No. I'm sorry,' Isabella said, amazed that Daisy knew what a "denominator" was. 'It's not going to happen.' With a loud scraping sound, Isabella slid her chair back and stood up. 'You two – by all means discuss it to your heart's content and do whatever you feel you've got to do. Me? I can find better things to get on with, like study.' She grabbed her plate and made her way to the sink.

'Hang on!' Archie said. 'What about Sue—?'

'And the fact that I sent her to her death!' Isabella snapped.

'You don't know that—'

'There's no way she survived—'

'*We did*—'

'That was luck, Archie,' Isabella shot back. 'Pure luck. I can spell it for you if you want.'

'No, it wasn't—'

Isabella shook her head. 'I'm sorry but I don't understand which bit of the last day you think wasn't.'

'That's ridiculous, you know what happened – you were there!' Archie said.

'Yes, of course I was. But there's no reasonable logical explanation for it, is there? No truth.' She washed her dish, placed it in the rack to the side and dried her hands on a tea towel. 'To be honest I'm not even sure it happened.'

'*What?*'

'It's an illusion, Archie,' she said staring at their shocked faces. 'Hasn't it crossed either of your tiny minds that what happened, might not have actually happened? That it's entirely a figment of your imagination.'

'Rubbish—'

'Guys, seriously.' Isabella smiled, 'It might have been a drug – or the vapours from the storm glass I made that led us, unwittingly, to imagine it.'

Archie shook his head. He could feel his hair turning steely. 'OK. Let's talk about the storm glass, Bells. When it blew up you thought it was important enough to go off to see the headmaster, didn't you? And blocking a lightning bolt and getting holes in your hands isn't simply a matter of luck. Look at my head and Daisy's eyes. I don't remember the cave being imaginary – do you, Daisy?'

Daisy shook her head. 'Nope. Nor the fact that the flooding stopped when Archie said it would.'

'Or a Jacuzzi that miraculously healed us—'

'And that I can hear lightning forming,' Daisy added, 'and see stuff you can't, and you can run up two hundred and twenty-two steps in the time it took me to go an eighth of the way. And, let's not forget, that you also repelled lightning.'

Isabella had been dreading this conversation. Her features darkened. 'These freaky things,' she said as she whirled her arms in their direction, 'can be explained by science. I'll grant you there may be some scientific wonders we experienced that aren't known as yet, but it's only a matter of time. Very soon, everything that happened to us will be seen as perfectly normal.'

'Bullshit,' Daisy said. 'That's utter rubbish.'

'No, it isn't, Daisy. Your hearing of strange, acute things must be something to do with heightened vibrations in your ear drum. Your hair, Archie, or wire or whatever you want to call it, must be an amalgamation of the electrical particles and the chemical atoms of the leather or rubber of the football combined with the huge voltage of electricity that narrowly missed you, and my hands – well, that's simple. It must be related to the anti-lightning conductor I made with Sue in the lab shortly before the football game.' She smiled triumphantly at them. 'So no, it isn't some kind of hocus-pocus weird dream magic as you're suggesting.'

'But Bells,' Archie fumed, 'look outside at the wreckage. The whole country has been utterly mangled. You – YOU dreamt about it—'

'Listen, Archie. It was a once-in-a-lifetime storm. They happen. Globally, big floods really do occur. America, Pakistan, Australia, China; they have massive meteorological activity just like this. It's quite possible that we somehow sensed it in our dreams – and remember, twins, these are *only dreams*. DREAMS for goodness sakes. And dreams tell you what you fear so it was perfectly natural for me, as a scientist, to make the connection.' She smiled at their furious faces, but her eyes were hard. 'It's your subconscious playing games with you, mucking about inside your head, telling you things—'

'So how come,' Daisy butted in, 'we saw the same things—'

Isabella sat down. Her eyes sparkled. 'Because people dream about the same things all the time. Dreams repeat themselves time and time again like ... like songs on the radio. Why do you think there are hundreds of books on dream interpretation?' she offered the question to the table. No one replied. 'It's because people have the same kind of dreams every single day, that's why.'

A silence descended. Isabella looked from one twin to the other.

'The trouble is, Bells,' Daisy said quietly, 'that no one knows what dreams are actually for – it's unclear what the purpose of dreaming really is.'

Isabella scoffed.

Daisy ignored her. 'Dream scientists who map our subconscious and study sleeping patterns and REM come to only broad conclusions because, hard as they try, they don't know why we dream.' She looked from one to the other. 'So it may be possible that *our* dreams have a purpose.' She slipped her pink glasses on and raised an eyebrow.

'Oh how awfully clever, Daisy,' Isabella spat. 'Suddenly you're an authority, are you?'

Daisy stood up and fixed her with an icy stare. 'Yes. I looked it up on the INTERNET. Do your own research.'

The girls eyeballed each other across the table.

'In any case,' Daisy said running her hands through her hair and puffing her cheeks out, 'I simply can't understand that you have the inability to link the dreams we've had about a storm, finding stuff and the murder of an old woman, with the pictures at the cave which quite clearly showed the first part of that exact same sequence.'

Isabella chortled. 'You're talking about those cave paintings?'

'Yeah, Einstein. Of course I am,' Daisy said.

'OMG. How typical, how cute that you managed to find a story in them. I hardly looked at those stupid pictures—'

'They were NOT stupid—'

'Oh, how sweet of you to think they had *meaning*,' Isabella responded. 'Of course they were cave-man scribbles! How dumb can you get? You honestly think you can derive a story, a narrative from them? They could be interpreted in any number of ways—'

'Really?' Daisy snapped, 'if you'd actually bothered to study them, you would have seen our dreams drawn out perfectly—'

'And,' Archie added, 'it showed us with our odd features—'

'And the Ancient Woman,' Daisy said.

'And the flood—'

'STOP IT!' Isabella screamed. 'STOP IT!' She hid her face behind her hands, her hair hanging like a veil over them. 'Stop going on at me,' she sobbed. 'Why are you two always having a go at me—'

'We're not—'

'Yes you are! Ganging up like … like Ant and Dec.'

Archie and Daisy exchanged glances. 'Ant and Dec don't gang up on anyone.'

Isabella flapped her arms about. '… thinking how funny you are all the time.' She wiped her nose with the back of her hand. 'Do you have any idea what it's like picking up the pieces after you two,' she raged, 'covering your backs?'

Isabella stood up, picked up her chair and threw it in the corner. 'None of this makes any bloody sense,' she yelled. She turned on Archie. 'God, look at you,' she seethed, 'You're a mess, and you,' she said, directing her ire at Daisy, 'are a stupid, idiotic tart. And you're thick. You're no better than that oaf, Kemp.'

She picked up a glass and for a moment, Archie thought she was going to throw it at one of them. Instead, she slammed it down, turned, and stormed out of the room.

CHAPTER TWELVE

A Problem Of Diet

Kemp detected another surge of Cain's energy tugging on his tendons and yanking at his muscles, threading into the fibres of his body. The heat radiated from the nerve endings of his fingers down to the tips of his toenails.

Kemp shrieked as the it hit him harder, forcing him out of his slumber, heat blasting over him as if he'd been tossed into a bath full of scalding water, burning him.

Why wouldn't Cain let him be? Did he have any idea of the damage he was doing?

Today, after another short sleep he woke up so weak that putting one leg ahead of the other was like wading through treacle. Tiny morsels of food and little or no water had passed into his stomach the entire time he'd been within Cain – nearly two days. It felt like a month. Kemp seriously doubted that the excuse for water really was water. It had the texture of slime and the smell of sulphur, like chemically manufactured eggy farts.

Every time he ate, and he tried everything, he spewed it back out.

Kemp stared at the breakfast – foodstuffs like nothing he'd ever seen before; slug-like creatures that wriggled, foul stinking jelly and cakes consisting of insects and flies; foods he did not recognise. Desperate for something, Kemp picked up a slippery purple ball. He could hardly bear to think about it. He shut his eyes and put it in his mouth. It tasted like tapioca with an outer shell as gritty as bark. His stomach heaved. He tried another – a thin hard-backed slice of cake with a soft gooey centre that smelt of oil. He put it towards his mouth. The odour was too awful. He shoved it in and chewed with his half teeth.

'… why … eat … slowly?' Kemp heard every second or third word, muffled, but he had no way of responding.

'Come … much … … little time. … world … … genetically useless … to sort … Hurry … … on.'

Was Cain talking to him again, urging him on?

Kemp chewed as best as he could. As he ground the cake between his teeth, a liquid suddenly burst out of the bark and flooded his mouth. He involuntarily vomited.

Kemp's swollen stomach gave a sharp pain, like the tip of a wooden stake jabbing his gut. His legs felt like lead weights. His head throbbed.

Kemp knew that his body was failing, as if his body wasn't even there. The pain of the burning seared him as if being sizzled in a frying pan and now his strength had gone, every last bit of it.

He stumbled and fell.

Then only blackness.

*

Cain's ashen exterior struck the floor and a large plume of ash soared into the air.

'What now!' Cain screamed. 'There's something wrong, I cannot feel the boy,' he yelled. 'Schmerger, Schmerger – where are you?'

Cain's chief of staff arrived. 'You called, Master?'

'This damnable boy is not working,' Cain said from his position within the ashen body prostrate on the floor. 'Do you think he does it purposefully? Does he do it to spite me?'

Schmerger made his way over to the bundle of ash, grabbed what he hoped was an arm and manoeuvred the ashen bundle into a chair. Stepping back, the servant coughed and dusted himself down. 'I am unsure as to how you mean to continue your relations with the being.'

'What are you talking about, Schmerger?'

'It appears the boy may have requirements of which, Sire, we are unaware. Can you feel if the boy is alive within you or dead?'

'I am unsure,' Cain replied, checking his limbs.

Schmerger rubbed his long black beard. 'How does your relationship with the boy work?'

'Work?' Cain said.

'Sire, I need to understand how the boy operates. It has come to my attention that he has barely ingested any of the food I have laid out for him. Maybe these humans do not eat what we eat. Or it might be that he requires another source of energy? All living things must feed to create energy, Sire. Or they fail.'

In his excitement Cain hadn't stopped to think this through. 'Then we must find out – and soon – for having this being within me is an absolute wonder, Schmerger. You have no idea – I *must* make it work. I have no magic, not yet at least, for I do not have eyeballs, but at long last I can see and my presence is as real as any other being. Do you have any idea how invigorating it is after so long?'

Schmerger was astonished by recent events. Never in his wildest dreams had he imagined that Cain would in some way come alive. And now he sensed the power of the man, the presence, the aura that once surrounded him. He now understood the stories that had been passed down by his ancestors, of Cain's imperious majesty and power.

Cain hadn't seen his palaces, his lands or the seas or the mountains for thousands of years. Even when he left the great palace for months at a time, roaming the lands of Havilah in his invisible form, he would return and continue searching for his branchwand. The branchwand which Cain believed might return a fragment of that old power.

Now that Cain had stumbled upon the boy, an energy and purpose returned to his master that was both thrilling and awesome. And his futile, eternal search for his branchwand was on hold.

When Schmerger had told his family of Cain's newfound body, they had told their friends and they told their friends and so on. Soon a buzz spread across the planet of Havilah that Cain was back.

A sense grew that this strange ruler of theirs, dormant for so many thousands of years, might finally help them. Schmerger wondered if it was fate. The people on Havilah had been weakening for some time, rife with disease and illness, and it wasn't because of anything particularly different, more that their bodies hadn't been able to modify, to change or evolve, since Cain's disappearance.

Havilah, once the melting pot of all the worlds, a hubbub of liveliness, a place where vices were ignored and ruthlessness admired and riches abounded now groaned in collective decay, a land slipping into waste.

'I've had the boy two days and now he is collapsing. What is wrong?' Cain asked. 'Why is Havilah failing? Why do the people here wallow in pity, why is there no life, no zest?'

Schmerger wondered if, like all the inhabitants of Havilah, this boy from Earth bore their sickness. He moved closer, inspecting the pile of ash. 'My Lord, this is a most unusual situation—'

'Of course it is, you fool,' Cain snapped. 'And I employ you to look after my unusual situations. How can I restore Havilah if the boy is faulty?'

Schmerger knew to tread carefully. 'The boy is made of flesh and blood? A human—'

'Of course.'

'Then perhaps he requires a diet to fit mankind?'

Cain was amazed he hadn't thought of this before. 'Of course! You're right. Just because I have no need of sustenance … what is the diet of man, Schmerger?'

'Our insect and fungus diet is not suitable, that is plain to see.'

'Obviously, you idiot. The boy needs earthly foods – where are they? He needs them NOW.'

Cain detected a faint glow of the body he had taken over. 'It is weak,' Cain said quietly as a terrible feeling washed over him. 'If the boy fails …'

'Surely you can remove yourself?' Schmerger asked.

'Indeed I can – and go back to how I was. But it is not good enough. No! I need a body that will *willingly* be a part of me. Understand this, Schmerger. It may not happen again. If I were to release the boy and he recovers, would he give himself to me again freely?'

Cain realised he had been reckless. He needed to act quickly.

Schmerger looked on anxiously. 'Is there anyone we can contact as to the boy's health?'

Cain thought for a minute. 'Do humans live here in Havilah?'

'There are some in the caves, but they are the old type,' Schmerger replied. 'Ancestors of the early people, from whom we are derived. They are troublesome and barbaric – I am not sure they would help.'

Cain groaned. 'Who else?'

'Perhaps you could return him to Earth, Sire, in the manner by which you arrived, through … a creature?'

'Alas, servant,' Cain said, 'Asgard the dreamspinner is reluctant for me to use his maghole as transportation until our plan is complete.'

Schmerger stroked his long black beard contemplating the situation. Suddenly a light sparkled in his eyes. 'As a spirit, Sire, a ghost, you are part of another world. You might summon a human spirit to advise you—'

'Yes,' Cain said as the idea sunk in. 'Brilliant, Schmerger. Of course. But who?'

'A spirit connected with him, one of his ancestors. Humans die so young there must be many.'

Cain sat and thought. 'You're right, humans have a bond like no other. I will call for them, Schmerger. You may live another day but be warned, you should not be here when they arrive.'

Every day since he'd returned Cain had threatened to kill him, part of the job, he suspected, but Schmerger partially heeded his master's advice, turned and walked to the door where he waited. If it got bad, he would leave.

The room fell into silence. Cain began chanting, his voice calling out into the universe.

'Spirits awaken, spirits come near.
Spirits come close you have nothing to fear.
I call to those who connect with this boy.'

He stopped and waited.

'O spirits from the reaches of time and of space
Come hither to connect with me here in this place.'

Schmerger trembled as he felt a wind envelop him. He hated it when Cain joined his ghostly companions. He looked about but there was nothing to see. But Cain looked upon a host of Kemp's family whooshing in and around the building.

'Spirits of this boy,' Cain called out, 'I call upon you as a spirit myself. I cannot ascend into the sky or feel the land but I will always live. This child of man, your relative on Earth, willingly joined with me and in return I have saved him from the great tempest on that planet.' Cain looked up at the spirits who floated round him. What an ugly bunch, Cain thought, with matted ginger hair, thrusting chins and thick red lips sweeping around the room.

'The boy is failing fast. I have fed and watered him but I did not understand his needs,' he called out. 'The child requires your help. I call on the newest of you to reveal yourselves now.'

In an instant, a silvery, opaque-looking man appeared, kneeling in front of them.

Cain noted the spirit's sadness – his youthful, bent head, his mournful face. 'Thank you. And you are …'

'I am the spirit of the boy's father,' he said, his voice deep and blowy like the wind.

The boy must have lost his father young, Cain thought. 'There is no more ideal person to help, other than a mother.'

'Indeed,' said the ghost. 'His mother lives though she knows not of her child. I was taken when he was an infant. We were together in an accident ...' the voice tapered off.

Cain suddenly realised that this information answered the question the boy had posed when he'd told him he had to save his mother – *because he'd never known his own mother*.

In the next second, Kemp's father reached into the ashen body, his body following.

Shortly, he flew out and settled over it. 'What have you done to him?' he roared. 'He is a child. His body is poisoned and burned almost to death. It is fortunate he is strong.'

Cain kept calm. 'Be assured, I did not mean to harm him. The boy means more to me than you know.'

The ghost snivelled. 'If this is true, you have only one option. Return him to Earth where they can nurse and nourish him. Can you do this?'

'I will try,' Cain said.

'There is little time,' the ghost said. 'The alternative is that he comes with us.'

'Should he go to his mother's side?'

The ghost shot into the air and swirled around before floating down. 'No. She may reject him. She does not recall ever having a son. Her mind was damaged in the car crash. And he is too sick.'

'Then where shall I leave him?'

'Somewhere he will be found and helped.'

'And there is no one else?' Cain asked.

Kemp's father swayed one way and then the other like a flag being waved, testing the vibrations. 'His friends will have the answers,' Kemp's father said as he drifted away as though on a breeze. 'His friends,' he repeated as he spiralled higher and higher and eventually away through the ceiling.

Cain watched him go. Spirits were a curious lot, but they did generally have their bloodline's best intentions at the top of their limited agenda.

Cain mulled over the ghost's words. Was he referring to that confounded Archie de Lowe as the boy's best friend? Cain could hardly bear to think about the de Lowes. He'd come so close to having Archie, with his power, within his grasp. The Heirs of Eden, children, surviving the great storm by the skin of their teeth. It was preposterous. But Cain knew that the prophecy demanded a great deal more; finding the three Tablets of Eden was an altogether different matter.

*

'Dreamspinner, dreamspinner, dreamspinner.' Cain shouted.

A second later and Asgard the dreamspinner appeared, long slender slivers of legs dancing by his silvery opaque body and the blue maghole of lightning burning in his middle in place of an abdomen.

'Ah-ha, my ugly dreamspinner friend,' Cain began. 'It appears I am within the dying body of a boy.'

Asgard walked on his eight legs across the air as if treading on an invisible grid. 'Then you must return him.'

'Yes,' Cain said, 'but how can our plan work if there is no flesh on me?'

Asgard dipped a couple of claws into his blue burning maghole as if thinking. 'The boy may recover and come back to you if he has access to the one thing he desires most in the world.'

'And, pray tell,' Cain replied, intrigued, 'what is that?'

'It is for you to puzzle,' Asgard said. 'There is no time to lose. When the boy lands on earth, you must return immediately. I am unable to transport at will any more. There are problems—'

'What kind of problems?'

'The boy burns me. I cannot be sure of survival.'

Cain's good mood evaporated. 'Then find me spiders who will sacrifice themselves for the cause,' he demanded.

Asgard stared at Cain. He did not like taking orders, especially from a spirit. Maybe he had to get used to it. 'The consequences are difficult for dreamspinners. We are not familiar with other species, other worlds—'

'If you are unable to transport me, Asgard,' Cain snapped, 'find others who will. If you want the Garden of Eden to open, if you want to keep making your dreams, I suggest you give me your wholehearted support. Use another.'

The ultimate sacrifice – death? This shocking idea had not even entered the mind of the dreamspinner. Asgard knew dreamspinners would have to change but he didn't realise how drastically. He recognised that the dreamspinners, the oldest curators of life, the givers of dreams, faced a stark choice: back the three children or line up behind Cain.

Asgard had been there when the children were given the Tripodean dream – the prophecy of Eden. But he knew the prophecy had been designed for the best of mankind, men who were strong, clever and wise in magic and nature. This prophecy heralded a new era for mankind, and as Asgard realised, for dreamspinners too.

Without dream powders of inspiration from the Garden of Eden, was there any point in being a dreamspinner? Asgard had seen it many times; species who failed to contribute to the fabric of life very quickly ended up extinct.

Havilah was now the only place that offered spider web powders of any note. Even if these spider web powders could only be spun into dark dreams, or nightmares, they were just as powerful as dreams from The Garden of Eden – depending on how they were interpreted. And although these dreams were not as fun to deliver, at least dreamspinners would continue to exist.

'Perhaps,' Asgard signed with his long, slender, opaque claws. 'Perhaps it can be done, for the greater cause.'

'Indeed,' Cain crowed. 'If you are to change, dreamspinner, then you must accept choices you do not like.'

Asgard knew it was so, but right now he needed to get them back to Earth. 'Master. Awaken the boy. There is one last thing to do. Dive through me once again. This time, save your strength for you shall bear the boy's weight and steer him through my maghole.'

Cain softly reached inside and for the very first time did not force the boy awake. He talked to him gently, as if to a child, and a glow – which wasn't particularly nice, nor unpleasant, just unusual – ran through him. He had to work with the boy, not force him, he reminded himself. Cain's thoughts turned to the puzzle Asgard had given him: what would make this human come back to him? What was the one thing the boy desired most?

Cain thought of the conversation with the spirit. His mother is alive, and the boy doesn't know it. The father who died in a car crash when he was an infant with his wife by his side. All this time, and the mother survived!

Yes, it made perfect sense, and Cain chuckled. It is the answer. I will search her out and when the boy is fit and strong he will come back to me, because I will give him his mother. And he will come willingly and I will look after him.

Cain's plan was building in his mind and already it pleased him greatly.

The boy woke and started to move as Cain gently coaxed him on. 'Together, little Earth being, we will start afresh. Together we will rule the universe.'

'Where shall I take him?' Asgard asked.

'Back to where he came from, dreamspinner. To a place they cannot fail to find him.'

'Then let us go with haste. I am ready.'

With the boy stirring, Cain summoned every ounce of his ghostly strength and threw himself and Kemp through the dreamspinner's middle.

CHAPTER THIRTEEN

Daisy Tries To Work It Out

'That is one seriously confused chick,' Daisy said picking up the chair and pushing it under the thick wooden table top.

Archie looked pained. 'You think she's wrong?'

'Doh, yeah. Of course she is, Arch!' Daisy replied. 'Come on, no one in the world has hair like yours or eyes like mine, or holes through their hands, for that matter.'

'True. Cool glasses by the way – they suit you.'

Daisy grinned. 'Bells has only to look at her hands to realise something odd is happening. It's just too freaky for her.'

Archie grinned. 'So what next?'

'Well, for starters,' she said smiling at him, 'you need to start wearing a hat.'

'Ha, ha!' He replied. 'No way!'

Daisy pulled a black hat out of her pocket and threw it at him. 'Try this – one of Dad's. Found it while rummaging around upstairs.'

'Have you been through their entire wardrobe?'

'Yeah, pretty much. Go on, try it.'

'No way!'

'Way! Pleeease!'

Archie put it on and Daisy clapped her hands. 'Fantastic!'

'I can't go round with a black beanie on my head.'

'But it's cool.'

Archie took it off and examined it. 'You sure this is OK?'

'Winkle, it's got *you* written all over it.'

'Don't call me winkle.'

Daisy laughed. 'Look, seriously,' she said, 'if we really think that our dreams actually mean something, we're just going to have to figure out the next part.'

Archie sighed. 'Great. Now *I* feel confused.'

'Well, let's start with those "cave-man" paintings on the wall?' she said. 'Did you study them?'

'They were just odd,' Archie said.

'No, they weren't. They were all about finding some tablets or books or pieces of rock. I've been searching already.'

'Found anything?'

'Nope. Just these glasses, your hat, and these cool fingerless studded leather gloves for Bells. What do you think?'

Archie couldn't believe it. 'They're so not her.'

She laughed. 'You think? Me too, but they might toughen her up a bit, make her look a little less like a nerd.'

Archie couldn't help himself and laughed. 'But I still don't get it,' he said.

Daisy put an arm round him. 'Don't worry, winkle. Trust me, it's a piece of cake. All we've got to do is get to the next stage.'

'Next stage?' Archie queried. Daisy's confidence was staggering.

'Yeah,' Daisy said slapping him on his back. 'Not sure how we do it, but don't worry, we'll figure it out. Somehow.'

*

'What do you think, Old Man Wood?' Daisy said as they entered the living room.

The old man was looking particularly pale and the lines on his face were deeper and more ingrained than usual. He simply continued to stare straight ahead at the wall. No words came out of his mouth.

'Woo-hoo. Anyone there?' she said, waving a hand in front of his face. 'Anyone home?' Old Man Wood blinked and rubbed his face.

Daisy shook her head, her hair bouncing in the firelight. 'A right load of zombies in tonight,' she said as she threw herself on the sofa. She opened the Bible, flicked through to the first pages and started to read.

Archie looked at her with his mouth open. 'You alright, Daise?'

'What do you mean?'

'Archie raised his dark eyebrows. 'Reading … *the Bible*?'

Daisy shrugged. 'Why not?'

'For starters, I didn't know you could read.'

'Ha-ha, hilarious aren't you? It's the Genesis story Headmaster Solomon's been banging on about – might as well get it over and done with,' she said. 'And anyway, in the cave you said we may have saved the world from forty days and forty nights of rain, right? Well then, in that case, the Bible's probably a pretty good place to start.' She turned the page, 'I've got a hunch, winkle. There's something in here. Something we're missing.'

Archie looked baffled. 'Missing?'

'Yup,' Daisy replied. 'And when things are missing, you need to look for them. Got to start somewhere.'

Archie slouched down by the fire. 'But what makes you think it's got anything to do with the Creation story?'

'As I said, it's a hunch, but there is an awfully well known flood-event in the Bible and the Koran and other religious tomes,' Daisy said mimicking Isabella's intellectual voice. 'You know Noah, animals in two by two, and all that jazz. When I think of those cave paintings I reckon we've hooked into a very old and very bonkers adventure that goes way back.'

Archie pulled a face. 'You really think so?'

'Yup,' Daisy said. 'Dunno why it's us, though. Beats me.' Her eyes sparkled. She rather enjoyed Archie looking confused. 'There's definitely a link between our dreams, the storm and the pictures in the cave; the images on the walls clearly showed we had to find stone tablets or a book, or something.'

'And what if we don't find these tablets,' Archie said as he threw another log on the fire and dropped into an armchair.

Daisy scratched her nose, rubbed her eyes and ran a hand through her wavy blond locks. 'Well that was the weird bit. It showed that if we didn't find the tablets we'd die—'

'As in the pictures below the images of the rain—'

'Precisely.'

A shadow crossed his face. 'So how do you think we're going to die? By plague or giant hail stones beating us to death?'

Daisy stretched her arms out. 'No idea,' she said. 'I couldn't make out what it was. But we definitely die—'

'Great—'

'… unless, of course, we find these tablety things,' Daisy added. 'Don't worry, winkle, it'll be just fine.'

'Oh, why should we worry, Daisy,' Archie said crossly. 'when we're only going to die! I mean is there anything else you'd like to share?'

'Come on. It's not that bad.'

'Yes it is! It's called *death*. The end of this thing we do called, *living*. And stop calling me winkle. You're just as bad as Kemp!'

Daisy pouted and returned to her reading.

Archie studied her. 'You actually think we're going to survive, don't you?'

'Yep.'

'How come?'

'Because, winkle,' she said, completely ignoring his name request, 'we beat the storm and it can't get any harder than that, can it? I also know that I very nearly died – and that you two got a zapping from lightning bolts, hence your hair and Bells' hands. But I didn't die because of you two. And I'm convinced that if we do this together, we're much stronger because if any of us fail, we're screwed. After all, that's what the pictures showed.'

'But Bells doesn't want to know. She's given up.'

Daisy closed the book. 'Then we're dead already.'

Archie leaned forward in his chair, his chin resting in his hands. 'You think she'll come round?'

'Yeah. She's having a wobble, that's all.'

Archie shook his head. Daisy didn't sound in the least bit worried. 'Aren't you terrified?'

'Nah,' she replied, momentarily opening the book. 'What's the point? Go with the flow, winkle, go with the flow.' Daisy nodded at her words of deep wisdom and returned to her reading.

Archie looked dumbfounded. 'Any idea how long we've got?'

Daisy lifted her head out of the page. 'What, before we die? Nah. No idea.'

'In that case,' Archie said, 'I'm going to write a last letter to Mum and Dad.'

'You do that,' mumbled Daisy who was now concentrating hard.

When Archie returned several minutes later with a pen and a pad of paper, Daisy was busy writing.

'What are you doing now?'

'Just had an outstandingly groovy thought,' she replied.

'Well, what is it?'

'I can't tell you till I'm certain …'

Archie scowled and began his letter, glancing up to study his pretty sister who was immersed in the Creation story and intermittently scribbling. He'd never seen her like this and wondered for a minute if this was the same Daisy he'd grown up with.

He couldn't bear it. 'Come on, Daise. Tell me, please?'

Daisy held the palm of her hand up in the air towards him and continued writing. Every so often she turned the pages forward and then flicked a few back before returning to her notes.

'Well,' she said at long last. 'You asked me how long we had, so I had an idea. In here there are loads of references to the creation of the world so I thought I'd count the numbers.'

'All I meant,' Archie said, 'was that supposing this is real—'

Daisy shot him a look. 'Winkle, it is real. You're going to have to wise up about this. Furthermore I'm sure the cave pictures are related to something in the Bible and my hunch is that the creation story is somehow linked to all of it. It's like the whole story is a massive clue. But in a weird way.'

'How?'

'How should I know! It's a hunch, right.'

'Oh,' said Archie. He was beginning to wonder which of his sisters was more insane.

'So let's say,' Daisy began, 'that the storm represents a new beginning aimed to wipe out the world for some reason. In here, it says that the Creation took six days plus a day of rest. That's seven days, OK. And there are more references to seven. Seven this, seven that—'

'Seven deadly sins,' Archie offered.

Daisy looked muddled. 'I'm not sure that's got anything to do with it, Arch.' She'd lost her train of thought. 'The thing is Archie, bottom line, I think we have seven days to sort this out.'

*

Isabella lay on her bed and stared at her cream-coloured book shelves crammed with books, all stacked alphabetically. She liked the regimented order of it, the neatness, the simplicity of her cataloguing. She noted that one of the books was upside down. How odd. The only person who'd been in was Daisy. She couldn't have rummaged through her bookcase again, could she? Isabella stood up, picked out the book and studied it. '*Evolution of Man.*' Goodness. What was happening to her sister? Isabella put it back in the correct way and sat back down on her duvet.

It was time to think; everything that happened could be linked scientifically and logically, surely? But her arguments had logic holes the size of France. She sighed and rolled over. She wished Sue was here to talk it through then it would be clearer, she was sure of it.

Sue had this skill of making complex problems easy to understand, like her explanation of particle physics, which she'd struggled to get her head around. Sue asked her to imagine how it was possible to look inside two cars that have no windows or doors. She replied that it was impossible but Sue told her that the answer was to smash them together. And that, in a nutshell, Sue explained, was what physicists were doing with particles in an attempt to find out what lay beyond.

Isabella swung her legs off the bed, stood up and sought her reflection in the mirror. Didn't her face look a

105

fraction thinner, her rather pointy nose a bit sharper than usual? Maybe it was worry. She looked tired and her eyes had a watery sheen on them, from crying. As she brushed her hair she mulled over the argument with her brother and sister.

To the twins, the events of the past twenty-four hours weren't a dream or a nightmare of any kind. They were real and deserved to be treated as such. These impossible things had happened. She held up her right hand and looked through the neat hole in the middle of her palm.

Perhaps she shouldn't have been quite so hard on them. After all, the twins were only trying to work it out and they were a lot younger and not nearly so clever. She'd apologise, especially for the chair-throwing bit, and make sure they didn't tell mum and dad about it whenever they returned. She picked up a picture of the family that sat in a simple silver frame by her bed. So odd her parents not being here, she thought. Not a word, either. She wondered if they had even the smallest inkling of what they'd been through and if they missed her even a fraction of how much she missed them.

The evening light outside had a creamy texture now that the sun's dappled rays had sneaked underneath the sheet of grey-stained white cloud that covered the valley. She opened her drawer in search of a hair clip and noticed her mobile phone. She'd put it there before she left for school on the day of the storm.

Now, as she stared at it, she knew it might give them contact with the outside world but as nothing had worked – no power, aside from the petrol generator, no communications and no TV – her hopes weren't high. And anyway, what would she say? After all they were alive and probably in a better condition than most of their friends. Her heartbeat quickened at the possibility of receiving news. Terrible news, she suspected. More importantly, she wondered if there might be a message from Sue or their parents. Could she take it?

She placed the phone back in the drawer, pushed it closed and walked away.

Then she hesitated, ran back and opened it again.

She pressed the power button and the phone loaded. First one, then three signal bars came up and the battery indicator showed that half the charge was available.

Messages bleeped in.

Isabella read the first and bit her lip. It was catastrophic. She trembled and levered herself off her bed; she'd need to walk around for whatever they'd been through, others, it appeared had experienced the same or worse and many were still going through an horrific time.

The difference was that while they were alive, most of the messages were about whether anyone had found Jimmy or Gus or Charlie or Poppy or Lara. These were heart-breaking messages from desperately worried people. The families of their friends who were in a frantic search for their loved ones. And she knew most would never get replies.

She'd recharge the phone with Old Man Wood's generator in the morning, but how long would the mobile signal hold? In no time at all, Isabella was downstairs and heading towards the living room. She poked her head around the door.

'Daisy, Arch,' she said, her voice quivering with excitement.

Daisy was still reading on the sofa and Archie was sitting in the smaller armchair opposite Old Man Wood looking bored.

'Firstly, I'm sorry I had a go at you,' Isabella said. 'I … was wrong to yell.'

Daisy turned her eyes up from her book and smiled. 'It doesn't matter. We'll work it out – you'll see.'

'You're reading?' Isabella said. She couldn't remember ever seeing Daisy read. 'Is that a book in your lap?'

Daisy rolled her eyes. 'Yeah, yeah. I thought I'd give it a try. Nearly at the end of the flood bit.'

Isabella moved in to the middle of the room and sat down on the floor next to Archie's chair by the fire. 'The other thing,' she said, her voice quaking, 'is that my phone's working – I've got some reception and a little bit of battery.'

Daisy and Archie's ears pricked up.

'Any messages?' Archie asked.

'Yes, tons.'

In a flash they were around their elder sister peering over her shoulder.

'Woah! Wait a mo,' she said, 'probably best if I read them out. I warn you, there's no good news. Seriously, we might need tissues.'

Daisy got the message, dashed off and returned with a roll of kitchen paper.

'Right,' Isabella said quietly. 'Our weird, bad week has just got officially worse.' She looked them both in the eye. 'Are you sure you want to hear this?'

Daisy and Archie nodded.

'OK, put your arms around my shoulders, we need to be strong.'

Isabella took a deep breath and let the air out slowly. 'Here goes: first up, a message from Alice: Mr Beattie's body floated past yesterday – face down so couldn't be sure – but identical blue and red tracksuit, same build.'

Daisy gasped. 'Coach … dead,' she said under her breath, her eyes welling. 'He can't be.'

'I'm so sorry, Daisy,' Isabella said. 'I know how much he meant to you. And just to think, Archie so nearly went with him after the game.'

For several minutes she read them out. Without exception these were heartbreaking messages of lost children and desperate parents. And between them they knew every missing child or adult.

As she read, the others stared into the fire, lost in their thoughts, tears rolling down their cheeks.

'Are you sure you want to hear more?' Isabella asked worried that this might not be helping them.

Archie and Daisy nodded, desperate to hear news of their friends.

'Another from Alice. She doesn't think they'll make it through another night. She reckons they've had it,' her voice began cracking. 'It's the rain that's getting them. There's nothing to eat, nothing but the wet and cold. Poisonous sewage in the water. Disease is beginning to spread.' Isabella dabbed her eyes with a paper towel. 'Here are the people missing or drowned.' She read out Alice's list, choking as she reached the people they knew. She couldn't go on.

Now there was a long silence, the only noise the gentle crackling of the fire, the slow deep snores from Old Man Wood and the tip-tapping of rain on the windows, which fell heavier tonight. The light from the flames licked the inside of the old room.

Finally Daisy spoke. 'Any news from Sue?'

'No, nothing, no,' Isabella said.

'What about the teams?' Archie said. 'They must have been the last ones out of there.'

Isabella scrolled down. 'Chitbury bus discovered five miles downstream.'

Then she read out another school message. 'Missing: Anderson, Petre, Hill, Allen and Alexander. Gus Williams missing too. Kemp's coat found, but no body.'

'This is terrible,' Daisy cried. 'What about little Jimmy Nugent, Jo and Cassie?'

'Sorry, Daisy. No word on them, I'm afraid,' Isabella said as she scrolled on. 'Here's one from the headmaster.'

'DUE TO FLOOD DISASTER SCHOOL ABANDONED – WILL NOTIFY IN DUE COURSE. GOD BE WITH YOU ALL IN OUR HOUR OF NEED – SOLOMON.'

'I'll reply that we're safe. At least they'll know.' Isabella began tapping away at the tiny keyboard.

'I wonder if the school even exists anymore,' Archie said as he recalled the storm. 'It happened so fast – the football match was mental—'

Isabella suddenly stood up and began pacing the room. 'That's it!' she exclaimed. 'THAT'S IT!' The others watched her, intrigued. 'OK, it might look like I'm backtracking,' she said, 'but you know Sue and I had been working on a worst case storm situation in the event of this phenomenon—'

'Uh-huh,' Daisy replied. 'The whole storm glass thing.'

'Well, yes. You see, Sue dreamt about the flooding as well, and she … she …'

'What is it?' Archie cried.

'Oh my God,' Isabella whispered, going pale and stumbling. 'It's … it's so obvious—'

'What is—?'

Isabella sat down. 'Sue—?' she began before stopping.

'Bells, are you all right?'

Isabella scrunched her eyes tight. 'Sue told me about her nightmare about a flood at the school. She said it was the most real and terrifying dream EVER. I told her I'd had one too, so we looked into it to see what might happen on a physical level. But she kept on wanting to tell me something else and I kept avoiding it – I thought it was something to do with a boy's crush—'

'Why was it so important?' Daisy asked.

Isabella stood up and resumed her pacing, talking as she went. 'OK. The thing is, Sue is meticulous about note-taking. And believe you me, she records loads of strange things. So the moment she woke from her nightmare she wrote it down, step by step, until the images in her mind blurred. It meant that she had a pretty clear idea of what she'd seen, whereas ours were basically a frightening assortment of images which were confusing and scary. And this stems partially from the fact that none of us wrote them down. Agreed?'

'Absolutely,' Daisy said.

Archie smiled. 'So are you saying now that there might be some purpose to our dreams?'

Isabella flashed him a wry smile. 'No, I'm not there yet, Archie.'

'So this would explain,' Daisy said, 'why she yelled at you on the football pitch?'

'How do you know that—?'

'I can hear everything, remember,' Daisy reminded her with a knowing smile, 'just before you did your "beat up the referee" act – she ran on after you.'

Isabella stopped still. 'You're right!' she said. 'I heard her too. What did she say? You've got to remember!'

Daisy put a finger up her nose and teased out a bogey. She looked at it inquisitively with her red eyes before popping it in her mouth. 'I dunno. Wasn't really listening.'

'Daisy, you really are revolting. Can you concentrate on matters at hand rather than the contents of your nose?'

Daisy rolled her eyes.

'Look, please try and remember, Daisy,' Isabella said. 'It's important.'

They sat down in front of the fire, the firelight flickering at their features as Daisy ran through what had happened. 'OK, I'd been hacked to the ground and lay still trying to keep out of the way when little Jimmy Nugent ran in and everyone started fighting. Archie joined in and threw one of their guys about four feet in the air – unbelievably cool – and I was probably the only person who wasn't getting stuck in. Then I heard a voice. Sue's voice – yeah, definitely now I think of it, screaming something like: *the rain – it's all your fault.*'

The three of them looked at each other.

'Our fault. OUR fault,' Archie said. 'That's pretty full-on. You sure?'

'No,' Daisy shrugged. 'Something similar, though.'

Isabella slumped to the floor. 'The thing is she desperately wanted to tell me something, and I kept putting her off—'

'No, wait!' Daisy exclaimed. Her eyes were literally glowing. 'I've got it wrong.' She slapped her forehead. 'It was about *you*. That's it. It's "*ALL ABOUT YOU.*" That's what she yelled.'

'Anything else?'

'Yes,' Daisy said turning to Isabella as it flooded back to her, '*you're the only ones who can stop it.*'

'*Me? Stop it?*' Isabella said incredulously.

'That's close, but it's not quite right,' Archie said standing up and clasping Daisy's shoulders. 'What she said was: *only you or your family – the de Lowes – can stop it.*'

'Stop the rain?'

Archie shrugged. 'Yeah, I suppose. The storm, the rain, everything. That must be what she meant.'

Daisy clapped her hands. 'And,' she said as more flooded in, 'that we, *must find clues in Eden Cottage.*'

'Clues? To what?' Isabella quizzed.

Daisy shrugged. 'I don't know. I thought she'd lost her marbles.'

'Maybe she had,' Isabella said. 'Maybe you two are making it up. It's not that convincing—'

'Perhaps,' Archie said, 'she was referring to the clues to finding the stone tablets that were in the pictures in the cave?'

'*You really think so?'* Daisy said, winking at Archie.

Isabella sighed. 'Look I really don't think it's fair to jump to conclusions about Sue's mental health state at that point by instantly linking them with your cave-man pictures. Do you mind if we don't go there right now?'

'But you just said how important it was—'

'Yes, I know I did. But before you two think I'm going to believe you, I need further proof, and proper science-based proof at that, not some crazed shouting in the middle of a football match or dubious links to Neolithic art. Sue could have been trying to say any number of things. It needs to be much more convincing if it's going to have any sway with me.'

'Yeah, right,' Daisy said, her voice cold. 'We've got seven days to find whatever we've got to find and your being like this really isn't helping.'

CHAPTER FOURTEEN

Genesis Quiz

Sometime later, after they'd read every message about the tragedy unfolding in the valley beneath them, Isabella read a message that had just arrived:

'THANK YOU FOR UPDATE. CAN ONLY APOLOGISE 4 NOT LISTENING TO U ISA. WISH I HAD. GR8 U SAFE. TERRIBLE LOSSES. ARMY ON SCENE. HELP TAKEN AGES 2 ARRIVE. SEEMS WE R LUCKY ONES. DISEASE RIFE. STRANGE POISON IN WATER. D & A WHY NOT LEARN GENESIS FLOOD – S.'

'I don't believe it!' Archie cried, 'half the school are dead or missing and he reminds us to do homework. The man's extraordinary.'

'No,' Isabella answered, 'he's a teacher. At least he apologised for getting the weather so spectacularly wrong. And the creation story is topical,' she said, 'and not exactly difficult. Everyone in the universe – even mice – know about Adam and Eve, the serpent and the flood.' She looked down at her sister. 'Please tell me you have an outline understanding about the Flood, with Noah?'

'Of course I do,' Daisy said staring at the floor. 'I've just been reading it.' Her eyes had narrowed and her red irises were like pinpricks. She hated it when Isabella tried to make her look brainless and foolish.

Isabella clapped her hands as an idea popped into her head and almost immediately a bleep from the phone meant a new text had arrived. Isabella studied it, her hair falling over her face like a curtain. She squealed in delight and thumped the air.

'What is it?' Archie demanded, leaning in on her.

Isabella removed the phone from his line of sight. 'Right you two,' she said, her face beaming, 'if you want to know about the contents of the text and I absolutely promise that you do, you'll have to battle it out in a Creation quiz.'

'You've got to be joking,' Archie scoffed. 'I'm not doing that.'

Isabella grinned back. 'Why not? This text is fantastic news.'

Archie's face sank. 'Because it's boring, and I'm not in the mood, that's why.'

Isabella looked at him earnestly. 'Arch, you're going to have to do it at some point. Why not do it now while we're actually thinking about it so I don't have to pester you with it ever again? And Daisy's just read it so it'll be fresh to our new scholar and if you don't know the answers I'll explain,' she said. 'That way you too might actually learn it and then pass the exam. Because if you remember, school disaster or not, you are both hanging on by a thread to your school places.'

Archie looked appalled. 'I'm not doing some stupid RS quiz.'

But Isabella wasn't going to let it go. 'Look, it's a bit of fun to kill the time.'

'I'd rather play … cards!'

Daisy joined in. 'Come on, Arch, let's do it – you can play cards anytime.'

Archie shot a disbelieving look at his twin sister. 'Daisy?'

Isabella knew Archie wouldn't argue with both of them.

'God. OK,' Archie said, knocking his head against the floor and denting a floor board. 'On condition that you never, ever mention it again.'

'Fine!' Isabella replied. 'It's a deal.'

A deep groan came from the armchair as Old Man Wood stirred. He yawned, stretched out his arms, blinked and rubbed his eyes. He smiled as he saw the children around him and he stretched first one leg out and then the other.

'Ah, good,' Isabella continued, 'now you're awake, Old Man Wood, you can judge.'

'Hmmm. What was that? A judge?' Old Man Wood said through half a yawn. 'Why, yes, of course – what sort of judge?'

'It's a homework quiz – and you can help me decide who wins. You know, you can be a quiz master—'

'Quiz master? What the apples are you going on about now, young'un?'

'Keep the score, see who comes first,' Isabella said. 'Like they have on buzzer rounds.'

'Buzzer rounds?' The old man had no idea what she was talking about.

'Yes,' Isabella said. 'Archie and Daisy will pretend to press a buzzer by making their own buzzing noise. It's pretty simple. All you have to do is tell me who gets there first – OK?'

Daisy and Archie proceeded to make strange buzzery noises.

Old Man Wood rubbed his hands and then his eyes. 'You and your games, hmmm. Apples alive. Whatever next? Well, before I do any judging of buzzery things, let me attend to the fire.' With a couple of groans Old Man Wood pulled himself up, made his way over to the fireplace and thrust a long steel poker into the embers a few times. He added a couple of lumps of coal from the brass scuttle and retreated into his armchair, the springs groaning under his weight.

Shortly, golden flames danced out of the fireplace. Daisy and Archie snuggled up to the old man, sitting either side of him on the arms of the armchair listening to the gentle crackle of the flames as Isabella rapidly scribbled out a selection of questions.

A flash from outside made their heads turn towards the window. For a moment, lightning illuminated the shiny wet flagstones in the courtyard, and they could see the outbuildings beyond, glistening from the water. Inside, shards of blue light bounced off an assortment of metal curiosities on the dark wood-panelled walls.

Now that Isabella was ready, she stood up, drew the curtains and returned to her position on the hearth rug.

'Archie, for goodness' sake stop reading and pass it to me,' Isabella said. 'Right, Bible quiz on Genesis, are you ready?'

'Oh. So it's the Bible you're practising?' Old Man Wood said, his deep grainy voice blending with the storm outside. 'Interesting choice. I can't remember the last time—'

'OK, quiet,' Isabella said. 'Question one on chapter two. Are you ready?' Isabella gave Daisy a look as if to say, *come on, concentrate!*

'When God made the universe, there were no plants on the earth and no seeds. Now, Daisy, is this true or false?'

'True.'

'Correct. One nil to Daisy. Second question to Archie. What substance came from beneath the surface of the earth?'

'Um, it's er ...water, isn't it?'

'Nice one,' Isabella said raising her eyebrows and ticking her score sheet smartly. 'You see it's easy-peasy.

So far, so good – one all. Right. Fingers on your buzzers,' she said glancing to Old Man Wood who leant forward in anticipation. 'Who came first, Man or the Garden of Eden?'

'The Garden,' Old Man Wood said, rather surprised by his instant response.

'You're the judge, not the contestant,' Isabella said scolding him. 'And anyway, you're wrong; it says here it was man.'

'Are you sure?' he replied.

'Yes,' she said.

'That can't be right,' he added.

Isabella sighed. 'Well that's what it says here.'

Daisy tilted her head. 'So – is the Garden of Eden a real place? Can you actually visit it?'

'No,' Isabella sighed, 'you can't.'

'Then, what is it?'

Isabella leaned back knowingly. 'This is the big question. No one really knows,' she answered. 'The Garden of Eden is a curiosity, a mythical place that if it did exist today archaeologists reckon it would be in Iraq.'

'Where Mum and Dad are?' Daisy said.

'Yes, I suppose,' Isabella said. Their parents never seemed to give them any precise locations, simply because they were constantly on the move from one archaeological dig to another. But in the last postcard their parents said they were in Mesopotamia and the children had figured out that it was almost certainly in Iraq even if the postcard wore a Jordanian stamp.

Isabella spotted Daisy's confused look. 'Look, if there once was a place of lush green vegetation there's nothing there now but desert and a river that swells during the rainy season. That's why it's a myth. OK?'

It was Archie's turn to look baffled, but Isabella continued. 'The other way of looking at it is that the

Garden of Eden is an allegory – a story – of how early man settled in the pasture-rich valleys of the area; also known as the paradise of the Garden of Eden. Carbon dating on bones and fossils tells us that man inhabited the earth for literally tens of thousands of years before. So you might think of Biblical creation as a method by which the writers and storytellers start our understanding of God.'

'Then it's all made up?' Archie said, wrinkling his nose.

'I suppose,' Isabella said. 'It's more than likely, but it depends on what you want to believe. Some people actually think that the world started at this point, some don't. Science has shown us that life has been evolving constantly for millions of years. So it depends on your religious belief and how you interpret the story.'

'What about the flood?' Archie asked. He'd never realised how complex it was. 'I'm sure I've read that a real flood happened.'

'Good point, Arch,' Isabella said as she thought out her reply. 'Flood stories have been recorded across different cultures – from Ancient Chinese to Aboriginal Australian, from India to the Middle East, so who knows, there might be something in it. Some experts reckon there was a meteor strike that created a series of tsunamis. Mum and Dad are basically experts about this – you should ask them.'

'I thought they were archaeologists, looking for relics and stuff,' Archie said.

'They are, but in a way it all amounts to the same thing,' she replied. 'They're trying to piece our history together. It's the sort of stuff they're mad about.' Her eyes turned to the book. She wondered if she should ever have started this. And all she really wanted to do was tell them her stunning news. 'Back to the quiz,' she said, scouring the page, her finger tracing down the text. 'Where in the garden of Eden do the trees of life and knowledge live?'

'In the middle,' they said at once.

'Correct.'

Old Man Wood furrowed his brow and shrugged his shoulders suggesting a dead heat. Isabella fired the next question.

'What does the tree of knowledge represent?'

'Er … knowledge,' Archie said with a silly smile on his face.

Isabella glared at him.

'Alright – *understanding* – the clue's in the name.'

'Nope,' Isabella said, 'it says here in the text: "of what is good and what is bad".'

'Hang on,' he said. 'That's the same thing.'

'No it isn't—'

'Yes it is. Of course it is. You must have knowledge to understand what is good and bad?'

Isabella thought for a while. 'A bit dodgy, but I see what you mean. Half a mark.'

Isabella fired in the next question before either could protest. 'OK. A hard one. How many rivers did Eden divide into?'

Archie and Daisy stared at each other blankly.

'Two?' Archie tried.

No response.

'Four or five,' Daisy said, trying hard to remember.

'Four,' Old Man Wood said softly as if not thinking. He scratched his bald head. None of this seemed right at all. But why did it feel wrong? Why did it throw doubt in his mind? 'There are four rivers,' he repeated, his brain in a spin. 'But—'

'Correct,' Isabella said with a tone of surprise, 'but please don't answer – how are they supposed to learn anything?'

'Sorry, just slipped out—'

'And can you name any of them?' Isabella asked.

Archie stared at the ceiling rolling his eyes while Daisy made an oooh-ing sound, as though it was on the tip of her tongue.

Isabella took this as a "no". 'Neither of you has a clue,' she said. 'The first river is called Pishon, which flows around the country of Havilah. And if you're lucky enough to be passing Havilah, you'll find gold, rare perfumes and precious stones. I am so going there when I'm grown up.' Isabella smiled. 'The second river is Gihon, which flows round the country of Cush, the third river is the Tigris which flows east of a place called Assyria. The fourth is the Euphrates.'

Just then, Old Man Wood exploded into laughter and long, deep guffaws echoed from his large barrelled chest. As the quiz had gone on, fragments of memories had returned and his extraordinary dreams were at last beginning to make some kind of sense, as though he'd found a vital piece to the jigsaw puzzle.

A thunderbolt crashed over the cottage. Isabella ducked and Archie and Daisy instinctively threw themselves behind the armchair but Old Man wood stood up and roared with laughter as if he hadn't a care in the world.

Isabella, Archie and Daisy stared at the large man with their mouths wide open, their hearts fluttering. Had the man they loved so deeply finally lost his marbles? Was it his eccentricity or simply the effects of his great age?

Suddenly a gust of wind shot down the chimney and blew out all the candles. The children froze as though darkness like a thick cloak had dropped out of the sky. As their eyes adjusted, the flames in the fire flickered with rich and vivid colours, the noise of the storm somehow louder.

'Are you alright, Old Man Wood?' Archie whispered.

'Fine, my boy. Fine,' Old Man Wood replied returning to his chair and then leaning forward towards the flames. 'Something smouldering in the back of my mind suddenly burst into flame when you were talking about those rivers,' he said. His weathered, bony features were greatly enhanced by the firelight, and his eyes seemed to shine like the stars and his wrinkles were deep and filled with experiences. 'It reminded me of … well, something from a long time ago, that's all.'

'Right,' Isabella said, gathering herself, trying not to explode with joy. 'Since there's no light and you both did reasonably well, would you like to hear who the text was from?' Daisy and Archie moved in next to her trying to catch a peek at the screen.

'It's from Sue!' she exclaimed.

'Sue? You're kidding?'

'NO! She's alive!' Isabella started dancing in front of the fire, punching the air. 'In fact,' Isabella continued, 'it's better than that. She's with Gus!'

'No way!'

'Yes-way! Together they made it through the storm.'

Archie was astonished. 'But how? Are they in hospital—'

'No, no it sounds incredible,' Isabella said, her voice singing. 'I scribbled on a piece of paper about the boat and shoved it in Sue's pocket. When Sue ran off, she bumped into Gus and persuaded him to join her and she found the note. They looted the shop, Gus built a shelter over the boat and because of that, they survived. Apparently Gus has been nothing less than heroic. They're out at sea and she just caught a fish!'

'Blimey,' Archie said. 'That really is incredible.'

'It's brilliant news, sis,' Daisy cried, and she hugged Isabella who was already hugging Archie.

'And there's more.'

'What do you mean, more?'

'Oh, so much more.' Isabella could hardly stop giggling. She found herself blushing and pushed her siblings away.

'What?'

Isabella found tears welling in her eyes. 'They've fallen in love.'

Archie reeled. 'No Way! Gus – are you sure?'

'Gus, with Sue,' Daisy added. 'Never.'

Isabella shook her head. 'They've kissed!'

Archie blushed just thinking about it.

'They've been snogging?' Daisy laughed. 'Epic!'

'Yup!' squealed Isabella. 'Snogging!' she repeated.

'Ooh-eeee!' and the girls squealed in delight.

*

While the joys of Sue and Gus' love affair dominated the conversation, Old Man Wood quietly picked his way around the room and re-lit several of the candles. Then he slipped out of the room to do the same in the hallway and kitchen.

For the first time in ages, his whole body fizzed with energy. It was as if a touch paper had exploded a great big memory-rocket right inside his mind and information had flashed in. It was almost too much to bear. He had forgotten so much – and yet so much still remained locked inside. How and when would he tell the children, and would they believe him? If they didn't, then what? Would it ruin everything? The old man was swamped by questions.

One thing had come to him with clarity. The answers to some of his questions lay with some special old friends who he needed to find – and fast. From what he had remembered, they might be able to fill in the blanks.

Maybe, he thought, his time had finally come.

*

Isabella was putting the finishing touches to her text reply and the twins were discussing the revelation of Gus and Sue's kissing which Archie thought sounded quite disgusting.

'Tell me,' he said, 'how do you actually snog?'

'OK, so what you do,' Daisy replied in a very educational manner, 'is put your lips together with your friend, shut your eyes, open your mouth a bit, poke out your tongue and swirl it around against the other one.'

'Oh my God!' Archie said. His look of revulsion said it all. 'And that's supposed to be nice.'

'Yeah. I suppose,' Daisy replied.

'What if you start dribbling?' he asked. 'And what if you bash your teeth?'

'You won't—'

'How do you know?'

Daisy pouted her lips. 'Cos I do.'

'And anyway,' Archie asked, 'if you're swirling away, how are you supposed to breathe? Isn't it all just a bit uncomfortable and awkward and what if the person you're kissing has bad breath, like Kemp.'

'God, Archie, *you're so ten*, aren't you?'

Archie frowned. How come Daisy knew all this stuff? 'Have you actually done it?'

'Might have,' Daisy replied coyly.

Archie eyed her suspiciously. 'I don't think you have, you're telling me a big fat porky pie, lie.'

Daisy winked at him with a smile on her face. 'That's for me to know, and you to find out.'

Old Man Wood returned and coughed. The children fell quiet. 'Time for bed. I'll put the generator on in the morning,' he said. 'But would any of you like to hear one of my special stories?'

'Oh yeah! But only if it's got absolutely nothing to do with snogging,' Archie said.

Old Man Wood's stories were fantastic tales full of heroes, magicians and witches, evil overlords and brutal wars. They nearly always contained adventures about Tree-men, who were always the bravest and noblest of creatures. The way he delivered them was like fire and ice blended perfectly together; his ancient face full of wrinkles alone seemed to express the meaning in the story. And when the stories were happy his eyes sparkled like the bright Northern Star. When they were sad, dark clouds cloaked his eyes and his wrinkles grew deep and long and the shadows from the wavering firelight dramatised the effect so much that the children would ask questions for days after, such as, 'What happened to the Warlbist, when her husband gave in to the Floak?' or 'How did the Spurtle get its fur?'

Daisy smiled. 'How about the Iso story?'

'We always have the Iso story,' Archie whinged.

'Because it's beautiful and she is so incredibly cool.'

'But it's sooo girly—'

'It's an excellent choice,' Isabella added. 'Just what we need – as long as it's only the beginning.'

'Ah, yes, the Iso story,' Old Man Wood said, winking at the girls. 'A story of love and friendship and derring-do! But afterwards, no questions, it's straight to bed.'

CHAPTER FIFTEEN

Old Man Wood And The Fire

Old Man Wood had always been old. His face was deeply lined by the journey of time; his teeth worn to dull stumps, his remaining hair random and straggly, his skin blotched and wrinkled. For this reason he was affectionately called Old Man Wood; because he looked as weathered as a rough piece of bark from a tree like an old birch.

Old Man Wood studied his rectangular four poster bed which jutted out into the room like a big wooden box. He noted with interest the strange patterns and shapes of the carvings on every upright and beam and wondered if they offered any clues. He examined the three rectangular panels at its foot, showing live pictures of the children. Old Man Wood scratched his chin. If it hadn't been for the panels he might never have found them … hadn't that been a stroke of luck?

On the floor lay five brown, dirt-ingrained rugs. Standing behind them, stood a large wardrobe where he stored his few clothes and in front of the window sat a brown leather sofa. Opposite the door an old metal fireplace with intricate scrolls saw regular activity during the colder months.

Classical wooden panelling made from many different tree species covered the walls and it glowed with an unlikely variety of colour. How unfussy it was, how strangely beautiful; how well it suited him.

Every night since the rain had begun he'd fallen into a deep sleep and later woken, sweating and yelling, gripping his sheets until his hands hurt – his fingernails digging into his palms. And last night it was the same: blinding flashes, searing heat followed by intense cold. Goosebumps appeared as he thought about the spider; that horrible, ugly, white, ghost-like thing with a blue ring of fire in its belly. He closed his eyes but the snapshots refused to go away.

Old Man Wood moaned. He stared out of the window at the dark early morning, with its dirty charcoal colours filtering through the grey clouds, and tried to make sense of it all. With nothing forthcoming, he frowned and stretched his arms out wide. Maybe he'd be better off in front of the fire in the living room with an early morning cup of tea. Might just fix my head and settle my nerves, he thought. He shuffled into the kitchen and boiled the kettle. With his brew in hand he ambled into the sitting room, grabbed some kindling and a couple of logs and placed them on top of the embers. The fire smoked before a small golden flame danced nervously around the wood as it tentatively took hold. Old Man Wood sank into his armchair and stared at the fire, trying as best he might to understand the images in his head.

He spied the local newspaper on the side table next to him. He read about a burglary in last week's Northallerton News where a thief, on making his getaway, had slipped on a banana skin and fallen down an open manhole into the sewer. Old Man Wood chuckled.

Then, out of the corner of his eye he noted that the fire needed a bit of a poke. A tune had jumped into his head, and feeling in a better mood, he reached out and grabbed the steel fire prong.

'Whoooosh, hummmy, sshhhhh,' he began humming. He didn't know why, but the song felt etched into him like a tattoo and came with ease. As he sang, he reached out and prodded the burning logs, enjoying the way the flames danced and licked yellow and tangerine with greater intensity. He hummed the tune a little louder, with more vigour, liking how it blended seamlessly with the rhythms of the crackles of the fire. He turned it up a notch until his singing was coming from a place deep within him, the tune filling him with a kind of inner strength that began in his loins and spread to his heart and then out to his fingertips and toes.

As he stared deeply into the fire, a curious rectangular object grew and appeared to be coming directly at him. *In all the apples*, he thought, what is it? A box, a lump of stone? Mesmerised, he found himself drawn towards it and moments later, the sound of humming still coming as if like a chant, he found himself stretching out a hand. And now his fingers touched it and much to his surprise he found that it was cool, not hot at all, and solid – as if it were made of a kind of stone. He stopped singing and pulled, but the object would not yield.

'Now then,' Mrs Pye's voice called out, shattering his concentration and the song. 'What do you think you're doing?' She stared at him from the doorway.

Old Man Wood suddenly felt the heat. 'OUCH! Blasted thing!' he cursed rubbing his hands.

'You alright?' she said. 'Messing with fire and at your age too – you should be more careful.'

Confused, Old Man Wood stood up and marched around the room rubbing his chin, hmm-ing to himself, trying to think. Then he made his way into the boot room where he donned his cap, threw on his green waterproof coat and, after a great deal of groaning, wrestled his boots onto his large feet.

After he'd seen to the cattle, it was well past time, he thought, to seek out his old friends.

CHAPTER SIXTEEN

Searching For The Bubbling Brook

Archie woke with a start. Darkness filled the room. He yawned, removed the sleep from his eyes and looked at his watch. Five o'clock. A bit early – but for the first time in ages he felt refreshed after a long and nourishing sleep with no dreams. In any case, he had knives to throw. He dressed quickly and trying not to disturb the house he trod exceedingly carefully on the ridiculously creaky floorboards and crept out of their attic room, down the stairs, along the corridor, down the main stairs and into the kitchen.

He wasn't the first up. 'Morning, Old Man Wood,' he said as he poked his head round the kitchen door. 'You're up early. Everything alright?'

Old Man Wood waved a hand in Archie's direction. 'Morning, littlun. Peculiar stuff going on in 'ere.' He pointed to his head and then stretched his arms out to pull down the cuffs on his coat. 'Very, very strange things,' he tapped his head again. 'I've been to see the cattle,' he said changing the subject, 'give them more feed. My oh my, they looked utterly terrified – which is hardly surprising, I suppose. None of them have eaten a great deal and I squeezed only a few drops out of Bernice and Burger, dear things.' He stopped and stroked his chin. 'It's as if they're trying to tell me something.'

He turned his attention back to Archie. 'What are you doing up so early?

'Might go and throw my knives, take my mind off stuff,' Archie replied rubbing the front spike on his head. 'Are you off out again?'

'Yes, littlun, I need to clear my head,' the old man said as he studied the boy. 'Is there anything I can help you with?'

Archie looked up at Old Man Wood. 'Actually, do you mind if I join you?' he said weakly. 'It's just I could do with some grown up company. I'm really missing Mum and Dad.'

'Of course you are,' the old man replied. He pulled him in for a hug. 'I've noticed that none of you lot are playing. Lots of arguing and funny conversations. What's up?'

'It's the rain, I think,' Archie said, wishing he could say more, 'and being stuck here and feeling utterly helpless and worrying about our friends and … and things like the cave and the pictures and my stupid hair that don't make any sense.'

'Hmmm,' Old Man Wood said. 'Think I know what you mean.'

'Where are you off to?' Archie asked.

Old Man Wood scratched his chin. 'I'm off to find some old friends – they might be able to help at a time like this.'

'Friends? Where?'

'Well, I don't know, down there, somewhere.'

'You're, er, quite sure about this?'

'Oh yes, Archie. I'm not fooling you.'

Archie thought for a while. 'Please can I come too?' he said.

Old Man Wood rubbed his mottled head. Taking Archie to find the Bubbling Brook could be a big mistake, foremost because he had no idea where it was. 'I'm not sure you're ready to come along, little Archie.'

'Yes, I am,' he said instinctively.

'If you come along, you're going to have to swear to me, Archie, that you won't mention it to your sisters. Especially Isabella. I heard her earlier.'

'Why?'

'Because I'm asking you, that's why,' he replied. 'Just for the moment.'

'I don't understand,' Archie said.

Old Man Wood felt himself getting tangled up with the words. 'Well, it might upset you, that's all,' Old Man Wood said gently. 'It would most definitely upset young Isabella.'

Old Man Wood draped an arm round Archie's shoulders. 'Many, many moons ago when the flood waters rose above the old steps by the base of the cliff, I discovered something and it struck me that I might find it again.'

'By the cave?' Archie looked puzzled.

'There or thereabouts.' Old Man Wood said. 'Somewhere in the valley.' The back door creaked open. 'If your come along, Archie, you're going to have to open up your mind.'

*

Dawn threatened as a soft murky light filtered out across the vale. In front of them the floodwaters stretched like a vast flowing silver lake starting behind the hedgerow in front of the currant bushes in the vegetable garden below. After slipping and sliding down the steep track, and squelching through the saturated fields, they were soon at the water's edge. Old Man Wood took a couple of deep breaths, shook some mud from his boots, furrowed his brow and peered into the rain.

'Now, where are those funny old trees?' he said out loud.

'Trees?'

Old Man Wood nodded.

Archie shivered. 'Blimey, we're looking for trees and you don't know where they are. There are thousands. Do you know what type they are?'

'Ooh yes. Willows, great big clump.'

'Willows?' Archie said avoiding a large puddle. 'The valley's littered with willow clumps.'

Archie scoured the vast expanse of grey water intermittently punctured with bushes nearer the water's edge. 'Most are underwater. What if it's one of those?'

'Must be easy enough to find, I reckon,' Old Man Wood said as he strode off, his boots squelching in the mud. 'Something tells me the clump's just around the headland towards Upsall. Come on, Archie, this way.'

Archie studied the expanse of water with tree clumps – mainly willows – popping out, like miniature crowns. This is utterly ridiculous he thought. Talk about a wild goose chase.

*

After a couple of unsuccessful attempts at entering the thick brambles surrounding one clump, and then doing exactly the same thing with another, Old Man Wood began to wonder if he had gone the right way. He stamped his boot down in the sludge and a shower of sloppy brown water sprayed over a clump of sodden ferns.

He stopped to think. It wasn't brawn that would lead them to the Bubbling Brook, it was brains, just as he often told the children. But Old Man Wood was well aware that his brain took a while to get going. In fact, he was amazed that his head worked at all considering his vast age.

He found an old tree stump, sat down, closed his eyes and concentrated.

*

Archie watched Old Man Wood with a mixture of curiosity and growing anxiety. His excitement bordered on madness, real madness. It was like watching a child at a fairground who couldn't work out where his favourite ride had gone.

Old Man Wood stood up and sat down again, all the while mumbling to himself. Then up. Now down. Without warning he shot off, following the waterline towards Upsall. Archie hurried to keep up. Most of the clumps that followed the line of the water were identical, their leaves stripped from the branches by the rain. Defeated by the first two clumps, they waded through the water, where at length they met a huge clump of brambles and fallen trees with twisted, smashed branches.

Close by, a mudslide with treacherous deep water pockets blocked their path. The pair slipped and climbed and squelched back up the hill towards the ruins, reverting down to the water's edge as soon as they could. Old Man Wood stopped every now and then and sniffed the air – or so Archie thought – as though searching out the best route before shooting onward at such a speed that Archie struggled to keep pace.

They walked along in silence for many minutes. Soon, they came across a willow clump consisting of new shoots and whips and three huge old trees. It was impassable. On one side several large and small trees stood half-submerged in the floodwater, on the other a mess of trees and rocks and brambles had collected where the ground had slipped away.

Archie caught his breath. 'Look, there's no way we'll get through there,' he complained. 'Why don't we head back—?'

Old Man Wood groaned. 'Maybe I'll use a bit of beef and bludgeon me way through the middle,' he said, ignoring Archie.

In no time, the old man had shinned up one of the large outer trees and was balancing on a thick branch that leaned directly into the middle of the clump. Archie climbed up after him and watched as the old man – his arms outstretched as if on a tightrope – moved one foot in front of the other along the branch.

Archie noticed that within the clump, directly below the trunk they stood on, was a crater filled with water. A creepy mist swirled around as if was in some way protecting it. Archie took a deep breath and pulled himself along.

*

'Blast!' the old man cried staring at his feet. He sat down on the branch. 'I thought there was something wrong. Look! A hole!' He bent his leg round, removed his boot and a stream of water splashed into the pool a metre or so below.

As Old Man Wood wrestled his boot on, he eyed a route across. It would take a couple of acrobatic leaps. Was he nimble enough? Apples alive, why not? Of course he could do it.

The old man took a deep breath and puffed out his chest. He leapt onto a low branch which swayed ominously before jumping on to the next one. He was halfway across.

'Hey, be careful!' Archie shouted. 'You sure you're alright?'

'Never been better,' Old Man Wood replied. 'Come on! It's a piece of Mrs Pye's cake.' But at that moment, for no real reason, he lost his balance and throwing his arms wildly in the air like a windmill, he swayed first one way and then the next and then back again like a pendulum. Each time, Archie's heart leapt. Then with a look of total surprise on his face, the old man disappeared into the pool beneath him and under the surface.

Archie, in spite of his gloominess exploded with laughter and held back his sides for fear of falling in himself. But seeing Old Man Wood struggle in the water he realised the pool was deeper than they'd thought.

'Over here,' Archie said offering his hand, tears blurring his vision. Old Man Wood recovered his wits and swam towards the side and when his feet touched the bottom, he picked his way carefully towards Archie, the water now up to his chest. When he was within a step of the branch Old Man Wood disappeared under the waterline again, as though he had walked off a ledge. Shortly he re-emerged looking, Archie thought, like a drowned rat and after plenty of splashing and coughing, he held onto the branch, spitting water out of his mouth.

Archie heaved him up. 'I think you swallowed some water,' Archie said, as he thumped the old man's back a couple of times.

'Thank you, Arch,' Old Man Wood replied. 'I most certainly did. That's better. Now out of the way while I shake myself dry.' The old man stood up and, like a dog, sprayed water in all directions.

*

Archie simply didn't know what to say. The surprised look on Old Man Wood's face made Archie's shoulders gallop up and down with laughter.

The old man wiped his face with his sodden clothes and sat down beside Archie on the branch. He shook his head. 'Getting a bit old for this kind of thing, I reckon,' he began.

Archie's frame hurt.

Suddenly, Old Man Wood's head twitched from one side to the other. Then he stood up and sidled further along. 'Is someone there?' he turned to Archie. 'Did you hear that, Archie?'

Archie scanned the pond.

Just the drizzle and the mist and drops of water splashing down from the branches overhead. He shook his head.

'Apples alive, there are more,' the old man whispered. 'Laughing like crazy. All round.' Old Man Wood's head shifted from side to side. 'Laughing like I've never heard.'

'I can't hear anything. You're sure you're all—?'

Old Man Wood had had enough. He climbed up onto the branch and folded his arms. 'You think that an old man falling down is amusing, do you?' he said furiously to the empty pool. 'Well, when I find you lot, I'll show you another type of entertainment!'

CHAPTER SEVENTEEN

Kemp's Rescue

Daisy woke, sensing a movement in the bedroom. It didn't take long to figure out that it was Archie. She felt a strange hollowness in her stomach. She laid her head back on the pillow, her curious thoughts staying with her. Sometime later, she sat up with a start. 'I've got to find Archie,' she said out loud. 'Something's happened.'

'He's fine,' Isabella yawned from behind her curtain. 'Don't worry—'

'No, Bells. It's not right. Not right at all.' She climbed out of bed. 'I can ... kind of ... sense it.' She flipped on the light which, much to her surprise flickered into action. The generator was working.

As she slipped into her jeans and shirt she tapped on Isabella's duvet. 'Bells, put your phone on charge. There's power but it won't last for long.'

'You do it. It's downstairs,' Isabella groaned before disappearing back under her duvet.

In the living room, Daisy plugged in the phone and headed into the kitchen where she found Mrs Pye doing the ironing in front of the telly. The hum of the generator and the drone of the morning news filled the room.

'The telly!' Daisy exclaimed. 'When did it come back on?'

Mrs Pye looked up. 'Good morning, Daisy.'

'Oh! Morning, Mrs P.'

Mrs Pye scrunched up her face. 'Now then, about ten.'

Daisy smiled. Mrs Pye never referred to time in its entirety, so it could have been seconds, minutes, hours, or days. Sometimes even months or years.

Daisy grabbed a bowl, ladled in a couple of spoons of porridge from the saucepan on the range cooker and sprinkled it with salt, stirring it in. Then she pulled up a chair and watched the screen as a banner ran below it with the words, *Yorkshire Disaster.* And next to it was: *helpline number.* Daisy wondered whether it was worth a call. Then again, they were fine, so why bother. By the look of things others were in a far worse state than they were.

' ... *experts are saying that the unprecedented flood in the north of the country is partly due to the effects of global warming. But what is baffling forecasters is that this freak storm did not blow in, it simply mushroomed out, growing at alarming speed from a position just to the west of the North Yorkshire Moors.'*

The camera panned to show a village almost totally submerged. Daisy gasped. It looked like Kettleby, just down the road. Only the spire of the church and a few rooftops were visible. *'This is the picture throughout the whole of Yorkshire, Cleveland and Lincolnshire. There is no power, no fresh water and sewage fills the streets. Disease is now a real threat.'*

The picture returned to the studio and a man stood next to a graphic of a map of the North of England. The presenter looked glum. *'It appears that a freak depression has settled directly over this area.'* The TV graphics changed. *'The problem, as you can see from our satellite image, is that this extraordinary weather doesn't appear to be letting up. Although there has been no torrential rain like we saw on Friday afternoon which, by the way, was the hardest rainfall recorded anywhere in the world – and for the longest sustained period of time – there is more rain forecast, which will cause further havoc as water levels continue to rise. And exceptionally high spring tides at York, with an already saturated water table, means the rising water doesn't have anywhere to go.'*

The screen snapped to helicopter imagery of the flooding. *'Early casualty estimates range from 3,000 to 30,000 victims. According to the emergency services it's impossible to tell. Ten counties are in an unprecedented state of emergency. Survivors within this huge area have been evacuated to the higher ground of the moors and the Yorkshire Dales. The death toll looks certain to rise as news filters in from stricken towns and villages across the country.'*

The picture reverted to the news anchor. *'We'll have regular updates throughout the day but right now we can go to our reporter in the submerged North Yorkshire town of Northallerton. Some of these pictures are of a distressing nature.'*

Mrs Pye watched the screen transfixed, her face even paler than normal.

'This pregnant woman was saved when a neighbour managed to break through an upstairs window and get her onto the roof. She was one of the lucky ones—' The woman, looking frightened and pale, told her terrifying story. Daisy recognised her as Sue's babysitter.

The reporter continued: *'Now that a partial service has resumed for many mobile phone networks, the emergency services are urging people to call the national emergency number to let them know of their whereabouts. Please be aware that the network operators have told us that only a limited service will be available.'*

Daisy was about to go when a news story flickered on the screen. *'Breaking News.'* The broadcaster cocked his head, listening to the mike in his ear. *'We're getting news of an extraordinary story of a boy who has been found at the top of a large tree.'* He smiled at the camera as he focused on his news feed. *'The boy, winched to safety by the North Yorkshire air ambulance, was found naked, hanging onto a top branch of a tree in the middle of the vast area of flooding. I'm told that it was close to the epicentre of the storm near to the ravaged village of Upsall. This remarkable footage has just come in from members of the helicopter crew.'*

The screen showed a helicopter cockpit and a man with a jumpsuit and mask. Through the windows, the chopper blades blurred. Below lay a huge expanse of water and as the pilot took the helicopter down; right in the very middle of the picture sat the top of a huge bare tree. Suddenly muffled noises from the crew cut across the whorl of the rotors. The camera lens cut back to the crew within the helicopter who were gesticulating wildly with their arms.

The camera panned back to the tree as the helicopter banked and then the lens zoomed in. For a moment there was a strange silence as the crew and viewers tried to see into the tree. As the helicopter swung to the left, there, draped over a bough, was a human figure hugging a thick branch.

Mrs Pye grabbed Daisy's arm and gripped tight.

Now the sound cut out altogether. The camera zoomed in even farther to show the boy, unmoving, his naked white flesh clearly visible against the dark water beneath him.

Daisy gasped. Who could have survived the storm and the flooding and then climbed up a huge tree? It didn't seem possible. Daisy could hardly breathe as the camera lens reached in until the only thing on the screen was the head and shoulders of the boy, gaunt and white, so utterly beaten. The boy had not a hair on his head; bald, like a big baby.

A shiver raced up her. The jawline, so familiar. And those fat lips. Like … who? In a flash it hit her. Kemp. It was identical to Kemp. She could tell his face from a mile away. But if it was Kemp then where was the thick ginger hair? So it couldn't be, could it? Her dislike for Kemp lightened. She wished the boy, whoever he was, hope.

She snapped out of it. If it was Kemp, Archie needed to know. Archie would confirm her suspicions.

Seconds later the images on the TV disappeared altogether. The satellite connection failed. Mrs. Pye waddled over and gave it a smack. She moaned at it and then returned to the ironing. Daisy swore she could see tears falling down Mrs Pye's ruddy cheeks.

Daisy slipped out of the kitchen to the bootroom and noted that both Old Man Wood's and Archie's boots were missing. Maybe Old Man Wood had gone to look for him as well. She donned her oilskin and lifted the hood over her tangled blond mop and headed out into the rain.

*

OK, Daisy thought, if I was winkle, where would I go? Dad's shed in the haunted garden? Not a bad place to start. Quiet. Dark. Horrible.

The shed by the haunted garden was part of a derelict area near the vegetable patch at the bottom of the garden. The children's father and Old Man Wood grew potatoes here but never stayed late. 'It's as if I'm being watched,' their father often said. 'Whoever it is, it doesn't like the fact that I'm there, and as a result I'm not too keen on staying either.'

Daisy knew exactly what he meant. She looked at the cold, damp, miserable place, intermittently wiping rainwater out of her eyes. 'Archie,' she called out. 'Archie. I think they've found Kemp!'

In the distance the drone of the whirring blades of a helicopter forced her to look up into the thick clouds. Must be the rescue mission, she thought, swinging into action, removing people to high ground. But they'd never come up here, where the forest was impenetrably thick and littered with broken trees and mudslips.

Behind the plum trees lay an expanse of thick bushes in the shape of a horseshoe. Daisy made her way gingerly towards the drooping, skeletal branches, her boots squelching noisily. Here, a small opening led to an old rusted gate.

She stopped and studied it for a moment. I don't remember that gate. Where can it have come from? More importantly, she thought, where does it lead? She looked up at the dark morning sky and wiped rainwater from her cheeks and eyes, removing a couple of sopping hair strands at the same time. Then she entered the pathway towards the gate.

Suddenly she caught a light glimmering on something in the bushes beyond the gate. Daisy peered at it, intrigued. A tiny jewel – a diamond? She walked closer until she was in front of the gate whose scroll-like pattern appeared strangely familiar, like a circular tree with its roots showing.

She noted that the jewel looked more like a pearl in the shape of a tear drop. It sparkled. She liked the thought of it around her neck, against her pale skin.

Daisy gave the gate a push. It was stuck, jammed by foliage and creepers. She tried again with the same result. It hardened her resolve.

Come on, Daisy, she whispered. On the count of three: One, two … THREE!

She slammed into the gate, but instead of meeting resistance, the gate flew open and Daisy hurtled straight into the bush. As she tumbled, she reached out for the jewel and before she knew what was happening, she crashed into a ditch full of water.

Daisy sank under, entirely submerged. Moments later she surfaced waving her arms and spluttered violently.

Phleaux, tchuch, she spat, coughing out the metallic, coppery-tasting water that had a hint of strong cheese. Her head swam and a dizziness overcame her as though a bee had shot into her brain and was struggling to find a way out.

She fell to the ground as a terrible thought washed over her. What if what she'd swallowed the deadly, poisonous sewage-water like the man said on TV?

She dragged herself up the bank on her elbows and knees moving to a patch of dry grass. She lay still with her eyes shut and wondered if this was how the poison worked. A gentle warm wind blew over her as the buzzing sensation between her ears grew more comfortable and then ebbed away entirely.

Perhaps, she thought, she'd died and gone to heaven.

*

After several minutes, her eyes still shut tight, Daisy placed her hand over her chest. Her heart thumped. She sat up and slowly opened each eye.

Stretching out in front of her was an area about twenty large paces across by twenty wide tapering in the further away it went. On each side, sat three wide-trunked and curiously gnarled old trees covered in pink, white and yellow petals. Behind these showy trees, sat a line of thick impenetrable-looking thorn bushes. Daisy realised that no one could see in and she couldn't see out.

At the far end adjoining the space stood a kind of old dilapidated greenhouse bereft of glass. In it sat a peculiar object, like a big Victorian garden roller with a curiously large handle.

She turned over and stared up at a rich blue sky. Bright rays of sunshine warmed her.

Daisy shot to her feet and dashed around in a frenzy. 'WHERE … am I?' she shouted out. But her cries were lost into the foliage and the blossom and the gentle wind.

She sat down and threw a handful of petals into the air which caught on the breeze and fluttered to the ground nearby. Maybe she was hallucinating – 'Am I dead?' she yelled out.

She tried again. 'Is this heaven?'

Still no answer. She kicked a pile of pink blossom then ran over and did the same to the white and yellow piles, repeating it again and again in a frenzy until petals filled the air and snowed down over her.

'WHAT IS GOING ON?'

Daisy lay down on her back and turned her face up to the sun as the last few petals fluttered to the ground. She wiped them off and sank back, enjoying the warmth on her skin as if it were a hot spring day by a swimming pool. She listened to the rustle of wind blowing through the petals and leaves and removed her wet coat, trousers and shirt, which she hung over one of the gnarly old trees. She took off her boots.

Since no one can see me, she thought, and I can't see anyone else, I can't offend anyone. So she lay back on the bed of petals in her underwear, took a couple of deep breaths and stretched out her arms. With the sweet fragrance of the blossom overwhelming her senses, she basked contentedly and considered her fate.

If this is heaven, I'm sure it'll be fine to lie here a little longer. I wonder if Archie and the others will miss me, she thought, a lump growing in her throat. And I never said goodbye … to anyone. Will Mum and Dad even notice …

Old Man Wood might. Just.

I hope they play football in heaven.

Daisy wiped a tear from her eye and looked around.

But I don't feel very dead.

She re-arranged herself in the blossom and inspected her body. This bump, she thought, feeling her shin, feels like me. She stretched her neck up. The wind blows in my hair and I can feel it. She sniffed the air and grabbed a handful of petals; my nose senses the perfume and my skin feels the warming rays of sun in each pore. So perhaps being dead is like being alive. Maybe that's what heaven really is. Daisy smiled. Got to be better than hell.

But it's a bit boring.

After a short while, she pulled herself up and scanned the area. She studied the bushes that fenced her in; thick hawthorn and blackthorn bearing inch-long needles interwoven with brambles and nettles. She groaned. They would tear her apart with or without clothes. The only other way out – and even then she wasn't certain of it – was to follow the line of the ditch under some bushes that looked like evil barbed wire. Definitely a last resort.

'So,' she asked out loud having completely forgotten that she was searching for Archie, 'What happens next?'

'You're after the Atrium, right?' a voice from the side answered back.

Daisy shrieked and covered her body with her arms and hands. She looked around. There wasn't anyone there. 'Er ... who's that? Who's there?'

The same voice spoke out again. It wasn't a nasty voice. This was a kindly old voice, rich in resonance. 'You're here for the Atrium?'

'What? I mean, pardon. I mean, I'm terribly sorry,' Daisy started burying herself under the petals, 'I don't understand, your Godliness.' If this was heaven, she reckoned she should be as polite as possible.

This time another higher pitched voice joined in from the other side. 'You're here for the Atrium, are you dear? That's all we need to know.'

Daisy tiptoed towards the tree where she'd left her clothes. 'What ... what, Aytreehum,' she said. Daisy was beginning to think her mind was playing tricks on her. 'Are whoever you are, angelic?' she asked. 'Perhaps you're the angelic invisible host?'

Daisy thought she could hear laughter, certainly sniggering. Her face reddened. Wrong question. She grabbed her jeans.

'The creature hasn't a clue,' said the higher pitched voice.

'Typical,' said the first low, kindly voice. 'The first person who comes along for an age, and it's by mistake.'

'What do you mean?' Daisy said, a little exasperated. *'Mistake? What creature?'*

Then a voice from right beside her said, 'Don't be alarmed, dear.'

Daisy nearly jumped out of her skin. 'Alarmed!' Daisy shot back. 'Of course I'm alarmed. Who are you?'

'Poor thing,' the kindly first voice said. 'I believe she's lost.'

Daisy, now with her top on, marched about peering around the trees. 'Where are you?'

There was a pause. Daisy listened. She could hear a kind of whispering.

'Now, a quick introduction,' said the voice that had come from next to her. We are the Cherubim of the Rivers of the Worlds. We guard the entrance.'

'Oh God. I'm dead, aren't I?' Daisy said.

'My dear,' said the higher pitched voice. 'I don't think you look dead. Do you think you're dead?'

'No, not really—'

'Well there you have it—'

The strange voices laughed again.

Daisy was confused. 'Hang on. Where … what entrance?' she said.

'Why, just look in front of you!'

'But all I can see is three gnarled old fat trees and a kind of greenhouse—'

'We're time-worn, NOT fat!' the second higher voice shrilled.

Daisy felt as if her head might explode. Either it's one hell of a dream, she thought, or a wicked hallucination. Dead or alive, what did it matter? She lay down in the scented petals, put her fingers in her ears to block out the noises that continued to babble on, and basked in the sunshine.

Shortly, thinking that the sun had disappeared behind a cloud, Daisy opened her eyes to find the tree with pink blossom leaning directly above her.

'Joe-crockers! You moved!' she said out loud to the tree.

The tree straightened, a flurry of petals swamping Daisy. 'Oh yes indeed! I haven't done that for a few thousand years. Apples it feels gooood.'

Certain that the tree had been talking to her, Daisy sat up and brushed off the petals. She shut her eyes and thrust out her hand. 'Hello, my name is Daisy de Lowe, from Eden Cottage, which I think is somewhere over there.' She found herself pointing randomly.

'I have absolutely no idea what's going on or how I got here but I'm looking for my brother Archie. He's about my height with strange spiky hair. And he's a little bit shy. You haven't seen him, have you?'

Then as an afterthought she added, 'and, your Godlinesses, please can you clear one thing up for me? I'd be most grateful if you'd tell me if I really am actually dead or alive?'

CHAPTER EIGHTEEN

Old Man Wood Finds His Friends

The laughter, for Old Man Wood, grew and grew. 'Haaahaaahaaaahaaa! Haaaaaaa! Ha! Woah-ha ha!'

His eyes darted from one direction to another. Old Man Wood crouched down and coughed the remaining water from his windpipe. 'They're laughing at me, Archie. Masses of them – in hysterics.'

'Cor, this is the most hilarious thing I've seen for years,' said a voice.

Old Man Wood's ears pricked up. 'Someone spoke. There! There it is again!' he boomed. 'Can you hear them?'

'Hear who?' Archie quizzed, trying to find the source of Old Man Wood's outburst. 'You sure you're alright?'

'Uh—? You can't hear it?' Old Man Wood whispered. 'You must be able to!'

'No, there's nothing—'

'There! There they go, loads of them. Laughing, talking, hum-humming.'

Archie strained his ears, 'Hum-humming? I can't hear anything – only rain.'

Old Man Wood scrambled across a branch, his head turning to and fro trying to locate the source of this invisible sound.

'You know,' Archie said, 'maybe you're hearing things. Is there water in your ears?'

Old Man Wood stared at him, his eyes bulging quite madly. He shook his head. 'Definitely not.'

'Look,' Archie insisted, 'there isn't anything here. I think we should go home for breakfast.' He scoured the clump. 'Really, there's nothing.' He watched Old Man Wood shuffle up another trunk.

'Oh yes there is, Archie.'

Archie sighed. 'Let's get back, please? You'll catch pneumonia if you hang around too long.'

But Old Man Wood had abandoned his boots and was now scurrying around the trees and bushes like a man possessed; dashing around the thicket, wading through the pools and peering through, under and around the trees.

'Reveal yourselves!' he cried. 'Where the devil are you!'

*

Archie waved and shouted at Old Man Wood. On his third attempt to grab his attention, Archie decided that the old man had totally and utterly lost the plot.

Brilliant! He thought. One half of our grown-up team has gone nuts. What would headmaster Solomon say if he saw this? They'd be whisked from the cottage and taken into care exactly as Solomon said. He snapped off a wet, dangling branch and tossed it in the water and stared at Old Man Wood who was still bouncing around the pool, ducking here and peering there behind the trees.

Archie felt empty inside. He's going to have to go mad all on his own, he thought. Making as little fuss as possible, Archie scrambled over the fallen tree trunks and returned out of the clump the way they'd entered, back towards Eden cottage.

*

To Old Man Wood, the giggling continued. Then, slowly it came to him as his old brain cells started functioning.

'Is that you?' He turned his head to the sky. 'Is it the sound of the old trees?'

This time, the trees collectively seemed to agree. And their laughter was now more of joy at seeing Old Man Wood than roaring at his antics.

'Archie! Here! I think I've found them. I told you so,' Old Man Wood yelled out before turning back to the brook. 'How come I can hear you old sticks?'

'Well, hello to you, too, Old Man Wood,' was the reply from the willows. 'The water is sooo high, way up, up over those steps, hum-hum. With any luck we have ourselves several days of the loveliest special water, hum-hum,' said a voice from the largest of the weeping willow trees. There was a general murmur of approval. 'Can you see us yet?'

Old Man Wood strained his eyes.

'Have yourself another good sip, dear old friend; you must have had a 'lil taster in the pool to hear us laughing at you, hum-hum. By heavens above that was one funny sight, you still can make a tree laugh, old man.'

Old Man Wood cupped his large old leathery hands and brought the water to his mouth. It tasted metallic and bitter as though laced with iron and sulphur, and the liquid fizzed and made his eyes wobble for a few seconds. He shut them as a buzzing sensation rolled in and tumbled about his mind. When he opened them again, he looked out over the brook.

Where before he noted an array of stems and boughs, now, and perched on each tree were tiny elf-like figures no bigger than shoe boxes, with small, pointed ears and sharp noses.

Each of the tree elves had rough course skin like bark and their tiny bodies were shrouded in mini clothes the colour of willow leaves. Tiny arms, like twigs, protruded from either side of their bodies and each had sharp eyes like polished wood that darted from place to place.

'Aha! Apples alive!' Old Man Wood exclaimed. 'The spirits of the trees. I see you!'

The old man noted that the larger trees had bigger elf-like creatures attached to them, and the young ones on the smaller stems ran up and down the trunks, their little legs disappearing into the wood and sometimes disappearing into the trunk of the tree altogether and then reappearing at the end of a branch dangling from their heads, or sitting at the foot of the tree trunk by the roots.

'Crimpers!' Old Man Wood said, as he hugged the biggest tree enthusiastically, the strange elfin creature standing with one foot attached to the tree and the other on Old Man Wood's head. 'How many are you?'

'We're now a family of sixty-seven,' said a deep voice from behind him. 'Loads of new little whips and a couple of small trees and, hum-hum, us big 'uns just keep on growing.'

Old Man Wood closed his eyes. 'Let me see if I can remember. Bethedi …'

'Well, well, well, hum-hom. Isn't that something?' said a wiry elderly tree-elf dangling off a big tree to the side of the brook. 'He remembers my name! So your memory is still intact, huh?'

'There's the thing,' Old Man Wood replied. 'It isn't. It's been an awful long time—'

'You mean,' the tree-elf said, ducking into the tree and reappearing at eye level with Old Man Wood, 'even with this great rain, you don't know what's happening?'

Old Man Wood groaned. 'I feel a yearning – an ache in my bones, but my brain gets all clogged up. And strange nightmares that I don't understand, with bits here and there that seem familiar and others that are a mystery. I've forgotten everything.'

'But you *do* know who you are?'

Old Man Wood frowned. 'I'm not really sure anymore.'

The noise of hum-homs and him-him's erupted around the brook as the elves absorbed this information. 'You quite sure about this?'

'Yes!' Old Man Wood replied.

'Then, hem-hem, you've come to the right place,' said a soft higher voice from the third large tree on the far side of the brook. 'And in the nick of time, it would appear. Do you remember me? I'm Crespidistra, hem-hem?'

'Crespidistra,' Old Man Wood repeated, nodding. He propped himself up on the tree and looked over the water as the slender feminine willow-spirit continued. 'We lost Jonix a few seasons back,' she said. 'He died from a painful canker, but he had time to pass on his knowledge. We miss him dearly … but lately, a whole raft of new willows sprouted. Let me introduce you to our saplings.' The elegant willow spirit turned to the nursery. 'Say hello to our oldest and dearest friend, Mr Old Man Wood, hem-hem; the greatest and indeed the only being of his kind on this planet!'

With that, a huge, 'Hello Mr Old Man Wood,' in an assortment of high and low voices called out over the gentle spring waters, followed by a range of 'um-ums and im-ims.'

Old Man Wood beamed back at them when he suddenly remembered Archie. He searched around. 'I've found them,' he yelled out, 'Archie, here, they're here,' he repeated. 'Come, look—'

'Your friend left a little while ago, while you were, hem-hem … figuring things out,' Crespidistra said gently, before disappearing into the tree and re-emerging higher up. She looked out towards the hill.

Old Man Wood followed her gaze and glimpsed Archie looking down at him from a distance up the bank. He waved enthusiastically but Archie waved back, rather half-heartedly, shaking his head. Oh well, the old man thought. Probably just as well.

'Can I say on behalf of all the willow-spirits, what a magnificent entrance that was, my old friend – you certainly haven't lost your style. Welcome to the Bubbling Brook, where all things speak as one.'

The smaller tree-spirits erupted into laughter, pulling their stems one way and then the other, so that very shortly, the noise of wood snapping and cracking on one another filled the Bubbling Brook, like applause.

'Took you a while to find us, though – the water's been high for a couple of days now,' the elf said as she sat at the end of a branch that hung over the water. 'It's been a long time since we last spoke, hem-hem?'

'I hope you've got some juicy things to tell—?' said another named Willip. 'It's so boring here. Did you ever manage to find your way into that storeroom?'

'How is that vegetable patch of yours?' said another. 'Some of the birds told us you'd grown star-shaped carrots.'

'And what of that young lady?' asked an elf called Shodwonk who, as his name suggested, was a little lopsided.

'And did you ever hear back from that friend of yours with all those ideas?'

Old Man Wood looked startled and scratched his head.

'You know, him-hom, 'bout five hundred and thirty two seasons ago. Mr Len Vinchi?'

'Oooh yes,' Crespidistra added. 'such a nice young man, hem-hem. And how are your apple trees? The apple spirits don't like to get out, always claim they're too busy—'

'Now, hum-hum,' said the deeper voice of Bethedi, 'fill us in, won't you. How have you been getting along, dear friend?'

Old Man Wood clapped his hands together as a smile spread from one side of his gnarled old face to the other. He beamed at the curious clump with their little tree elves homming and humming. Then, after a bit of a fuss, he sat down respectfully on one half of Jonix's stump, took a deep breath and began by telling the trees about the children, and how he'd found Mrs Pye in the woods at the bottom of a gorge, mangled and covered in blood and that they still didn't know who she was, or where she'd come from.

He followed this by telling them about his beloved vegetable patch and his trusty cattle. He went into limited detail about his struggle with bolting purple spinach and how the answer to his carrot fly problem was to grow the vegetables in containers on the roof. All the while the willow spirits listened, asking questions when appropriate, and laughing at exactly the right moments.

Old Man Wood felt as if he was talking to his oldest friends. And in a way this observation wasn't so far off the truth. For no matter how ancient Old Man Wood grew, the willow trees had the ability to remember in astonishing detail each and every word he'd ever told them, from the day they had first met. And this knowledge had been passed on from generation to generation.

These willow tree-spirits were information sponges – a perfect living memory bank. And if Old Man Wood asked a question about his past they would tell him because they held the answers within their sap … but this information would never be given freely.

If Old Man Wood wanted to know something, he had to ask the right question.

∗

Just then two ducks flew through the branches and with a minimum of effort dropped into the middle of the pool of water. Automatically, the ducks dunked their heads and moments later surfaced shaking their heads from side to side.

'Hey! You gnarled-old-pieces-of-timber,' the first duck said. 'What do you give a sick bird?'

'Tweetment!' the other said before any of the tree spirits had the chance to respond. 'Hey, and did you see that duck who came in here? He really … quacked me up! Woahhh! I'm on form today,' the duck continued. 'And what about the owl, huh?' said the second duck. 'He couldn't give a hoot!' They both quacked with laughter. 'Ha-aha, oh boy, oh boy, oh boy we're good,' the first duck said, 'anything to liven up you boards, Woah, geddit – *boards* – that's terrific, ha ha!' the birds sang as they lifted themselves out of the glade.

'Cres,' Bethedi said, 'can't we stop those blasted ducks flying in here, telling their appalling jokes?'

'You know there's nothing we can do and they're a great deal better than the blackbirds who simply repeat things over and over again if they like the sound of it.'

Old Man Wood shook his head and laughed – the sound of his rich voice echoing around the brook. He'd forgotten how wonderful the world was when everything could talk – and spell – given the right circumstances.

He was overjoyed to be with old friends.

Right now, however, he needed to put the trees' memory to the test and think of some good questions.

But where would he begin? And what sort of questions would be most helpful to all of them?

Just thinking of this quandary made his head pound and his eyes heavy with worry.

CHAPTER NINETEEN

Archie's Knives

Archie squeezed between the old oak upright and the wooden door that had jammed tight against the cold concrete floor of the garden shed. Inside, he felt for the familiar course fibres of a pile of old empty sacks and fell heavily into them. His cheeks, red from running in the cold wet air, stung with the salt of his tears and the walk up the slippery hill had made his legs burn. He found the light on his watch. Not yet ten. It felt like lunchtime especially as he'd forgone breakfast. Archie tried to get himself comfortable, to settle himself but he couldn't think clearly for the noise of the rain which now drummed hard on the tiles above his head.

He reached behind one of the sacks feeling for a bundle tied in a package of cloth.

Archie untied the layer of cloth, pulling out five stunning silver-coloured knives. He ran his hand over the sharp tips and shivered as he thought about the strange ghost, Cain, and the ruby-encrusted knife. He touched the scar on his chin. The power of a horse and the courage of a lion, he thought – ridiculous – even if he couldn't get it out of his mind. And he smiled as the image of himself, deeply muscled, entered his mind and he wondered if somehow, impossibly, he really had acquired strength of some sort. How had he managed to pull that tree out and carry Daisy and push the boulder out of the way? And yet here he was, still his reasonably puny self. He tensed his arms and the muscle bulge wasn't impressive. He patted his head and felt his spikes, which were hard. Maybe it had something to do with his spikes – something to do with being partially hit by lightning?

Archie's knives were like secret friends. He knew how to hold them, care for them, balance them and hide them away. It was his one secret, albeit a badly kept secret, for Isabella knew and she hated them with a passion that Archie thought was way over the top.

He remembered the day he found them. It was two days after his seventh birthday and they were playing a game of hide and seek in the ruin. He spied a dark space beneath an outcrop of stone and without thinking, crammed himself under it, working his body under until he had all but disappeared. As he scraped the earth furiously to give himself more space his hand touched upon a cloth.

Instantly his curiosity was aroused. As he feverishly reached in and dug further, he realised that inside this cloth lay hard objects. Treasure? He remembered his excitement but just then and much to his annoyance Isabella rounded the corner, saw one of his feet and dragged him out. He had left the bundle there, but even now he wondered why he hadn't brought them out and shared his excitement with the others. Somehow, this was his own little secret. His, and no one else's.

A few days later, he returned. His fingers touched the bundle again, and the same thrill passed through him. Using a trowel from Old Man Wood's potting shed, he teased the package from the hard earth. Bit by bit, more and more came. And as he scraped, he found that the cloth was bound deep in the chasm holding the treasure within it. Archie pulled until eventually the bundle popped out like a cork from a bottle. With the evening drawing in he ran home and hid his treasure under the bed. Archie's excitement meant he could barely talk through supper and the following day, with the girls in town, he opened the package.

The cloth itself felt unusual, certainly like nothing he'd seen before. Wound neatly round and round, the fabric was light and strong even though he'd tried to rip it and pierce it. Inside, were three knives, each one about ten inches in length made from slender sticks of metal, the points of which were slightly rounded like leaves off a plum tree. The knives shimmered as he touched them.

The blade ends were slender with sharpened edges leading to a point. The other ends were flat, like a wider version of an ordinary kitchen knife. And he noted that as no water had penetrated the metal, no rust or discolouration showed, so he figured that no air had entered either – or the metal wasn't steel. As he inspected them, right in the middle of each one, he found a pattern, a circle of lines swirling – mirrored – top and bottom.

It took him several days to work out how they should be used. As a hunting knife they were all wrong; the blades weren't long enough and the handles ungainly. In the woods as he ambled along figuring it out, he held one in his hand, balancing it. As he rounded a corner, there, besides the carcass of a rabbit, was a rat. Without thinking Archie cocked his arm back and let the knife go. It flew through the air and landed with a thud, killing the rat instantly. Archie stared in shock as a thrill passed through him. How had he managed to do that?

From that moment on he knew knife-throwing would be his thing. He wanted to be the best in the world. At first, when the house was empty, he threw the knives from the end of his bed onto an old cork noticeboard that he kept hidden under his bed.

What he discovered, by a process of elimination and frustration, was that each knife had a different weight, and he figured that each one had to rotate through the air at either a different speed or at the same speed but from a different distance.

Archie spent hours trying to work it out. And slowly it came to him. Soon he could automatically judge the weight and the throwing speed of each knife. Then one day, much to his surprise, he rubbed the emblem in the middle and is if by magic, a smaller knife unfurled itself from the body of the big knife. The same thing happened on each, but as with the larger knives, the smaller ones bore different weights. Now he had six knives to play with; three heavy and three light.

Archie played with the smaller ones indoors against his cork board and the larger ones on an old wooden log in the forest. He didn't want anyone to know because he sensed that all hell would break loose, and he was right. In the end, it did.

One day, in the woods while Archie thought the others were fooling around in the house, he set up a target which consisted of a woolly mop head and one of Daisy's old shirts which he pinned against a tree. Archie had mastered his throw from ten feet and now he was attempting a new distance – thirteen feet, which meant holding the knife the other way round. The first two had clattered into the bark and fallen to the ground. Archie weighed up the final one. The heaviest of all. He pulled his arm back and throwing a little harder, let go. But at that exact moment, Isabella's head suddenly appeared by the tree.

Archie gasped.

The knife whistled through the air and to his enormous relief, with a gentle thud, the blade nestled into the wood. For a fraction of a second Archie wondered whether Isabella knew what he was doing. She looked at him curiously. Then her eyes followed his – to where he was looking. She moved around the tree and saw the end of a knife straight through the breast pocket of Daisy's old shirt.

Isabella went berserk, screaming at him for being reckless and stupid and for plotting to kill them. Archie protested but Isabella gathered the knives and ran inside.

From that moment on, his knives were forbidden and it was made clear that they would not be tolerated in or around the house. Finally, on his eighth birthday he was allowed to have them back on condition that he always told a grown up when and where he was throwing, and never, ever, anywhere near Isabella.

*

In the dimness of the musty, rickety shed, Archie focused on the large log. He balanced the first knife in the palm of his hand, a sparkle of gleaming metal catching a ray of light that had crept nervously under the gap in the door.

Thud.

The knife flashed into the thick wood. Archie wanted to throw it quicker – venting this curious anger that kept welling up in him.

He rubbed his front hair spike that stood as hard as iron. He knew he would have to throw it twice as fast. The next kicked out a splinter of wood. Nice one, he thought, much better. Exactly in the right spot.

And while he did this, it gave him time to think, time to reflect, time to work out what his dreams were all about.

*

On the one hand, his dreams had made him feel like a bloodthirsty thug intent on the destruction of everything. Then, a moment later, he remembered how the sensation departed and he'd be laughing and joking with his sisters and friends and he couldn't remember being happier. And then his dreams would swing back to

162

violence and this curious desire for power, which made his bones shiver because Archie's violent feelings were contrary to his laidback approach to life.

He was an average kid; scruffy and carefree; "horizontal" and "chilled" were words often associated with him. He was friendly too, to … well, everyone; he got on with people – he always had – preferring to walk away, or talk, rather than head into a fight. Perhaps that was why Kemp liked him?

What shocked him most was how utterly real his dreams were, particularly the murder in which he had killed the Ancient Woman with a strength and anger he could not resist. He couldn't tell how he'd done it, but she had died by his hand. And yet, in a strange contradiction, he wondered if this Ancient Woman wanted to die, enticing him to kill her, even if she meant no wrong.

And did Daisy's dream – where she had screamed at him as though possessed by demons – mean that he was different? And what about the ghost of Cain, the weird spirit who had visited him, the ghost he'd run away from? How did Cain fit the puzzle? Cain knew all about them – and about the Ancient Woman and this crazy Prophecy of Eden – but if Cain truly existed, where the hell was he from? Could Cain really be the same spirit left over from the Bible story, the son of Adam and Eve?

If so, Archie thought, what did Cain want? And how did Cain know about the "strength of a horse and the courage of a lion". Archie toyed with this thought. He had strength, yes – possibly. But courage? No, not really.

It didn't add up.

Archie twisted the knife in his hand, flicking the dull blade around his fingers. He didn't have Isabella's cleverness to try and work it out nor Daisy's easy going nature to forget. To Archie, these confusing thoughts filled his soul with darkness.

And now, to top it off, Old Man Wood had gone totally stark-raving bonkers. Sure, you could talk to trees in dreams, but at 8:30 in the morning – to a clump of willows?

They'd have to get the old man seen to – proper medical help. Northallerton had a decent geriatric ward, at least that's what Gus Williams said. He used to visit his great-grandfather who got everything muddled up before he passed away.

The unfamiliar anger brewed in his veins again; his neck throbbed as a pain shot into his head. 'Why?' he said out loud to the dank air in the shed. 'I'm a twelve year old boy, and I'm sitting in a cold potting-shed in North Yorkshire, scared out of my mind. Why me?

'WHY ME?' he yelled. 'WHAT IS HAPPENING TO US?'

Annoyed that there were simply no answers, he weighed up his heaviest knife. He summoned every ounce of strength in his body and with a cry, threw it as hard as he could at the old stump.

Archie walked across the floor and ran his hands over the two foot-thick log which now lay on the ground, split clean in half.

He smiled, picked the knife off the floor and for a reason he couldn't explain, rubbed the centre over his jeans. He looked at it again and just as he was returning it to the cloth, he realised he'd seen it before.

In the centre of the knife lay the circular emblem of a tree, with branches arching out above and roots mirrored identically below. The emblem of the Tree of Life.

He'd seen it in the cave, the exact same emblem. His heart beat quickened. The emblem at the beginning of the mural bearing fruit, and in the middle depicting death and finally by the images that reminded him of rebirth – of a new beginning.

Archie gasped and for the first time he wondered if the words of Cain should be taken with deadly seriousness. In his mind he ran through the meeting in the alleyway again and again trying to remember every word until he realised his bones were aching.

Cain told of a prophecy – that the storm was only the beginning. It blended in perfectly with what he'd seen in the cave.

Niggling at the back of his mind was another thing; what had become of Kemp? Did he die, or run to high ground, or, and his pulse raced at the thought, did he actually join with Cain? Poor Kemp. Whatever happened, it must have been a nightmare. He was probably better off dead.

He rolled his neck and took a deep breath.

Whatever was going on, Daisy was right. All these things were somehow linked and they were right bang in the middle of it. And if only he could remember the general gist of Cain's speech to Kemp because, he realised, it was absolutely pivotal to the outcome.

Like it or not.

CHAPTER TWENTY

The Miracle Boy

With his mouth and nose enclosed by a clear plastic breathing device, Kemp sucked in a large mouthful of oxygen and opened his eyes. Slowly Kemp's brain began to wonder where he was.

He listened. A gentle churning noise like the dull throb of an engine, of machinery gently running through its processes followed by a regular bleep.

His body felt lighter and as he ran a check over his anatomy, he noticed the burning didn't hurt compared to the agony he'd experienced before. Perhaps he'd died after all.

Kemp searched his body for signs of Cain.

None.

For a moment his mind and body leapt for joy. Then he remembered that Cain might be asleep. And Cain never slept for long. His eyes felt heavy again.

His ears picked out noises nearby.

He listened. Voices, deep voices, whispering, occasionally louder. Concerned, anxious tones. One higher pitched than the others. He tried to move his hands but they felt leaden, as though fixed down by weights. He yearned for someone to hold him and love him, for the comfort of a warm hug, of gentle words and soothing kisses. He pined for the mother he never had.

A terrible sadness sank into him and a tear rolled down his cheek. He needed to sleep.

Kemp felt his mind drift off once more.

*

Prime Minister Kingsford was basking on his sun lounger in Italy when the news broke. Three days into his break and the phones went crazy. Typical, he thought. Of all the weeks! Here he was with his family, gradually unwinding from the rigours of government, when there's an emergency of simply epic proportions to deal with.

It was true; you never got time out in this job, he mused, and with an election looming, he had needed a week to recharge his batteries. And now this. Oh well, what did he expect? Running the country, he thought, was like looking after thousands of plates spinning on sticks and making sure that each person twiddling a stick kept it moving. If one plate fell, it became an event or an outcry or a scandal. When a whole pile of them crashed, the pointing finger of the media spotlight inevitably turned on him.

He caught a helicopter the following day to find out what was happening. By the time he arrived the damage had been done and England's heart lay in ruins. As the chopper flew north from London, he saw at first hand extraordinary scenes beneath him. From as far south as Lincolnshire, through the Midlands, into South Yorkshire then on and up through the Vale of York between the Moors and Dales he looked out of the window to find a country underwater. Entire towns were submerged, fields transformed into huge, muddy lakes, only variously interspersed by protruding islands of high ground.

His leadership hung by a thread. It was typical, he thought. Those damn media people. What on earth could he do about a biblical-style freak flood? Furthermore, the damage had been so sudden, so brutal. Coordinating a rescue effort in these conditions and setting up COBRA, the emergency government office, took time. Time which they didn't have. To the rest of the country, their efforts appeared disorganised and uncoordinated … *'Too little action, too late'*, the papers screamed. It must look, he thought, like a shambles. But they were doing everything they could.

Victims of the storm were found every hour, bloated and floating in the waters, thousands of people displaced, homes ruined, infrastructure wrecked, businesses destroyed and lives shattered. The difficulty was that the rains hadn't let up enough to enable the waters to recede, while high tides meant the water had nowhere to go. From his vantage point in the chopper, the Prime Minister fully understood how desperate the situation truly was. The military faced an uphill battle to coordinate a salvage operation in such adverse conditions. But as the hours went by, fingers pointed accusingly at the Prime Minister.

Worse still was the latest development. A deadly virus was spreading. World governments and the media were clamouring for updates and yet there was very little he could tell them. The only option was to meet the experts in North Yorkshire, find out what they knew first hand, so he might understand what they were up against.

Soon enough he found himself wearing an anti-contamination suit and staring through thick glass at a sick bald boy in an isolation unit; the miracle boy, found naked in the top of a tree right in the middle of a huge expanse of water. The images, already a sensation around the world, represented a glimmer of hope; a good news story amongst the carnage as the disaster spiralled out of control.

The Prime Minister recognised this and wondered how long he could put off facing the press and their questions. The media were baying like hounds for a story, and he needed it to be a positive one. The boy's survival remained top priority.

*

Dr Adrian Muller instantly struck everyone who met him as a kindly man. His sharp nose, thick mop of dark hair that flopped across his forehead and his jutting jawline that moved from side to side when he talked, gave him a curiously academic air. He took hold of the clipboard and ran his finger down the boy's chart. Without meaning to, he raised his thick dark eyebrows which dislodged his half-moon wire-framed glasses. He nudged them back into place without even noticing.

He studied the data again. The boy's survival simply didn't make sense. 'Are you sure these are correct?'

The nurse, her mousy hair tied behind her head in a bun, confirmed the data. It had been triple checked she told him. And keeping her voice low, she said, 'His condition is unlike any of the flood victims. Typically, what we're seeing is a combination of hypothermia and a form of viral infection. This is nothing like that. Now that he's come out of his coma – we're hoping to talk to the boy later today.'

Dr Muller shook his head as he looked beyond the sheet of glass in front of him.

The boy lay on the bed, his mouth and nose covered by a plastic mask, his arms pricked with drips that dangled from him like flexible plastic straws. Littering his body were bandages, liberally administered as if he were part human, part Egyptian mummy.

Two other men stood next to the medics in the gallery room with the window that looked in on the boy. One was Charlie Stone, the tall, thin, silver-haired Police Commissioner and chief coordinator of the flood relief, and the other was Prime Minister, Ed Kingsford.

And the PM was more than a little irritated by the whole thing.

*

'He's been looked over by the pathologists,' the doctor said.

'Good,' Commissioner Stone nodded. 'When will their findings be available?'

Dr Muller cocked his head. 'In roughly two to four hours,' he replied. 'They're working on it now.'

'And is this the same illness as the others?' said the Prime Minister.

'We don't know, sir,' the doctor replied, his jaw jutting one way and then the other. 'At the moment, it appears not. The symptoms common to the majority of victims are not evident – at least not yet. That's what makes him intriguing. We have the world's leading scientists evaluating this type of influenza, yet the boy here has none of the rashes, skin discolouration, acute vomiting or bowel dysfunction seen in the others. This little fella's main problem is malnutrition, poisoning and burns.'

'Burns?' Commissioner Stone quizzed.

'Indeed,' Dr Muller replied. The news of this had surprised him too. 'Small burns covering all four limbs, front and back and around the neck up to the ears. We think his hair has been singed off – not a single follicle can be found on his body. In his mouth we discovered traces of soot and burn-blisters. It's as if this boy has been in a fire or been sprayed with a flammable substance.' The doctor raised his eyebrows. 'Were any fires reported?'

Commissioner Stone thought for a minute. 'Further south from where the boy was found there were two big blazes. But the boy would've had to swim or row a raft several miles against the current to get to where he was found. And remember, he was found naked. Are there signs of hypothermia?'

Dr Muller shook his head.

'And no major flesh injuries,' the nurse added. 'Not even minor scratches or bruises, just burns.'

The doctor strummed the glass with his fingernails. 'When his samples come back, we'll know if he's a carrier. If he is, then we might be able to monitor the effect of the virus through his body. We'll try and trace the viral elements and isolate it. At the moment he's our mystery boy and the only hope for a cure.'

'What if he came from somewhere else?' the nurse asked.

'Are you suggesting he fell out of the sky, like an alien?' the Prime Minister said with sarcastic bite.

The nurse blushed.

The Prime Minister noticed and immediately regretted his sharp tongue. 'Oh, forgive me, I'm sorry,' he said. He smiled badly. 'Doctor,' he said, 'how many patients have symptoms of this … disease, and how quickly does it affect them?'

The doctor stared at the floor. 'It acts fast; ten to thirty hours at most from incubation to death, depending on the severity of the strain and the constitution of the patient. There are sixty-two dead at the moment, each victim pulled from the water, all with the tell-tale skin rash and signs of acute vomiting and diarrhoea. In truth, Prime Minister, we have no idea how many are infected.'

'Is there any way of knowing?'

'None, I'm afraid. We don't know if it's waterborne or airborne, or both. And we don't know where it originates, but our guess is somewhere near to the epicentre of the storm, possibly the village of Upsall.' He raised his eyebrows and looked over the top of his spectacles. 'At the moment we can't tell whether it's an animal-based virus or a toxic chemical misnomer released by the floodwater.'

The Prime Minister sucked in a breath. 'What about some form of chemical or biological agent?'

'Unlikely,' the doctor replied. 'Though there are similarities to the untrained eye.'

'Have the initial life-savers, doctors and nurses shown any of the symptoms?'

'No, not yet, but many are in the containment zone, just in case,' Dr Muller continued. 'The common factor is that it appears to associate from contact with the floodwater—'

'Which is being analysed as we speak,' the Commissioner added. 'And the boy has obviously spent time in the floodwater, which makes him unique.'

A nervous quiet fell over the gathering. Then the PM asked, 'Do you know where he comes from?'

'No, I'm afraid not, Prime Minister,' Dr Muller said. 'No distinguishing marks, no clothes, nothing. We can't even tell what colour his hair is, though, from the paleness of his skin we suspect he's a redhead.'

'And strangely,' the Commissioner said, 'no one has come forward to claim him, even though footage of the boy has been shown repeatedly on every single TV channel in the world.'

The team continued to stare at the boy, working out the next move.

'Alright, hear me out,' the Prime Minister began. 'The boy's story has captured the imagination of audiences around the globe … and you think he might come around in the next few hours. Is there any way we can use this as a media event so we can buy some time until we have a clearer idea what this disease is? I mean if it's contagious we'll need to work round the clock to start the process of containment, correct?'

'Indeed, Prime Minister,' the doctor said. 'Can I suggest that before the scientists divulge their reports tonight, we begin the process of sealing-off the infected area. If we take into account the movement of people during this time, the cordon needs to cover a significantly larger mileage than just the flood zone.'

Commissioner Stone nodded. 'With the known geographical spread of the flooding stretching for such a vast distance, this operation will be bigger than the evacuation of Dunkirk during the war.'

The Prime Minister coughed. 'Hang on a minute!' he said, a frown covering his face. 'Let's not run before we can walk, eh? Shouldn't we wait until the scientists report back? What if it's imminently curable?'

The doctor twiddled his thumbs. 'Prime Minister, I urge you to start the process as soon as possible. This outbreak is from an unknown pathogen and more cases are being reported on an hourly basis. We are fighting a battle with an unfamiliar enemy and time is against us. The flooding is spreading. It is not going to get any easier.'

Prime Minister Kingsford had gone pale. The potential calamity of the situation was sinking in fast.

Commissioner Stone noticed. 'We have already begun it … quietly,' he added. 'The last thing we need is a media-led panic. I have taken the liberty of putting in place a "containment zone" around North Yorkshire – travel bans to the area for everyone and I've cancelled leave for all civil servants, doctors, nurses and emergency crews. I realise this goes above my jurisdiction, but as the flood disaster tsar I had to trust my judgement.'

A murmur of agreement.

The Prime Minister's mood lifted a little now that a plan appeared to be coming together. 'Good thinking. Well done, Stone. Use whatever powers you feel necessary to get to the bottom of this bloody mess. I will make sure all the relevant authorities are aware.' One of the Prime Minister's personal private secretaries scribbled on his pad and slipped out of the room.

'So, first things first,' the Prime Minister continued. 'We invite selected media in and show them the child,' he turned to the doctor. 'You happy with that, Dr Muller?'

The doctor moved his jaw and nodded slowly. 'Sure. We can try to get the boy talking, it's a long shot but worth a go—'

'Don't you think it might appear a little bit see-through, a touch desperate?' the Commissioner asked.

The Prime Minister turned on him. 'Look, Stone, we've got the world's press outside clamouring to know what the hell's going on,' he snapped. 'Many are already sniffing about and jumping to conclusions. If the word gets out before we have any evidence, think of the consequences. Think of the panic. Imagine the morning's headlines. "Britain – Quarantined".' The Prime Minister paused for effect. 'In the rush to leave the disaster zone, the disease may go with it and that, my friends, will be a total catastrophe. We need to buy time.' The Prime Minister kneaded his temples. 'The fact is this: it's our very own biblical mess and we're going to have to deal with it. It's as simple as that.'

'You're correct,' the doctor said. At least the officials were now taking the situation with the deadly seriousness it deserved. 'Good to hear you're right behind us.'

'Call a press conference for midday,' the Prime Minister ordered. 'You'll have the boy's blood results by then, so see if you can add a positive spin. Expand on the fact that this boy was found against all odds, burnt and naked up a tree, a miracle among the carnage, to give you added time. Speak to the press team. Commissioner Stone – you've got a day – more if we're lucky – to find out as much as you can and continue the "quiet" work you've started. After that – and when there's a fuller picture the COBRA team will put a wider containment plan into action.'

Dr Muller nodded and nudged the Prime Minister gently to the side. 'If it is the start of an epidemic, Prime Minister, you are aware that you have been in an infected area and you must go through a de-contamination programme. For safety's sake, I urge you to do this and leave immediately after the press conference.'

The Prime Minister cocked his head. Years of being in the firing line of politics had given him a nose for judging people. 'Is there something you haven't told me, doctor?'

Dr Muller shifted and drew the PM and the Commissioner to one side. 'So far, we've only been able to reach a small number of people – namely those from Northallerton. We have no knowledge of the situation in the smaller villages which have been all but eradicated.' He frowned as his voice fell to a whisper. 'Early reports indicate that animals too have been found with plague-like symptoms almost identical to the human condition.'

'What is the relevance of this in relation to the outbreak?'

'Well—'

The Prime Minister stared at him open-mouthed as the truth hit him. 'You're saying that the disease – or whatever it is – is wiping out everything in its path.'

'Perhaps … we can't rule it out,' the doctor replied. 'As I mentioned, these are only rumours and of course we don't know how the virus spreads – who is likely to catch it – or the conditions of infection. It could be—'

'Why was I not briefed about this?' the Prime Minister snapped. 'Have COBRA been notified?'

'There's a unit heading towards the village of Upsall – they left this morning. They are due to report back this afternoon.'

'God, almighty,' the Prime Minister said under his breath. 'Isn't this where the storm started?'

'Indeed. Satellite recordings show that the weather system came from directly above the village—'

'Yes, I heard it was unlike any other storm formation ever recorded. What do we know?'

'As far as we're aware, it's the location of a well known local school that inhabits an old monastery and the village is a popular tourist attraction for walkers in the summer. My cousin happens to be headmaster there. Man called Solomon.'

The PM pursed his lips. 'We need a thorough investigation of this place, and I mean thorough. Anything suspicious, anything ever recorded – police records, hospital records – must be analysed and re-analysed. We'll need details of farms, cattle stocks, any previous outbreaks of disease, bird populations … anything and everything.'

'I have a team working on it already,' Stone said.

'Good. All survivors must be brought into the containment area and questioned. We need answers and quickly – like yesterday.'

The commissioner nodded.

'And pardon the pun, Stone, but leave no stone unturned. If this Godforsaken crisis cannot be explained by usual methodology, we need to work on something outside the box. Understand? 'And if the storm and the disease both spilled out of Upsall, then I want to know why. Is this perfectly clear?'

Stone smiled. 'Yes, Sir. I understand completely.'

The Prime Minister nodded. 'Call on anyone – and I mean anyone you need in order to assist you. Let nothing get in your way. As far as I'm concerned, Stone, you have whatever power you need to get the bottom of this.'

CHAPTER TWENTY ONE

Isabella Makes A Discovery

For a considerable time, Isabella remained under her bed covers, waking up. She'd slept like a log. She sat up and rubbed her eyes before stretching her arms out and yawning. There must be a reason for all these odd things, Isabella thought. I'll work it out logically, starting with Sue's dream and then go through everything I can remember. Then, when I'm done, I'll present a logical, scientific report to the others.

As she headed downstairs for some porridge, she grabbed her notebook and a pen and began to think hard about the chain of events that led up to where they were now.

She decided to concentrate on what she had discovered from the others, write it down and then work out which bits were linked and why they were connected. She opened her notebook, took the lid off her pen and began to write.

A LIST, OF WHO IS / ISN'T IN MY DREAM(S).

Parents:

Not involved. Definitely remember seeing them, but can't place them anywhere.

Daisy hasn't mentioned them and Archie nothing. So they are fairly hopeless in not being here to help!!!

Sue:

Hasn't appeared in my dreams – WHY NOT?? So why did she have a dream ... friend??

Is she relevant? Probably. Don't know why.

She predicted the rain and knows about something we have to do ... according to her, it's our fault! Why are we to blame for the rain? Don't think so – IF SO, HOW?

Something else about clues ...? in Eden Cottage. Have to find something. What? Tablets? Paintings?

Is Gus involved – NO. (Don't think so.)

Old Man Wood:

VERY VERY important.

Crops up all the time. Seems to be more than one of him, but why oh why would Old Man Wood want to be in my dreams??

Resplendix Mix is weird (but amazing). From an apothecary, apparently (they don't exist). Need to get a sample. His funny apples are a bit weird, too.

Somehow found us in the rain. HOW WAS THAT POSSIBLE???

Looks freaked out by what's going on. But not bothered by the ridiculous pool and Resplendix Mix.

Why did he laugh when doing the Bible quiz?

How old IS he?

Mrs Pye:

Comes into it at some point (I think) though is it actually her? Something not quite right about her. Don't know what it is.

Ancient Woman:

Vital to the whole thing. Daisy's common dominator (!!) but keeps on being killed. Mainly by Archie. URGH? No idea why. She seems lost, desperately ill and frail.

Where is she from??

The Cave: (According to the twins)

Paintings on the wall similar to Sue's comments about finding ... what – tablets? (according to D). V Odd healing water.

Gears on stairs and boulder at top. Must have been designed. But WHO designed them and WHY?

Daisy:

Can hear acute things like lightning bolts forming and see astonishing detail, (though is she making it up?) Scientific explanation: Electrical charge from lightning bolt altered nerve motors in these areas. Eyes and ears suffered semi-permanent damage?

Also, utterly convinced that cave paintings are relevant ... D was dead? All V. odd.

Archie:

Moved the boulder – though would it have gone anyway?

Hair stiff and wiry like a mace club. Scientific explanation: A mix that happened when the lighting struck between the particles of the football and lightning strips we gave him.

Very freaked out by murder of Ancient Woman.

Knew about sunset and rain ceasing. HOW? Did he dream this or ... ? Seems to know something else

Is a bit lost and has doubt.

Isabella read her list and realised that she still had no idea. It struck her that she needed to interrogate Old Man Wood and quiz him relentlessly until he gave her proper, reasonable answers.

She'd start by grilling him about Resplendix Mix, which was both real and yet totally extraordinary. Then she'd ask him what he knew about the Creation story and also try to figure out how old he was.

Why not run a couple of tests on the Resplendix Mix to see if she could identify some of its properties? But then she realised she'd need a lab and light and heat and test tubes and all manner of things.

Realising her frustration, she thumped the table and threw her notepad across the room.

She'd just have to find out what she could, and prove – beyond doubt – that these were freak events that they were caught up in and nothing else.

And then she remembered that the old man said he'd been dreaming too. Perhaps she'd ask him about that as well.

*

Isabella took off up the main wooden stairs towards his room and knocked on the solid oak door. 'Old Man Wood, are you there?' she began. 'I really need to talk.'

There was no reply. Isabella knew he wasn't in. When he was at home, either huge snores would reverberate through the door, or he'd be padding about, or rustling a newspaper on his great big bed; or the curious odour of pine-scented smoke from his homemade pipe with its strangely reassuring woody aroma, would drift into the corridor from under the door.

Isabella waited a moment longer and turned the door handle. She peeked behind her, closed the door and entered the room. In the middle sat Old Man Wood's great bed. She tiptoed over the musty little carpets and jumped high in the air landing in the soft pile of the feather-down duvet and cushions.

With her head propped up by large soft pillows she lost herself in thought, and stared at the rain tracing its way down the windowpanes. Her attention turned to the beautiful wooden carvings that depicted strange scenes and images of animals and creatures which adorned every upright and joint on the old four-poster bed. She smiled as she remembered how, as younger children, they had spent hours creating outrageous stories with the wooden characters and now that she thought about it, the carvings were never quite the same from one day to the next. Probably, she thought, just their childish imaginations running wild.

Isabella studied the three wooden panels at the foot of the bed. She couldn't remember seeing these before. Three panels, each the size of a large rectangular place mat. The harder she looked, the deeper the array of colours; dark and light reds, pale and ocean-deep blues, soft and rich browns and a mixture of subtle creams and yellows. But overall, if you looked quickly, the wood was light brown.

Isabella pulled herself up and helped herself to a sip of water from Old Man Wood's glass. Then she laid back again.

Hang on! The figure in the first panel moved!

Oh. No, it didn't.

She smiled. But as she journeyed down memory lane, she stared at it again and noticed a girl sitting in a bed. She laughed. It looked quite like her but probably prettier and thinner. Weird or what?

She turned her attention to the second panel, the wood lighter in colour than the others. The harder she looked the clearer she could see another girl lying down, somewhere where the sun was shining. The girl sunbathing but lying in snow in between three fat, rather deformed trees.

Isabella felt a little jealous. How nice to feel the sun, she thought, but odd that the girl was semi-naked in snow. Just as Isabella lifted her head to see what else was on the bed-head, she detected a movement in the panel.

It changed! It definitely changed. She laughed nervously. Come on, Isabella, don't be an idiot. Bed panels don't move. She shut her eyes and lay back. But a part of her brain wouldn't let the imagery go.

She looked again and it was still. She breathed a sigh of relief.

Then the image moved again.

In shock, Isabella felt her head going numb. She stared, her bottom lip hanging, forgetting to breathe.

At length she exhaled. 'It's moving. It's really moving ... like a ...' she muttered. Isabella sat bolt upright, shut her eyes and swung her legs off the bed. 'Like a ... telly.'

She walked past the wooden panels and over to the window where she sat down in Old Man Wood's armchair and shook her head. She must be seeing things.

After a few minutes, she reaffirmed that she was normal. There was nothing wrong with her eyes or her brain, and although her stomach felt hollow she took herself back to the bed.

She lay back, closed her eyes and then slowly opened them, hoping like mad that she'd been seeing things. But to Isabella's horror, the girl in the wooden relief stood up, walked first one way and then the other before heading towards a frame of something that resembled a large greenhouse.

Isabella felt sick. But however much she didn't want to believe it she couldn't tear her eyes away.

The girl, now clothed, walked into this strange looking area where, across the floor lay another object, rather like Old Man Wood's old-fashioned garden roller but with a flat ledge, like a table. If it wasn't a roller, what was it?

Isabella rubbed her eyes, swung her legs off the bed again and this time faced the mirror above the fireplace. She looked deeply at her reflection, particularly at her eyes. Then she pulled her hands up to her face and slapped each cheek as hard as she dared.

'OW!' she cried, surprised by the force. 'Wow, that hurt,' she said, rubbing her cheek, feeling a little foolish.

'OK. I'm real and this is real and that slap was definitely real,' she said to her reflection. 'So how has Old Man Wood managed to do this?' she continued. 'Is he a secret agent, a spy? Does he work for a space agency or something?' Isabella laughed. Old Man Wood as a spy, hilarious. Spaceman – even more hilarious. She walked across the room and lowered herself into his armchair.

A frown filled her face and her eyes narrowed. What if he's a … a wizard, or a witch doctor, or an ALIEN?

A thrill swept through her. It would explain the Resplendix Mix.

Isabella returned to the bed full of trepidation and settled back in the cushions. She closed her eyes and then half opened them hoping the images had gone. They hadn't.

So this time, she sat up and examined the subtle movement of the panels and the more she studied it, the more enchanted she became.

If it's a kind of wooden telly, she thought, then it must have power going to it. She began searching for wires, or a transmitter or anything that might make a bit of sense. But again, she drew a blank.

Isabella sighed, clambered back onto the bed and returned to her viewing. For some time the girl in the middle panel sat on the roller-object and nothing happened. Every now and then her arms were thrown in the air in a familiar gesture that Isabella recognised from somewhere. Then the girl stood up and with considerable effort began to pull the roller-object's handle and as she did so a hole opened up where the table had been.

This is more like it, Isabella thought, pleased to see some action. The girl in the panel returned to the space where the table had been and appeared to look at it. Then she knelt down and swivelled as if she was talking to someone.

I'm sure I know that bum, Isabella thought, and the way that body bends forward so easily, like a doll, but who is it?

Isabella moved her attention to the third panel at the end of the bed which, up until then, had remained lifeless. But now that her eyes were accustomed to the colours, she could make out an outline of a body curled up in the corner of a darkened room.

Suddenly she saw a movement – an arm cocked back and then slammed quickly forward.

'Woah!' she cried. 'What's that all about?' She watched again and shuffled closer to the screen. Moments later the exact same motion happened. She suddenly realised what she was looking at. Her heart raced.

'It's Archie!' she whispered, 'with his stupid throwing knives. I knew he hadn't got rid of them.' She watched closer. The figure stood up and there on the top of his head were his extraordinary hair spikes.

Isabella put her head in her hands. If that's Archie, then the middle one … she looked at the picture of the girl in the sunshine again. That bum! Of course! It was …
Daisy's bum!

Isabella clapped her hands together. The third panel is Archie. The middle panel with the roller-object and that lovely bottom is Daisy's, so the last panel is … she threw her hand in the air and the image on the relief copied her.

It was her!

A strange dizziness started to rush in.

It's me! Here, in Old Man Wood's bed!

Isabella stared back at herself hardly daring to move. A dull ache jammed her brain.

Keep calm, need to think. Come on, brain; what … OK … who was Old Man Wood, really? And why this bed? For spying on them? Why though, for heaven's sake? For perving on them? No. It couldn't be. Old Man Wood wasn't a pervert, not one little bit.

Perhaps it was a kind of child-monitor while the parents were away? No – way too expensive and ridiculous and impossible.

But why did he have it and what did it mean? Why did it exist?

Her heart thumping, she turned back to the wooden screens. Archie's arm flashed forward throwing another stupid knife. By the dinginess of it he's probably in that horrible old woodshed.

But where was Daisy? On the panel it appeared as sunny, whereas outside, and she looked out of the window, it was dank, rainy and horrible. In her mind's eye she ran through every place on the farm and by the ruins but no place came close.

She took a deep breath and, totally absorbed by the spectacle, viewed her sister. But a moment later, Daisy disappeared.

One minute she was there and the next … *where is she?*

A lump grew in Isabella's throat and her heartbeat quickened. Was the panel faulty?

Suddenly the wooden screen came back to life.

Phew. Panic over!

Isabella breathed a sigh of relief as she watched Daisy scuttle about on her hands and knees trying to move the roller thing.

She's talking again.

Then Isabella watched as Daisy stood up like a sentry and pointed towards the ground, her mouth open wide as if … screaming.

Slowly her body lowered into the ground; first her legs, then her chest, until all that remained was her head. Moments later she vanished entirely.

The screen went blank.

Isabella stared at the panel for several minutes, transfixed, until her large eyes filled with tears. But there was no mistaking it; while she and Archie remained on their panels, Daisy's wooden panel lay empty and lifeless and dull, like an ordinary section of their dining room table.

Daisy, she realised, had quite literally vanished.

CHAPTER TWENTY TWO

A Bee and a Leaf

Daisy squeezed her eyes shut and sucked in a lungful of air as if it were her last.

Suddenly her legs were pulled from under her as she tore off, a combination of whizzzooming at breakneck speed down the fastest water chute in the world, being thrown around in a tumble dryer and blown about by an enormous hairdryer all at the same time.

Two seconds later she found herself lying on a cold dusty floor, her heart racing.

Those ridiculous trees encouraged her, she thought as she gathered her wits; and she'd taken their advice! Idiot! She should have tackled the undergrowth by the ditch like any normal person.

With her eyes clamped tight and her head spinning, she spread her fingers and collected a thin velvet substance on her hands. Dust. Fine dust. She pushed her hand in. A lot of dust. How long had this place been empty? She sniffed the air. It smelt like a combination of decayed cheese and old newspapers.

Slowly, she opened her eyes. 'Where am I?' she whispered.

Her voice echoed back to her several times, eerie and ghost-like. She shivered now that the heat of the warm glade had gone.

A deathly silence surrounded her.

Daisy picked herself off the dusty floor and began to survey the area. The first thing she could tell was that there was no one around, simply a flat surface that went on and on and on. Apart from the indentations of her marks in the thick layer of dust there were no other footprints or signs of life.

She turned and gasped. About fourteen football pitches away a huge wall shot up from the floor reaching high into the air. Under closer inspection, at the foot of the wall, a series of huge arches concealed dark mouths.

Daisy looked up and squinted, her eyes adjusting to the change in light. She was in a vast cathedral-like room, bigger than anything she'd ever seen – so big that she couldn't make out where the sides ended and the roof began.

If I'm really dead, and this time I absolutely must be, she thought, I don't think this is heaven, or hell for that matter. Maybe God couldn't decide so he left me in between. In purgatory.

Some way off, near to what she suspected was the middle of this vast, dull construction, stood a strange-looking dust-laden object. Daisy imagined it looked like an old grey tree with, as far as she could tell, spindly branches that poked out rather sadly as if they were dead. Like a skeleton tree.

She stood up and headed towards the gaping holes along the walls. As she approached, she frowned. Some were big enough for a ship to pass through and took minutes to walk past, their cavernous openings cold and black, while others were as small as fox holes. She walked gingerly down a tunnel that could have easily accommodated a pair of elephants, but after a short distance, found it blocked by rocks.

She tried another, and another, but they too were sealed. After five tunnels Daisy felt lonely, frightened, lost and very, very small.

'What … what is this place?' she said, her teeth chattering as her words echoed back. 'How do I get out?'

She took off towards the strange grey tree but after a few steps she jumped in the air and squealed as something gave way underfoot and snapped. Her heart raced. Underneath the dust, lay a skeleton. She worked the dust away from the bones and found it to be human. Daisy winced; someone died here a long, long time ago.

'Sorry,' she said out loud. 'Didn't see you there.'

As she studied the bones, her senses on high alert, she heard a rasp – a strange wheezing noise.

Was it the ghost of the skeleton? She listened again, putting all her concentration into it. The more intently she listened the clearer the sound. Now there was a grating – a kind of breathing – getting closer.

Fear grabbed her.

She had to get out. *But how?*

The beginnings of a panic attack grew; the combination of hopelessness and fear, like a feeling she'd had in her nightmares. She jogged towards the wall.

In the next moment, a terrible CRACK cut through the air like a huge branch snapping in two. The crack was followed by a scream and its shrill echoed around the huge room like deathly wailing spirits.

Every hair on Daisy's body stood to attention. Her eyes bulged.

'Oh my God. I'm not alone!' she whispered to the room. 'The devil's coming to get me!'

She ran.

First towards the large holes to the side and then blindly, searching for a glimmer of light, a way out – a place to hide. After a few minutes, she drew up in front of a slightly different tunnel with worn markings surrounding it and caught her breath.

She wiped her forehead and listened. The sound of wailing, or screaming filled her eardrums. How the heck would she get out?

She took a deep breath and readied herself to go when she noticed the stonework. It was a real arch, not the crude arch of a cave hole, but more a built arch – of stone – with carvings. Under the brow of the arch was the outline of a gate and below this a familiar looking motif, like a crest you might see on a shield with the curious circular tree emblem exactly like the ones in the cave.

Below the circular tree were two distinct icons. She studied them. One bore a leaf, like an oak's, and the other, the picture of a bee.

As she looked around she heard a new noise, a terrific shrill that seemed to be growing.

The oak leaf and the bee, she thought. She realised she'd seen it before, but where?

She stared hard, her heart thumping. Where and what did the bee and a leaf mean?

She concentrated on the images as the piercing high-pitched noise filled her ears. She had to work fast. Then it struck her like a bolt of lightning – it was a clue from her dream. She remembered it now. She had to join the images! That was it!

"BEE-LEAF."

'Bee leaf,' she said out loud. It struck her. 'It's about BE-LIEF! That's it!

All I have to do is believe!

Without looking back, she took a deep breath, shut her eyes and walked straight towards the doorway without hesitating, thinking only of Eden Cottage.

*

The next thing she knew, the wind was blowing and the rain pouring down. She was back in a ditch but this time the other side of the gate, way below the house. She shrieked with relief and punched the air as if she'd scored the best goal of her life.

She didn't care that she was drenched through. She laughed aloud and splashed the water, crying with joy. Daisy de Lowe had just escaped from Hell itself.

She had to tell the others. But as she went, doubt filled her. What if they don't believe me? I mean, it's a bit … nuts. Actually, she thought, it's totally bonkers. But they must believe me. They have to.

She'd make them believe her, whatever it took, and then they'd start making sense of things and begin the search for the tablets.

Daisy ran, slipping and sliding as fast as she could up the hill towards Eden Cottage

.

CHAPTER TWENTY THREE

The Yorkshire Strain

Commissioner Stone was proud of his accomplishments on the Force, proud that he had the respect of his team and proud that at the age of fifty-two he could still fit into the suit he had bought with his first pay cheque aged nineteen: a sharp black pinstripe. He prided himself on his fitness, his well-being, and his full head of hair. He liked the fact that others complimented him on his sense of fair play and his ability to understand and uphold the rule of law in an uncomplicated manner. He liked the way ladies half his age stole admiring glances at him. But this, this silent and deadly enemy, which was growing at an alarming rate, terrified him. Nothing, no charm offensive nor training manual could combat it, even if operations for this kind of "natural event", had been planned years in advance.

Biblical happenings here in God's own county of Yorkshire. Storms! Plague! It was unbelievable.

Ironically, he'd been looking forward to the day for some time. His older cousin, known only by his surname, Solomon, was headmaster at Upsall school and had sent him an invitation to a banquet in celebration of his twentieth anniversary in charge. Rumour had it that it was to be quite an occasion.

In any event, he didn't get as far as his local town of Masham, on the edge of the Yorkshire Dales.

Only an hour after the rains began he found himself stranded. Fortunately, it was as he drove past the front drive of the Swinton Park Hotel that he decided enough was enough and took refuge.

It was a huge stroke of luck.

Geographically the hotel was perfect. Directly across the Vale of York from the village of Upsall, the hotel was isolated enough to prevent unwarranted intrusion and perched high enough in the dales to be out of danger from flooding. Furthermore the hotel was big and comfortable; able to house the army of experts summoned at short notice from around the UK.

Over the following day, as the hotel guests were airlifted out, his team and their equipment moved in. The luxurious facilities were turning into the headquarters of the largest police and medical operation ever seen in the country.

He stroked his moustache as he drew himself up, patted his pressed uniform and addressed the team in front of him.

'Right. I need speech analysts in to try and fathom what the boy was trying to say. If it was the word "Algae", maybe the boy is referring to the water, so I want results from those water samples today, please. I need to know what the "Dunno" is – if it's a thing, a person, a piece of rock or if the boy simply cannot speak clearly – I need to know. I want teams to work on his family, figure out where he's from: blood samples, DNA screening – whatever it takes. Understand so far?

'I need an up-to-date on the boy's burns – who or what could have given them and how. And we need to understand if this is a terrorist attack on the country – a form of international sabotage or simply a freak, biblical phenomenon. Find out what you can even if it there's a possibility it's an alien attack – is this all perfectly clear?'

The officers nodded. Two ran out of the room.

'OK. Has everyone arrived for the briefing?'

'Yes, Sir. They've been flying in all morning. The last guest put down ten minutes ago.'

'Good.' He made his way out of the reception area and into the grand hallway where a large white sheet hung neatly over the paintings of the past owners of the once-grand ancestral home. Crammed in the hallway were a mix of scientists, military and civil servants. Top brass. Commissioner Stone made his way up the wide staircase.

'Ladies and Gentlemen – Doctors, Generals, I appreciate your coming here at such short notice. I trust you saw the scale of devastation from your helicopters. You'll appreciate we don't have much time.

'The situation in regards to the viral infection is far worse than anticipated.' Stone paused as he caught the eyes of the people spread out below him. 'In fact, it's worse than our biggest nightmare. Not only are the contagion rates astonishing, but worse still, we have no idea how it is spreading. I'm handing you over to Chief Medical officer, Harries. He'll give you the latest update.'

Harries was one of the thinnest, leanest men you could imagine, with a pointed nose and a large ill-fitting pair of spectacles on his nose. His thinning, scraggly hair made him appear far older than his forty-five years and the way he wore an almost permanent frown didn't help matters. But he was the leading authority on viral strains in the country, if not the world. He made his way to the front, a bundle of files tucked under his arm and nodded to the projectionist. The lights dimmed and the white screen above them burst into life.

'This plague, the Yorkshire strain or Ebora, from the Latin *Ebor* meaning *York* – and I do believe that this will become the common noun – is a most curious one,' he said as the first slide came up. 'Here are the strains of the virus that we've been able to map so far. You will notice how many there are.' A new image slid into place. 'Now, here is the Yorkshire strain in comparison with the Plague of Athens, Spanish flu and Ebola.'

'These pandemics spread through touch or via carriers – the virus moving from one organism to the next. The difference to the Yorkshire strain is multi-fold. Our Ebora strain is smaller and considerably more aggressive. Moreover, it appears to mutate both randomly and rapidly. As I've shown you, we have already identified several varieties of the strain. And we believe there are many others out there.' The slides moved on.

'See here the effect of the Ebola virus on a victim in twenty-four hours. Now compare it with ours.' A loud gasp came from the onlookers. 'Yes, indeed, the Yorkshire strain is a great deal deadlier. Worse still, we've found animals – cattle, foxes and birds – bearing similar symptoms. So it appears that this outbreak doesn't stop with humans. It has the ability to attack every living thing.'

Another slide came up. Harries straightened. He looked pale and drawn. 'This slide will try and explain our current understanding of how the virus spreads.' He pointed his cane at the newest image. 'The known area of infection is coloured in blue.'

The map showed the entire area between the dales and the moors, reaching from Teesside at the top to Nottingham at the bottom. 'Two hundred miles and counting. This inner red ring, is a five-mile radius around the likely source at Upsall, the exact same place as the epicentre of the storm. We don't know why, or even if there's a connection, but we're working on it.'

On the slide, a geographical map showed the flooded region of Yorkshire. 'Now here's the truly worrying part.' On his signal, an overlying translucent sheet was placed over the map. 'This,' he continued, 'shows us the known victims as of early this morning.

The lighter green circles around the dots indicates the victims' approximate movement.'

On the map were a number of random marks stretching north, south, east and west.

A voice rang out. 'Sir, what does it all mean?'

'I was getting to that,' Harries barked. He straightened and smiled thinly. 'In simple terms we think it means that the virus is spreading arbitrarily.'

A murmur spread around the room. Harries raised a hand in the air. 'The virus is spreading in a way we haven't seen before. By contact, by wind and by water. Perhaps, it is a combination of these. The incubation period is like nothing we have ever come across. There will be thousands of people with the symptoms already and I am afraid that until we know more about it, we are at its mercy.'

An explosion of questions shot out. Harries absorbed them and then raised his arms for silence. 'We can only work with what we know,' he said. 'Scientists from all around the world are battling night and day to try and understand how this virus works so that a vaccination can be hurried through. But as I mentioned, the Yorkshire strain is mutating fast and the sequences are enormously complex.'

'How long have we got?' yelled a female voice.

'In two days,' Harries said, 'the virus has spread uncontrollably. I'm afraid I don't have an answer.'

'Do you have any leads, any positive news?'

Harries looked glum. 'Even with the best scientific minds working flat out, we are unable to pinpoint the cause and effect of this strain. The common denominator is the fact that the outbreak appears to have started at the storm's epicentre. And that, my friends, is the small village of Upsall.'

CHAPTER TWENTY FOUR

Isabella Rushes Out

Isabella hoped like mad that when she looked again, the panels wouldn't be there. She opened her eyes.

They were.

She groaned. She could see her outline in the first panel and Archie's in the last, but the middle panel showed only a blank empty space. She waved her feet in the air and the panel reflected her movements. If the panels were a true reflection of them at this exact point in time, she thought, then where was Daisy?

She leapt off Old Man Wood's bed and raced down the wooden stairs three at a time and into the hallway. Then she dashed along the corridor, through the door to the kitchen, where she all but crashed into the table. 'Have you seen Archie or Daisy?' she demanded, as her eyes searched the room.

Mrs Pye was not impressed. 'Good day to you, too, Isabella,' she said.

'Well? Have you?'

Mrs Pye puffed out her chest and faced her. 'Good afternoon, Isabella.'

'Oh. Good afternoon. Well—?'

'Why, not for a little while. Archie went out early and ...'

Isabella didn't need to hear the rest. In a flash, she was pulling on her boots and donning her coat. She found her leather wide-brimmed hat and as she drew the toggle under her chin she flew towards the door, inadvertently slamming it behind her. As she turned the corner she narrowly avoided smashing into Archie.

'Oi! Watch out!' he said.

'There you are!' she said clasping his shoulders. 'Great! Good! Fantastic!'

Archie reeled. 'What's going on?'

'Quick question – honest answer,' she panted. 'I'm not going to be cross.'

Archie didn't know what to say.

'You've been throwing your knives, haven't you?'

Archie bowed his head. 'Er, well—'

'You have – great!' she said. 'That's fine, excellent, good. Next question. Have you seen Daisy? She went off looking for you ages ago.'

Archie shook his head.

'OK. Didn't think so,' she said. Isabella knew that if what she'd seen was correct Daisy wouldn't be found anywhere. But she had to be sure.

'Where are you going?' Archie asked.

'Up to the ruin and then round the farm. I'll meet you in the cupboard, in twenty minutes … I've got to find Daise. It's important.'

Archie was confused. 'Right round the farm? It'll take you an hour at least. If you want Old Man Wood, he's in a bunch of willow trees by the water's edge. He's gone totally dotty.'

But Isabella wasn't listening and in a flash she'd shot off towards the ruin.

*

Isabella thought hard about which direction to take. She'd head up to the ruin first, check around the rocks and then make her way back down the hill, circumnavigating the garden.

She charged off gritting her teeth and running as fast as she could through the mud and spitting rain, jumping and hurdling branches and boulders with ease. She was amazed at how little time it took her to get there, how her feet seemed to take on a life of their own. She knew the distance was about five hundred metres. And she reckoned it took less than a minute. Was that right? She did a quick calculation. That's around thirty miles an hour. That's faster that Usain Bolt!

She stood by the remains of the old stone wall, which jagged here and there, its grey stones covered in ferns and creepers and small trees that had tucked their roots deep into the crevices. The battlements jutted out before disappearing into the grass below, then rose up like dark shadows until they ran along at twice her height for several metres.

Isabella followed the stones looking for footprints. Had only two days passed since they had limped home from the cave? It felt like a lifetime; so many confusing, bewildering events crowding her brain. She stopped by a section of masonry half-submerged in the ground, layered with moss and lichen. Was this the entrance into the old body of the castle? A gateway? She checked for footprints. There weren't any, just large, tyre-track markings, that weaved in and out of the scattered boulders. Maybe, she thought, these were the residual patterns made by the movement of water finding its route.

Isabella called out but the sound of her voice bounced back off the walls. She hurried on. It was hauntingly silent, too silent, even with the rain pit-patting onto the leather rim of her hat.

She walked through the centre of the ruin towards the gnarled battlements on the far side. As she went she wondered where the cave entrance might be.

She followed the thicker walls, turned the corner past the low-lying walls until eventually she was back in the same place. Had she missed it?

Isabella circumnavigated the ruin again, this time paying even closer attention. No gaping holes nor tell-tale tracks where a boulder had once been were in evidence at all. But the cave had to be there – the old ruin wasn't that big – and there were only three places where the walls were thick enough or tall enough.

Isabella sat on a rock and stared out into the valley at the hulking grey body of water. Had they imagined the cave or emerged from an alternative pile of rocks? She turned her hands over and for a brief moment her heart leapt as she thought she saw skin covering her palms. Her heart sank. The neat symmetrical holes were still there, reminding her.

What if some parts were real and other bits … made up, invented? What if the terrible experiences they'd had, had made them imagine things? What if they had some kind of post traumatic stress disorder? She'd read about this kind of thing in her textbooks. The brain was a powerful tool, a living computer with an unlimited ability for imagination. Perhaps that would explain the dreams and things like the bed and Daisy disappearing.

She took a deep breath, put her hands out on the rock and leaned on them. As she did, a strange noise interrupted her thoughts. She gasped as a terrible chill ran through the very marrow of her spine and the image of a vast serpent with glazed green eyes flashed into her head. Her skin prickled and instantly she vomited, a nauseous feeling washing right through her.

She started walking.

It's only in your head, she told herself – in your imagination. She stood tall and stretched her arms out wide then swung them around in a windmill motion as if to swish away the awful feelings.

It didn't work. She still felt nauseous and the chill remained deep in her bones. She hardly dare admit it, but the flash was identical to the image she'd dreamt about before the storm. Every bit the same, if not worse. The beast with the same green eyes that had latched on to her mind and made her head swim. But why here of all places?

And worse, what did it mean?

She looked around. Had the light dimmed? She noted another cloud brewing overhead. Wasn't it strange how this once happy place now had such a deep aura of evil, of darkness.

A rustling noise further along reminded her to check on Old Man Wood's cattle. She followed the strange tyre-track markings a short distance until they ran under a large rock. She thought briefly about her theory of how channels of water made the marks. But if this was the case, then wouldn't the tyre-track marks be in a different place?

She hurried on and before long came to the other section of the ruin, a large rectangular courtyard, dotted with crude rocks and the occasional scraggly bush and tree. Almost certainly this would have been the outer courtyard to the main castle keep. At the far end in the corner was a shelter for the herd, crudely constructed by Old Man Wood from large rocks and tree trunks and covered by a moss-covered roof of jumbled slates and tiles.

As Isabella approached, a terrible noise erupted – a frantic mooing and bleating building up and up. She crept forward, wondering what had unsettled them only to hear a stampede of hooves as the cattle bolted, scattering in different directions, mud flying.

Isabella knew the animals well; they were never afraid of her. But now they looked terrified, their eyes wide and shining more than she could ever remember. She talked to them in a soothing voice, and slowly they calmed down. As the noise abated, and they moved back under the shelter, she counted them.

Two missing. How come? She counted them again. Perhaps the noise of the storm had incited two of them to bolt. They might escape from the rough enclosure of the courtyard, but the ground slipped away sharply on each side. In poor weather they always came up here.

Isabella tried to work out which ones were missing, and holding her nose, she took a step inside to see if they were hiding at the back. No luck. She made a mental note to tell Old Man Wood and offered some comforting words to the herd. Then she headed back towards the house.

And still, no sign of Daisy.

CHAPTER TWENTY FIVE

Daisy's Disappearance

Isabella quickly removed her waterproofs. Noting that the kitchen was empty, she reckoned Archie had sought the warmth of the cupboard.

"The cupboard", drew its warmth from the flue-pipe of the range cooker directly below in the kitchen. It was a small room, used by Mrs Pye as a walk-in airing cupboard, for drying and storing towels, sheets and linen, and the children used it as their own personal snug – for chatting, hiding and warming themselves up on a cold winter's day.

Isabella approached and knocked on the door three times and rattled off last week's password, 'Carrots, cauliflower and courgettes.'

Archie clicked open the latch, which was screwed on from the inside so that when they occupied it, no one could barge in.

'Any luck finding Daisy?' Archie said.

Isabella settled in her corner on a soft bean bag and stretched her legs out. She shook her head. 'But I know where you've been.'

Archie reddened. He knew this was coming. 'Me?'

'Yup. I saw you curled up in the shed, Arch, throwing your knives.'

Archie frowned and felt his hair starting to wire up. 'Bells, there's no way you could have seen me in the potting shed. You saw me coming in and before that you were in bed.'

'You were in there, though, weren't you?'

'So what?'

Isabella didn't want to upset him. 'Look I'm not going to go mental on you, OK.' Her eyes widened. 'But aren't you curious to know how I know?'

Archie was confused. 'A wild guess?'

'Nope. You could have been with Old Man Wood for all I knew.'

'Well, I was, until he went crazy. He went to find some weirdo trees ... have you seen him—'

'No. And it's him we need to have a talk about. I'm afraid there's properly bad news.'

'I know. He needs putting in a geriatric home.'

Isabella smiled. 'Spot on.'

Archie cringed. 'Bells, you're not making sense,' he said. 'First you say that you've seen me throwing knives and then we need to talk about Old Man Wood. What's up?'

'Well, I don't know how to explain it,' she started, her voice barely controllable, 'but Old Man Wood has been tracking us ... spying on us, and... and I've found out how he does it—'

'What are you talking about?' Archie said. 'That's ridiculous. He'd never do such a thing. I'll admit that he has gone insane, but he's our best friend and he wouldn't harm a bug.'

Isabella leaned in. 'You may think so, Archie, but I have evidence.'

'Get real!' he replied. 'Why would he do anything like that?'

'Listen to what I've found – and trust me, every single word of what I'm about to tell you is true.'

Archie's hair had now achieved full wire status. He was agitated. It didn't feel right.

Isabella went on. 'I was bored and wanted to ask him a few questions, so I went down to his room. He wasn't there so I let myself in and jumped onto his bed. At the end of his bed are three screens that show every move *we* make. EVERY SINGLE MOVE, for each one of us, Archie.'

Archie sat listening, stroking his hair-spikes.

'And that's how I know you were in the potting shed, bundled up in the corner feeling sorry for yourself, throwing your stupid knives. On the final panel was Daisy. I could tell by the way she moves, by her bottom. And me, I was there on one of the panels, sitting on the bed.'

Quiet filled the small cupboard, only broken by the faint sounds of the range cooker drifting up to them and the hum of the generator.

'You've gone mad,' Archie whispered after a while. 'Just like Old Man Wood.'

'No I haven't, Archie. I couldn't make this up. I don't have an imagination, you know that.'

Archie groaned. 'Well, if you must know, I think we're missing a link to Old Man Wood.'

'What do you mean?'

'Well, our freaky dreams showed that Old Man Wood is connected to us, so there has to be a reason for his odd behaviour.'

'Archie, if Old Man Wood is spying on us then something is definitely not right. He might not be who we think he is—'

'But really—'

'Look, I'm serious – deadly serious,' she said, her voice quivering.

'Old Man Wood?' Archie chuckled, his memory fresh from Old Man Wood's fiasco with the trees.

'Yes! Maybe he's part of some sort of conspiracy—'

'So why not ask him?' Archie said. 'I mean, he's hardly likely to deny it.'

'That's exactly what I was going to do,' Isabella fired back. 'I mean think about it. That medicine of his, the way he blunders about looking like he's lost at sea staring aimlessly at the walls—'

'But he used the medicine to help us, didn't he? Look, I just can't believe he would do anything that would in any way be harmful—'

'There's more,' Isabella interrupted. 'You know I told you about these panels with each of us on.'

'Yeah. So?'

'Well here's the shocking bit—'

'Shocking—?'

'Yes. Just listen,' Isabella demanded. 'One minute Daisy looked as if she was sunbathing—'

'Sunbathing? She couldn't have been.'

'No, really, she was. One hundred percent the truth. And can you please stop interrupting me. Then she talked to someone or something and then she totally … disappeared.'

Archie stared at Isabella. 'You have completely lost the plot—'

'No I have not, Archie. Her screen went blank – I'll show you. And anyway, why do you think I tore off round the farm, huh? To find her, of course, and she wasn't anywhere. I checked the place over.'

'But why would she disappear—'

'Ssshh!' Isabella said. 'What's that noise?'

Below them they could hear the sound of the door shutting followed by voices, as though the telly had been turned on. They listened.

'It's only Mrs P,' Archie said.

'It isn't. Mrs P headed off ages ago. Old Man Wood doesn't watch telly and Daisy's missing.'

Archie frowned. 'Then I think we'd better investigate,' he said.

They flicked the latch and slipped quietly down the stairs.

*

The kitchen was in its usual immaculate condition but with no sign of Mrs Pye.

Splashes of neon from the TV lit the otherwise dark room as the latest news bulletin showed pictures of the disaster.

Archie and Isabella sneaked in.

Archie crept past the oak table and chairs, past the island and looked beyond it. Nothing. He moved farther forward, turned to Isabella and shrugged.

Then they heard a sniff. Archie took a pace forward as Isabella went for the light.

In a wet heap on the floor beneath the island sat Daisy, watching the news. Archie gasped. She looked terrible.

She turned her head as she heard him but quickly refocused on the news, ignoring him.

Archie didn't know what to think. She was drenched from head to toe, and shivering, but she wouldn't take her gaze off the pictures.

'You alright?' he said softly.

'Sssshhh,' she replied and with a shaking hand she pointed towards the screen.

Archie turned his gaze up.

On the screen the image of a room inside a hospital showed a patient lying in a bed. The patient's eyes were open but dulled. A caption ran along the bottom of the screen in big letters.

LIVE: FLOOD CHILD OUT OF COMA

Archie sat down next to Daisy – offering her a couple of drying up cloths. Daisy grabbed them without taking her eyes from the screen. Why, Archie thought,

207

was Daisy so preoccupied with this bald, sick-looking boy covered in drips and bandages?

The news continued.

Earlier on today, the commentator said, *the miracle boy who has been nicknamed Jonah by the medical team, came out of his coma. The boy, his real identity still unknown, his body hairless and covered in mysterious burn marks, was found hanging on to a branch at the top of a tall tree surrounded by the floodwaters. Jonah, thought to be a local boy, was discovered by the air ambulance team earlier this morning suffering from serious malnutrition. Police and medical staff are urging anyone who might know him to ring this hotline number.*

The camera panned in on the boy, who happened, at that moment, to blink, quite slowly.

Archie reached in a little. That movement.

Then the boy smiled faintly, his lips parting a fraction. Archie gasped and peered in even more, and turned to see the reaction of his sister. She was doing the exact same thing.

The camera zoomed in even closer. The screen filled with the lips and eyes of the child, who had no hair, no eyebrows, nor eyelashes and who bore a curious red rim mark on his head as if he had squeezed into a hat that was too tight.

The boy closed his eyes. It appeared that he was trying to speak. He swallowed, struggling to form a word. After a great effort a sound emerged.

It was barely audible, but sounded something like, *Arjjie.*

Archie and Daisy knelt forward, watching keenly.

A voice from one of the medical team, her face covered by a white medical mask, gently said, 'Hello. Can you hear me?'

'*Algae*,' the boy repeated. His eyes opened wider, the struggle to talk seemingly beyond him. '*Dunno*,' he said before closing his eyes.

The boy swallowed again, the camera highlighting his considerable effort. '*DUNNO*,' the boy said again, with as much urgency as he could muster. Then the boy collapsed back on his bed as a machine above him started to bleep and a team of medics rushed in, surrounding him.

Immediately, the TV pictures cut out and shot back to the studio, where, emblazoned in big writing along the bottom of the screen were the words:

THE PRIME MINISTER WILL ADDRESS THE NATION AT 18:00hrs GMT.

CHAPTER TWENTY SIX

Headmaster Solomon

Commissioner Stone stood up. 'Thank you, Chief Medical Officer.' He faced the throng of anxious faces. 'You now have an understanding of the situation. Coming round the room is more information – essential documents – in regards to what are the likely outcomes. Also, there is an outline of the strategic operation that is about to come into place. None of it makes for easy reading. All of you have been assigned roles in relation to your skill set. When this meeting is over, please collect your briefing papers from the drawing room which is along the corridor.

'These papers contain sensitive information, links and passwords to several Government archives and the main COBRA operations portal on the web. In order for this to remain out of the public domain, you will sign official secrecy documents before you depart, or you will not leave Swinton Park. Is this quite clear?

'Ministers and civil servants are being briefed as we speak. Regional and emergency councils are gathering. The main headquarters for the operation will be here and at Downing Street, London. As the virus spreads operational headquarters will be situated in locations like this outside Cardiff, Exeter, Manchester, Cambridge and Edinburgh. The heads of all the emergency services are meeting in strategic locations shortly. Across the country emergency stores are being placed in aircraft hangers and distribution systems are being organised. In our hospitals, isolation units are being prepared. Non-life-threatening operations have been cancelled. Every town and village will run their own health centres manned by local doctors, nurses and volunteers. Only dire emergencies will be accepted into hospitals.

'Later this afternoon the media will be thoroughly briefed by the Prime Minister, who will then address the nation. You will not talk to the media from this moment on. All press and interviews in regards to the virus and operations will be made through official channels.

'Most of you will be flown out of here to help. You will be given smart-phones that run on a special service connection so you can be kept up to date. Parliament went into an emergency session early this morning and the Prime Minister is chairing a cross party emergency cabinet. At the moment other heads of state are being briefed, particularly our neighbours in Europe and in the United States.

'At eleven o'clock this evening, all airports, ferry crossings, railway stations, waterways and motorways will be closed. Access in or out of Great Britain will be prohibited unless authorised by one of you. As of midnight tonight, there will be a total media blackout. The Internet will be temporarily suspended with access at specific times to be announced. Television and radio stations will play films and repeats and be the source of all news updates. Supermarkets will come under state supervision and armed military units are already moving in to areas where civil unrest is likely. Yes, we do envisage serious panic in towns and cities as people rush for supplies.

'To that end, a curfew will come into play in every town and city across the country and a zero tolerance approach will be forced upon the citizens of the country.' The commissioner could feel the sweat on him. 'You will need to work fast. The security of the country is at stake.'

Stone remained standing, looking into the eyes of the people below him. 'We believe that so long as the disease is confined to the north of the country, these measures might contain the spread both south and farther north. Every available expert is working on a solution right now.

He pushed his glasses along his nose. 'As Britain goes into lockdown, be assured the world is watching with bated breath, and even then, it may be too late.'

*

The commissioner drew in a deep breath and mopped his brow. The stunned crowd in front of him began to disperse, heads buried in folders.

'Is a chopper available?' he said to the smart young officer next to him.

The officer, Dickinson, made a quick call. 'Ten minutes and it's yours,' he said as he hung up. 'Can I brief the pilot where it's headed?'

'Short trip – Upsall. Want to take a look for myself and there's someone I need to get out – the headmaster at the school, name of Solomon. Can you run a check and see if he's made contact with anyone.'

'It's bang in the middle of the zone, Sir,' Dickinson said. 'The area suffered badly.'

'I don't care.' The commissioner snapped back. 'I need that man out of there, dead or alive!'

Dickinson raced off. Stone glanced at his watch and dusted down his jacket. He studied his mobile. Still no word from the scientists. When would they come back with something – anything? They were so lost in their own world, scientists, what they needed was a bang on the head to sort them out. He spotted Dickinson returning.

'This Headmaster Solomon,' the officer said, 'actively used his mobile when the signal became operational. Nothing since 21:00 hours yesterday. Maybe he ran out of battery.'

'Good. At least we know he survived. Are we ready?'

Dickinson nodded and knowing that the Commissioner liked to stride more than walk, marched quickly ahead.

*

'Good Lord above,' Stone said as he viewed the brown smear of water and debris that was the Vale of York through the windows of the helicopter. 'Now, pay attention. I want details of everyone in this area, starting with Upsall. I want names and addresses. I want to know who is in the school, pupils, teachers, caterers, who runs the newsagents, who blows the candles out in the church. I want medical records, death records, birth records and a history of the place from as far back as you can get. I want to know the occupations of all the families that have been around the area, I want contractor information.' He paused as he waited for the team to catch up with their note taking. 'I want a pattern. Have you got that?'

'Sir,' one of the officers nearby said, 'this kind of investigation takes weeks.'

Stone fixed him an icy stare. 'Understand this, money is no object. Hire everyone you goddamn can. Use the universities of Leeds, Durham, Newcastle – Timbuktu – for all I care. We need results and we need to find something that connects Upsall to this plague, do you understand? We need this last week, goddammit.'

The chopper wheeled to the right. 'And I want everyone, and I mean everyone, who was found in Upsall village put in quarantine. Are the military in there yet? Good. Make arrangements for a mass evacuation of all the people up into the moors.' He rubbed his chin. 'Try using the outcrop at Crayke – use the castle there.' He fixed each of the people with eyes that told them to trust him implicitly. 'Your status as part of this team means we can access anyone. *Anyone*,' he emphasised. 'So get on your phones and get about your business. NOW.'

In no time the crew were relaying messages from their communications devices.

A message came through from the pilot. 'We're approaching Upsall, Sir.'

'Good. Can you get near the tower?'

The helicopter whirred and levelled out. Beneath them was a slurry of debris where the pretty village once stood. Grey water swirled below. Sticking out was the old tower of the school and the top half of the tall chapel.

Before long one of the marines was being lowered down, onto the parapet. A couple of people were there welcoming him in.

One was the familiar figure of the headmaster, Solomon.

*

To the Commissioner, his cousin looked pale and drawn. Weight had dropped off him, and his face, rotund at their last meeting was now angular and coated with a grey, stubbly beard.

'You have to get the others out,' the headmaster said. 'You can't leave them there. You don't know what it's like.'

Stone nodded and patted his shoulder reassuringly. 'We'll get everyone out, believe me,' he said and then added, 'I'm sorry about your party. I know how much it meant.' The chopper soared into the rain. 'Was rather looking forward to it, myself.'

The headmaster shrugged. Tears welled in his eyes as he stared out of the window.

'I'm going to come straight to the point, Solomon,' Stone said. 'We've got a pandemic on our hands and it stems from here.' He stared out of the window as if sharing the older man's grief. 'You need to tell me everything you know about Upsall.'

The headmaster gathered himself together. 'Of course. I'll tell you what I know, but I'm not sure if it'll help.'

The chopper climbed high and from here the devastation was truly remarkable. Water stretched from Teesside in the north as far as the eye could see to the south. Dotted at various points were outcrops, islands, full of tents and makeshift dwellings, like mini shanty towns.

'Were there any unusual circumstances prior to the storm?' Stone asked.

Solomon thought for a while. 'None. We thought, the storm was, for all intents and purposes, just localised. That's what the Met Office said.'

'So you called the Met Office?'

Solomon remembered the incident with Isabella. 'No. Not exactly. I watched the forecast on the television, but there was a girl – one of my brightest students—'

'She thought otherwise?'

Solomon admired the way his young cousin had the knack of picking up little leads like this. 'Yes, probably nothing,' he said. 'A smart kid. You know, just interested—'

Stone lent in. 'And she said what, exactly?'

'Well, she'd made a barometer and insisted there was going to be a terrible storm. Why, I don't know. But she did it on three occasions.'

'Her name?'

'Isabella de Lowe,' he replied without flinching.

Stone scratched her name in his pad and handed it to the officer next to him. 'Get this checked out,' he said. 'Find out if she's alive, what family she has.'

'Oh, I wouldn't worry about her,' Solomon said. 'Her parents are stuck in the Middle East – archaeologists—'

'Look, I need answers and at the moment there are none,' Stone said. 'Everyone and I mean everyone is being checked out.'

An alarm bell rang in Solomon's mind. 'But she's only a child—'

'I don't care if she's a bloody donkey. I need to know about everyone.' His tone was tough and unapologetic. 'Where is she from? Upsall or—'

'All I'm saying,' Solomon said in his most headmasterly way, 'is that this girl came to me wanting to talk about a storm, which she said was going to be bigger than everyone thought.'

'Why?' Stone pressed. 'Do all your students do this?'

'I have no idea,' Solomon replied racking his brain. 'Perhaps she was being intuitive. Some children are remarkable in that respect. She's a bright child, one of our best.'

'Do you know where she lives?'

Solomon didn't like the way this was going. 'In the hills,' he said, waving a hand roughly in the air. 'Extraordinary family, very eccentric.'

'In what way?'

Solomon had forgotten what a persevering human being Stone could be. It was, he realised, one of the reasons he'd climbed to the top. 'Look,' he said. 'I'm tired, exhausted and hungry and I don't think this is helping.' He turned his head away. The headmaster needed to think, to run the conversations through his mind before he'd give his cousin anything else to work on. He certainly wasn't going to allow Stone to hound his students. 'I simply think you're barking up the wrong tree,' he added.

Stone surveyed his haggard cousin. 'De Lowe. Is that the name?'

Solomon grunted disapprovingly.

Stone turned to the officer. 'Find out everything about the de Lowe family. History, academic records, family records – the whole damn lot. Understand?'

Solomon was too tired to respond. In his heart there was something about Isabella and her ranting that struck a chord with everything that had happened – as if she knew. But what and why her? How could that family, living in a curious old cottage perched high up on the moors, with the strange old man looking after them, and a heritage as old as the hills, have anything to do with this disaster?

But deep down, Solomon supposed that if anyone had a clue about strange goings on in Upsall – it might be them. He slumped back into his seat and shut his eyes. He'd find out when they landed and he'd slept, washed and eaten. Until then, the last person he would tell would be Stone and his cronies.

Stone had a fearsome reputation for extracting information and he wasn't ready to hand over his students, or his friends.

Not yet at any rate.

CHAPTER TWENTY SEVEN

Cain's Plan

Cain amazed himself with his supreme intelligence. And his latest ruse smacked of pure genius.

OK, so he lost the boy. But did he really need him? No, not right now. In a way, the timing couldn't have been better. You see, he'd discovered a way of speeding up delivery of the plague, so that the world was plunged into misery even before the water had receded. Four days early! That was the strange thing about those dream-giving spider things, the dreamspinners. They knew everything but at the same time, they knew nothing.

And yes, he did miss having the boy around. What a wonderful feeling! Walking, dancing, beating people up, just like the good old days. When the boy was better, he'd return and tell him all about his mother – for a price, of course. He looked forward to it. But this time, he'd look after him and get the boy to utterly trust him.

Cain couldn't believe that he had ignored the boy's most basic needs. For a brief moment he felt a twinge of regret but his current excitement made him overlook that emotion. Next time, he'd find a way of talking, perhaps by opening up a path in his brain, and they'd communicate and wouldn't that be fun? And he'd feed him – like a king. Already, huge lists of foods were being sought out. Things he'd never heard of. Things with extraordinary names like *fish fingers* and *roast chicken* and *Coco Pops* and *prawn crackers*. A kitchen to prepare this food was under construction along with a well of water sunk deep into the palace earth and filtered in exactly the necessary way for humans.

Next time, he wouldn't force the boy to do anything by burning him. He'd only burn him if he didn't do things *his* way. Sure, it might be tricky, but he'd communicate and then win him over.

Anyway, the boy would understand that he had an opportunity to wield real power. And if he was honest, Cain wondered about letting himself be dominated, controlled like a sleeping partner – take a back seat and see what happened. He could switch off for a year or two, have a break from being a spirit; take a sabbatical, become a non-executive.

Cain danced around and swished through the air even if it wasn't half as enjoyable as having an actual, real body to do it in. He thought about the Heirs of Eden and laughed. So they survived the flood. Big deal. They have seven days to find the three tablets, and as of day three, those wretched children are still moping around their strange little home while a very horrid plague is rearing its ugly head to the unsuspecting world.

And it's all their fault!

He laughed. Well, they were just kids. The only person who could guide them was the old man. And what a failure he was turning out to be. Worse than useless! He had no idea, even if he had discovered the old cellar and the trees at the brook. It was like watching a snail in a running race.

Cain ran through the sequence of events on Earth. By the time the Heirs of Eden failed, as they were bound to, every living thing would have succumbed to the plague and died. He laughed. It was so easy: just let them be themselves. The dreamspinners would take him to the Ancient Woman, his dear mother, and he'd open up the

Garden of Eden himself. He couldn't believe he hadn't thought of it before.

Then he'd have control of every living thing, every being, every cell of every being and he'd nurture the ones he wanted and put them onto a new Earth and revitalise his dear Havilah. He would create any creature he wished, just the way he wanted. And would the old man stop him? No, because he wouldn't know how.

But what if those children managed to succeed? He toyed with the absurdity of it. On the remote chance that they did manage to find the stone tablets, could he deny them passage to the Garden of Eden? No, not really. But it made no difference. The prize would still be his because he'd steal it. In any case, children of the human race would never commit murder, I mean, they could hardly bear to even dream of it.

With these happy thoughts, he summoned Asgard. 'Dreamspinner, dreamspinner, dreamspinner,' he called. Moments later the large opaque spidery creature appeared, his blue middle fizzing with electric light. 'Aha! There you are. How is our little plan coming along?'

Asgard's legs moved rapidly. 'Master, the particles have been mixed into the new stocks of spider web dream powders deep in the caves of Havilah.'

'Excellent!' Cain said. 'What will these dreams be like?'

'Havilarian spiders are different to those of the Garden of Eden and Earth. They are clever, brutal, manipulative and easily roused. These qualities are reflected in the action of the dream powders made from their spider webs.'

'Nightmares?'

'Bad dreams are as rewarding and enriching as the pleasant,' Asgard said, flicking his legs. 'After all they are only dreams. Remember, creativity and enlightenment comes from the darker side of life too, master.'

Cain was intrigued. 'Why not spider webs from Earth?'

'Earth spiders are bland and lifeless. These spider web powders do not nourish dreamspinners as deeply.'

'Why so?'

'Dream powders are as vital to us as the breathing of air is to mankind and water is to creatures of the sea. Dreamspinners will spin more dreams from Havilah from now on. I guarantee it.'

'Your band of dreamspinners has grown?'

'Now there are many,' the spidery creature signed, speaking through the vibrations of his legs. 'Each day, as the sun sets, more join. Dreamspinners cannot resist a dream.'

'Even bad ones, eh?' Cain loved this creature. 'You are most enlightening, Asgard,' he said. 'And wise,' he added.

Asgard was unsure of Cain's meaning. 'In the event of the boy returning to you,' Asgard continued, 'I have found a way of transporting you from place to place.'

If Cain had ears, they would have flapped. 'Are you suggesting there are dreamspinners who would sacrifice themselves?' he asked.

'Indeed. Some who are too old to give dreams do not wish to see the world shaping as it is. They believe a new time is coming. They are prepared to go to their deaths early.'

Cain jumped up, invisibly, and thumped the air repeatedly. 'Phenomenal news! Truly, Asgard this is wonderful! I am delighted with you.' He lowered his voice. 'Tell me, dreamspinner, how long before the plague particles in your dream powders are ready to go?'

'The new spider web dream powders are free to use as the sun sinks over the western horizon.'

Cain gasped. 'Tonight? Already? My goodness.'

The ghost danced an invisible jig. What a turnaround! Nightmares stuffed full of plague and a few days early at that. 'Poor, dear little earthlings,' he crowed. 'They have no idea what is about to hit them – and not a helping hand in sight.'

Damn the wretched Prophecy, damn the old man and damn the Heirs of Eden, he thought. Very soon there won't be a world worth saving.

CHAPTER TWENTY EIGHT

Lockdown

While showing footage of the hairless boy in his hospital bed, the TV screen started to flicker, soon blacking out altogether.

Isabella flipped the light switch, but it wasn't working either and she noticed that the buzz of the generator no longer filled the air. She shot out of the house to see if she could restart the motor.

Silence filled the kitchen. 'Was that who I think it was?' Daisy said quietly.

Archie had gone pale. 'What do you mean?' he stammered trying to hide his face.

'That boy!' Daisy said.

Archie didn't know what to say.

'*It's Kemp*! It has to be.'

'You think so?'

'Yes, winkle. Of course. But without hair. Bald and burnt. It's Kemp, your horrible friend.'

For a moment Archie wasn't capable of uttering a word. 'But how could it be Kemp? He'd been in the alley—'

'Where?' Daisy cut in.

Archie hesitated. 'Well, you know ...'

'No, I don't know what you're talking about,' Daisy said, as she started to remove her wet clothes. 'What alley?'

Archie wondered if he should come clean and tell Daisy about the meeting with Cain, and Cain's offer. 'No, it's nothing,' he heard himself say. 'He just said he was going shopping in town, *down the alley*, that's all.'

'Strange, isn't it?' Daisy said as she removed her top, 'I saw the rescue on telly this morning and at the time I thought those ugly lips could only belong to one person. Do you think his burn marks are from a lightning strike or a burning building?'

'Dunno,' Archie said.

'Is that "dunno" you don't know, or are you just repeating what that dimwit Kemp said?'

'Eh? Oh, sorry, just trying to work out what he was saying.' Archie's said as his brain raced. Was this Cain's doing? Even so, how on earth did he end up in a tree? Kemp could hardly swim.

Daisy felt like smacking Archie round the head. Talking to him was like chatting to a goalpost. 'Come on, winkle, it's a desperate cry for help. Shouldn't we phone the helpline and tell them we know who it is? Don't you think that's our, like, duty?'

Isabella came back into the room. 'Can't seem to get it going. Arch, why don't you have a try? You're good at that kind of thing.'

'We're going to phone the number,' Daisy said, addressing her sister.

'Phone who, about what?'

'Call the emergency number and let them know we think the boy is Kemp.'

Isabella turned on her. 'Why? Why the hell should we do that?'

Daisy hesitated. Isabella sounded unnecessarily sharp. 'Well, he's Archie's friend—'

'And my enemy,' Isabella snapped. 'No way. If anyone wants to claim him,' she said, 'let them.' She turned away. 'Come on, Archie, the sooner we get the generator going, the better.'

*

Daisy's heart thumped. She desperately wanted to tell them about the enormous chamber, but this revelation about an unknown virus had to be the same as the images portrayed on the cave wall.

If she was going to talk about it she'd have to pick her moment carefully; Isabella was in an argumentative mood and best avoided until she'd calmed down. She headed upstairs for a shower, which drizzled cold water.

As she rinsed her hair, she thought about the huge building and for a fleeting moment wondered if she had simply imagined being there. Nah, that was impossible. It was as real as the water running down her back.

And what were those funny old trees that spoke to her, Daisy mused, and where did the terrible screams come from? She dressed quickly and skipped down the stairs.

When she walked in, Archie was washing his hands in the sink and Isabella was sitting in a chair with her arms folded tight across her chest, staring at the floor. Oh well, she thought, better now than never.

'Right,' she said pulling up a chair. 'We need to talk.'

Archie sat down. 'The Prime Minister's on in ten minutes,' he said. 'We should watch him.'

'We'll do that after I've explained what happened to me earlier,' Daisy said. 'This is important.'

Isabella yawned. 'Fire away, twinkle toes.'

'OK, so this is going to sound a bit crackers,' Daisy said, pulling off her pink glasses. 'I went to look for you this morning, Archie, and when I reached Dad's old potato patch, I found a gate with a pearl hanging from a bush.'

Isabella tutted.

'Please, Bells, let me finish. I tried to grab the pearl and as I reached out, I somehow fell into a ditch. When

I'd dragged myself out, I was in sunshine on a small glade with three really old trees totally covered in blossom. I know it sounds impossible but the trees asked me questions—'

Isabella groaned theatrically.

Daisy shot her a look. 'At first I thought I'd died, you know swallowed some infected water or something, and ignored them – but the trees insisted and eventually pointed me towards a strange platform. After a bit of hesitation, I went on to the platform and then flew off to a … a new kind of place.'

Isabella guffawed. 'Yes, yes, I know you disappeared, Daisy. Nice story, by the way.'

'Eh? What …?'

'You disappeared?'

'Well, yeah.'

'And do you know how I know?'

Daisy shook her head.

'Because I saw you. I watched as you moved an object on this platform of yours and then you vanished.'

Daisy was flummoxed. 'How do you know all this?'

'I found some magic panels on Old Man Wood's bed—'

'Magic—'

'Yes. Panels, like TV monitors, which showed that you'd slipped away.'

Daisy's face had turned puce. 'What panels, Bells? You're talking bull,' she said. 'It's not possible.'

'I'm afraid it is. Happy to show you if you like.'

The children sat silently round the table. Isabella smiling.

'It's a joke, right. You're making fun, aren't you?'

But Isabella's face didn't change.

Daisy was seething. 'I knew you wouldn't believe me but it's true, it's all true. One hundred percent.' She stood up and paced around the table. 'My dreams – our dreams – are really, really happening – right now. Everything we've seen, Bells, is real, not imaginary. And we're running out of time—'

'Daisy, shut up!' Isabella snapped. 'I told you, I saw you, OK? There's really nothing more to say on the matter.'

'Anyone fancy,' Archie began diplomatically, 'a slice of Old Man Wood's starlight apple crumble? I don't know about you, but I'm starving. Nothing like a good pig-out to calm the nerves because it's becoming perfectly clear that we're losing the plot – big time.'

Archie stood up, pulled some milk from the fridge and a pushed a cake tin onto the table. Then he pressed the button that turned on the TV.

Much to their surprise, it flickered into life.

*

Prime Minister Kingsford looked tired. No amount of make-up could disguise this. He was flanked by senior government ministers and his COBRA team as he stood in front of an oak lectern.

'People of the United Kingdom,' he began, *'Never in the annals of our history has this country faced a crisis as severe as the situation that confronts us now. This afternoon, I speak to you as your leader. I also speak to you as a husband and a father and an ordinary man. I don't doubt that the words and actions that are about to follow will be met with shock. But I ask you all, before I say any more, to understand that the measures that are about to be imposed have been thrust upon us as a very last resort. And therefore I urge you to listen to what I have to say with level-headed understanding.*

'It is with a heavy heart that I tell you this. But I tell you so that together we may face the threat in front

of us with the decency and common spirit that I know resides within the marrow of each and every one of you.'

He shuffled nervously, his eyes hollow, his skin pale.

'Following the devastating flooding of the Yorkshire area,' he began, *'a virus known as Ebora has emerged. It is a strain that has never been seen before. It is a freak. There is no rhyme nor reason as to Ebora's aggressive nature. It is a silent enemy that we do not, as yet, understand, but rest assured, we will. As I speak to you now, top scientists from around the world are trying to identify its complex properties in order to find a vaccine. But they require more time.*

The camera zoomed in on his face. *'Earlier today I met with the COBRA team who have been working non-stop to provide the framework necessary to protect as many lives as possible. Their work is being actioned as I speak on the orders of the Government following top-level consultations.*

'In order to give ourselves the best opportunity to narrow its destructive path our first step is to limit the movement of people in and around the country,'

The Prime Minister mopped his brow. *'By morning, our hospitals will be ready with contained areas for those showing symptoms, though you may decide, as responsible citizens, that remaining at home is the best solution.*

'In the meantime the following limitations are to be forced upon every person in these isles.' The Prime Minister shuffled his notes and held a long pause. A global audience of billions, reached into their sets.

'From midnight tonight a great safety net will be pulled over our land and drawn around our borders. Every airport in Britain, every railway and waterway

will be vacated. Motorway traffic will be limited to emergency use only. Supermarkets, power companies, media organisations and their distribution partners will fall under the control of Government departments.

'These measures are to ensure that food and necessary supplies can be provided to everyone, at the right time, without panic and without preference so that the fundamental elements of our existence can continue.

While we learn how to combat Ebora, life must go on. So, this evening, do not rush to your local stores, do not go outside for unnecessary errands or social occasions. Consider everything closed. Civil unrest will not be tolerated and the penalties for such acts will be swift and severe.' The Prime Minister paused to sip some water. *'Many will have noticed the presence of the military in the cities and the towns. I urge you not to be alarmed. They are there to protect you and to enforce law and order upon our nation – and for no other reason.*

'Local travel will be possible, but ill-advised. For the benefit of safety, internet use will be limited. Updates will be posted regularly on television channels and radio stations.

'Until a vaccine is found, I cannot tell you how long these measures will be in place.'

He paused again and looked directly into the camera. *'In this great country of ours we have overcome many things. Together, we shall persevere. Together, we will win this fight.'*

Tears welled in his eyes.*'Go now to your loved ones. Be safe, responsible and ever mindful. God bless you all. Thank you.'*

*

For a minute or two, the children stared open-mouthed at the screen.

It was Daisy who broke the silence. 'Bollocks!' she said.

Isabella turned on her. 'Daisy, there's no need to swear.'

Daisy was shaking. 'Yes there bloody well is!'

'No,' Isabella replied icily. 'There isn't!'

'Yes, there shitting well is!' Daisy yelled.

'Daisy! Stop it!' Isabella cried. 'And anyway, there's nothing we can do about it, you heard what the PM said.'

'Isabella, how unbelievably thick are you?' Daisy said. 'Don't you understand? Don't you get it yet?' She stood up, stamped her feet and growled. 'This is our problem, you daft idiot. This is OUR BLOODY PROBLEM.'

'No it isn't,' Isabella replied calmly, 'and for God's sake, stop swearing. Didn't you listen to anything, *anything* on the telly? It's a national problem—'

'Yes, but it started here! Right here in Upsall. Don't you see—?'

Archie moved in. 'Woah! Cool it, Daise,' he said.

'Cool it!' she roared. 'What's got into you both? Have you lost your minds? Seriously, which bits don't you understand? You think you get freaky hair like that or bloody great holes in your hands or glaring red eyes *every bleeding day?* Really? You think these strange things happening to us are *normal?* Do you?'

Isabella wasn't having any of it and stood up abruptly. 'Well, it looks like I'm not the only one who's lost my bloody mind,' she snapped back. 'This virus has nothing to do with us.'

'It has EVERYTHING to do with us, der brain,' Daisy spat. 'If you'd bothered to look at the cave paintings you would have realised it is *exactly* what was shown. It showed a plague, like in biblical times, and three stone tablets like … like books, and they needed to be found or everyone dies.'

'Oh belt up, Daisy. You're completely overreacting.'

'Me, overreacting? You're kidding, right?' Daisy said as she stood up and swept a mass of blonde curls off her face. She faced her sister, her face puce with anger, her red eyes burning like fire. 'Take a hard look at yourself, Bells, and think of everything we've been through. Overreacting? Jeez, I really don't think so.' She gave both of her siblings a piercing look. 'Seems like you two are suffering from total memory failure.'

'Stop being so irrational and stupid—'

'Stupid? You're the daft ones, not me!' There was no reaction. 'We have to find those things that were clearly painted on the walls. This is about the three of us. It's about all of us doing whatever we've got to do, together. Why don't you get it?'

Daisy stormed out and slammed the door. Then she opened the door again and marched back in. 'And there's one more thing.'

Isabella tutted.

'Yeah,' Daisy said, 'I've worked it out.'

'Worked what out?' Archie said.

'What Kemp meant. You know, when he said those words, "dunno" and "algae". I know what he was trying to say.'

'What are you talking about?' Isabella said.

'Kemp – in the hospital bed, your holy thickness.'

'Most likely he was simply trying to alert them about the water,' Isabella said coolly.

Daisy shook her head.

Isabella smirked. 'Go on then, spit it out, Professor Stephen Hawking.'

Daisy smarted. 'Why should I?'

'Oh don't tell me – it's yet another thing that's sprung out of your fertile imagination,' Isabella said, smiling thinly.

'No. I know alright,' Daisy fired back. 'Why should I tell you when you will not open your eyes?'

'Try me?'

'Sod you, Isabella. Where the hell is Old Man—'

The door opened. Old Man Wood's head popped round the doorframe. 'Have I missed something?' he said, as he went over to the range and put the kettle on. 'Everything alright?'

'*No, everything is not alright!*' Daisy roared, fixing him with an icy stare. 'An epidemic is about to sweep the country following the worst flooding ever, and LA-DI-DAH we're the only ones who seem to know anything about it. You're part of this, Old Man Wood, so it's time you started telling us; *what the hell is going on!*'

CHAPTER TWENTY NINE

Leo And Kate

Gus was relieving himself off the end of the boat, when all of a sudden a shriek and a wobble very nearly made him topple overboard.

'Woah!' he shouted. 'Give me a break!'

Sue was yelling. At first Gus thought she was in trouble but it quickly dawned on him that these were howls of joy. He zipped up and looked under the canopy. Sue was holding her phone, the back-light illuminating her face, tears rolling down her cheeks.

'They're fine,' she said. 'Look!' she handed him the phone.

S + G, wow!!! U did it. So so happy – dancing at UR news! Survived. No idea how! scary + mad – not sure how real. At cottage. Phone works every now n then. Weird stuff happening. Any idea where u r? National catastrophe. SO pleased 4 U!!!! Hugs I, D, A

Gus whistled. 'I knew they'd do it.'

'You did not,' Sue replied, hitting him.

'Course I did. They're tougher than you think, cleverer than you think and a lot madder than you think. Not sure which goes with who, though. Must be a few stories about how they got back. No word on the other message?'

'Nah. They must think I'm cuckoo.' She wiped a tear from her eye. 'Time for sleep, Mr Williams. It's knackering doing nothing.'

Gus looked up at the night sky, which for the first time since they had been at sea showed a wide range of stars occasionally blotted out by a woolly cloud. 'Bit chillier tonight, and windier,' he said. He put his hand out. 'I reckon the wind's changed. Can you button down the other end if I do this one?' He pulled the sail about and jammed it into place. The boat sped forward in perfect union with the wind. He bent down under the canopy and tied off the makeshift end sections.

Then they lay on the planks, shivering a little as he studied the compass on Sue's phone. Set fair, South West.

'I could do with a warm fire,' Sue said, 'wrapped up in my furry onesie watching a good movie.'

'Drinking a cup of hot chocolate,' Gus added, 'with a pile of cream frothing on top.' He sighed as he turned the phone off, noting the two power bars.

'And marshmallows,' Sue added.

Gus wriggled closer. 'Move over. You're the worst bed hog ever—'

'Me?' Sue cried. 'Yeah right! Your snoring keeps the fish awake.'

Gus chuckled. 'At least I don't fart in my sleep!'

She hit him on the chest. 'Don't be vulgar. That smell is the skanky fish guts at the bottom of the boat.'

Gus yawned. 'Oh, sure!'

Sue pulled the two thick dust blankets up and rolled over so they were facing. They'd given up trying to do the lookout – it was simply too cold and for two nights not a light or another boat had been spotted. Their body warmth was a necessary comfort.

In the pitch black, Sue put her arms around Gus and very slowly moved her head towards his. Their noses bumped and a soft snigger came out. A moment later their lips met and this time, now that he'd relaxed, it was a far more pleasant experience. Shortly, Sue broke off and rolled over. 'Night, Gus,' she whispered. 'Hey, and Gus, if we don't make it through the night, thank you. Thank you for everything.'

He groaned.

'Sweet dreams,' she said.

＊

A murmuring came out of Gus' mouth. He rolled one way, then the next, knocking her. Then she heard a noise. Was it Gus, or wind on the canopy?

Sue woke with a start. 'Gus?' she said, listening to the strange noises coming from him. His head rolled one way and then the other. 'Hey, you alright?'

The boat wobbled and pitched. A sense of being terribly small and insignificant, of being a tiny speck of life in a vast ocean, filled her. She reached across him for the torch, her fingers dabbing at the heavy cloth of the dust sheet. As she did so, her hair brushed across his face.

A moment later he sneezed violently, waking himself up. He sat bolt upright.

Sue flicked on the torch. 'You OK?' she said. 'I think you were having a nightmare.' She yawned and rested her head on his chest.

Gus blinked. 'Yeah. Yeah, that's all.' He said, trying to get his bearings.

Sue raised herself up and smiled. 'I think my hair tickled your nose.'

The boat pitched as it rode a larger wave and then rounded the crest and headed down again. For the first time, Sue detected a look of anxiety in Gus' eyes.

The wind thudded into the side canopy as the boat plunged into the next wave, the doffing sound of water colliding with the wooden helm filling their small cabin.

'There's a storm coming,' he said. His blue eyes were now wide open and in place of his usual, happy demeanour with his big toothy smile, he wore a frown.

The boat lurched and spray showered the canopy. 'It could be pretty unpleasant.'

Sue spoke very calmly, trying not to betray her nerves. 'We've had it, haven't we?' she said.

'Oh, I don't know about that,' he said, regaining his bravado. '*The Joan Of* survived the worst storm since Noah, so there's no reason it can't withstand a wee North Sea gale.'

Sue shivered. 'So what you're saying, in Gus-speak, is that we're stuffed.'

Gus took too long to reply. Finally he sighed and smiling boldly said, 'Nah, not really. We beat the odds last time, who says we can't do it again. And anyway, after all we've been through, it'll be a walk in the park.' He shook his legs out, encouraging blood back into his toes and shuffled down the boat. 'I'm going to see what's happening out there, and then we need to batten down the hatches.' He opened up the makeshift canvas door and slipped outside.

Gus' over-confidence simply confirmed her worst suspicions. The boat lurched into a bigger wave and water thudded onto the canopy. Sue grabbed her phone and pressed the power button. The phone display lit up.

Moments later she was tapping away furiously. Her first message was to her entire address book:

SOS. Sue Lowden here with Gus Williams. In small rowing boat in the North sea. Sucked out in storm. Gale coming. No idea where we are. HELP!

Her second was to Isabella. A thought had been niggling away at her.

Me here. Not looking good. G being v brave me less so. Have you found clues? In your house – like pictures. You MUST find them. Sounds mad but think important. If don't speak, love you very much. Sue – n Gus. xxx

Sue noted the bars of the battery sinking to red. One more.

M & D, love you so much. If you get this, I'm stuck out at sea. Don't worry – never been happier. Thanks for all you have done. I love you xxx

*

The Joan Of jolted viciously and Sue, off balance, dropped the phone. It landed in the water at the bottom of the boat with a splash.

Gus put his head back under the canopy, his head soaked. 'Do you want the good news or the bad news?'

'Uh,' Sue said as she picked up her phone.

'I said, good news, or bad news?'

Gus sat on the end of the bench and waited for her response. If he could have seen her face he'd have noticed tears trailing down her cheeks. 'Anyone there?' he asked.

Sue wiped the handset and then her eyes. 'Bad news,' Sue croaked.

Gus smiled his big toothy smile. 'Ace. Right, the bad news is that it's quite a big one.'

'Big what?'

'Bag of bananas, you monkey! Storm! What do you think?'

Sue shivered. 'And the good?'

'Lights! I can see lights!' He was shouting. 'Look … there, can you see it? A lighthouse.'

Sue crawled down the boat and for a moment, as she popped her head out, she caught the blink of a light way off in the distance. Her muscles tensed and her eyes widened. Was it one mile off or ten miles away? 'How far?' she shouted.

'I don't know,' he yelled back. 'I'd get a better idea if the waves weren't so big.'

For the first time now that her eyes had fully adjusted to the murky gloom, she could see the wild seas frothing and chopping nearby. A huge dark wave loomed up. Before she had a chance to move, it broke. She dived inside. The canopy sagged for a moment and then sprang back.

Gus immediately pulled the sail, the umbrella they used as a water holder and other odds and ends into the boat. He secured their food package with a rope, tying it against the bottom of the seat. 'Here,' he said, 'have some.' He threw her a bag of crisps and a water bottle. 'Drink.'

Sue did as she was told.

'Now,' he said, handing her an assortment of chocolates. 'Tuck these in your pockets. Just in case.'

She grabbed them and pushed two into her jeans and another lot into her jacket.

'I'm scared, Gus,' she said.

He grinned back. 'Have no fear, we'll be fine,' he replied as another wave assaulted the canopy. Quick as a flash Gus was bailing water. Sue joined in and for the time being at least, the water in the boat took their mind off the storm.

He lay down, Sue next to him gulping in air. She was shaking. He draped an arm round her. 'Sue, believe me, everything will work out, fine and dandy,' he said softly.

She trembled. Gus knew it wasn't from the cold. He needed her to be strong. 'Look, it's like at the end of the film, *Titanic*,' he said. 'Remember? When Leonardo DiCaprio holds Kate and they're in the freezing cold water but they keep going until they get rescued—'

'*But HE dies*,' Sue shot back.

'Yeah, but he kept her alive, somehow, right to the bitter end. And you know what, I'm going to keep you alive too. Anyway, in our version, it isn't that cold, we're very close to land and you've put out an SOS – haven't you?' He held her harder and turned to her, his eyes wide. 'You have, haven't you?'

'Yes.'

'Good,' he said. 'So there you go, it's tons easier. And we're not in a hulking great boat in the middle of the North Atlantic, we're in a tiny rowing boat, somewhere off the coast of … somewhere. So safety is pretty much guaranteed. It's a piece of cake. And, there's another thing,' he said, his grin returning, 'you're way prettier than Leo's Kate.' He kissed her forehead.

Sue snuggled into his chest as the boat groaned under the thrust of a wave which bashed the boat first one way and then the other. It lurched wretchedly, like a ride at the fair, and she felt they might suddenly tip over.

A horrible sickness swept through her.

Gus' eyes sparkled and then he started laughing. He got up and stumbled to the end of the boat, grabbed the large container that was filled with fresh water, took a deep swig and filled up his water bottle. He turned. 'You want some?'

Sue hardly dared move but she reckoned a bit of water might make her feel less queasy. She nodded and slid along the bench not daring for a minute to let go. Sue gulped at the water, instantly regretting it. Her stomach churned.

Gus tied the rope around his wrist, pulling the plastic barrel after him. Then he pushed the barrel out and began pouring the water out into the sea.

'What the hell are you doing?' Sue screamed.

'Buoyancy aid,' he grinned. 'If we go down, and of course it's a massive "if", it would be a shame if we were to drown.'

'But we need water, Gus!'

'We've got enough,' he shrugged and tapped the water bottle as a wave threw him against the canopy. His grin grew and his eyes shone.

'We'll freeze!'

'Nah! Course we won't.'

A roller smashed the canopy and Sue cowered down, trembling.

Gus stumbled over. 'The fact is,' he said, 'we're near the coast. I can sense it. So either it's a short swim, or *The Joan Of* gets wrecked, and a boat comes along and picks us up – or a helicopter – wouldn't that be cool?'

'No, it would not be!'

'Aw, come on, liven up a bit. We're on the verge of getting out of the boat.'

'You're insane, Gus Williams. Totally bloody bonkers.'

Gus mocked a pained look.

Sue thumped him on the arm. 'OK – utterly gorgeous, but still bloody bonkers,' she added.

Gus tied a section of wood onto the handle of the barrel with some rope and settled into his construction mode.

Sue watched, admiring his speed and concentration.

'Oh God, I'm going to be sick,' she said her hand moving to her mouth. Holding tightly onto the seat and using the rocking motion of the boat she slipped towards the canopy entrance. As she leaned out a wave smashed her in the face. She reeled and put her head back in and shrieked, shaking the water out of her hair.

Gus laughed.

'Oh shut up,' she said as she put her head back outside and let fly. Her body felt green and deathly. When she opened her eyes, she tried to figure out what she was staring at. A large black towering hulk right in front of her. And then it was lost behind a wall of water. Was it a boat, a cliff or something else?

She scrambled in as Gus was tying the other end of the plank onto one of the buoyancy containers. 'What is it?' she said.

'What's what?'

'The big – sodding great thing – out there.'

Gus smiled. 'Cliffs, probably.'

'Cliffs? Is that good or bad?' her attention turned to his contraption. 'What are you doing?'

Gus' eyes sparkled in the torchlight. 'This, my little vomit comet, is our life raft.'

'That!'

Gus looked taken aback. 'Yeah. It's brilliant. You got any better ideas?' His eyes darted to the bottom of the boat where, for the first time, she noted there was a considerable body of water swishing around.

'Bail!' she cried. 'We've taken on too much water.' Immediately Sue reached for the bailing bucket, her arms flailing in the darkness. She found it but as she bent to scoop she was thrown to the other side of the vessel. A strong hand pulled her up. Gus looked deep into her eyes.

'Sue. The boat is leaking. There must be a small hole somewhere. No amount of bailing can save *The Joan Of.* Not now, not in this.'

After all they'd been through, she could hardly believe it. 'So we're going to sink?'

Gus pushed on the torch. 'Nah,' he said shining the torch in his face in a mock spooky way. 'This is the part where we disembark. You just have to hold on, you understand? Do exactly as I say.'

Sue summoned her strength and nodded through her tears.

'So now you're Kate, like in *Titanic,* and I'm Leo.' He kissed her. 'OK? Whatever you do, don't let go. Promise me you won't let go.'

Sue threw herself at him and hugged him tight. Somehow, deep down she trusted him with her whole soul. If Gus said they'd survive, they would. Everything else had worked. Why not this?

Gus noted the water up to the knees of his trousers. He slipped out of their embrace, opened his penknife and thrust it through the canvass, the blade ripping the canopy in a neat line.

In no time the full force of the gale was upon them, blowing hard, the vessel filling with water. In the dim light they could see into the night beyond. On one side loomed a cliff and on the other ... a boat. Sue's heart soared. Did the boat even know they were there?

She turned to Gus. 'Look!'

He turned back, his face bursting with a smile and his eyes dancing like little stars in the dull night sky. 'Hold on, my Kate,' he said. 'That's all you've got to do.'

Sue smiled back. She'd hold on for Gus this day and every day henceforth.

And before she had the chance to dwell on it, a huge wave engulfed *The Joan Of.*

Gus' big toothy smile was the last thing she remembered as her world was churned upside down and inside out.

CHAPTER THIRTY

Stuck For Eternity

She heard the noise while they were playing a game she had made up many centuries ago. The game centred on a bundle of cobweb silks the size of small peas: on the poke of a leg, she made a faint clap of her old hands or a wheezy cough, and on that signal, the little dreamspinners flicked mini balls of spider web silks towards each other's magholes. If they succeeded, a small puff of smoke burst out on a very surprised little dreamspinner. So the best effect was when a multitude of pellets exploded on one maghole and as such a sophisticated game of sending secret messages about ganging-up on one another had begun.

Smaller dreamspinners never tired of this simple amusement. The powdered remains were shared out and re-manipulated into balls by the baby creatures and the game continued until fatigue overtook them or the spider web bundles ran out or an elder dreamspinner told them to quieten down.

After the Great Closing of Eden the dreamspinners discovered the Ancient Woman in the small rooms below the vast storage area of spider web dream powders. Her eyes had been gouged out and she could never leave. She was part of their family now and they looked after her with food and water as she required.

She was immortal, and the dreamspinners knew she would never die, so this nourishment prevented her body withering away to nothing. But many long years of solitude had left her physically wretched. Her skeletal

243

frame was overhung with her own coarse over-sized skin, her bony skull had but a few wisps of hair, her empty eye sockets hollow like dark holes and the nails on her fingers long and curling like spiders' legs.

To the Ancient Woman, the dreamspinners appeared in her mind as clever, shy, solitary creatures concerned only with making and giving dreams. As the trust between them grew, and as a great passage of time crept by, she understood the immense influence of these strange, unknown dream-giving spiders. And slowly she learnt about dreams.

She discovered how dreamspinners blended old and new spider web silks into all sorts of powerful and exotic concoctions. She was amazed to learn that these strange creatures had no interest in manipulating their power and begged them to allow her to try out new dream powder combinations in order to understand what effects they might have.

Much later, she manipulated their dream powders to give herself dreams that lasted for days, dreams where she could lose herself, free her imagination to wander and forget the perpetual darkness, the anguish and her desperate boredom. In this state she could fall in love again, dance in the fields of the Garden of Eden once more, ride the giant horses on the glorious pink Tomberlacker Plains, talk to her children … kiss them, hug them and teach them all the things she knew … and do it again and again.

And she did, until her heart ached like a balloon at bursting point.

In the Atrium of The Garden of Eden, the dreamspinners provided her with a degree of comfort from the solitude and darkness, while she waited and waited for the arrival of the Heirs of Eden. Yet ever at the back of her mind was the knowledge that if Eden was to open, she would never see its beauty and splendour.

She heard it again. A sound from the outside; a sound that had haunted her for thousands of years. She listened harder.

The gentle thuds both thrilled her and injected her with unimaginable dread. Someone or something walked in the dust in the great chamber above.

Her mind sparked into life. Instantly, she pulled her tiny, bony frame off the ground and made her way up the curving staircase. Her body, so ancient and pathetic, made it hard for her to move. With every step her wasted muscles screamed out in pain. She forced herself on, her heart pumping furiously, energy flowing through each and every vein as she diligently struggled up the worn treads.

At about the halfway mark, she paused for breath, exhausted. All she could hear was her thumping heart and the rasping sound of air trying to squeeze into her withered lungs.

After recovering her poise, she listened again. Yes, she could quite clearly hear footsteps walking in the Atrium.

An Heir of Eden, perhaps? But why only one? Had they failed already?

She urged herself on, each step more painful than the last. At the top she felt for the wooden cane. With this she could guide herself into her half of the great chamber. She leant hard on her stick, her body begging for a rest. She shuffled a few paces and stopped to listen, her lungs wheezing like wind through dry leaves. She sensed the person moving away.

'Come on! MOVE legs, MOVE body,' she cackled.

Then she heard a sound she hadn't expected. A loud—

CRACK!

The stick, which had supported her for so long, gave way beneath her snapping clean in two. The old woman landed awkwardly. A strange pain ricocheted through her body.

She ran a hand down her leg. She felt something sharp and fragmented. It wasn't the stick, it was her thighbone – a shattered piece that had speared through her flesh.

When her brain realised the extent of the injury, pain coursed through her and she screamed in agony.

Moments later, as she regained consciousness, she heard another sound so haunting that it chilled her to the core. It was the unmistakable noise of a giant whirring fan, a sound she had often heard before she was abandoned; a noise that had troubled, haunted and eluded her ever since – the distinct whirr of the Great Door for those *leaving* the Garden of Eden.

Her wails that followed spoke of utter misery; of agony on a totally different scale and intensity. 'When will this wretchedness ... this cruelty end?' she cried out to the empty cavern. 'Finish this. End this. PLEASE ... please,' she implored. Her sobs trailed off unheard along the empty tunnels. 'Haven't I suffered enough?'

Lying at the top of the stairs, thoughts tumbled back. She recalled how her family had been so happy in the Garden of Eden before the punishment of immortality. She remembered their love, and, although she hadn't minded it at first, the emptiness she felt after Cain, Abel and Seth had flown the nest, left her with a sadness that grew like a cancer.

The memory of Cain's betrayal, his alliance with the serpent, his ever increasing lust for power and his embracing of darkness made her shudder as did the shock of her capture and torture and the agony of losing her eyes. She thought of the chaos and muddle when Eden closed and the magic that had vanished.

And all that was left was cold, desperate endless emptiness.

WHY DID I DO IT?

Why had she offered herself as the ultimate sacrifice? Possibly because there was no alternative. Probably because it put an end to the conflict.

In the end, though, she had spent a life in purgatory so that one day there might be a fresh start for life in a new Garden of Eden.

While she mulled over these thoughts, several dreamspinners bound her leg with tough dreamspinner silks and gave her dream powders to soothe the pain. Soon she knew she would spiral off into a comforting dream. The dreamspinners would take good care of her – even if her injured leg made movement impossible.

She realised that if Eden could not be woken, she would be stuck in the Atrium forever, disappearing into dust, her heart the last organ to survive in this empty world.

As she drifted off, a curious feeling of hope washed over her: whoever had worked out how to get in to the Atrium of The Garden of Eden had discovered how to get out. No one had done this since the Great Closing.

Calm swept through her like a gentle breeze. The person who came – and went – must possess, she thought, truly great qualities, magical qualities that would solve the riddles to opening the Garden of Eden. Perhaps he or she would return with the other Heirs of Eden? From the depths of her heart she felt convinced of this.

Next time, she would be better prepared and ready for them. And it wouldn't be long, she was sure of it.

Her heart began to glow like an orb of fire within her, blood pumping around her veins like molten lava.

Her brain filled with a new kind of energy that brimmed with confidence, hope and desire. It was a sensation she hadn't felt in eons.

Maybe, she hoped, her sacrifice will not have been in vain.

Perhaps my story will be told after all.

CHAPTER THIRTY ONE

Unanswered Questions

Mrs Pye followed Old Man Wood into the kitchen and quickly sensed there was an 'atmosphere'. In no time she'd delved into her fridge and larder but her heart was heavy and her movements pained and sluggish.

Archie noticed it first. 'Mrs P, did you watch the speech?' he asked.

Mrs Pye snivelled. 'Aye. Worrying, I reckon,' she sniffed, pulled out a white handkerchief and dabbed her eyes. 'It's … it's that poor boy I feel for. Makes me come over all strange every time I see him, everyone waiting for him to wake up.'

Archie went in for a big hug and was rewarded by a squashing from Mrs Pye's ample bosom. 'Thing is, Mrs P,' he said as he resurfaced, 'we think that boy might be my friend Kemp. What do you think?'

Mrs Pye released him and rubbed her eyes again. 'Well now, that be something.'

'It's amazing if it is,' Archie continued, 'I can't believe it. Can you? I thought he'd be dead, like all the others.'

She burst into tears.

'Oh, heck, I'm sorry,' Archie said. 'I didn't mean to upset you.'

'Never you mind,' she said wiping her tears on her sleeve. 'Every time I see his dear little face I get an upsetting feeling in me bones, that's all.' She dusted herself off and pulled herself as upright as possible. 'I think,' she declared, 'that a special Mrs Pye sandwich is what you lot need tonight, followed by a slice of starlight apple crumble. Might have one myself too, you know – help get over this terribleness.'

And in no time, as she always did, Mrs Pye shooed everyone out of the kitchen. 'Come back in fourteen,' she said as she ushered them out of the door, and the children dispersed to different parts of the house.

*

Mrs Pye took her meal over the road, for she was too upset to see anyone. The three children and Old Man Wood ate their MPS sandwiches – pronounced *emps* – in virtual silence, aside from an occasional slurp or clatter of cutlery. An MPS was the abbreviation for "Mrs Pye Special". It was a slice of French bread with layers of melted cheese, ham, tomato, and crowned with a poached egg. Mrs Pye insisted that it was washed down with Old Man Wood's apple juice, which the old man had spent a lifetime perfecting, and which contained no less than nine different varieties from his very old and very gnarled apple orchard. He pressed his apples every year always using the same, precise quantities of each apple variety.

Old Man Wood probably knew more about apples than anyone. He had a selection of twenty-seven ancient and highly prized apple trees in his orchard. Each variety was different and each tree bore fruit for a multitude of ailments and purposes: there were apples for headaches, apples for indigestion and other medicinal matters, apples for confidence, apples for energy, apples that were thought provoking and then there were apples that made the mind sharp or made it wander. Old Man Wood was besotted by apples.

When they had finished, a sense of calm filled the room. Archie, after licking his plate, broke the silence, 'So, Daisy, what did happen to you yesterday that makes you certain this involves us and us alone?'

Daisy took a deep breath, closed her eyes and began to tell her story. As she spoke, she tried to catch their eyes, but whenever she did, both her siblings stared at the table.

'It was huge,' she said, 'like ten Wembley Football Stadiums wide and, well, I couldn't even see the top. It just went on and on forever. In the middle I saw a tree with no leaves and smothered in dust. So thinking I might be dead I walked off, only to tread on a skeleton … and the bones crunched under my feet as if I'd trodden on a pile of sticks,' she said, trying and failing not to laugh. 'Poor thing must have been there for years. Moments later I heard this truly terrible noise piercing my eardrums. I panicked and ran round trying to find a way out. All around the edges were tunnels, thousands of them, some big, some small, but they were all blocked up. I ran and ran until I found a gateway with a couple of pictures on. I realised I'd seen the gate before – from my dreams, I think – and I figured that all I had to do was believe I could walk through it.' She stopped and tried to gauge the reactions of her brother and sister.

Isabella, Archie and Old Man Wood stared at her in complete silence.

'So that's what I did,' Daisy croaked. 'I simply walked through it and found myself in a wet ditch. And here I am.'

Old Man Wood turned on her. 'Daisy, you are a right daft fool!' he said, the colour draining from his face. 'What on earth do you think you were doing?'

The children looked at Old Man Wood, astonished. He had never, ever raised his voice at any of them. He was clearly as startled as they were, if not more so.

There was an awkward silence.

'Er … well, it was very exciting,' Daisy replied trying not to burst into tears. 'I rushed straight back and found this shocking news about Kemp and the plague …'

'Daisy, don't you get it?' Old Man Wood interrupted, and he moved round to her side putting an arm gently round her shoulders. 'You see, that person never saw the motif. He never worked out the way home. He died a horrible death all alone. That could have been you, my littlun. You're not ready for that, yet.'

'But I saw the clues,' she argued, feeling a bit confused, 'and it was easy, so parts of my dreams are true aren't they, so I know it really exists … doesn't it? It all adds up.'

*

For once, Isabella was quite moved. 'Right!' Isabella said. 'I think we need answers. Home from *where*, Old Man Wood? And how do you know it was a *he* who died?' she demanded.

Old Man Wood looked rattled. 'Oh, apples! I can't remember,' he answered, his face scrunched up and his deep wrinkles more pronounced than usual.

Isabella eyed him suspiciously and turned to her sister. 'Look, Daisy, first off, I owe you an apology.' She met her sister's eye and sighed. 'There are some strange wooden panels on the end of Old Man Wood's bed that follow our movements, like TV security monitors, I'll show them to you later. That's how I knew you'd disappeared.'

'Uh, really?'

'Yes. And I absolutely promise you I'm not joking,' she said and turned to Old Man Wood who waved a hand in acknowledgement.

'That's how I saw you sucked into the ground and when you didn't return, I ran off looking for you. And I'm sorry I yelled at you earlier, but there is a part of me that simply will not accept that these strange goings on are in any way real. Do you understand me?'

Daisy nodded as Isabella continued. 'Part of me cannot and will not believe all these peculiar things that are happening. That's me, Daisy. It's how I'm made and there's nothing you or Arch can do about it,' she said. 'My whole life has been built around reason and fact, cause and effect, and it's very difficult for me to see anything else.' She smiled at Daisy, noting her disappointment. 'But if we're to explore your fantasies, then so be it.'

Daisy half smiled.

Isabella turned abruptly to Old Man Wood. 'Right, here goes. First off, Old Man Wood, we need answers because otherwise we're going to end up in a lunatic asylum and you will be the first one in.' She tapped the table with her fingertips. 'What is the story of your bed, are the images in the cave anything to do with us, and why did Sue insist the rain is *all our fault*? We need explanations, we need answers and we need them now!'

The children gazed at the gnarled old face expecting a spectacular response. But all Old Man Wood said was:

'Mmm … perhaps. Oh dear, my little favourites.'

'Old Man Wood, this is not helping.'

'The bed is a bit of a mystery,' he said. 'But perhaps it's time we found the riddles.'

'*Riddles! WHAT riddles?*' chorused the children.

'The riddles to finding the Tablets of Eden.'

'Like the ones Sue was yelling at us about?' Archie said. 'And the pictures in the cave?'

'Hmmm.'

'So this plague *is* something to do with us?' Daisy said, her eyes glowing like lasers.

'Well, now,' the old man said, staring at the floor, 'it's been an awful long time.' He opened his eyes wide, as if attempting to welcome the world into his mind. 'That's the problem, my dear littluns.' And he rapped his knuckles on his head. 'There's nothing in here anymore. I just don't remember.'

*

The problem, as Old Man Wood kept telling the children, was that he really had forgotten everything.

There was nothing in his old grey cells but an empty void. But he knew he had to try, so he pulled himself together and, with Archie and Daisy in tow, headed upstairs to his room and began searching the large assortment of carvings hoping that something – anything – might jolt his memory.

The willow trees had told him that he himself had hidden the tablets a long time ago using complex magic. More importantly, he discovered that the tablets were a link to the rain and that the children were the Heirs of Eden, as he suspected.

But because the trees made the process sound so obvious and straightforward, he hadn't deepened his questioning and now he regretted it. He wondered if he shouldn't go back and talk to them again. But doing that meant he would have to think of the right questions and he didn't know what those questions were.

In due course, he announced to the disappointed faces of Archie and Daisy, who had followed his every move, that he simply couldn't find the riddles.

And with this, he looked at the time, ordered the children to go directly to bed, dropped his shoulders and headed outside to check up on the cattle.

*

Isabella, fast asleep in the attic room, stirred. She rubbed her eyes and found herself staring at the old man.

'Wake up, wake up,' he whispered.

'Whososse that?' Isabella groaned.

254

'It's Old Man Wood, my dear,' he replied, as softly as his coarse, deep voice would allow. 'I need to talk. Come downstairs, if you don't mind.'

Isabella slipped into her dressing gown and stumbled downstairs to the living room. A steaming mug of hot chocolate was waiting for her.

They sat alone, comforted by the gentle crackle of the fire and the pitter-pattering sounds of rain on the roof tiles. Old Man Wood's face looked pained, his deep wrinkles prominent in the firelight.

'What's up, Old Man Wood?' Isabella asked. She figured she'd better come clean about finding the panels on his bed. 'Old Man Wood, um, I've got a confession to make …'

'I know. I know all about your little … discovery.' He glanced up catching her eye, reassuring her. 'To be honest, I don't know how it works myself. But it's how I found you on that ledge in the storm when you were coming back home after the football match.' Old Man Wood scratched his chin and took a gulp of hot chocolate. 'Strange things, Bella … are going on. I know you're worrying yourselves stupid about it but I'm sure all will be revealed soon.'

'But it's so confusing,' Isabella said. 'I don't know what to do – or what to believe any more. What's happening to us, Old Man Wood?'

'My dear child. You are like a blade of grass. One of many, un-trodden, fresh, pure. Hmmm. So pretty, neat and clever—'

'Stop humming, and talking in riddles and tell me, WHAT is going on?'

'Things not so clear, eh. Rain. Endless … dreams … troubles? Have you all been … dreaming?'

'Yes, you know we have,' she replied. 'Unbelievably vivid ones if you must know.'

'About an old woman?' Old Man Wood quizzed.

'Yes,' Isabella began. 'How did you know?' He didn't respond. 'Look, what exactly is all this about, Old Man Wood? You know, don't you?' She let the question hang and blew on her hot chocolate. 'I think we're going crazy even if the others don't. I'm not convinced anything is real anymore. And anyway, where have you been? Archie told me you'd been talking to trees. What good is that?'

Old Man Wood harrumphed.

She continued. 'Without Mum and Dad here, we could really have done with your support. It was unfair and frankly selfish of you to abandon us.'

Isabella felt slightly foolish for letting it all spill out and an awkward silence hung in the air.

Old Man Wood's furrowed brow seemed even deeper than usual. 'Let me try and explain a little bit ... Right, well, where to begin ...' he mumbled. He hadn't expected her mini-outburst and his brain worked so slowly that he was unable to think of a response.

'Have you had them too?' Isabella asked.

'Had what, littlun?'

'Well, a dream, like ours!'

'Oh yes! Many, many wonderful, strange and exciting dreams. Some sad, some terrifying, some exhilarating and some of well ... of nothingness. Those are the worst dreams of all. Quite often I dream that I'm king of the most beautiful place you can imagine with a beautiful queen. These are fine dreams, young'un. Then again once I was swallowed up by a large, terrifying white spider with electric lightning bolts coming out of its middle.' He laughed and his whole face lit up with his kindly character. 'You know, little Isabella, dreams show you the things you desire or fear most in this strange life. They help you make choices.'

'But these weren't like MOST dreams, Old Man Wood, they were real. I've never felt anything like it.' Isabella's eyes lit up like candles. 'There were dreams where I felt passion swelling in my chest like never before. I tasted tears of despair and joy. I saw terrifying scenes and odd creatures, conflicting emotions … more. And, all condensed into small flashes.' She sat back and ran her fingers though her hair.

'You know, Old Man Wood, I could even feel my blood rushing through me, which was so wonderful … but totally alien. And there's so much I can't remember – you know how it's all there, and then not there. And do you know the strangest thing,' Old Man Wood raised his eyebrows, encouraging her. 'I even had a dream about stuffing myself with banoffee pie!'

Old Man Wood chuckled and pushed a log farther into the fire. In a low voice, just louder than a whisper, he spoke, his rich tones resonating in the dark room. 'Look into the fire, Isabella. Tell me, what do you see?'

Isabella stared for a minute at the flickering flames as they danced out into the room.

'Nothing … burning wood, I'm afraid. Why, is there something I should see?'

'Perhaps,' said the old man sighing deeply, 'but maybe not tonight.' He uncoiled his large frame as he extracted himself from the armchair, yawned and stretched his arms out wide. 'You know, Isabella, I believe you may have been given those dreams—'

'Given them? Oh Lordy, not you as well—'

'Oh yes, Isabella. You need to pay them due attention, young lady.' He yawned. 'The universe isn't as black and white as you think it is. In the morning all will be clearer, but right now best if we both get some sleep.'

He followed Isabella up the stairs to the children's attic where he straightened Archie in his bed and rearranged Daisy in hers.

Old Man Wood made his way back to his room, sat on his bed and looked around at all the curious wooden panels. There, on the screens at the foot of his bed, were the children, fast asleep, their eyes shut tight. Old Man Wood ran his hand over the old wooden carvings and as he did they seemed to move and whisper and he felt twinges of familiarity that made his skin prickle.

He lay down, tired and worried. How on earth could he explain what was going on, and get the children to believe him, when he couldn't recall anything himself?

But the thing that concerned him the most, was that the willows had told him there was very little time.

Something about seven days. Seven days to find these tablets? Was that it? If so, time was running out fast.

CHAPTER THIRTY TWO

New Powders, New Dreams

That night, no one in Eden Cottage dreamt.

Gaia, the dreamspinner, knew Asgard had opened up a new source of spider web powders in Havilah. She was well aware that dreamspinners were flocking there. But she wanted nothing to do with these new powders.

She made sure that the dreamspinners she oversaw produced simple staple dreams from the spider web powders made from the spider webs on Earth.

Her band of dreamspinners appeared disappointed, for the vibrations coming back indicated that these dreams weren't as bad as the nightmares Havilah normally produced. But how could they know, Gaia thought, and she insisted that her dreamspinners worked faster, giving dreams to as many people as they could.

She suspected Cain was behind this new dream powder source and anything involving him spelt trouble.

*

Prime Minister Kingsford climbed into bed. His limbs were tired and his mind fizzed with information. He studied the clock. Three in the morning. Damn. He was up at six and three hours sleep was not nearly enough. He needed to be on top form tomorrow. His head hit the pillow hard as he toyed with the huge death toll of storm and plague victims. He tried to put it out of his mind and thought of his family holiday in the sun as he fell asleep, the images of feet splashing in calm, clear Mediterranean waters.

*

A short while later a dreamspinner hovered invisibly above the Prime Minister, its long opaque legs anchored beside the man's face. The dreamspinner extracted tiny powders from its maghole and filtered a dream which the man sucked in with long, slow breaths.

The dreamspinner wondered how this human would react to her new dream powder. She'd been told that this spider web powder was from the webs of a recently discovered arachnid found deep in the caves beneath the mountains in Havilah. And these powders gave dreams not too dissimilar to those of the Garden of Eden; stimulating and enriching, with a twist – an extraordinary twist – Asgard had claimed.

It was a pity that the spider web powders from the Atrium in the Garden of Eden had ended. She had loved these dreams, knowing what joy they'd give. Perhaps these powders would do the same. At least the dreamspinners had a decent dream to give – and the excitement had been catching on everywhere. In milliseconds she was by their child, and when she'd given the little boy a dream she sensed a dog sleeping. She checked her powder stock and there was easily enough for at least a thousand dreamers, including the canine. This dream powder stretched a long way.

She inverted herself back to the man, to see if his dream had begun.

He groaned and turned in his sleep. Then he laughed. Now he flailed his arms.

Excellent, thought the dreamspinner. Their dreams are rich, just as Asgard said they would be.

She checked the vibrations of life in the area and flicked her legs time and time again, giving dreams until her dream powders ran dry.

She'd missed several out, their sleeping patterns too erratic or their sleep too shallow or where a dream had already been given. She would return in the next few nights, but right now her stocks needed replenishing, from Havilah, not the Garden of Eden.

As the Earth rotated on its axis, as each country slipped into darkness, she would begin afresh on the other side of the world.

CHAPTER THIRTY THREE

Clues

Isabella sat in bed, running through her conversation with Old Man Wood the previous night. Her phone bleeped and she read it and re-read it before rushing downstairs. She found Daisy and Archie curled up on the sofa in front of the fire.

'Look! Another message from Sue. What do you think?' She handed Archie her phone.

He read it out loud:

Gus total hero. Now lost at sea. Have put out SOS. Supplies OK for few days. Boat holding together, just. Fish vile, but is food. U saw Kemp on TV? G saw K acting weird b4 storm with old man. Dunno how u "stop it" but stone tablets = v good, I think. Clues in pictures? Hurry. Phone dodgy. Hope near coast. Love u all S xxx

Archie's heart skipped a beat; *Kemp acting weird with old man.* That had to be Cain. So maybe he had joined …

Daisy interrupted his thoughts. 'So Sue thinks the clues are in the pictures.'

Archie read the text again. *Clues in pictures?* There's not a great deal to go on. Do you think she means in the actual image of the picture itself – or within the frame of the picture, like a piece of paper stuck behind it?'

Daisy shrugged. 'I guess we'll need to study every picture in the house. Come on, winkle, no time to lose.'

Isabella stepped in front of her. 'If you're going to do this, do it properly. You need a process. If there's no method it'll be chaos.'

'So you're in?' Archie said.

'Only because I've got nothing better to do,' she replied. 'If you really think there's something in this madness, I might as well organise you.'

'Great, thanks, Bells.'

'I'll do upstairs and you two do downstairs.' Isabella ordered. 'Bring all the pictures into the sitting room and line them around the walls starting from the door and working round the room. I'll go the other way. Then at least I can catalogue them and return them to their correct position later.'

Archie and Daisy hared off and before long an amazing assortment of oil paintings and watercolours lined the walls of the sitting room. Isabella flew around upstairs and emerged with several older-looking canvases and more importantly, they thought, antique-looking oil paintings on wood. They were so old the paint had cracked like a mosaic.

'Look,' Isabella said, 'I found them in the spare room.' She studied the paintings. 'These ones *must* have a secret message on them. Old Man Wood ... over here! Do these trigger *anything?*'

Together they leaned over them, trying to see if there were a series of scratches or markings that might be clues, or if the backs had writing on them.

Archie suggested that secrets were often added by invisible ink. He'd read stories where clues had been written in milk and that heat would show the markings. He tried his theory by placing the flame of a candle close to the canvas of a landscape oil painting. The others looked on in anticipation. All of a sudden Archie noticed a plume of smoke as the landscape burst in flames.

Archie squealed but Isabella reacted fast, grabbed the painting, tore outside and threw it in a puddle.

'Thanks, Bells,' red-faced Archie said. 'I'm not sure we need to do that again.'

*

The majority of the paintings were ancestors who bore an uncanny resemblance, Daisy thought, to a slightly younger Old Man Wood. The rest were landscapes or seascapes.

For over an hour they studied the pictures. Isabella decided that they ought to be moved into groups: pictures with water and pictures with trees in that corner, abstract pictures in another, still life oils on the sofa, portraits with people near the window and those with animals on the adjacent wall. But even when they'd studied them twice, there wasn't a single distinctive element that they recognised from their dreams.

'What about the carvings in Old Man Wood's room?' Archie said, his voice betraying his frustration. 'Would you mind if we have a look? You know, a fresh pair of eyes.'

'Be my guests,' said Old Man Wood, and as a group they headed up to his room.

'Look!' Archie said jumping on the bed. 'The screens! We're still on them.'

It was the first time the twins had seen themselves on the curious panels.

'How very cool,' Daisy said as she pouted and tossed her hair. 'They are awesome.' She watched Archie admiring his spikes.

'Basically, we've got our own TV channel, ,' Daisy said. 'I wonder if we can record stuff?'

'Oh, grow up,' Isabella scolded. 'Stop admiring yourselves and check if there's something in here. Daisy, you start over there.'

The twins slipped reluctantly off the bed and started to inspect the carved panelling. But although the gnarled wood and odd-looking animals and curious faces were intriguing they once again came up with nothing.

Isabella slumped to the floor. 'This is ridiculous. How can we find what we're looking for, when we don't have even a single clue?'

'I bet you,' Daisy said as she scratched the carpet with her fingernails, 'whatever we're looking for will be right under our bums.'

'The expression,' Isabella sighed, *'is right under your nose* – not your bottom.'

'You,' Archie said, his dark eyes sparkling mischievously at Daisy, 'should know that, 'cos you're such an big arse!'

'Hilarious,' Daisy replied screwing a face at him.

'Come on kiddoes. No good hanging round here,' Isabella said and she began to usher them out of the door.

But as Archie scoured the room one last time, something caught his eye. 'You know what,' he said, 'Maybe Daisy has a point. Look!' He pointed at the floor.

'Where, what do you mean?' Isabella said.

'There. The rugs.'

'Rugs?'

'Yeah … look at them. They're old patterned ones, Persian or something, aren't they, Old Man Wood?'

The old man squinted at them, a look of surprise on his face.

'So what,' Isabella scoffed. 'We're looking for a picture not an old mangy carpet.'

Archie reddened a little. 'But look carefully,' Archie said kneeling down where they'd been sitting. 'There are marks on them. They might be part of an old picture. We shouldn't write them off just because they're not on a wall.'

Isabella sighed. 'Those marks are probably stains, right, Old Man Wood?'

Old Man Wood shrugged and turned for the door.

*

But now it was Daisy's turn to stare at the rugs. 'Archie's right. Surely it's worth a look, isn't it, Bells?'

Isabella tutted. 'They're filthy – they probably haven't been washed for—'

'Ooh, I say,' Daisy said. 'There's something on this one,' she scanned it further, 'and this one's got a kind of tree in the middle … wow, maybe you're right, Arch. What if *these* are the pictures?'

'Oh for goodness' sakes. Fat chance,' Isabella said. 'You know as well as I do that those marks are years of ground-in mud and grime.'

Daisy picked up one of the rugs and draped it over the end of the bed. Archie copied her and in no time, the five little rugs were folded over the end of the wooden bed-end.

The children stood back only to find themselves admiring five grey-brown mats. But the faintest outline of a pattern where Daisy had been picking the fibres with her fingernails had begun to show.

'They're disgusting little things,' Isabella declared.

'I'm not so sure,' Archie piped up. 'But I do know that the best way to clean a rug is to give it a massive whack.' He grabbed one, threw it over his shoulder and slung it down hard on the bed end.

A plume of dust exploded, filling the room. They ran for the door, coughing and spluttering.

'Genius,' Isabella said scathingly and she smacked Archie on top of his head. Much to her surprise and irritation a hair spike shot through the hole in her hand.

266

'This is quite ridiculous,' she said ignoring Daisy's laughter as she struggled to extract her hand. 'Oh do stop it,' she said, turning on her. 'Come on, guys. Isn't this a little bit desperate? I mean we haven't even analysed all the picture frames yet.'

Isabella shook out her hand and found her hand-hole shrinking back to its original size. 'Sometimes you two really don't possess a single particle of intelligence. We clearly need to look harder.'

Old Man Wood gathered the five little rugs. 'I'll beat them outside and hang them out on the line. These little things could do with a freshen up,' he said. 'With any luck, the dirt will wash out naturally.'

*

A little while later, Mrs Pye waddled across the courtyard, her feet splashing in the puddles. She hummed to herself and then stopped and stared at the washing line. Five rugs hung like wet towels, muddy water dripping from each one. Had she forgotten them?

She racked her brain. She was sure she'd brought them in a while back, dried them and replaced them on Old Man Wood's floor. She tutted to herself and bustled over, removed them at arm's length and placed them in a washing basket. She couldn't imagine the old man suddenly wanting to clean them, so had one of the children…? But those children weren't exactly forthcoming in the laundry department.

Before long, she found herself scrubbing each rug in the old stone sink in the washhouse. She was amazed at the steady flow of filthy dark water coming out, but realising the time, and without really giving it too much thought now that the generator was on, she gave up and threw all five rugs in the washing machine.

Mrs Pye had never seen a material quite so light and so tough, and yet so extraordinarily filthy.

When the wash came to its juddering conclusion, she hung the little rugs out to dry in two neat rows on the Sheila's maid above the range in the kitchen.

Mrs Pye was delighted with their spectacular colour. Each rug shone radiantly and felt soft and clean. She smacked her hands together in a moment of washing triumph and feeling rather pleased with herself, picked up her bag and returned to her flat across the courtyard.

*

A few hours later, the children were in front of the fire surrounded by piles of pictures that seemed to cover almost every square inch of floor. They'd inspected the antique ones over and over again to see if a message had been left on the back or if there was mystical writing or indeed if it simply rang a bell inside their heads.

'This is hopeless,' Archie said as he stroked a stiff hair spike. 'We still don't have a clue what we're looking for and we've been at this for hours.' He picked up a modern landscape painting which had hung in their parents' bedroom. As he studied it, a sudden yearning to see them went through him and his heart stretched like the strings on a bow until his eyes watered.

'I love this picture,' he said quietly to Old Man Wood. 'A house set by a vineyard, the sun going down. A distant fire, the colours of the vines. Somehow,' he said, 'it reminds me of Mum – lovely, calm and pretty, just like her.' His bottom lip quivered. 'And what I'd do for some sunshine right now.' He sniffed and shut his eyes. 'Do you know where they bought it?'

'Hmmm,' Old Man Wood said, placing a comforting hand on Archie's shoulder. 'I'm certain that it came back from a holiday some years ago,' he said softly. 'It won't be long before they're back.'

Archie turned it round so he was now looking at the back. There, much to his surprise, he found a picture postcard stuck with tape to the top and bottom corners. The picture showed a deep, crimson-red rose set on a white background. That was all. Archie gently removed the tape and turned it over.

A typical red rose from the vineyards of Tuscany, was the description, and below it, in his mother's neat handwriting, was the following:

My darling,
I want you to know that we love you very much, and our hearts and dreams will always be with you.
Best of luck, whichever direction you choose.
Your loving,
Mother and Father

Archie massaged a spike which had gone soft. What a weird message, he thought. I mean, it's lovely, but peculiar; "Best of luck in whichever direction you choose". What was that supposed to mean? And why was it addressed to just "My darling", and not, "My darlings"? It was as though it was addressed to him and him alone. Archie smiled.

Maybe it was meant for him.

Quietly and with his back turned to the girls he closed his eyes, kissed the postcard and slipped it into the back pocket of his jeans.

*

'No time for getting upset, young'un,' Old Man Wood said to Archie.

'I know,' he smiled bravely back. 'What do you think we're looking for?'

Old Man Wood stroked his chin. 'It must be old, really old,' he said, 'perhaps with writing you won't understand, so look for a strange script or peculiar scribbling.'

Daisy tutted. 'We have,' she replied in a bored voice.

Isabella groaned. 'Are you sure it's not on the wooden panels in your bedroom?'

'I don't believe so,' Old Man Wood replied. 'They appear to be stories, not instructions.'

'And are you *sure* there's not a wall painting behind your wooden panels —'

'No, but there were some in the church—'

'What about a ceiling painting?' Daisy added, 'like the Michael-whatsisface one?'

Isabella laughed, although Daisy felt it sounded more like a scoff. 'Michelangelo? Here in Yorkshire, by the moors?'

'Yes, even here by the moors, Bells. Why not?'

'I'll tell you what, Daisy,' Isabella sneered, imitating her voice, *'why don't you search out with your eyes, man.* Or are they not working?'

Daisy fixed her sister with a stare. *'Why don't you go feel for it, holy hands?'*

'Will you two please shut up and get back to looking for the clues,' Archie said. 'Your bickering really isn't helping. It's giving me a headache.'

*

Old Man Wood slumped into his chair. He ought to return to the bubbling brook; the trees would know, but what would the children think? Then again, did it really matter.

He lifted himself out of his chair when he caught the familiar sound of pots rattling from the kitchen. No doubt Mrs Pye was fishing out saucepans, preparing tea. Was it so late already? A bit of nourishment to get his brain in gear was just what he needed to help him think of the right questions for those funny old willows.

*

Mrs Pye sauntered into the kitchen and released the rope on the Sheila's Maid. She folded each rug in half and then half again, and piled one on top of the other and placed them in the washing basket. She noted the unusually fine fabric, the lightweight silk-like textures with delicate stitching and neat embroidery. Why oh why had they sat disregarded on Old Man Wood's floor?

She filled a saucepan and placed it on the hot plate. Then she picked up the basket and headed out of the kitchen towards the "cupboard". As she walked past the living room, she peeked through the gap in the door and gasped.

She pushed the door open. 'What in heaven's name above have you been doing?' she cried.

The children stood up, a sure admission of guilt, and looked around them. Frames of oil paintings and portraits and sketches and watercolours lay scattered all over the room.

'We are trying, dear Mrs Pye,' Isabella said, in her smartest voice, 'to find something in a picture. The problem is, we're not sure what it is, but we do know it is vitally important.'

Archie and Daisy nodded in agreement.

Mrs Pye turned from one to the next and back, her already ruddy face getting redder.

Isabella, oblivious to the housekeeper's glare, added quietly, 'Sue said so.'

'Sue said so. *Sue said so!*' Mrs Pye cried. Her face was now bright red as though someone had turned up a heat dial. 'Your friend Sue, who lives in Northallerton said you should gather all the pictures in this house and leave them in one room. Because you're looking for something! AND YOU DON'T KNOW WHAT?' she tutted in disbelief. 'Now come on, Isabella you can do better than that.'

271

The children instinctively turned towards Old Man Wood.

'The thing is,' the old man hesitated as he pulled himself up, 'Isabella's right. But I'll … er … tell you about it later. This,' and he gestured around the room, 'is all my doing, Mrs Pye. Don't worry, each and every picture will be put back in its proper place, I promise.'

'I should hope you will,' she replied, her eyes boring into each of them. 'You ought to know better, the lot of you. If you're missing something, ask me. I'd be surprised if I don't know its whereabouts. I want this room and all these pictures back where they belong by tomorrow night, even if you haven't found what you're looking for. I'm responsible for the domestics while your parents are away and they would not be happy.'

A long embarrassing silence hung over the room. Eventually Archie piped up and said sweetly, 'what we're trying to find is a picture with some sort of old writing or marks on it, something that might be connected with this rain? Maybe you could help?'

Mrs Pye's face instantly melted into a smile. 'I'll keep my eyes open.' She exited out of the room carrying the basket. But something in the back of her mind made her stop. She opened the door. 'Any of you lot know anything about some ruggy things left out in the rain?' She looked at the blank faces of the children, '… on the washing line?'

'Ah, yes! Those are mine,' Old Man Wood said, 'thought they could do with a clean.'

'By leaving them out in the rain? Tuh. Typical!' Her small eyes lit up. 'Well, I've had a right proper go at them. You should see the difference. Beautiful things. Come alive they have. I'll put them in the airing cupboard.' She turned smartly and marched off along the corridor, humming to herself.

And if he doesn't want them, she thought, I'll have 'em for myself. She stroked the top one and it seemed to reciprocate her touch, like the warmth of a sleeping cat.

*

'What was Mrs Pye going on about?' Archie asked as he prised open the back of an old wooden portrait with a screwdriver.

Old Man Wood walked over and held the frame. 'She's given my old rugs a clean,' he said. 'Tickled blue about it too.'

Archie tried not to laugh. 'Why?'

'She said they'd all come alive. Don't you listen to anything she says?'

'Not really!' Archie said, staring at the next family portrait. 'How long have you had them?'

'Had what?'

'Your filthy old rugs!'

'Oh! I can't remember,' Old Man Wood scratched the back of his neck. 'It's a long time, though.'

Archie moved on to the next portrait. 'So how old are these?'

Old Man Wood walked over. 'I've no idea. Sorry, Archie.'

'The date on these portraits,' Daisy shouted from across the room, 'is on the back or on the right bottom corner. It's the same with all of them for some reason. This one's from 1638 … and here's one from 1702.'

Archie joined in by holding up a very delicate portrait. 'Oh, I see. Look … 1595!'

Isabella who was in the hallway listening in, said, 'I can beat that. This shield goes back to 1382, I think that's right? It's Roman numerals.'

A sense of excitement and expectation filled the room. The notion of being surrounded by such antiquity built up a sense of awe, as if the people in the portraits had somehow gathered into the room and joined them in their search.

'Isn't it funny,' Archie said as he studied a series of individual portraits, 'how each of these have the same kind of creamy rectangular backgrounds with pale little swirls on, while the actual images on the paintings are only slightly different.'

Daisy stared at the pictures, her concentration intense. 'My God,' she whispered. The others leaned in.

'What is it, Daise?'

Daisy's eyes were glowing. 'The backgrounds are the same, like five light … panels.'

'Panels?' Archie said, 'I can't see anything like that, just sort of, blurs.'

'Aha,' Isabella said, 'I knew it. I told you there were wall panels somewhere in the house.'

Old Man Wood sighed. 'Isabella, wall paintings would never last, young'un. They simply wouldn't survive—'

'Oh, come on. What else could they be?'

Daisy looked up. 'If they're not panels, then we're missing something. What else hangs on a wall, has colour and could last the test of time?'

The children sat down in a circle, their brains working hard.

'Of course!' Archie said, a smile filling his face. 'We've been complete idiots!'

'What is it?'

'Tapestries—'

'Like those massive carpets on church walls?' Isabella said. 'Don't be ridiculous—'

Archie shot up. 'I think I've got it,' he said. And before anyone could blink he flew off down the corridor, then up the stairs, the floorboards creaking at every footstep.

CHAPTER THIRTY FOUR

Kemp Awakes

Solomon was grateful for the shower and change of clothes. He ate his lamb chop with mashed potatoes, remembering to chew every morsel otherwise his hungry stomach would hurt him later.

'I'm going to be honest with you, Charlie,' Solomon said, sipping a glass of water, 'there is no way my school has anything to do with this.'

'That's all very well, but the evidence suggests the storm's epicentre was directly overhead. And it's from here that this blasted pathogen started.' Stone pulled out a graphic. 'Have a look at these satellite images. The reason the meteorological geeks didn't pick it up was that it appeared like a localised storm. And combined with the humid weather prevalent in the area it generated its own peculiar entity and "boosh", in a matter of hours it built and built. Here.'

On the screen Solomon viewed the weather graphic. The storm was coloured in red, its centre a much darker hue, which ballooned out until a massive area was swathed in black. There was no mistaking that it stemmed from Upsall.

'No one's ever seen anything like it.'

'But why Upsall, Charlie? We're a small community with an old school built on the foundations of a monastery just like the Abbeys at Fountains, Rievaulx and Byland. Have you checked them out?'

The commissioner nodded. 'They're underwater – like Upsall – but the difference is, all the others are ruins,

Upsall isn't.' Stone picked his nails. 'Something makes me think this disaster begins here and ends here. I don't know what it is, but I'm going to find out.'

Solomon wiped his lips with a paper towel. 'I'll help you all you want, my dear old friend. You know I will. But as I said earlier, I think you're barking up the wrong tree.'

'You mentioned the girl coming to you,' Stone said, his eyes boring into the older man. 'Tell me more about this de Lowe family?'

Solomon shifted. 'Well, the mother and father are archaeologists, currently out in the Middle East on a dig and the children are popular and gifted. There's not much more to it than that.'

Charlie rubbed his chin. 'Why did that girl come to you knowing the storm was about to happen?'

'I have no idea.'

'I do,' Stone replied. 'She knew something. Something about all of this and she wanted to let you in on it.' Stone rubbed his hands. 'What else did she tell you?'

'We've been over this before,' Solomon said, smiling thinly and leaning back in his chair. 'She simply bustled in saying that her homemade barometer was indicating undue pressure. She's a scientist, and a good one. We encourage pupils to act on their instincts and she did just that.'

'But don't you think it's uncanny?'

'No I do not,' Solomon bristled. 'We teach students to be decent responsible citizens, and reacting to her findings is a part of that. It isn't complicated, you know.'

Stone sensed unease in the headmaster, 'When their parents are away, who looks after these kids?'

Solomon tensed. He hoped Stone wouldn't bring this up. 'There's an elderly uncle and a housekeeper. I saw them myself only the night before. In their circumstances, they do a terrific job.'

Stone opened up the folder in front of him, pushed on his reading glasses and scanned the document. 'There's no mention of an uncle.' He thumbed through another couple of pages. 'Ah. It mentions that a woman, named here as Mrs Pye, was taken in by the family eleven years ago. She was found with terrible injuries in the forest beneath the moors.' He looked up and said slowly, 'and has possible brain damage.'

'That's ludicrous,' Solomon snapped. 'I don't see what this has to do with your enquiries.'

Stone's lip curled. 'I'm trying to find out what the hell is going on. Just doing my job.' He smiled. 'So who is this old uncle? Why no record?' Stone pulled out some historical documents. 'After all, they're an old family in the area, right?'

Solomon stared out of the window. 'I suppose.'

'Says here there's a whole stained glass window in the church dedicated to the de Lowe family. Seems they go back a long, long way. So I repeat my question. Who is their uncle?'

'I don't know how this is relevant,' Solomon replied, feeling the heat. 'He's a loner – a hermit who lives with them. There's probably no record of him because he's never been on record for anything.'

'He was born, though,' Stone fired back. 'There's been a legal duty to record all births for more than two hundred years. Why is he not mentioned?'

'Perhaps,' said Solomon, 'you should ask the parents. I am the children's headmaster, I do not study the historical records of every child in my care.'

'But it says here that the school has given a bursary to the de Lowe's for centuries,' Stone countered. 'And in fairness, the school was started by the family, was it not?'

Solomon couldn't deny it. He shrugged and scratched his head.

'Strange, isn't it,' Stone said, 'the name *"de Lowe"*. Where did that come from? I mean it's not exactly common?'

Solomon pursed his lips. 'Probably a Norman conquest knight, given land here by William of Normandy.'

'French, huh,' Stone said leaning back in his chair. 'With that name, I thought it might be Flemish, or Dutch.'

Solomon suddenly sat bolt upright. A thought struck him like an arrow through the eye.

Stone noticed. 'Is there something you want to tell me?'

Solomon regained his composure. 'Oh, I was just thinking of those poor children. They wouldn't have stood a chance.'

'How come?'

'All three de Lowes were on the playing field when the storm broke. Little Archie was struck down by a huge lightning bolt. It was that moment that made me realise it was no ordinary storm.' Now that he remembered, it was Sue and Isabella yelling on the football field that had given him the creeps; they were having a private, though very public screaming match about the storm as if there was something they knew. 'I gathered up a whole bunch of children and we headed to the relative safety of the school.'

Stone eyed him curiously. 'So the first part of the storm went for one of the de Lowes. I'm intrigued.'

But Solomon's thoughts were elsewhere. Why hadn't he thought of it before? It was staring them right between the eyes. The name, *de Lowe*. Stone clearly didn't know his French; de Lowe, or should it be, *de l'eau* – French for *water* – the essential ingredient of life. Was this a coincidence or part of some ancient code?

And not for the first time, the headmaster realised there might be something a little different about those children and their old man. The stained glass window in the chapel! It had been staring him in the face for twenty-five years. A beautiful but rather grubby artwork with three panels showing three figures bearing gifts. And filling the background: *water*, or *de l'eau*! He realised he had to get back to Upsall as fast as he could.

'Charlie,' Solomon said. 'I'm very tired and I am afraid it has been a shattering and overwhelming experience. Would you mind if I slipped off to bed? You know where I am, if you wish to question me further.'

Stone clasped the papers together. 'Very well. It's late and there's a hell of a day coming.' He stood up smartly. 'If there's anything you need, shout.'

Solomon knew this was his chance. 'I'd be happy to do some investigations into some of the school books if you like. Being high up in the tower, the library was relatively unscathed and there are several large old volumes which may shed some light on the history of the area. Perhaps there are plague records from the Black Death.'

Stone eyed him suspiciously before his face lightened. 'Great. That's exactly what I need. An academic with local knowledge. I'll get you back in there first thing in the morning.' He pressed his phone. 'See to it that Headmaster Solomon is returned to Upsall at first light. Give him a linked phone and full access to the site.'

The order was confirmed.

A rap at the door made both men turn. The young officer Solomon had noticed from before came in. 'Sir,' he said, 'there's been a development with the boy in intensive care. He's awake.'

279

Solomon raised his eyebrows. 'Tell me more.'

'He's made a very quick recovery. It looks like we might be able to talk to him after all.'

Stone checked his watch. It was nearly midnight. 'Reports are due in for the next two hours and I've got to brief the PM at seven tomorrow morning. I'll get a few hours' sleep if I'm lucky.' He yawned and addressed the officer. 'Let's try and talk to the boy at nine. Make sure he has everything he needs. It'll give him more time to recover before the scientists get their hands on him.' The officer nodded and left the room.

'It's the boy they found in a tree, hanging on to life with some extraordinary injuries. Burns covering him. It's been all over the news – we've been waiting for him to come round so we can talk to him.'

'Yes, I heard,' Solomon said. 'Was he an Upsall boy?'

'I doubt it,' the commissioner replied. 'Found too far downstream to be one of yours. The strange thing is, there's no sign of the virus on him which, given his position, is quite frankly astonishing. In fact his whole survival, in line with the injuries he sustained, doesn't add up.'

Solomon breathed a sigh of relief. He'd lost so many it hurt him to think about it. He stood up. 'Well, good luck, Charlie. I don't envy you but I'll do my best.' He headed for the door.

'Excellent – thank you,' said the commissioner standing up to conclude the meeting. 'Report in if there's anything unusual or suspicious, especially with regard to the de Lowe family.'

*

Commissioner Stone stretched his arms out as the door closed behind his cousin.

He re-ran Solomon's reaction through his mind especially the bit when he'd mentioned the de Lowe family. Something didn't stack up.

He pressed the intercom. 'Dickinson.'

Shortly, the officer strode in.

'The headmaster leaves at dawn for Upsall. Do something for me, will you? Fit him with video surveillance. From the moment he lands, I want a handpicked member of your team to monitor *exactly* what he's studying. You know the score.'

Dickinson nodded. 'And mike enabled?'

'If done without trace.'

Dickinson straightened. This kind of work was his speciality. 'Does the schoolmaster wear glasses?'

'Is there a headmaster who doesn't?'

Dickinson feigned a smile. 'Then I'll add micro gram lenses to them. Consider it done.'

'Good. And keep this to yourself, Dickinson. Report back to me at lunchtime. We'll run over his findings then.'

*

Over breakfast, reports bombarded his office, while earlier, his link-up with the Prime Minister had been dreadful. The PM sounded ill and in a foul mood, so that by nine o'clock an early-morning fatigue swept over him. He needed at least five hours sleep, not two. The news was awful: Astonishingly awful. The plague, even at this early hour, appeared to have spread randomly across the country. Thank God the media had been shut down or the pandemonium and unrest throughout the United Kingdom would be unthinkable. But, conversely, unless they found answers soon, panic across the world was a real possibility.

His entourage swept into the confines of the hospital unit and surgical masks and gloves were put on following a spray down with a fine decontamination mist. It reminded him of the outbreak of foot and mouth disease on cattle. He pulled in a secretary. 'Is there a report on livestock? I want one in an hour.' The secretary scurried off, phone at the ear.

Kemp lay in the same bed, in the same room behind the glass. This time he was sitting up with all manner of medical equipment plugged into him: drips from his arms and patches that covered his head and upper torso where the burns had been most severe.

Commissioner Stone turned to Doctor Muller. 'What progress? Is he ready to talk?'

The doctor contemplated his answer. 'He's hardly said a word, just stares into space. Whatever he's been through has scarred him terribly.'

Commissioner Stone clenched his fist. Interrogating people was a skill he prided himself on. From a young age he had had the knack of prising information out of people, whether by charm, force or by verbal intimidation. But a sick boy? He contemplated his approach.

Doctor Muller showed him into the changing cubicle. 'Sorry, Prime Minister but not a sniff of germs allowed in here. You'll need to pop these on,' he said, handing him a sterile set of overalls. 'He's doing fine in a medical sense, but we've got nothing out of him so far. Not a jot.'

'Can he speak, though?'

'Oh yes. He's been repeating the words, *"Go away"* in his sleep – and various other short, garbled sentences. To be honest nothing that makes any sense.'

Minutes later Stone, looking like a plastic yeti, entered the boy's room. He walked round the bed, nurse and doctor flanking him and noticed the boy's eyes, wide open and just as the doctor said, staring fixedly at a point on the wall.

*

Stone didn't feel sorry for many people. In truth, he despised those who portrayed any form of weakness and that's why, as a rule, he disliked children. But as he took a seat next to this boy a sense of sadness filled him. Here was a boy who no one knew – who no one claimed – but who had clung onto life so bravely.

'Hello, my name is Commissioner Stone,' he began. 'I'm thrilled you've woken up at last.'

The boy didn't move a muscle.

'You've been on quite a journey by the looks of things,' he went on, noticing a strange shift in the boy's eyes – a small sense of panic, perhaps. 'But we're here to make you better, get you back on your feet,' he continued chirpily, 'with the best medical staff looking after you. And you're safe here, we'll make quite sure of that.' Stone looked at the nurse and doctor for encouragement. They nodded. 'We would like you to tell us what happened – as much as you can remember, OK?'

Still the boy stared into space.

'I'm going to tell you some pretty scary stuff about what's been going on, so it'll really help if you can answer some of my questions. Then we'll try and find family and friends to come and get you. How does that sound?'

The boy remained impassive, but he licked his fat lips.

A sign that his mouth works, Stone thought. 'Can you tell me your name?' he asked.

He waited for a response.

The boy closed his eyes.

'Can you tell me where you live?'

The boy opened his eyes, this time fixing the commissioner with his gaze.

That's a start, Stone thought. 'What do you remember about the storm – can you tell me anything about it?'

The boy stared into the distance, his eyes unwavering.

Stone sighed. He wasn't going to give anything away. He was wasting his time. Perhaps he needed a different approach. 'Look, buddy,' he began raising his voice. 'There's a disaster happening outside these walls which might affect the whole world. Somehow, and Lord only knows how, you survived with inexplicable burns all over your body. We are here to help you, but we must find out what you know.'

The boy shut his eyes again and swallowed.

The doctor, nurse and commissioner waited with bated breath for some words. The doctor made as if to speak but Stone shot him a glare. Aside from the bleeping of the monitors, silence filled the room.

'Alright, I understand,' he said. 'I understand what you've been through. But we know you can speak. You see, you've been talking in your sleep.'

The boy's eyes narrowed.

'And the longer you refuse to talk,' Commissioner Stone added, 'the more I think you're hiding something. Because experience tells me that people who don't say anything have nasty little secrets. What do you think, boy?'

The boy swallowed again but continued to stare at the wall. They waited.

'You're scared. I can tell,' Stone said lowering his voice. 'Come on, fella or I'll be forced to fill your veins with a truth serum and you'll be singing like a bird before you know it.'

'You'll do no such thing.' Doctor Muller said.

It was exactly the response Stone had hoped for. 'Yes I damn well will!' he yelled. 'I have the authority to do anything to get to the bottom of this mess, so back off.'

Doctor and nurse wore shocked expressions.

The boy moved his eyes from the doctor to the commissioner and back again.

A tiny indication of fear. Good, Stone thought as he leaned in. 'And the other thing you need to know is that we've found your friends,' he lied.

The patient's eyes widened but still he uttered not a word.

But Stone was just getting going. 'Let's start again. Your name, your school and how you ended up at the top of a tree when everyone else was swept away. You've got till the count of five to answer me or I'm throwing you out of this hospital.'

Next to him, the nurse gasped. Commissioner Stone turned on her. 'You, out!' he commanded. 'Get out! Both of you.'

'Never!' the doctor replied. 'You have no right – we have a duty of care to the boy.'

'Oh really,' Stone said sarcastically. 'How frightfully honourable. For your information, I have a duty of care to the rest of the bleeding world.' His eyes were cold. 'Security!' he yelled.

Within seconds the doctor and nurse were man-handled from the room.

Now it was just him and the boy.

For the first time, the boy's face looked scared.

'Five. Four. Three,' he counted down leaving longer and longer pauses.

'Two.'

'One.'

Still nothing.

'Kemp,' the boy croaked.

The Commissioner thought he'd misheard. 'What?'

The monitor by the boys bedside started bleeping faster. 'My name is Kemp.'

Stone smiled, marched over to the monitor and switched it off.

'What else?'

The boy's face was contorting. Was he in pain? If so, he deserved it.

'What else?' he demanded.

'If,' Kemp tried to work up enough saliva to speak.

'If what, Kemp?'

'If you want to know,' the boy said, his voice shallow and faint, 'find Archie de Lowe. If he isn't dead.' Kemp's head fell back limply on his pillow.

Commissioner Stone turned and stormed out of the door ripping at his overalls as he went.

'Damn that Solomon!' he cursed. 'He knew. He bloody well knew it was de Lowe after all. Archie bloody de Lowe!'

CHAPTER THIRTY FIVE

Clean Rugs

Archie appeared with the basket and the gleaming rugs and they gathered round as he unfolded them and laid them on the floor.

'Where did these come from?' Isabella asked. 'They're beautiful.'

'They certainly not the rugs from Old Man Wood's floor,' Daisy said as she stroked the soft downy material. As Mrs Pye had also noticed, they seemed to purr with pleasure. As she took in the bright patterns her heart beat with excitement. 'Let's hang them up – perhaps there's a map on them.'

Archie found a box of tacks and climbed up the stepladder with the first one. He pushed the tack into the corner of the rug and as he started to push it in, the weight of the rug forced him to drop it on the floor. Archie frowned. He tried it again with exactly the same result. On his third attempt, as he pushed the tack into the corner he felt it almost wriggle free. 'We're going to have to come up with another plan,' he said. 'I can't get these in.'

Daisy moved beside him. 'Come on, winkle. You're normally pretty good at this kind of thing.'

'I've got a much better idea,' Isabella said. 'Lay them out in the hallway. Then we can examine them from the stairs. Old Man Wood is there any chance of a bit more light? And can you make the generator run a little longer?'

As Old Man Wood strode off to find a lamp in his store and check the fuel in the generator, Isabella, Archie and Daisy laid out the five carpets neatly below the stairwell.

Isabella climbed a quarter of the way up the staircase. 'Archie, move that one along a bit. That's it. And make sure this one isn't overlapping. Good. Where's Old Man Wood, it's too dim under the stairs. I can't see them clearly. Is it me or are they a little blurred?'

Old Man Wood returned with two lamps which he lit and placed at the foot of the stairs. From higher up Isabella directed Archie and Daisy to move the lights into the optimal place, and then the twins joined her in peering over the banisters. From here, the colours reflecting back were brighter and sharper

A sense of excitement filled the hall.

Daisy ran up a couple more steps, peered over and then climbed up three more, then a further four until she was almost at the top. Then down one – her head jigging backwards and forwards.

Likewise, Archie moved up two steps, then down four and up five. Old Man Wood, who was much taller, stayed on the third step but then decided to copy the children.

Isabella moved a couple of steps down and stayed there staring at the five rugs – her lips moving but no sound coming out. It was a most peculiar sight; the four of them shuffling up and down the staircase and, apart from a bit of polite barging and the occasional muffled gasps there wasn't a sound from them as they racked their brains.

Finally, it was Daisy who broke the silence.

'There's writing,' she announced, tremendous excitement in her voice, 'all over them and it changes at varying distances.'

Daisy climbed to the top of the stairs. 'OK. Archie get a pen and write this down.'

Archie scampered off and in no time was back armed with a sheet of A4 and a pen.

'Right,' Daisy began. 'This is a bit complicated. It appears to work at different levels so I'm going to scoot up and down, OK.'

She skipped down a couple of risers and then up to the top as if double checking. 'We'll start with this one, the second rug along.'

Archie moved next to it.

'From up here,' she began, 'this is what it says:-

The first you hid in the heart of the house,

And now if I move down here, the same writing changes to:

That warms you night and day.'

Daisy daintily skipped down another four stairs, *'Get it out by poking me—*

And singing your favourite song along the way!' Old Man Wood finished off with her from the foot of the stairs.

*

'How did you read that?' Archie quizzed, staring at Daisy's blazing eyes. 'I can see that each rug seems to change like a kaleidoscope as we move nearer and farther away. But in pictures, NOT words.'

'Same,' Isabella said. 'I see tablets and scrolls and fire but ...'

Daisy smiled. 'You know, magic eyes, remember! Did you write it down, Archie?'

He nodded.

'Perhaps it's got something to do with sex,' Daisy said lightly.

'Don't be ridiculous!' Isabella snapped.

'Per-lease! Can we not have a conversation about that,' Archie said, turning purple.

Isabella was slightly irritated. 'There's nothing about sex here. It's merely an allusion to something. Just because it has the words "poke" in it, Daisy, doesn't mean ...'

Daisy ran up the steps again. Why couldn't she keep her thoughts to herself. 'Right Archie, let's have a go at that one. Yup, there.' She pointed at the rug adjacent to the first and he moved beside it. Are you ready for number two?'

He nodded.

'For the second one you find,' she read before skipping down a couple of steps, *'burp it from the family belly.'*

'Are you sure?' Archie quizzed.

'Yes! That's exactly what it says. Just write it down, OK.'

'To do just this,' Old Man Wood continued from the bottom step, *'you have to eat—'*

'... *Blab-ister-berry jelly!'* Daisy said.

'Blabisterberry Jelly?' Archie repeated, pulling a face as he wrote it down. 'What's Blabisterberry Jelly? Is it really, *jelly*? Or an edible jellyfish? It's nonsense. Read it again.'

Daisy did. And this time she even spelt it out.

'Blimey,' Archie said scratching a hair spike. 'How are you supposed to burp jelly without it coming back through your nose?'

'Maybe you have to do a nose trick?' Daisy said.

'I'm quite sure ancient riddles didn't have nose tricks in mind when they were created,' Isabella said.

Daisy shrugged. 'Who knows? Maybe they did, Isabella.'

'What if it's something to do with marmalade?' Isabella added.

'Nah,' Archie replied. 'I wouldn't have thought so.'

'Well it's quite ludicrous,' Isabella said, shaking her head. 'Archie's right, none of it makes any sense.'

Daisy ran upstairs again. She nodded down to Old Man Wood.

'Are you ready for the next one, Archie?' she called out. 'It's that one over there.'

Archie signalled with a thumbs-up.

'Right here we go: *The third you search,*' she began, '*is underneath your nose. It is clear, pure and cold.*'

She waved at Old Man Wood.

'*In order to draw it out,*' his deep rich voice boomed, '*you need to send a rose.*'

'Send a rose?' Archie repeated as he scribbled on the pad. 'What the—'

'Gibberish,' Isabella said running her hands through her hair, 'written by someone with absolutely no aptitude for poetry. It has to be … must be, a red-herring. How can anyone take this seriously?'

Daisy scampered up the stairs once again. 'OK, next one coming up. Ready?'

She leant over the banister and stared hard, her red eyes glowing. '*Put them all together, then get out of the way …*' she ran down a couple of stairs, '*what you will find will prove a guide—*'

Old Man Wood joined in, '*for all the other worlds.*'

'Have you got that Archie?' Daisy asked.

'Yeah, yeah. All down. Pretty weird, though.'

'Final one coming up. Ready?' Daisy said. 'Hang on a mo, this one's a bit faded.'

'I can't believe you can see anything,' Isabella said. 'I reckon you're making it up.'

Daisy shot her a look which with her red eyes wasn't something you could ignore.

'You have but seven days and seven nights, as Earth moves in its cycle, from first lightning strike and thunderclap,' she began, *'the world waits your arrival.'*

*

Old Man Wood sat down heavily on the step next to Archie and very quietly read the poem from Archie's sheet of paper:

> *'The first you hid in the heart of the house*
> *That warms you night and day*
> *Get it out by poking me,*
> *And singing your favourite song along the way!*
>
> *For the second one you have to find*
> *You burp it from the family belly.*
> *To do this, you have to eat*
> *Blabisterberry jelly!*
>
> *The third you search for is underneath your nose.*
> *It's clear, pure and cold.*
> *In order to draw it out*
> *You need to send a rose.*
>
> *Put them all together,*
> *Then get out of the way*
> *What you find will prove a guide*
> *For all the other worlds.*
>
> *You have but seven days and seven nights*
> *As Earth moves in its cycle*
> *From first lightning strike and thunderclap*
> *The world waits your arrival.'*

'Apples alive!' the old man exclaimed after the first verse. 'Blast!' after the second, and when Archie had finished, 'Extra double blast!' he spluttered, his face ashen and twisted. He put his head in his hands and started to sob.

The children looked at each other – their eyes wide.

'Good Lord. What's the matter?' Isabella asked, taking hold of his hand. 'Is it bad …?'

'Bad, oh yes, my dear,' the old man replied, his lips trembling. 'It is VERY BAD.' Then he looked at them earnestly, tears forming in his eyes. 'It appears that so great is the stretch of time that has passed … since I wrote it,' he pointed at the rugs. 'The greatest length of time you can ever imagine, that I have already failed in the task that was set upon me so many, many years ago.'

There was an uncomfortable silence. The children looked at each other, and then Old Man Wood as if he had completely lost his marbles.

'I know the poems are pretty awful, but they aren't *that* bad,' Isabella said gently, playing along with him. 'The rhymes are actually quite sweet. Dear Old Man Wood, I wouldn't get too hung up on it.'

'But these *are* the clues, aren't they?' Daisy added.

Old Man Wood shook uncontrollably while muttering. 'I suppose I just never thought that this … would ever happen. I'm so sorry. I'm afraid I may be to blame for the greatest catastrophe to befall the world.'

Old Man Wood pulled himself together with a shrug and blew his nose extremely loudly, which in any other situation would have made them howl with laughter.

'Why don't you try,' Isabella began softly 'by telling us everything that you do know? Perhaps it will make things easier.' She exchanged nervous glances with the others.

'Hmmm … yes,' the old man sniffed. 'Good idea.'

He lifted his head and stared deeply into the eyes of each one of the children in turn. 'As you may have worked out by now, I am not who … who … er … who you think I am.'

'Then, who are you?' Daisy squeaked.

'Goodness me,' Old Man Wood replied. 'It's almost impossible for you to understand my littluns. And it's going to sound a bit barmy – well, utterly appley barmy, so you must promise you won't be afraid.'

The children nodded.

'Good, right,' he said picking himself up off the stairs. 'I'll tell you what I can remember – and fast – for if I'm not mistaken, the sands of time are already moving against us and have been for far too long. Now, you know that bible story you read, Isabella, the one about creation and all that?' the old man began.

She nodded.

'Well it's got a little to do with all that – and more. Goes back before – a long time before. Oh dear.'

'Go on,' Isabella said.

'There's a whole history, lost and forgotten … until now. It was my role, I think, to help out when the time came.' He began sobbing again.

The children guided him to his armchair where he sat slumped in a sad heap with his head in his hands and tears rolling down his cheeks.

'And this history is related to the flooding and the plague isn't it?' Daisy asked.

This was met with more groaning. 'Apples, yes!'

'And we're the link, aren't we?'

Old Man Wood turned his wrinkled face and bloodshot eyes to them. 'Oh yes. Yes indeed, my littluns. You three, my favourites, are the key to the whole appley thing.'

CHAPTER THIRTY SIX

Stained Glass Windows

Headmaster Solomon pulled another heavy leather-bound book from the library shelves. In Latin the book translated as, "Stained Glass in the Churches of Northern England."

He carried it to the desk where it thudded down. He pushed his glasses up his nose and flicked through. Plates of stunning, intricate drawings filled page after page. Finally, he came to the end where he found one last entry:

Upsall Church, Date: Medieval. Designer: unknown. Fabricator: Local.

He read the description, translating the Latin out loud as best he could:

*

'This is an unusual triptych, in the medieval style with adaptations of ancient symbolism, possibly pagan. It is recognised for the strong use of natural elements in its design and of curious detailed seated figures. One figure is similar to that of Christ, with hands showing holes from the cross, another holds a mace above his head and the third bears eyes like fire. Embracing all three is a large disjointed emblem of the Tree of Life. Below each figure smaller scenes show of an apocalypse, namely flooding, disease and famine.

Positioned in the laps of the figures are three books, or stones, each one bearing a repeated motif of the Tree of Life. Above, angels feed the figures from the clouds.'

*

Solomon's heart nearly stopped.

He stared at the old images of flooding and disease. Wasn't that uncanny? And three of them were being fed. But fed what exactly?

Frankly, he thought, they were pretty rotten images, as if drawn from memory by someone not in the least bit interested. He needed to get in there and see it for himself. Drat. It meant he'd have to get wet.

Solomon closed the book and made his way down the stairs until he reached the foul smelling water that licked the walls and stairs.

He removed his clothes bar his underpants and vest, took a deep breath and lowered himself into the water. He swam easily on the flat surface, the noise of splashing reverberating off the vaulted ceiling in touching distance above him. At the end of the colonnade he ducked under and dived under the door arch and into the aisle of the chapel. On surfacing, he kicked off to the side and hoisted himself up onto a stone ledge.

From here he had no choice but to climb up over the stone screen that separated the aisle from the nave. He spied an opening above which he reckoned he could crawl into. But halfway through, Solomon realised this gallant approach was a tactic for a younger man. He tried to pull himself back but remained wedged. He had no alternative but to go headfirst and pray the water depth in the church was same as in the colonnade.

He puffed out his cheeks, wiggled his bottom, wobbled his belly and slipped forward.

A moment later, with a cry, Solomon plunged through the air, belly-flopping into the water below.

*

'Sir,' came a voice from the doorway. 'I think you'd better take a look at this.'

Stone looked up to see Dickinson walking towards him.

'What is it?' he snapped.

'Your headmaster friend, Sir … I can bring the feed in here if you wish.'

Stone ushered him in. 'It'd better be worth it.'

'You won't be disappointed.' A smile crossed the officer's face.

Stone stared at the screen trying to work out where he was. A church. High up. A window perhaps?

Dickinson filled him in. 'So he's climbed the wall and looks as if he's going through the window.'

'Why?'

'He's been flicking through a load of old books on stained glass windows. I'm not sure he's found what he wants. Knows his Latin, though.'

'Of course he does. He's a ruddy teacher—'

Suddenly the image moved fast and filled with water. For a minute all they could make out were dark stains and a flurry of watery activity.

Dickinson could hardly suppress his laughter.

'Is the feed—'

'Yes, watertight, Sir. Not sure about the mike.'

Solomon swam over to the side and found a jutting beam which he climbed on. He looked around. In front of him the tall stained glass windows reflected light upon him.

From the office the two men followed his eyes. 'There,' Dickinson said. 'It's those windows he's after.'

And as Solomon stared at the ancient glass pictures, trying to deduce their meaning, so too did Stone.

*

Solomon began laughing. The deluge had cleaned the window! These weren't the grimy windows he'd seen in the book, nor the ones he'd seen every day for years, but vibrant, shining coloured glass – bursting with life – especially with morning light beaming through them.

After a while he removed his glasses, folded them and tucked them under the elastic of his pants. He rubbed his eyes.

In front of him, laid out like a comic, was a window that told a story. Here, there were three people, a flood, a plague, and even the old de Lowe castle, now a ruin. Common factors. Perhaps the three figures were ancestors of the three de Lowe children? But who, he thought, are the curious angelic creatures sitting above them, giving them a substance that looked like dust? It reminded him of Isabella's dream about the storm. A premonition perhaps?

As the sun brightened, illuminating the window further, Solomon gasped. Another layer of detail shone through. He reached for his glasses. 'So these are gifts, and here are challenges or, it appears … the world … fails,' he said out loud. 'Curious. And unless I'm very much mistaken, lying at the foot is a long snake-like beast with a dragon's head.' He wiped his forehead. Could this be part of the de Lowe myth that one of their ancestors had slain a dragon, or something else?

He counted the notches – seven. 'Seven days? Seven days of creation. Seven days of de-creation.' He stiffened at the thought. Was it a coincidence? After all, the nucleus of the storm and plague began right here.

In his bones he knew that for some strange reason this terrible event centred around those de Lowe children. This window absolutely had to be linked to them.

*

Temporarily they lost Solomon, and then, just as Stone thought about giving up, the image came back, this time sharp and clear.

The microphone picked up every word.

Stone listened and looked. Then he leant back in his chair with his arms behind his head. 'You know, Dickinson,' he said as he stared out of the window. 'This is the only thing we have, the only damn thing we've managed to trawl up: an old stained glass window with some hocus-pocus images and a mad old headmaster going on about the creation story.'

Stone stood up and grabbed his jacket. 'You know what. I need to see that boy again. The boy who calls himself, Kemp. I need to find out what he really knows about young Archie de Lowe.'

*

Kemp stared at the ceiling, bored. His recovery was speedy and now that his drips had been taken away he could move about, but to where? And why oh why did he tell that weasly man about Archie? What would happen to his friend if they found him? Would he too be paraded in front of the TV cameras, subjected to interviews, get put on drips and given endless blood tests?

Kemp rolled his legs off the bed. 'I need the toilet,' he yelled through the glass. 'And not in the piss pot.'

The nurse came through. 'You're feeling perkier, young man,' she said.

'Yeah. I certainly am. Any chance I can stretch my legs?'

The pretty nurse smiled and shuffled out. She rang a number, talked for less than a minute and returned. 'There's a toilet just around the corner. Why don't you pop along there. I'm sure no one will mind.'

As he walked slowly along the corridor, Kemp noted guards at every door. Were they all for him? Was he seen as a threat?

He found the toilet and opened the door. It was a large cubicle with a loo, basin, mirror and shower. He locked the door and stared at his reflection.

'Boy,' came a soft voice.

Kemp froze. It couldn't be.

'Take off your gown, so you can see me.'

Kemp removed his dressing gown and let it fall to the floor. But before it hit the ground, it was scooped up.

'Cain!' Kemp snarled. 'What are you doing here?'

The ghost put it on. 'I wanted to apologise,' Cain said, his voice just above a whisper.

'Too bloody right. Now get out—'

'In my excitement, I cared for you poorly. Despicably. But I realised my mistake just in time and managed to save you.'

'So why are you back?' Kemp whispered.

'Because I want you and I need you,' Cain implored, his voice silky.

Kemp guffawed. 'Why do you think I would ever go back to you after the way you treated me?'

'Because I made a terrible error.'

Kemp sat down on the loo seat. 'That's not enough.'

'Because, together we can be powerful.'

'Still no! No way!'

'Because I will give you food and water. I will let you sleep. Because I know we can do this together.'

'NO!' Kemp hissed. 'Piss off!'

Cain sighed. 'Then you will remain here as a medical phenomenon, getting poked and prodded and things pushed into you. And eventually you too will get the disease. Everyone will. And you will suffer a horrible, painful death—'

'It'd be better than living in you, in your hell.'

Their conversation was interrupted. 'Is everything alright in there?' a voice called out from the corridor.

'Yeah, got a bit of constipation,' Kemp replied, thinking quickly. 'I'm going to have a quick shower in a mo. I won't be long.'

'Jolly good. Shout if you need a hand. If you're really struggling, pull the emergency cord.'

Cain tried again. He had one last card. 'Join me, boy. This time it will be different. I swear it. I have made arrangements—'

'Yeah, right. You said that before.'

'This time, I swear it … on your mother's life.'

'My *mother's* life?'

'Yes,' Cain said slowly. 'Your mother lives. I have found her.'

'It can't be true,' Kemp squealed. 'How?'

'It's a long story, boy,' Cain said sensing his moment. 'But every single word is true. Come with me and together we will see to it that she lives with you for the rest of your life.'

Kemp put his hands over his bald head. There was nothing, *nothing* he wanted more in the world. The revelation left him lost for words.

'You need to come with me now,' Cain urged. 'I will not fail you. You know what to do. Put on the robe.'

Cain hovered to the door and plucked a see-through bath cap from a shelf. He put it on. 'Do it just as you did before the storm.'

Kemp switched on the shower and removed his nightshirt. 'My mother, huh?'

'You have a few seconds to decide.'

Kemp moved under the cold water. When he was fully drenched, he stepped out, shivering.

'Have you made your choice?'

'Yes.' Kemp said and he grinned through his shivers. 'But this time, cold water will ease the pain.'

*

Stone marched into the sealed-off compound and through the usual procedures of sanitation.

301

'He's having a shower,' the nurse said, smiling at him. 'He's feeling an awful lot better.'

'Excellent,' Stone replied.

The nurse nervously examined her watch. 'He's been in there a little while. I'll hurry him along.'

Several minutes later, she returned. 'I can't get a reply, I wonder if he's alright?'

Stone sensed worry in her tone and moved in front of the toilet door. 'It's Commissioner Stone here. You OK in there, young man?'

They listened. Just the running of the shower could be heard.

'How long?' he said to the nurse.

'Ten minutes.'

'TEN MINUTES! Rats! Dickinson – open the door.'

The officer sized up the door then ran to the fire extinguisher and pulled it off the wall. Moments later he smashed it against the lock like a battering ram.

The door swung open.

Stone ran in and searched the small cubicle. On the floor was the boy's medical gown.

'Oh, Christ alive,' Stone said as he slumped against the wall. 'He's gone.'

'What do you mean, gone,' the nurse said. 'It's impossible.'

But they could all see it was empty.

'What the hell is going on?' Stone yelled. 'Where is that bloody boy?'

Stone leant down and picked up the flimsy garment. As he did, and much to his astonishment, a pile of fine grey ash fluttered to the floor.

*

Cain desperately wanted to jump, run, thump the air, kick something, beat someone up. But he knew he needed to keep his energy level in check.

The boy was back. Ha, ha! I knew he'd come – I was right – I knew it!

He hadn't worked out quite how they might communicate but thought it was worth a try.

'Boy, can you hear me?' he said, and then repeated it, booming out the words.

Cain listened. Nothing.

So in his head he thought his question very precisely. *I would like to know your name, boy!* A tingle came back. Slightly gibberish, but definitely worth developing.

He listened again. There … just. He scrunched his face up. Yes, definitely a noise, though a bit echoey. Perhaps this wasn't going to work.

Suddenly another absolutely brilliant idea struck him. It was risky alright, but the boy had nowhere to go and couldn't leave so it had to be worth a try.

Cain ushered their ashen body onto the floor. Then, in the same way as before when he'd left the boy in the tree, Cain pushed out of the body trying not to do it so fast or with quite as much force. Slowly he squeezed out, as though plying himself out of a thick, tight rubber mould. When out, he clapped his hands and looked down at the boy's naked torso sprinkled in ash.

Kemp stared back, spitting ash from his mouth. 'You let me out?'

Cain audibly sighed from beside him. 'As I said, this time it will be different. This time, I need to look after you, I have to earn your trust, boy.'

Kemp realised the ghost genuinely meant it. 'My name, by the way, is Kemp,' Kemp said.

'Ah, so you heard?'

'Yes. And please don't yell. I can hear you easily when you speak. Were you trying to think it, too? Didn't really come through.'

Cain smiled. 'Hmm. Just as I suspected.'

Kemp stood up and began to dust himself down. 'Any chance of some clothes?'

'Of course.' Cain picked up the bath cap. 'I'll put this on so you know where I am, Kemp.' A floating see-through bath cap hovered nearby. 'Schmerger!' Cain yelled.

Shortly, a tidy manservant appeared with a long neat pointed black beard and a strange black hat that muddled between a skull cap and a beret.

Kemp covered his privates.

'Find a robe for your new master, Schmerger. Quick, quick!'

Schmerger frowned, his long nose bending even further down. 'Sire.'

He returned, with a thick, silky burgundy red robe adorned with golden snakes. Kemp slipped it over him, and being several sizes too large it fell over the floor.

'Now for your welcome home surprise!' Cain said.

'Surprise?'

'Yes, yes. Come along. Follow the strange hat!'

Kemp strode through an extraordinary building that looked somewhere between a vast cave and a palace. On one side jagged mountain-side rocks were inlaid with jewels and gold, and on the other, a vast chimney breast was flanked by windows and shelves filled with drawers, and all covered in dust.

'Go on, open it.'

Kemp pushed the door. As he did, the smell of roast chicken and fried bacon and all sorts of delights wafted over him. 'Food!' he cried. 'Real food. Tons of it!'

The table was covered in an assortment of chocolates, fruit, cake, meats of all sorts. Kemp made his way over, his eyes wide. 'All this, for me?'

'Indeed. You now have a kitchen and chefs, to use as you wish.'

Kemp stuffed himself until he could eat no more.

All the while Cain watched, intrigued. 'You know, Kemp, I think our relationship is going to be quite splendid. Tell me your hours of sleeping, your meal times and what you like doing so that when you're not with me, you'll have that time to do as you wish, unless I require you for an emergency.'

Kemp reckoned this beat hospital a million times over. 'As long as there's a cold shower nearby before I join you.'

'Yes, good thinking. Was it easier this time?'

'Oh yeah. Miles. Hardly felt a thing.'

'Any other demands?'

Kemp licked his lips. 'The deal with my mother. She must be saved. She could come here?'

'Of course,' Cain said.

'And I'd like to see my mate, Archie,' he said.

'That would be Archie de Lowe?'

'Yes.'

Cain grinned. He was liking this Kemp boy more and more. 'Perhaps we could get him to come here permanently – if we play our cards right.'

'That would be ace,' Kemp said. 'Just imagine it. We'd have a blast.'

Cain nodded. 'Wouldn't we just. But all in good time, Kemp. All in good time. I truly feared that after my terrible treatment of you, you would shun me for death. So I could not imagine a better way in which we have patched up our differences.'

The ghost was ecstatic, but there was one thing that would make this day even more perfect. He remembered the poison, the lethal Havilarian Toadstool Powder that he'd poured into the sugar bowl at Eden Cottage when he'd visited Archie in his room.

Cain had been rather surprised by his quick thinking, nipping into the kitchen and finding sugar – the perfect mask for this poison – just like that. Ha! The mark of a true genius.

Havilarian Toadstool Powder, made with tiny, microscopic, squealing little toadstools. Useless on humans but lethal to those from the Garden of Eden.

The only substance in the universe that could reduce that Old Man Wood to a little more than a shadow.

What were the chances, he wondered, that the old man would help himself to a nice sugary drink?

CHAPTER THIRTY SEVEN

The Song Of The Trees

From that moment on, however hard he tried, Old Man Wood simply couldn't speak properly; words stuck in his throat or twisted in his mind.

The children looked at him with an equal sense of significant awe and worry.

'Would you like a cup of tea?' Archie asked. Wasn't that what grownups had when they needed comforting. That or alcohol. Perhaps he needed both.

The old man smiled and Archie took himself off to the kitchen. He pulled out the largest cup he could find and brewed a strong cup of tea. For good measure he added a dash of rum, knowing that every now and then Old Man Wood enjoyed a tipple. Archie took a small sip, grimaced, and spat it out in the sink. Ugh. Repulsive, bitter.

He found the sugar bowl, stirred in a couple of heaped teaspoonfuls, sniffed it, then dipped his finger in and licked it. Finally he returned to the sitting room where he handed it to Old Man Wood who sat in his chair being comforted by the girls.

The old man beamed as he took the cup and blew on it until it was cool enough. Then he took a large gulp. 'Interesting tea, Archie,' he said as his few remaining head hairs began to curl. He winked at Archie. 'Touch of rum?'

Archie nodded.

Clever boy, Old Man Wood thought. And in no time, his face had returned to its familiar woody, ruddy complexion.

'If you're feeling ready to chat,' Isabella began softly, 'tell me about the bed, and why you've taken it upon yourself to spy on us,' she said.

'Hang on! I want to know about the Glade and Atrium thing-a-me first,' Daisy butted in, irritated that Isabella had sneaked in first. Hers was easily the most important event by far. 'I mean it's a whole other world, isn't it?'

'What about the poems and the rugs?' Archie said. 'And what and where are the clearly vital tablets?'

They all seemed to talk at a hundred miles an hour, their questions getting louder and louder. Old Man Wood listened quietly to their increasingly hysterical arguing while sipping his rum tea.

Finally he spoke, very quietly and with a certain authority they had not heard before. 'First off, young'un's,' he said, 'we must find these tablets – as a matter of urgency.' The children instantly ceased their bickering. 'As we go, I'll try and piece things together for you; I'll tell you what I know as we search, because, believe me this goes back a heck of a long time, and it won't be easy.' He looked each one of them in the eye. 'Do you understand?'

They nodded.

He took a deep breath. 'Right then. As you may have suspected I am not exactly your "Uncle". I'll tell you now that I am in fact your great, great, great, hmmm, great, great … well, to be honest it's an awful lot of 'greats' – more than you can imagine in fact … grandfather.'

'WHAT!' they cried.

'DON'T be silly,' Daisy laughed. She patted him playfully on the back. 'Heard it all now—'

'You'd be dead,' Archie said.

'It's impossible!' Isabella said standing up. 'Stop being so dramatic. Archie, how much rum did you put in—'

'Ahhh. Hmmm, now young'un's this is a great problem. What can I say?' he looked at them all lovingly. 'We are ... how can I put it ... a little bit special in this family. I have lived in this house on this hill through the ages of mankind for an awfully long time. Since way before your records like the Bible even began. As a family we moved over the years, several times in fact, to look around and see places and there have been many, many adventures, but, on and off, I suppose I've been here on this hill in Yorkshire for thousands of years ... waiting, I believe, for this very moment.' Old Man Wood paused and his crinkly face seemed to lighten as the magnitude of what he was saying sunk in.

The children stared at him, not certain they'd heard him correctly.

'Of course,' he continued, 'I've had the very greatest pleasure in bringing up generation after generation of my family. You three are the last in the line, it would appear.' Old Man Wood cupped his mug between his large weathered hands, took another sip and beamed at each one in turn.

'And this house alone has seen many, many re-buildings. Spent a great deal of time doing it, all by myself,' he laughed. 'And you know what, most of them are pretty similar to the original, I suppose. It's been all manner of things from a school to public house to a shop. And there used to be houses nearby once upon a time. Now, what else? Well, not a lot at the moment, but I reckon it's coming back slowly.'

He held Isabella and Daisy's hands. 'You must realise by now that all of these strange events, like your hair and eyes and hands have something to do with the rain and the rising water. I found that out from the trees at the bubbling brook; the ones I took you to see, Archie,' he said, turning to the boy who was staring at the old man with his jaw open. 'I did find them – but I'm not sure I asked the right questions. You see they're clever, those trees, they've memorised everything I've ever told them and they'll tell it back if you ask right. But as I couldn't think what's going to happen or what I'm supposed to do or who I really am … well …'

Isabella had had enough. 'This is madness!' she yelled, getting up. 'You're insane or sick. I can't bear it anymore.' Tears welled in her eyes. 'He's cracked, totally cracked. We need to get him urgent medical attention.'

Archie pushed her down firmly. 'Shhh, Isabella. Let him finish.' He'd noticed how Old Man Wood's eyes widened as he sipped the strong tea and hiccoughed as if it were doing something to his brain. Now was not the time to interrupt him. Madness or not, he needed to be heard.

'You see,' Old Man Wood continued, 'when I read those passages in Genesis in your Bible and laughed my head off, well, it's just that whoever wrote it must have had more than a couple of rums in 'em and I know that for sure.' He flicked a glance at Archie.

'Pl-eeee-ase,' Daisy squealed, 'what are you talking about?'

'Genesis – you know the bit about how the world was created and all that, well, hmmm, the thing is, it doesn't say that much. In fact it doesn't say anything really, just a story to start you off at a not-too-embarrassing-point. You'd think the greatest events of mankind – your creation and the creation of every other living thing here on Earth would be given a few more believable lines. But, *hic*, oh no, all you get is a story I told to some strange bloke sitting round a campfire as a bit of a joke – ha, ha – because life was more than a little complicated before – oh yes – *hic*. Very tricky. It was after a few too many jars of Walterbrew – as it happens. Cor, now there's a drink.'

He slurped on his tea, which had the effect of sending his hair curling outwards and his eyes bulged even more. 'Can't believe I remembered that.'

'Old Man Wood, I don't think you're well,' Isabella said before addressing her siblings. She pointed at her head and twirled a finger. *'Seriously, we need to do something – he has totally lost it.'*

The old man ignored her and carried on rambling. 'This bloke, you see, quite a clever fellow – terribly serious and, hmmm, well, it just seemed a good idea at the time – couldn't resist it I suppose, fantastically entertaining.' He hiccoughed again. 'There is truth in that passage, though; Havilah is full of treasure and things beyond your wildest imagination. And Cain and that serpent of his are wretched,' he spat, 'and the other thing is the flood …'

On the word "flood" he slurred quite badly, and Old Man Wood checked himself before hiccoughing very loudly. But now he was on a roll, a mere hiccough wasn't going to stop him.

'Oh yes, I do feel a little guilty, if you know what I mean. Well, you may say it's not possible but I tell you it's true. I was there. Amazing isn't it? I wrote those poems, did I say that? Such a long … what actually happened is quite different because, well … hmmm … all those places exist or used to, rather like here. Otherwise you might get … now what was I talking about?' he continued, forgetting himself.

A blink of lightning followed by a ripple of thunder sent a message that another storm was close by. It seemed to intensify the situation.

'Stop rambling and tell us, in plain English, what on earth you're talking about,' Isabella demanded.

Daisy, however, giggled and leaned in on him. 'Go on, tell us Old Man Wood. Tell us your story …'

But unfortunately Old Man Wood, whose few head-hairs were standing erect like the threads of a worn brush, started to hum a strange tune which sounded as if the wind was rushing through trees, its rhythm building all the time.

He clambered out of his chair and stood tall in the room, his big trunk filling the space in front of the fire as strange whooooshing and swissssshing sounds came out of his mouth and vibrated round the room.

Moments later, his hands and body moved in a slow, graceful way as a breeze appeared to blow through the house.

The children sat down and watched as the old man hummed the song of the trees.

*

Suddenly Archie had an idea.

He slipped out of his chair, and while the two girls listened, mesmerised by Old Man Wood's extraordinary movements and the swishing, whooshing noises of his song, he crawled on all fours behind the back of the armchair to the fireplace. He found a poker and thrust it into the fire, shifting the logs in the embers. There was nothing and for a brief moment, he felt rather foolish.

Under his breath he recited the words of the poem.

'The first you hid in the heart of the house
That warms you night and day
Get it out by poking me,
And singing your favourite song along the way!'

Archie looked up to see Daisy standing, copying Old Man Wood, humming away and moving her arms in slow controlled waves, somewhat, but not exactly, mimicking the old man's motions.

She wore a huge smile on her face.

On the contrary, Isabella lay on the sofa, her knees up to her chest and her head between her hands.

Archie picked up the rhythm and began to hum along, and as he got the hang of it, he decided to bolster the fire up anyway and thrust the poker in once again.

With a tiny flash, a strange flicker came out at him. Archie's heart skipped a beat.

He poked with a little more urgency and the light intensified.

He looked about. Had anyone else seen it? Daisy and Old Man Wood were singing as if in a trance; Isabella cowered on the sofa.

He turned his eyes back to the fire and found that right before his eyes an object very slowly approached. He could hardly breathe. But Old Man Wood had come to the end of his song, and the moment he finished, the "thing" receded back into the orange glow.

*

Seeing Old Man Wood like this made Isabella feel as unhappy as she could ever remember. As his song ended, she slipped off to the kitchen where she heard the gentle drone of the generator. She worked out that it might run for another fifteen minutes or so if they were lucky.

For a while she thought she might slope off to bed; leave them to it. Perhaps, first, she ought to check the TV for any up-to-date news.

She flicked on the remote control and as the telly warmed up she opened the fridge to see if Mrs Pye had left anything worth snacking on. She peered inside.

Nothing she fancied, so she grabbed an apple and sat down on the chair and took a large bite.

For a minute or two she watched the news repeats that had been going round and round in a loop.

She bit in hard again wiping the juice off her chin as a message ran along the bottom in bold red letters. *"Important announcement coming up."*

What was so important that it had to be flagged?

Daisy and Archie came in just as the picture changed. It now showed a live feed from the same press office with oak-panelled walls, but this time full of weary-looking officials.

A tall man, with grey hair and a pointed nose, made his way to the lectern. An elegant smart lady, the deputy prime minister, introduced this man as the chief coordinator of the flood crisis, Commissioner Stone.

'First of all,' he began, a subtle Yorkshire trace in his voice, *'I speak on behalf of the COBRA team to offer my thanks to all of those who have dug deep in protecting and keeping the citizens of our islands safe at this terrible time. The help and resolve given by so many continues to touch the lives of millions.*

'I will be frank,' he said, looking directly into the camera, *'the epidemic, the so called Yorkshire Plague or Ebora, reached all parts of the country overnight. It strikes at will. There is no logic to its method nor is there a cure for those affected. Not yet. Medical centres are overwhelmed as our few doctors who do not have symptoms themselves, struggle to keep up. If you think you may have symptoms, please ring our helpline number at the bottom of the screen. Our advice is, be patient, drink plenty of fresh water and keep warm. And please, stay at home.'*

He shifted and smiled, *'While many are suffering there are stories of incredible bravery and heroism. We're going to share some real life stories from the flooding. These are tales of extreme courage and dogged resilience. Above all,'* he said, his voice quivering, *'they are stories of hope.'*

The screen cut from the press conference to a scene on a beach, waves crashing someway behind the sand. On it a reporter with his microphone at the ready waited for the link up.

'Here I am near the beautiful Suffolk coastal town of Southwold.' The camera panned to a lighthouse and then away to colourful beach huts. *'Famous for its beer and upmarket holiday resort, last night was the scene of an extraordinary rescue off the coast, where two names will surely be remembered for an awfully long time. I'm handing you over to Serena Strutt who continues the story.'*

'Thank you, Bill,' said Serena, her perfect smile beaming at the camera. *'On the day of the storm two children from the village of Upsall in North Yorkshire found a rickety old rowing boat, built a canopy in a manner of minutes from odds and ends found in a shed, and then, miraculously, they survived what is now understood to be the most vicious storm of all time before being sucked out into the North Sea.*

Against quite incredible odds, they survived. Three nights later, their boat sank in a fierce gale last night off this very coast. The coastguard spotted them and these, frankly remarkable children, were rescued.'

The children watched in silence, mesmerised by the images, huddled together, their arms locked around one another.

'*I have with me here, one of the survivors, Sue Lowden.*'

The moment the words were out of the reporter's mouth the kitchen erupted. Daisy and Archie leapt up and down screaming their heads off. Isabella sank to the floor, tears falling freely down her cheeks.

'*Sue,*' Serena said, '*what an amazing story. I know you're still quite numb from your experience especially as Gus Williams, your partner on the boat has gone to hospital, but please tell us more?*'

The camera moved and Sue came into shot. She'd lost weight but her eyes sparkled. '*I just want to thank Gus,*' her eyes began welling up, '*he was amazing.*'

'At snogging,' Archie quipped.

'Oh shut up,' said the girls in unison.

Back on the screen, Sue recalled some of their adventures, how they'd built the canopy and caught fish to eat.

Serena Strutt shook her head. '*Sue, what a truly astonishing story and of course, our thoughts are with Gus. Is there anything else you'd like to say?*'

Sue looked down at her feet as if trying to rein in her emotions. Then, very slowly and as the camera zoomed in on her face she looked directly into the lens and very sadly said. '*Infected now,*' before adding, '*lush.*'

For a second, Serena looked confused, but being a professional she draped an arm around the girl. '*Thank you Sue – I know this is a very emotional time, and we really do wish Gus a speedy recovery. Back to you in the studio.*'

*

The sense of relief in the kitchen was extraordinary. But while Archie and Daisy danced around, Isabella sat down at the kitchen table with a pen and paper. She was instantly struck by the oddness of Sue's response. Sue never ever used words like "lush". That was a Daisy kind of word. Not a Sue word.

Daisy pulled a chair up. 'What's up, sis. Thought you be jumping over the moon.'

Isabella shook her head. 'Inside, I am, believe me. But there's something wrong, that sentence wasn't right in any way.'

'Know what you mean,' Daisy said. 'Sounded like something she'd planned, if you ask me.'

Isabella pushed the pencil through the hole in her hand and spun it round. 'Yes. You're right. But what did it mean? I thought 'lush' meant, kind of cool.'

'Yeah, that's right. Gorgeous – lush.'

Isabella twiddled her hand in the air, the pencil making a strange starry shadow on the paper. 'Maybe you're right. Perhaps she had planned it.' Isabella wrote down the sentence on the paper and looked at it.

She rearranged the letters in a circle and tried to see if there was a pattern or some obvious code. As she pondered the letters she asked? 'Is Old Man Wood alright? It might be an idea to check on him.'

Archie slipped out of the kitchen and returned a couple of minutes later. 'He's wandering around with his hair sticking out on end. I think he's, sort of, OK.' He hesitated. 'Look, while you were singing that hummy song, a weird object came out of the fire—'

'Holy moley! I think I've got it,' Isabella exclaimed, ignoring him.

Daisy and Archie crowded round.

'Look. Take the word, *'Infected'*. In it is the word, *'find'*. She crossed out the letters. Now what's left. *'The'*. She crossed that out as well.

They stared at the paper. Daisy clapped her hands. 'Look – the word, *'uncle'*.'

317

'Excellent,' Isabella said, surprised by her sister's grasp. 'Which leaves', she continued, '*S, O, W.*'

'*Find the uncle sow,*' Archie said, 'or, '*wos*'. You think she means Old Man Wood?'

'Possibly,' Isabella replied, pulling the pen in and out of her hand-hole. 'But it's not like her to make a glaring error like that. She knows perfectly well what his name is. Hang on, what if it's, '*clown*' and then you've got, *E, U, S.*'

'*Sue.*' Daisy said. 'That's it. *Find the clown, Sue.*'

Isabella shook her head. 'No. It just doesn't stack up.' She stood up and began pacing the room. 'I mean what could she possibly be referring to?'

Daisy sat down and played with the letters, her eyes glowing, a gentle pink light forming over the paper.

She rearranged the final letters and clapped her hands.

Isabella ran over. She studied the paper, squeezed Daisy's shoulders and took a deep breath.

'Archie,' she ordered, 'make another cup of tea for Old Man Wood, exactly like before.'

'You sure?'

'Yes! Just do it, now!'

'God. OK – why? You saw what happened to him. He'll go properly bonkers.'

'Sue's message.'

Archie skipped over and read it out loud.

'*FIND THE CLUES, NOW.*'

CHAPTER THIRTY EIGHT

Rum Tea

'What were you saying about the fire, Archie?' Isabella asked.

Archie grabbed the bottle of rum and poured in a generous measure. 'Oh, yeah. An object appeared to be coming out of it,' he said, 'but when Daisy and Old Man Wood stopped singing, it retreated.'

'Have you finished with that?' Isabella asked sniffing the tea. 'It smells gross.'

'Not quite, it needs some sugar to sweeten it up,' Archie said. 'Pass it over.'

Daisy picked up the sugar bowl, took a long, hard look inside and handed it over. 'Are you sure that's sugar?' she said.

'It was the last time I looked.'

Daisy shuffled on the spot. 'Just curious. Looks like something else, bit weird, that's all. Sounds like it's wailing.'

'Wailing?'

'Yup – like it's crying.'

Archie heaped a couple of teaspoons into the cup and stirred it round. Daisy peered into it and shook her head. 'What is sugar, anyway? she said. 'Is it, mushroomy?'

'Oh, for goodness' sake, Daisy.' Isabella said. 'Now is not the time to start learning about sugar and mushrooms. Now,' she said addressing the twins, 'here is the plan.'

*

Just as they were about to head back into the sitting room with the tea, Daisy's ears tuned into the TV. She turned and faced the screen.

Commissioner Stone was thanking the various officers around him and trying to placate viewers that the nation shouldn't be too worried. He sounded confident. *'One final thing,'* he said, a crooked smile crossing his face, *'we now know that the epicentre of the storm centred on the small moor-side village of Upsall.'*

'Archie, Bells,' Daisy called out. 'You dudes should watch this.'

The Commissioner continued as Archie and Isabella returned through the door. *'We'd particularly like to speak to anyone who was in the area of Upsall the day the storm broke. We know that most were tragically lost and almost certainly swept away, like the brave Gus Williams and Sue Lowden who we heard from earlier.'* Another camera honed in on the lean moustachioed face of Commissioner Stone. Clumsily Stone turned towards it.

'There is one family we know of, whose three children were on the football pitch at that time. There's little doubt the water took them but if anyone has seen or heard from any of them, particularly this young man on your screen now, Archie de Lowe, then please get in touch with your local authority representative.'

A picture of Archie, a couple of years younger, filled the screen.

Archie put the tea down on the table. 'Jeez,' he said. 'Why me?'

'Who is the only person,' Isabella said, 'who they know, who knows you?'

Archie squinted. He could feel his hair hardening.

'Kemp. That's who,' Isabella said as she wheeled away. 'You're a fool Archie. I told you not to trust him.'

'My God,' said Daisy. 'I forgot to tell you. You know when he said those words in the hospital—'

'*Dunno* and, er … *Algae*, wasn't it?' Archie said.

'Those exactly. I think he was trying to contact you.'

'What do you mean?'

'For *Algae,* read, *Archie,*' Daisy said. 'And for *Dunno*, read—'

'*De Lowe,*' Archie finished.

They looked at each other. 'Do you think he was trying to warn me?'

'Almost certainly,' Daisy said.

Isabella shrugged. 'Looks like we'll never know. But what we do know, is that because of him, they're now hot on our case.'

*

The news that they were being searched for felt like a body blow to Archie. He'd slightly hoped that his first appearance on national television might be as goalkeeper for Leeds United, not as someone wanted by the authorities. What had Kemp said to the police? Had he spilled the beans and told them about Cain and the coat? Even if he had, though, they couldn't possibly have believed him, could they? They'd have thought he'd lost his mind.

He sank down in his chair, trying not to worry about it, conscious that his hair was as hard as steel while his blood coursed through his veins. He had that angry feeling that pricked him every time he thought about Cain.

Daisy sat on the arm of Old Man Wood's chair. 'Tell us more about your song,' she began. 'It's beautiful.'

Old Man Wood smiled a little drunkenly and sipped his tea. 'I don't know where it comes from,' he said.

'Reminds me of this whole other place. A time long ago. Feels apple-marvellous, though, doesn't it.'

'Teach it to us,' said Isabella, who was sitting on his other side.

'Really?'

'Oh yes,' the girls said at once, smiling sweetly.

'Liked it, did you?'

'Absolutely,' Isabella lied.

Old Man Wood beamed. He couldn't refuse smiles like these and after taking another large swallow of tea he climbed out of his chair.

'Whooooosh, swissshshhh, swissshy, swoosh,' he began, his eyes closed in concentration, his arms pulling slowly around like a gentle breast-stoke motion.

The girls stood up and copied him. Daisy was immediately right on track with Old Man Wood, as if she absolutely understood it.

Isabella, on the other hand, found it rather embarrassing. Try as she might the song and movements didn't register.

The pace built up.

As before, the deep vibrations of Old Man Wood's voice made the whole room tremble and when the music reached its climax a curious wind curled around them and through them and up their spines.

Archie crawled over to the fire and, as planned, began poking around, but his thoughts weren't with the song, they were still fixed solely on Kemp and Cain and he hadn't hummed or sung a word.

Nothing happened. No bright light emerged from the fire.

The children looked from one to the other and then back again, confused. Why hadn't it worked? Had Archie lied?

'Encore, encore – more, more!' Isabella clapped as she danced over to Archie and whispered into his ear. 'This time, Arch, you've got to sing it too. It's all or nothing. Understand?'

As the lights failed and the noise of the generator departed, they heard only the sounds of their breathing and the distant cracks and rumbles of the storm overhead. Archie ran off and found the lamps Old Man Wood had used to highlight the rugs. He lit them, and positioned them either side of the room, where they cast a deep orange glow.

Old Man Wood's face, now greatly accentuated by the soft rays, beamed from ear to ear.

Daisy, who hadn't noticed Archie's lack of vocal involvement clapped encouragement. 'That was utterly lush,' she said, winking at Isabella. 'Encore, encore, Old Man Wood. More, more!'

Old Man Wood remained standing, drained the rest of his tea and put the mug down with a clatter on the mantelpiece. He breathed in deeply and smacked his chest. 'This time,' he said, 'you go a wee bit higher, girls. You'll feel it in your blood. The song will take you there, if you believe in it.'

'Can I start?' Daisy said. 'It's so beautiful and moving. Rather like being in paradise.'

Old Man Wood's booming laugh rebounded off the walls. 'That's exactly what it is. Clever littlun. Well of course you can. I'll take it up as you begin.'

Daisy began. She closed her eyes and extended her arms. 'Whoooosh, swishes, swiffy swissh whoooosh,' she hummed.

Old Man Wood smiled. Even if the children didn't have a clue what the song meant, it thrilled him that the song resonated well with them. He couldn't think how it had come to him, but it reminded him of a time when things in his head weren't quite so foggy, as if the song unlocked a hidden door to a room full of secrets.

He joined in, this time even more enthusiastically, whirring the strange noises in and out of his mouth and gesticulating, slowly at first, with his strong arms and hands, building up his movements as the song increased in tempo, so that before long it sounded exactly like wind rushing through leaves in a big tree.

Isabella stood up and shut her eyes. 'Swiffy swissh whoooosh.' Goosebumps ran up her back.

Archie, poker in hand, sensing the power of the song, stood up and began as well and in no time was consumed by the mesmeric, chanting tones.

Suddenly, from rather sad embers, the fire burst into life.

Isabella and Daisy, without even realising, raised the tune up an octave with the hummy, swishy and whooshy noises, and the momentum grew.

'Swiffy, hummm swish sshshh. Swiffy swissh whoooosh, swissshshhh hmmm ...' Louder and louder it grew, the four of them consumed by the music.

Old Man Wood suddenly took the piece to a whole new level, roaring the song out. Daisy and Isabella climbed an octave higher and as they did wind gushed over them like a tornado.

Archie opened his eyes. Old Man Wood's hair stood fully erect on his head and his face had the look of a wild sea-worn pirate; his ruddy complexion setting off his thick frown-lines, his face flickering in the firelight, his concentration intense. His dark eyes, unblinking, fixed stonily to a point on the wall as if he wasn't looking at the wall at all; but looking back through time at another world.

The storm outside now crashed about the cottage. Rain lashed violently down onto the tiles of the old building and flashes of lightning illuminated the room as a massive crack of thunder shook the building.

Old Man Wood's movements with his long arms now became more expansive, flailing around like a mad conductor who had lost control of his orchestra and was trying wildly to get them playing together.

'Has anyone opened a window?' Daisy shouted over the din, trembling a little in awe as wind started to whirl around her. But her voice was drowned out by the music and the bangs and cracks of thunder. She rejoined the singing. Suddenly an extended gust of wind picked up a bundle of papers and scattered them around the room, like confetti.

Now, noise, air and paper whirled wildly about as if a thousand ghosts had suddenly flown into the room at once. Every hair on the children's bodies stood to attention as Old Man Wood stared crazily at the wall, his brow furrowed, his body upright and his face majestic.

As the song mellowed, bits of paper floated gently to floor.

Daisy and Isabella, soaked in sweat, looked over to Archie, lost amidst the muddle of paper and debris.

From out of nowhere they saw a fabulous smile spread across his face. And they could hardly believe what they saw; for in his hand was a tablet; a dusty, stone tablet which was very, very old. On the top, etched in gold was the emblem of the tree of life – a tree with roots that joined with the branches, like a globe.

'Oh my … oh my,' Daisy cried. 'Look! Bells! Look at Archie! *It's true*! The tablets from the clue in that silly rhyme.'

They said it together:

'The first you hid in the heart of the house
That warms you night and day

Get it out by poking me
And singing your favourite song along the way.'

Archie thumped the air as they hugged. 'One down, two to go, what a result! Old Man Wood, you aren't so hopeless after all!'

They turned their attention back to the old man, but the combination of the song and Archie's brew had got the better of Old Man Wood. He lay collapsed in his armchair, snoring heavily, sweat sheening his gnarled face, a few strands of hair still erect off his old head.

'I hope he's OK.' Daisy said.

'Sure he is,' Isabella replied. 'He just needs a good sleep, that's all.'

CHAPTER THIRTY NINE

A New Belief

Golden brown in colour, hard as steel and inlaid with beautiful scrollwork, the tablet from the fire was roughly the size and weight of a small paperback book. As Archie touched it a cosy tingle, like the warmth of love, enveloped him.

He traced the engraved surfaces, running his fingers along the lines of the symbol of the tree of life, its characteristic swirls mirrored up and down, and he noted that it was the same artwork as they had seen on the walls of the cave.

They passed it round, marvelling at its beauty.

'Look, guys,' Isabella said as she handed it over to Archie. 'I don't know what to say.'

'Well, you should be thrilled to bits that Sue's alive—'

'And Gus,' Daisy added. 'He's a hero.'

'Yes, of course, Gus too,' Isabella said, beaming. 'But what I meant to say,' and she stuttered trying to find the right words, 'what I really meant to say, was, thanks.'

'Thanks? For what?' Daisy replied.

'For not believing a word I was talking about,' Isabella said.

'We never do, anyway,' Daisy responded raising her eyebrows. 'Here, your turn, Bells.' Daisy handed her the tablet and rose from the kitchen table.

Isabella pulled it to her lips. Like with Archie, a glow, a rush, a joyful sensation shot into her like a fizz of confidence that pushed her fear and worries sideways.

Isabella smiled and pulled it to her chest. 'Look, I'm sorry I didn't believe you, I just couldn't. Now, I can see how massively wrong I've been. By the way, where's the paper you wrote the poems on?'

Archie pulled it out of his pocket and handed it over.

Isabella read it and frowned as Daisy returned to the table.

'Problem?'

'Just a bit,' Isabella said and she proceeded to read the last poem:

'You have but seven days and nights
As Earth moves in its cycle.
From first lightning strike and thunderclap
The world waits your arrival.'

'I was right,' Daisy said. 'Remember, Archie? I told you I thought we had seven days—'

Isabella put her hands up. 'I've been holding this whole thing up, haven't I?' She bit her lip. 'And we've got to find two more of these little beauties in three days.'

'What's the problem?' Daisy said.

'It took us three days just to find this one.'

'Only because you were poncing about, being all sciencey and dull.'

On another occasion Isabella would have punched her. But not today. 'I know, and I'm sorry.'

Daisy smiled and pulled out a bag. 'We'll find the next one in the morning. The Blab-is-ter-berry Jelly one, or whatever it's called. Right now it's about time we started to look the part.'

Daisy reached in and slipped on her metal-rimmed pink-lens spectacles.

She tossed the bag to Archie who pulled out a hat and he passed it on to Isabella.

'What is it?' Isabella asked.

'Just put it on. You too, Archie.'

'Oh God!' he said. 'Do I have to?'

Isabella opened the bag, her face full of questions, and removed the contents.

'Go on,' Daisy insisted.

'Studded fingerless, black leather gloves?'

'Absolutely!' Daisy clapped. 'Mrs Pye and I have made some adjustments. Same with yours, Archie. Hope they fit.'

Isabella slipped them on and was amazed to find how comfortable they were. 'What's with the stud popper thing in the middle?'

'Oh, that's a trouser popper. Mrs Pye's idea, so your gloves don't slip off.'

Isabella didn't know whether to laugh or cry. 'Oh, Daisy, I don't know—'

Daisy leaned over the table and put a finger to her sisters' lips. 'Sshh. No more excuses, Bells. If we're going to save the world we may as well try and look the part. In any case, it's way time you got a bit more bling, sister.'

She turned. Mrs Pye had reinforced Archie's beret with leather patches for his spike-ends and added three studs around the rim. 'You do look handsome, my dear Archie, in a rugged, French kind of way,' she joked.

Isabella was impressed. 'That, Daisy, is a very good idea.'

'Yup,' she agreed. 'No more getting poked by those silly spikes, right?' Daisy shot off next door and came back holding Isabella's phone.

Isabella knew exactly what she was thinking and burst out laughing.

Archie protested, 'Please, Daise. What now?'

'I think,' Daisy said, mischievously, 'that it's time for a very special selfie!'

*

As the shutter clicked on the camera, they heard a deep groan. The children turned towards the door.

'Old Man Wood?' Archie said. 'He was fine a minute ago.'

'Oh heck!' Daisy said. 'He's probably drunk on your rum-based tea and crashed out.'

The children smiled at one another.

'The least we can do is make sure he's comfortable.'

They trouped back into the living room, a room they barely recognised as paper, canvas and pictures littered every inch of the floor.

'Lord almighty,' Isabella whispered. 'If Mrs Pye sees this, she's going to go utterly mental.'

'It's a warzone—'

'Chill, guys,' Daisy cut in. 'If we don't find the tablets, then there won't be a world left in which she can offload her tidiness anger. We'll deal with it later. Hey, there he is.'

Archie re-lit a couple of candles and joined the girls next to Old Man Wood on the sofa.

'He's fast asleep,' Bells said.

Daisy wasn't so sure. 'Old Man Wood, you there?'

He groaned.

'Hi,' she said, resting a hand on his forehead, 'you should go to bed. Busy day coming up.'

A flicker at the corner of his mouth. 'I ... I think—' he whispered before slumping back.

'What?' Daisy said. 'You think you're a bit tiddly, eh, Old Man Wood?'

The old man suddenly looked grey and withered and terribly old as he tried to sit up. The children gasped.

'Poison,' he spat. 'You've got to—'

'Poison?' Isabella exclaimed. 'What poison?'

Old Man Wood tried to speak but the words wouldn't form. His bony hand grabbed Isabella's wrist and she squealed as he gripped it hard and levered his head off the pillow. He stared at her with watery, scared eyes, 'Y-o-u ... y-o-u-r ... p-o-w-errrr—'

And then his grip loosened and his head fell back slowly onto the pillow, like a rock falling through water, and his eyes shut.

A look of peace descended over him.

The stillness in the room was deafening.

Stunned, the children instinctively stepped back as a huge rumble of thunder rolled out over the cottage rattling the glass in the windows.

'Holy crap,' Archie trembled. He fell to his knees and wiped a tear from his eye. 'I think we've just killed Old Man Wood.'

To be continued ...

There's an apple-load of spectacular adventure coming for Isabella, Daisy and Archie ... and if you'd like to find out more, visit James' author website:

www.jameserith.com

... and sign up to the mailing list.

Subscribers will receive the first few chapters of the next instalment before anyone else, for FREE.
(and other cool stuff as well!)

***

James Erith

James Erith was born in Suffolk in the UK in 1970. He travelled the world extensively, worked briefly as a journalist in the 1990's and then turned to his passion for the great outdoors, designing and building gardens for several years.

James moved to North Yorkshire where he lived between the Yorkshire Dales and the Yorkshire Moors. It inspired him to use these beautiful areas as the location for the EDEN CHRONICLES series.

James is easily distracted by the sound of leather on willow. In 2013 he rowed across the English Channel and the length of the Thames to raise money for MND and Breakthrough Breast Cancer.

***

Review

To help the author and other readers, spare a moment to give
SPIDER WEB POWDER
your honest

REVIEW

at the online store of the shop from where you purchased it.

Thank you.

***

Readers' Comments on:
Eden Chronicles, Book One
THE POWER AND THE FURY

LOVED IT!!!!! THE best book I have read. And I am positive that you will agree!
Rose, Aged 10

Gripped ... wonderful characters, intriguing story, great pace, evocative locations ... funny, clever, surprising, insightful, ... A Very Good Read Indeed.
Neil, Scotland

Our daughter loved it, captivated from beginning to end.
Mrs S, UK

A fast, pacy adventure with jumps and thrills.... I can't wait for the next book.
Ludo, Aged 9, Sussex, UK

This grandmother was engrossed in the adventures of Isabella, Daisy and Archie ... Bravo.
Iona, South Africa

Wonderful, exciting and totally un-put-downable ... I am giving every teenager I know a copy for Christmas.
ACB, Ireland

... if you like Harry Potter read this next. A great debut, this series is going to run and run!
John, UK

(From: Amazon.co.uk)

Made in the USA
San Bernardino, CA
02 December 2017